C000174882

TH

BROKEN

ONES

BOOKS BY CARLA KOVACH

The Next Girl
Her Final Hour
Her Pretty Bones
The Liar's House
Her Dark Heart
Her Last Mistake
Their Silent Graves

THE

BROKEN

ONES

CARLA KOVACH

bookouture

Published by Bookouture in 2021

An imprint of Storyfire Ltd.
Carmelite House
50 Victoria Embankment
London EC4Y 0DZ

www.bookouture.com

Copyright © Carla Kovach, 2021

Carla Kovach has asserted her right to be identified
as the author of this work.

All rights reserved.
No part of this publication may be reproduced,
stored in any retrieval system, or transmitted, in any form or by
any means, electronic, mechanical, photocopying, recording or
otherwise, without the prior written permission of the publishers.

ISBN: 978-1-83888-868-8
eBook ISBN: 978-1-83888-867-1

This book is a work of fiction. Names, characters, businesses,
organizations, places and events other than those clearly in the
public domain, are either the product of the author's imagination
or are used fictitiously. Any resemblance to actual persons, living or
dead, events or locales is entirely coincidental.

The Broken Ones is dedicated to those who are grieving. Sometimes that grief can be filled with regrets of things you did or didn't say or do, but don't be too hard on yourself. X

PROLOGUE

Friday, 18 January

Ten years ago

I tap on Hailey's bedroom door hoping that my mother can't hear me. The last thing I want to do is wake my mother up. 'Hailey,' I whisper, but I know that isn't enough. If she's asleep, there's no way that would have woken her but what I have to say can't wait the few hours until morning. I have the solution to all our problems. There will be no school tomorrow or ever again. I have a plan and everything is in place, just like I promised her. I asked you to be patient and you have. Our nightmare will soon be over and we can start again, somewhere else, away from all the hurt that we've endured.

A creak comes from my mother's bedroom and I hold my breath. A trickle of sweat slips down my forehead and eventually bounces off my nose. Quietly exhaling, I grip the door handle and pull it down. Hailey's perfect nose and the curve of her forehead is lit up by the moonlight that comes through her bedroom window.

Something's odd. She normally has her curtains closed, preferring to sleep in pitch-blackness. She always said she couldn't sleep if there was the faintest bit of light coming through. I creep across the floorboards, purposely missing the squeaky one and I stare at her face. Her skin has a serene blue hue, like an almost white baby blue. I reach out and move her hair from her mouth then

I tuck it behind her ear. She still has her earphones in. She must have fallen asleep while listening to music. I pull the one bud out and place it to my ear. Nothing. I pick up her phone and play the last thing she was listening to as she fell asleep, hoping that my movement and presence will slowly wake her. The last thing I need to do is startle her and make her scream. We need to get out of the house quietly before Mother hears us.

'Beautiful Dreamer.' That's the song she was listening to last. That's weird too. It was one of Nan's favourites. Hailey normally prefers the Black Eyed Peas. Her bedroom is testament to the fact that she is their number one fan. There are posters of will-i-am and Fergie on every wall. As I remove her other earbud by reaching under her head, I flinch and gasp for breath. 'Hailey.' I nudge her. She's freezing cold. I reach for her arm. That is cold too. I nudge her again. 'Hey, wake up.'

Nothing. No breaths, no reply, no movement.

'Get up. Hailey, we have to go.' Tears begin to slip down my face as the realisation of what has happened dawns on me. 'No!'

I grab her stiff body and place her head on my chest and I can't hold my sobs back. It was all going to be okay. I'd fixed everything for us but now she is gone forever. We were finally going to be safe and happy. I spot the empty blister packs of tablets on her bedside table, the water glass is on its side and some of the packs have fallen onto the floor. I let out a distraught yell and grip her ice-cold hand, knowing that she's not coming back from this. Everything I've done has been for nothing. I've lost her.

I draw her quilt up to her chin before rushing out of the bedroom and into my mother's, turning the main light on. I can feel the veins on my head pulsing and my hands ball into a fist. I'd always held back at Hailey's insistence, but not this time.

'You did this.'

I grip the sides of my head and pull my hair as she stirs. At the back of my mind, I hear Hailey's voice, telling me she doesn't want anyone hurt. She doesn't want trouble and she doesn't want to be punished. She won't be punished again. I left it too late. I should have done something earlier.

'What? Go back to bed. It's the middle of the night,' she murmurs and yawns under the blanket but I can hear what she's saying. My mother. My lovely mother. 'Turn the light off.'

I jump on the bed and reach for her neck under the top blanket, my hands gripping her windpipe to a squeeze. She flails and wriggles beneath me. I hate her. I've never hated anyone so much. I feel her fist hit my nose and I fall to the floor, landing on the rug. She has a punch on her that would rival a boxer, Hailey and I have felt the strength behind her fists on many occasions. 'You killed Hailey.'

My mother looks puzzled as she rubs her neck. 'What?' My blood is smeared over her knuckles and I just want to pound her head to a pulp.

'You heard me.' I'm back on my feet, seething, and my own fist hits the side of her head, and I don't stop there. I hear a rib crack and a shriek as I catch her jaw. She goes to fight back but I am no longer a kid. I'm a man now. After a few blows, I feel a weakness run through my body. So much for being a man. That didn't save Hailey. Another punch and another. I can't stop myself as I think of Hailey's cold body.

Mother has to pay for what she did and I'm making her pay, right now.

'Stop! You're killing me.'

If only I cared.

CHAPTER ONE

Friday, 22 January

Now

Amber sifted through her clothing rail and held up the pale pink jumpsuit. 'How about this one?'

Scrunching her nose, Lauren shook her head. 'You should go with the blue dress, it really suits you and it will be easier to take a pee.' Her friend giggled. She remembered the time that Lauren had got so drunk while wearing a jumpsuit that she'd almost peed herself outside a nightclub in Birmingham.

'No! The blue looks like an old lady dress. I wore it for a job interview. Why don't you make us a drink while I get ready?'

Lauren padded out of the room, pulling a comedy face as she glanced back before leaving the room.

Grabbing her phone, Amber smiled as she spotted another message. She didn't give this phone number to anyone, but he wasn't anyone. She liked him, a lot. He definitely wasn't like the others.

I seriously can't wait to see you for real. You don't know what you do to me. Xxx

She twiddled her finger through her curls. That's what student life was all about, trying new things, new men, new women. She'd tried it all and only regretted the one and that was Lauren. She shrugged as she pulled the jumpsuit on, pairing it with leopard print heels and a long winter coat, which she knew she'd be able to remove when she arrived at the restaurant. Grabbing a chunky necklace to finish off the look, she was as ready as she'd ever be.

She typed back.

Bring it on!

She finished the message with a wink emoji before hitting send. Maybe that sounded too forward. No, it was exactly what she meant to send and it sounded perfect. She unclipped her hair, allowing the rest of her long black locks to flow down her back.

'Oh my goodness, you look beautiful, Amber. Your eyes are so… feline.' Lauren placed the cup of mint tea on her bedside table, kicking a few items of clothing aside to get there.

'Thanks, and thanks for the drink.' Amber knew she wouldn't be drinking it. As soon as she could get Lauren out of her apartment and back into her own, she'd go.

'I may or may not be home this weekend. We'll see how things go.' Amber winked. Insensitive maybe, but Lauren needed to get the message.

'You know, you do look hotter in the pink. Go have a good time. If I don't see you tomorrow, then I'll know you're having too much fun.' The forced smile on Lauren's face told another story. 'Catch you later. I'm off to FaceTime my mum before she turns up uninvited to check on me.'

She listened as Lauren left and the door slammed.

One last spray of her hair and a splash of her favourite perfume, and she was ready to go. Bending over, she picked up the tiny overnight bag she'd packed earlier, containing the bare minimum. It looked like a going out bag but larger. Nothing would be assumed by its presence but she'd be prepared if she needed her toothbrush and some clean lacy underwear.

As she locked her door, Lauren opened hers. Her pale face had blotched up a little bit. 'I'm going to miss you.'

'You said we were okay.' Amber didn't have time for this. Regretful, that's how she felt. She had crossed the line with Lauren and damn, she wished she hadn't. All that 'have a good time' was a front. It was now obvious that Lauren had wanted more. 'I have to go.'

'Please stay.' Lauren reached out and placed a hand on her arm as she passed, her fingers stiff and cold.

Her phone beeped in her pocket. He'd be waiting for her at the restaurant. 'We'll talk about this when I get back, I promise.' Amber broke away.

Wiping a tear from her cheek, Lauren slammed her front door.

As Amber navigated each step in the most impractical shoes she owned, she couldn't get the look on Lauren's face out of her mind. *Let it go for now,* she thought.

She pushed through the creaky main door and an icy gust filled the hallway. It hadn't snowed yet, but the weather forecasters were threatening it. If only it could hold back for the next hour, she'd be fine.

The sound of someone yelping made her stiffen and stop. A man leaned over the boot of his car at the back of the car park, holding his back as he tugged something. She squinted to see into the darkness. As he yanked again, he slipped and stumbled backwards onto the kerb, screaming out as he hit concrete.

'Oh my goodness. Are you okay?' She teetered towards him, almost slipping on the ice in her stilettos as the contents in her bag jangled. An icy blast whipped up the bare branched trees that surrounded the car park, whistling through the underpass opposite.

'Hi, Amber. I'm lucky you came out when you did. My leg, it kills. I was just trying to get my crutches out of the boot and now look at me, I'm a mess.'

'I didn't know you'd hurt yourself.'

'It only happened yesterday. I had a few too many and you know how it goes. The pavements have been icy and I just went. Whoosh. Just like that. Looks like I'll be trussed up for a bit.'

Her gaze was immediately drawn to his pained smile. She checked her watch. She could have him back on his feet in a minute and still make the bus. 'Right, I'm going to have a go at helping you.'

He yelped again and began breathing heavily as she tried to pull him up. 'I'll be okay, honest. Just go for it.'

She winced as she imagined what pain he must be in. She knew all too well how much a broken leg hurt after she'd fallen in PE at school and broken her own. 'Right, let's try again. Are you ready?' He nodded.

'I tell you what, can you just get my other crutch out of the boot? I think I wedged it in a bit tight. That's how I fell in the first place.'

She nodded and glanced into the boot. He was right, the crutch had been jammed between the two sides of the car; the rubber nugget at the end was firmly pressed on its interior. She tugged and tugged but it wouldn't come free. It was definitely stuck. 'I can't seem to budge it.' Warm breath, that's what she could feel on the back of her neck.

Shaking, she turned only to be faced with his nose almost touching hers. The grin on his face told her that he didn't need help. It was a trap and she'd fallen straight into it. A sharp pain flashed through her head as he struck her with something hard. As she stumbled to the frozen ground, her trouser leg caught on something, she heard the tear. Glancing across at her apartment block, she knew no one was looking. All the curtains were shut and she was all alone with a man who was trying to kill her.

The moon above appeared to be spinning. Climbing to a standing position, she tried to turn and run but the dizziness sent a sickening wave through her body. Her heel caught in a pothole and she stumbled back into his arms. She went to punch but he batted her fists away.

'You're not going anywhere.'

Any sign of his limp was now gone. All she could see was his seething mouth and his penetrating stare.

'Why are you doing this to me?' She paused, knowing that her words were slurred. 'I'm meant to be somewhere. He'll call the police if I don't turn up.' He grinned and shook his head. She tried to pull her phone from her pocket. 'You won't get away with this.'

He snatched it from her hand and popped it in his pocket. 'You won't need that any more.'

Another flash of pain seared through her head as he brought the rock down again before forcing her into the boot. Pinpricks of light filled her vision as she fumbled for anything but there was no room to move. When the boot lid slammed, she knew she was in trouble. Her shoes were catching on everything and her coat was twisting. The other crutch was sticking into her side. Jammed in, she was stuck. The car trundled over a speed bump, then it carried on and on. Then nothing but the sound of a dual carriageway followed. The whooshing past of fast-moving cars and a horn in the distance.

She was going to die, she knew it.

CHAPTER TWO

Monday, 25 January

The thaw had begun and there was an icy chill in the air. DI Gina Harte sloshed across the car park at the station, headed through the main door and along the corridor until she reached the ladies. She ran her fingers through her tangled brown hair and tied it up at the back with an elastic band, the very thing that kept ripping it to pieces.

'Ah, guv.' DC Paula Wyre headed towards the sink and ran the tap. Her jet-black hair fell down her back and her fringe had almost grown out. It wasn't like Wyre to let herself become even remotely unkempt.

'Are you okay?' Gina leaned against the sink waiting for a reply.

Wyre began fiddling with her cuff. 'Me and George, we're over.'

'I am so sorry. The wedding?' Stupid thing to say and Gina instantly regretted it. She glanced down at Wyre's ring finger. The shiny rock that had recently adorned it was no longer there.

'It's as over as it's going to be and…' She shrugged. 'I had no idea, not an inkling that anything was wrong in our relationship. He wasn't keen on my hours but I told him from the start, I'm a police detective. People don't just commit serious crimes between nine and five. Anyway, shit happens but another day waits for no one. I've just got to get on with things. Maybe I'll get myself back out there, back in the saddle as they say.'

'Look, if you need to take a short break to—'

She shook her head. 'No. What I need is a distraction. It is what it is. At least the tenancy on the flat was in my name so I sent him packing yesterday. He is gone.' She sighed. 'Anyway, I just want to get on with things so less talk about me and George.'

'A distraction would be most welcome. It's been a bit quiet lately, not that I'm complaining.'

'Not as quiet as you might think.'

'Do tell.' Gina finished pulling her hair into the elastic band and checked out her appearance. It wasn't good but to hell with it. At the moment, she didn't really care. It was January, it was gloomy and it was freezing cold. On top of it all, the boiler at the station was on the blink and they were relying on fan heaters in every room to keep hypothermia away. She almost revealed her smile, the one that might reveal that last night she was with her DCI, Chris Briggs. That night shouldn't have happened but history had repeated itself. She enjoyed his warmth and the fact that he always managed to press her right buttons, but no one would know. She didn't want to be moved from Cleevesford Police and neither did he.

'A woman called Lauren Sandiford is coming in to report her missing neighbour as she hasn't come back to her apartment all weekend. They're both students and live at the large converted house on Bulmore Drive.'

'I know the one. There's been a lot of trouble there in the past but I don't recall any incidents there over this past couple of years. Do we know anything more? Is it just a case of uniform following this one up?' Gina straightened her back, undid her heavy woollen overcoat to expose her grey suit jacket.

'As you say, we've been a bit quiet but uniform have been run off their feet with volume crime lately so I thought we could take the pressure off them for a change.'

'Sounds good. I hope that our missing woman is just staying with friends.'

Wyre leaned against the sink. 'Lauren Sandiford did say that she and Amber Slater had become close friends and that she's not answering her phone. It may be something, it may be nothing. Let's hope it's nothing and Amber turns up.' Wyre reached into her pocket again and pulled a proper hair bobble out. 'I got this for you, guv. It pains me to see your hair being ripped to shreds when you remove those elastic bands.'

Gina snorted out a little laugh, prompting Wyre to follow suit. 'Thank you.' She wrenched the elastic from her hair, pulling out a few more strands, and replaced it with the lovely padded bobble. 'Better.'

Wyre nodded.

'I think we'll interview this woman together when she gets here?'

'Great.' Ever the professional, Wyre had left whatever heartache she may be suffering in the toilet block.

Gina hoped that their missing woman was just having a wild weekend with some guy she'd met. After all, she hadn't been gone long. A little cold shiver prickled on her neck. Hope was pointless. What she needed to do was find the woman, then she could relax.

CHAPTER THREE

Lauren Sandiford nervously sipped on the tea that Wyre had made. Her face was blank, giving nothing away, but her fingers nervously traced the grain on the wooden table. Gina had chosen the room she considered their best, although none of them were particularly inviting, such was the result of the cuts to their budget. The fan heater whirred away, making a clanking noise every now and again. The smell of burning dust filled the room.

'I feel stupid for being here.' The young woman threw her mini backpack to the floor but kept her khaki duffle coat completely zipped up to her round double chin. Her mousy hair fell from the sides of her fur-lined hood. After grabbing a tissue from the box on the table, she wiped her red nose and blew.

'You shouldn't feel stupid. It's good that you're concerned about your neighbour.' Gina leaned forward as Wyre flicked over to a fresh page in her notebook. 'Can you tell me a little about her?'

'We're friends. Really close actually. She left to go on a date on Friday night and I haven't seen her since. It's just weird that's all, and she's not answering her phone. I've tried calling loads of times.'

Gina checked the details she noted down. Lauren was twenty. She was studying the Early Years foundation degree at Worcester University and she worked part-time at the chip shop in Cleevesford. 'Okay, we'll start with her name.' They'd been told when Lauren originally made the call but Gina needed to clarify that they'd taken it down correctly.

'Amber Slater.' She cleared her throat and had another sip of tea.

'How old is Amber?'

'Same as me, twenty.'

'And what does she do?'

Lauren dragged the chair along the carpet tiles and placed her gloved fingers on the table. 'She's a student and she works behind the bar at the Angel Arms. She's studying accounting and finance, year two.'

Even with the heater on full, Gina shivered and she knew everyone else in the room would be as cold. 'Do you have a photo of her?'

Lauren pulled her phone from the outer pocket on her rucksack and prodded at it with her gloves on. After realising it wasn't going to respond, she pulled them off and started again. 'This is her Facebook profile picture.' She held the phone out across the table.

'May I?'

The woman nodded and handed Gina the phone. 'Of course.'

Gina clicked on the photo and pinched it to make it larger. The smiling young woman on the screen exuded confidence in her orange jumper. Her wavy hair shone with health, giving her a model-like appearance. Her eyebrows were definitely painted over to give them a flattering arch and her tight jawline and her heart-shaped face was finished with a pointy chin. 'Could you please email that photo to me once we've finished.'

Lauren nodded and unzipped her coat a little. 'Yes, no worries.'

'You last saw her on Friday night, when she left you to meet someone for a date? Is that correct?'

'Yes.'

'Can you tell me what time that was?'

'Erm... I think it was around seven. She was getting the bus to meet this man at a restaurant outside Cleevesford. It's called the Fish and Anchor. She was meant to be on the twenty past seven bus.' She paused as if thinking. 'It pulls up at the stop a little further down Bulmore Drive.'

'We can certainly contact the restaurant and the bus company to check her whereabouts that night. Are there any reasons she may not be answering her phone or could she have just stayed with someone over the weekend?'

Lauren paused and went to speak but then stopped as if trying to carefully compose her next sentence. 'Maybe. She could have stayed with her date but she would have called me by now? I know she would.'

'Did she usually call you if she was going to be staying away for a couple of days?'

'She's never stayed away like this, except when she's been home to her dad's house. But still, she's always called me or sent a message of some description.'

'So would you say this was out of character for Amber?'

'Yes. Something's happened. I know it has.'

'Can you tell me what she was wearing?'

'A bright pink jumpsuit and leopard print heels. She has a gold nose ring too. I can't remember which coat she had on now.' Lauren scrunched her brow in thought.

There was a tap at the door. Gina stood. 'Excuse me.'

She opened it gently and DC Harry O'Connor stood in the corridor, his bald head shining under the strip light. 'Can I have a word, guv?'

She allowed the door to gently close as she let go. 'Of course.'

'A walker has found a body at the lake.'

Gina swallowed, knowing that it could well be Amber Slater. The woman who was younger than her own daughter, Hannah… Her heart rate began to speed up. They had to get over to the lake, now.

CHAPTER FOUR

Gina passed the play park and headed towards the outer cordon that PC Smith was finishing off by tying it to a tree. 'Morning.' Wyre gave him a smile.

'Morning, both.' Smith's bulky fluorescent police coat made his frame look twice its size. 'Hey, get back, please. There's been an incident. You can't get through.' He held his hand up, pointing to another path that the jogger could use. His other hand gripped the scene log.

The sweaty jogger held his arm up and ran back the way he came.

'Where's the person who found the body?' Gina glanced around but she couldn't see anyone speaking to the PCs.

'He's on the other side of the path with PC Kapoor. He came from the other side of the lake.' He began writing Gina and Wyre's names on the log, the words looking skewered as he kept his gloves on. 'Right, I have you on the list so enter.'

'Thank you.' Gina lifted the cordon up, allowing Wyre to duck underneath first.

A couple of mothers parked their pushchairs behind Gina. She ignored them and followed Wyre under the cordon. In the distance, she spotted Bernard Small, the crime scene manager, along with his team of assistants who had all donned their white forensics suits. His name certainly didn't match his appearance. He was the tallest person she'd ever come across, his wiry frame always hunched above her when they spoke. His once long grey beard had now been neatly trimmed since he'd started dating again. A PCSO darted past them, chasing an errant dog as its owner waited behind the cordon while trying to gently call the terrier's name.

'Time to suit up.' Wyre took a suit from one of the CSIs and passed Gina one.

The CSI shifted her facemask slightly. 'They're just finishing taking the photos and video, if you could give it a couple of minutes that would be great.'

Gina tried to glance over her shoulder. 'Do you have a description as yet?'

'I haven't seen the victim. I just know it's a woman. We'll have all the stepping plates down in a minute. It shouldn't be long.'

Cameras clicked away and another clean CSI walked around with a video camera. Two PCs had started walking up and down the path that led to where the body was, looking for the tiniest of clues beyond the cordon. People were beginning to gather. From the corner of her eye, Gina spotted Kapoor standing under a leafless tree with a man who looked to be about fifty. That had to be their witness. Even more people began to crowd. A sea of bobble hats, raincoats and damp mops of hair added to the crowd. Gina glanced across, wondering if one of them was the murderer coming back to check out their handiwork. Maybe it was the woman who was peering over, wearing a yellow mac; or the man with the maroon bobble hat covered in white knitted snowflakes who was standing behind her. The man in his sixties with the yappy terrier. The two young men in track bottoms and sweatshirts. All of them, going about their business along with twenty or so other people. As more faces joined the crowd, it became impossible to take them all in.

Wyre crept up behind her. 'Guv, Bernard is calling us over.'

'Good. We need to get that body moved with some dignity while this lot are around.' She zipped her crime scene suit right up and pulled the hood over her head, finishing up with boot covers and gloves. Several people had their phones out and were filming and taking photos. Kapoor spotted them, then left their witness for a moment to move the crowd on. '*What's Up Cleevesford* is going to be the busiest Facebook page around any minute now with all the theories and photo uploads. People annoy me at times.'

'Too true, guv.'

Gina almost slid down the slimy bank that led to the lake. Only a few days ago, this same patch of earth would have been rock solid with ice, now that it had thawed it was nothing more than a mudslide. 'Morning, Bernard. Can I see the body?'

'Yes, come with me. Step on the plates when you reach the bank. They're a bit slippy so be careful. We've managed to screen the body off for now while we continue to work around it, but we keep spotting people from the other side of the lake with their cameras and phones out. It's making everything take that bit longer.'

'Wyre, will you ask Smith to send someone over to the other side of the lake and move everyone on? Take their details first.' A list of everyone at the scene would no doubt be useful later.

'Yes, guv.' She nodded and hurried back towards the cordon.

Several ducks quacked and swam over, thinking that everyone was there to feed them. Gina took a few careful steps and finally reached the screen. A bitter breeze caught her face, almost taking her breath away. The thaw wasn't set to last.

Bernard clanked on the plates as he followed, his awkwardly large feet looking like they were spilling over the plates.

'Anything I need to know?'

He cleared his throat. 'Well. I've barely had a chance to look at the body let alone examine it, but there's no mistaking the stab wound to the victim's chest. The post-mortem will hopefully reveal the type and length of blade and if this was the cause of her death. We'll know if she drowned by the presence of diatoms in her body;

a sample of the lake water will be taken. Again, we need to do the post-mortem to confirm this. She's a young woman, maybe even a teenager. I'd place her age at between sixteen and twenty-two. There's no evidence of blood or body tissue found on the banks as yet but, again, we're still looking and testing. She would have bled a lot from this assault. I'd expect to find something on the banks if it happened here.'

'Any signs so far of a weapon nearby?'

'Nothing as yet but the search goes on.'

Gina glanced back. In the still of night, a car could have pulled up at the cut behind her and brought the body down to the lake, or did the girl walk here and become the victim of a vicious attack that led to her death? She also knew there was CCTV at the main car park, which she'd already asked for in her call before leaving the station. It would be a miracle if their killer had used this car park though as the cameras were so visible. The public had been campaigning for more security in this area but, as usual, cuts meant it wasn't possible.

'Any idea how long the body has been in the lake?'

Bernard shook his head. 'She would have been well preserved by the cold water and both yesterday and today have been cold. One thing that does stand out is the post-mortem lividity. She is facing downwards on the bank. You will see that post-mortem lividity has occurred in her buttocks and the back of her thighs and calves. Not long after death, blood pools where there is contact pressure. It appears that the victim may have been sitting with her legs elevated at the time of her death or very soon after. Bear in mind that her heart would also have been pumping blood out of her chest, unless the killer left the knife in place for a while, possibly plugging the wound a little. As you can see, there are so many factors to consider which is why we have to do the post-mortem ASAP.'

'ASAP, I like those words.'

'There's something else.'

'What?'

'Ligature marks on her ankles, wrists and neck. She's been tied up, possibly to the chair that she died in. There are also marks at the corners of her mouth and cheeks. She'd been gagged. One other thing, the skin on her lips has been torn. I'd need to examine her further but I'd say her lips were glued.'

Gina shuddered. All those injuries and it was the thought of the skin ripping from the young woman's lips that turned her stomach. Why would her murderer glue her lips together?

She closed her eyes as she tried to recall what Amber looked like in the photo that Lauren Sandiford had shown her and she hoped that the woman in the lake wouldn't be her. She crept around the screen, wobbling a little on the last plate and stared down at the heap of a body that lay on the muddy shore. She could see what Bernard meant about the purplish shade on the woman's buttocks, visible where her nightshirt had ridden up. Dumped in a lake after being stabbed in the chest. An assault that was so final that Gina shuddered and looked away. 'Any sign of sexual assault?'

'None that I can see but that doesn't mean anything at the moment.'

Glancing across the lake, Gina could see an officer moving the photographers on. She wondered if any of them were from the press. She turned her head back to the young woman and bent over slightly so that she could see the side of her face better. Her long black plaits mingled with the muck and her pointed chin was covered in a gunky film. Her nose ring glinted in the light and her lips had patches of missing flesh on them. 'That's our missing woman.' She grimaced as she took in the waxy appearance of the woman's skin. 'Can you tell me how long she's been here?' Gina looked away.

'The cold water makes this difficult. Given her temperature and the condition she's in, I'd say at least eight hours but that wouldn't be accurate.'

Wyre clanked on the stepping plates as she came up behind them. 'Is it her, guv?' Wyre sniffed.

Gina nodded. 'I'm afraid so. Thanks, Bernard.' She headed back up the bank, ushering Wyre to go ahead as she spoke. 'She was last seen about seven in the evening last Friday and she entered this lake at least eight hours ago. That would be two in the morning on Monday. The killer would have had all day Saturday and all day Sunday to do this. We need to refine this timeline a little more. I hope the post-mortem will be able to do that for us.'

She glanced back at the crowd, albeit a much smaller one. Some of the earlier watchers had gone and a few new ones had replaced them. So many people were coming and going, Gina knew it would be impossible to keep a track of everyone. She removed her forensics suit and started walking towards the witness. 'We need to know what happened to Amber Slater after she left to catch the bus that evening.'

Wyre's brow furrowed. 'Poor woman. Goes out for a date and never comes home. That could happen to any of us.'

Gina swallowed as she thought about her own past dating disasters. One of them had even become embroiled in a case, making her wary of dating again. Besides, no one had ever matched up to Briggs. She'd tried and each time she was with someone else, all she could see was his face. She shook those thoughts away. 'I want to know who this man was. Did she arrive for her date? We need to get everyone back at the station up to date with an initial briefing, then I want to head over to the Fish and Anchor when we leave here. That's where she was meant to be meeting her date. You going to come with me?'

Wyre nodded. 'Definitely.'

Gina shivered as she glanced back. She pictured Amber in a seated position being stabbed in the chest while prising her stuck lips apart; that almost made her stomach turn. The ligature marks made it all the more sinister; an abduction. She ground her back teeth as she imagined the life seeping out of Amber and a slight dull headache began to throb above her brows. Amber must have begged and pleaded for her release and her killer thought nothing of stabbing her. Then, they'd callously dumped her in the lake, semi-naked. All for what?

'Can you contact her friend, Lauren, and ask about next of kin? If she doesn't know, the university should. I remember Lauren mentioning that Amber went home to stay with her father sometimes. We definitely need to speak to the university too. Maybe one of her tutors can lead us to more of her friends or they may have heard or noticed something.'

Wyre nodded and walked to one side to make the call.

'Guv!' Kapoor called to her in her screechy voice.

'What is it?' Gina began removing her crime scene suit.

Kapoor shuffled from foot to foot to keep warm as she pulled her gloves on. 'The witness is talking. I think he saw the killer.'

CHAPTER FIVE

I can't bear to think about it. On Friday, the empty chair had been filled with so much hope but we weren't meant to be. I now see that you weren't Hailey. Deep down, I know the failure was my fault but that's what second chances are for.

My hands itch for more and my head screams failure. That word won't leave me alone. It could have all panned out so differently but now I have nothing. The cold is biting and I really want to be inside and warm but I know my failure will be brought up as soon as I walk through the door.

The park was always a place I loved to visit but now, with Amber being pulled from the lake, it will always be tainted. There are two women at the murder scene that I can't get out of my mind. The one, sleek, black hair, petite and pretty. The other one is definitely senior in position and age. She has an air of authority in her mannerisms, hair wavier but still dark. She stands tall and looks strong. Her face tells a story. Maybe there's pain in there somewhere. The way she tilted her head while looking at the body, I know she cares. I need someone to care about me. She's a little pale, possibly not wearing make-up, but she doesn't need it. I like her and I'm torn. I like them both.

Glancing around, my gaze locks on to one of theirs for the briefest of moments but that's just enough to transfix me. I've decided who the best one is and I know I've made the right choice. I'm in a quiver and I shake my head a little. I can't go there. It's too risky. She's in the police. I have to get out of here before I make a huge mistake. Walk and think, that's what I'm going to do. There's nothing like a wintry day to clear the mind. My boots crunch on a stack of undergrowth and I become still. I have to fade back into the background before someone wants to speak to me or take my address.

Confused. What should I do? I need guidance. I need a plan. I need something. Anything. My mouth is dry and my heart beats fast. A distraction, that's what I need. I pull my phone from my pocket and log on to my favourite app as I disappear from the crowd. AppyDater is the way to go. This is where I will find what I'm looking for, not here.

Forget what I saw here today and keep looking for someone new. Leave the police alone. I search through the listing of local women once again.

Keep looking and don't give up. I will find her amongst this sea of women.

She's out there and if she won't come willingly, I will take her and I will transform her, like a caterpillar becoming a butterfly.

CHAPTER SIX

The witness was sitting on a park bench. He nodded as Gina approached and popped his phone in his pocket. His smart attire seemed unusual for a walk around the lake on a freezing cold January morning. Dark corduroys met brown boots. His blue tie and shirt underneath a charcoal grey woollen coat made him look like he was on his way to work. She glanced down at his footwear, the mud had almost reached his shins and the creeping damp soaked up the material.

'I'm DI Harte and this is DC Wyre. Can I just confirm your name?'

Wyre blew on her fingers before snatching her pad and pen from her pocket.

The man leaned back and stared at the dull sky. 'I've been through this with one of the officers.'

Gina's attention became fixed on the sovereign ring he wore on his right hand, very similar to the one that her deceased husband Terry used to wear. She would never forget its imprint on her cheek after she'd forgotten to put his favourite shirt in the washing machine. Terry might be dead but his memory never left her and that ring was like him saying, *I'm still here.* She shivered.

'Look, I know you must be shaken but I need to know what to call you.' There was something in his tone that wasn't sitting well with her. He was the person who discovered the body. For a person this smartly dressed, what had prompted him to head down to the shore of the lake? She glanced back at the crime scene in the distance knowing she needed to tread carefully. Right now, he was nothing more than a witness and there was no reason to suspect him of anything.

'Otis Norton.'

'Thank you, Mr Norton. Address?'

'Thirteen Bloomsbury Avenue.'

'Can you just go through how and when you saw the body? Please start at the beginning.'

He tapped his foot repetitively on the pavement. 'Seriously? I've already been through all this and I've got things to do.'

'And I'm sorry I'm asking you again but a woman has been murdered. Please, start at the beginning.' A gust of wind blew an icy chill in their direction. Gina rubbed her hands together. He was beginning to test her patience.

His phone rang. He ended the call, looked at his watch and leaned back on the wet bench. 'I got here about an hour ago. I parked back there.' He pointed to the trees behind them that led to a path. This path fed into a gritty track that led to the lake. The very road that had no CCTV monitoring the comings and goings of people who chose to park there.

'On Cedar Lane?' Wyre spoke up.

He nodded. 'Yes, my car's obviously still there. Anyway, I walked down to the lake following the only track that leads from Cedar Lane.' He emphasised the name of the road and stared at Wyre.

'Go on.'

His phone rang again. He muted it and dropped it in the pocket of his overcoat. 'I came out onto the lake and it was quiet, apart from a few joggers and a couple of people walking dogs. When I reached the path, I noticed something that looked like the shape of a human washed up. It wasn't obvious to begin with as I was quite far away and it was a bit misty. Not being sure, I ventured down the bank to the shoreline. I walked past those fishing pegs and that clump of bushes until I reached her. I trod in the mud at the edge of the lake and reached down for her wrist hoping to find a pulse. One look at her told me she was dead.' He stared at his boots and stopped tapping his foot.

He'd contaminated the scene. Gina knew that he would be asked to provide samples so that he could be eliminated. Something wasn't adding up. Most people who found a body were more than happy to assist the police. He seemed like he'd had enough. Glancing back and forth like he was looking for someone wasn't helping her to rule him out. 'Are you waiting for someone?'

'Erm, no. Can I go?'

Gina ignored his question. 'You said you had something to tell us.'

'Yes. When I found the body, I glanced back and saw someone rustling in the bushes back by the path, the one that leads back to Cedar Lane. All I could see was dark clothing but there was definitely someone there. I told your officer just as you were coming over.'

Gina glanced back. PC Kapoor was already cordoning off the spot.

'When I caught them looking, I stared over thinking maybe that's the murderer and I suppose I froze. It felt like they were there for ages but it must have only been a minute, maybe even less.' He glanced at his watch. 'I have to go.'

'Where is it you're going?'

'Seriously? Am I under suspicion?'

Gina felt an eye roll coming on but managed to hold it back. 'Just take a look over there.'

The man glanced at the uniformed officers who were taking notes and speaking to onlookers.

'We are asking everyone the same questions. You are all witnesses and we wouldn't be doing our job if we didn't ask. The woman in the lake is someone's daughter. She has friends and family. Imagine if she was a member of your family. You'd want us to do a thorough job, wouldn't you?' If she had a pound for every time she had to use that in her explanations, she'd be rich.

He undid a button on his coat. His face was reddening and he took a couple of deep breaths. 'I was just walking. My wife is ill and sometimes I just need to get out of the house for some air. She's terminally ill so you can imagine how hard things are at home. She's been trying to call me, which is why I need to get back home. I don't normally leave her for long.'

'Thank you, Mr Norton. Is there anything else you can tell us about the figure you saw in the bushes? Did you see which direction they left in?'

He shook his head. 'No, they were just there one minute and gone the next. That's all I know. I really have to get back to my wife. You have all my details.' He pulled his muted phone out of his pocket. 'She's trying to call me again.'

'Okay. PC Kapoor is heading back over. She'll take over from here. We'll need you to go to the station to make a formal statement after finishing here and we'll need your clothes and to take some samples.'

'Oh, bloody hell!' He stood, towering above Gina and Wyre.

'Thank you.' Gina met Kapoor halfway. 'He's not a happy man but we need his clothes and fingerprints for elimination purposes. Can I leave him with you?'

The uniformed officer smiled. 'Of course, guv.' Her voice pierced through Gina's ears. She headed towards Wyre and gave Bernard one last wave as he headed behind the screen.

'What do you think of our Mr Norton?' Gina exhaled and a plume of white mist told her that the temperature was already starting to drop again.

'I'd say there's something he's definitely not telling us. He's caring for his seriously sick wife but he comes out in what looks like his best clothes for a random walk around a lake that he has to drive to. While you were talking, I checked where Bloomsbury Avenue is. It's a fifteen-minute drive from here and is surrounded by lots of scenic walks and the river runs alongside it.'

'Why would he drive all the way here for a walk?'

'Exactly.'

'We need to dig a bit deeper on him, that's for sure. I don't buy his reasons.' She glanced back. As Kapoor was speaking to Otis Norton, his gaze met Gina's for a moment longer than was comfortable.

CHAPTER SEVEN

The Fish and Anchor stood proudly on the country road just outside Cleevesford. Gina glanced at the bus stop before she pulled in. 'That's where Amber Slater should have alighted the bus to meet her date.'

Wyre nodded. 'And now we'll hopefully get to find out if she made it here. I called ahead like you asked and they have the CCTV on a hard drive that we can take away with us.' She paused. 'You know, George brought me here after he proposed.'

Gina had never been taken out anywhere this nice on a date or during her marriage. Terry had soon conditioned her to stay at home while he went to the pub before coming home to hit her. She remembered one particularly bad time she'd been screaming hysterically and he'd clasped his hand over her mouth, nearly suffocating her. She shivered as she thought of Amber Slater's glued lips and knew that her panic would have been much worse. Was she being silenced in the worst possible way? Gina glanced at Wyre who seemed to be deep in thought. 'Are you sure you're okay?'

Wyre shrugged. 'Maybe I seriously need to get back out there, have some fun and just think about myself.' Wyre paused. 'I now know how you feel when we all ask if you're okay.' A smirk flashed across Wyre's face.

Gina pushed her past to the back of her mind and smiled at her colleague. 'I'll try not to ask again but just know that you can talk to me if you need to. I'll shut up now.' She parked the car in front of the building. The empty hanging baskets squeaked as the wind blew their rusty hinges. The walls were painted in a crisp white. Gina was sure she'd seen it mentioned that the gastropub had been shortlisted for the 'Cleevesford In Bloom' trophy. A cute loveseat greeted customers beside the huge door and everyone entering had to walk under an archway that was surrounded by climbing roses in the summer. But today, everything was bleak and the opaque skies that were filling with snow covered the landscape in a blanket of mist. The licensee's name hung above the door: Lennie Dack.

'Something smells good but I don't know if I could face it after seeing that poor woman's body.' Wyre stood behind Gina and followed her into the pub that had barely been open five minutes.

The smell of frying onions oozed from the kitchen as a door burst open and a woman dashed out to place candles in bottles on the intimately separated wooden tables. Gina's stomach began to rumble despite the horror of what she'd seen earlier, but now wasn't the time to consider stopping for lunch, not with a murderer on the loose.

A short man with a bald patch and a circle of fuzzy speckled black hair started cleaning the bar. Gina squinted to read his name tag. Lennie. Just the person she wanted to see. His dark flawless skin had a shine that reflected the fairy lights dangling from the bar. This really was the perfect place for a romantic meal. His nose twitched and he turned away and sneezed into his elbow. 'Excuse me. It's the cleaning fluids. I'm allergic. Can I help you?'

Gina held her identification up. 'DI Harte and DC Wyre. We spoke on the phone just now.'

A wide smile filled his face. 'Ah, yes. I have the footage ready for you to take. It's timestamped and all that and it covers the back of the pub, the front and the car park. We have CCTV on everything here so hopefully you'll get what you need. Has something happened to one of our customers? I know the staff have all checked in.'

Gina smiled. 'We hope not. We're just following up on a lead at the moment.' Gina opened her bag and pulled out the photo of Amber Slater that Lauren Sandiford had sent her only a few hours ago. 'Do you recognise this woman?'

The man pulled a pair of glasses from underneath the bar and wiped them clean with his crisp white apron. He took the photo from her and held it under the light of the bar. 'I've seen her in here before but not on Friday night. Maybe she was our no show. In fact, bear with me. What was the name again?'

'Amber Slater.'

He grabbed a diary and flicked through a few pages. 'Yes, no show.'

'Is there another name on the booking?'

'All we have is Amber Slater. She definitely didn't turn up on Friday. I was working all day from open until close and I personally greet each customer who comes here for evening service. We pride ourselves on making our customers feel special. We even make an effort to remember their names on arrival. We only have twenty covers and most people who book to dine stay for the evening. We're not McDonald's.' He smiled. 'We're hoping to achieve a Michelin star soon and I'm proud to say, it's on the cards.'

Gina took the photo back from him. 'Can you remember when you saw her before?'

'That's a tough one.' He scrunched his eyes up and turned again only to catch another sneeze. 'Excuse me. At the back of my mind, I think I remember her coming in a couple of times but it was over a month ago. Of that, I'm sure. It was definitely before Christmas. She's been in at least twice while I've been on duty and I can say for certain that she was with different people. Both male. I wish I could remember what they looked like. I am so sorry. We will have written over that footage too.'

'But you definitely remember seeing her?'

He undid the top button of his shirt, shifting his black tie slightly. 'I mean, she's a really pretty girl. I know that sounds bad and I'm not a perv or anything but I remember her because of that. She was also polite too. Not all our customers use their ps and qs when we serve them etcetera but she called me Lennie and, along with the men she was with both times, left me a big tip. We always remember the big tippers.'

'Did she seem intimate with either of these men?' Gina hoped his liking of Amber might have made him take a little more notice.

'I couldn't say for sure. Our diners don't see behind the scenes, but it can be chaos on a busy evening, which is why I probably don't remember. I can't remember anything about them except the men were handsome and well built, if you know what I mean. Looked like they went to the gym. One was white and older and I recall one maybe looking like he could be of Asian descent, maybe Indian, that part of Asia. I know Asia is a huge place but that's the best I can do. Now I remember all that because I envied those men.' He patted his slight pot belly. 'I like my food too much. Never going to happen. I'm so sorry that I can't give you more information but it was a long time ago. She definitely wasn't here last Friday night.'

'Thank you for your help. We'll send someone to take more thorough statements from your staff at a more convenient time, maybe earlier tomorrow morning, before service begins.' Gina glanced around the room. The woman was still tending to the tables and a young man wearing chef's whites popped out from the kitchen. He glanced over, catching sight of Amber Slater's photo.

'Hey. Excuse me,' Gina called as he turned to leave. 'Do you know this woman?'

He shook his head and wiped his sweaty brow with his sleeve. 'No. I've never seen her before. I best get back to prepping the aubergine.'

Whatever he'd come out for he'd swiftly forgotten. Gina glanced through the little circular window that divided bar and kitchen. The chef caught her line of sight and quickly turned away. 'What's his name?'

'The chef?' Lennie wiped a few crumbs from the bar.

'Yes.'

Wyre stood poised with her pen.

'Jake Goodman. Is there a problem?'

Gina smiled. 'No, and thank you. As I said, someone will be here to take statements from the staff soon.' She glanced back. A whoosh of steam filled the air as Jake deglazed a pan. Something about his demeanour told Gina that he knew exactly who Amber was but why would he lie about knowing her?

CHAPTER EIGHT

New day, new dating profile! Time to become someone else.

I flick through the collection of online photos that I've saved and settle on a square-jawed male who claims to be six feet tall. Dark hair and coffee-coloured skin. He's the epitome of perfection, everything I aspire to be. He's shiny, sculptured and just the bait I need on the end of my line. This physique was mine a few years ago but life drains a person. I'm not that person any more.

Profile – add. Hmm, what do I put as a job? Doctor or paramedic. Paediatrician – loves children and animals. Vet, maybe?

Ooh, I recognise her but why wouldn't I? Cleevesford is a small town. Is she the right woman? I'm not sure. She's helped me to choose a profession though, I'll go with doctor. I wanted to be a doctor, but then again, I wanted to be a solicitor then an architect and then a writer. I'm a person of many faces.

I can be anything, I always did think that until life presented me with a plan of its own, one that I hadn't chosen. But I'm free now, free to make my own destiny and it feels like I can breathe again. All my baggage is finally in the past where it belonged. I've taken care of it.

Only last week, I thought I'd found what I was looking for, but she wasn't right. The one I choose has to be perfect.

Today was a new day and it was as if by magic, you've returned to me. There's someone else I can't get out of my mind, only she would be difficult with her being in the police, but she's an even closer match.

I'd do anything to feel close to you again and hold you again. I didn't think that was possible but it is, I know it is.

A shiver of excitement travels through my body as I think of the woman I saw at the lake. What's life without risk?

Shaking my head, I continue with the doctor profile. I'll go with sporty. Women like a sporty man. I begin to type. *I play squash with my friend Jed every week.* I really feel as though my character would have a friend called Jed so I add that detail in. He'd be a handsome high-flyer, like me. Maybe we have drinks at the clubhouse after. I type in squash. I like books too. I know the stories of a few classics from seeing films like *Oliver* and *1984*, I can blag that if the conversation takes us there. Of course, that's if we chat online. Thank goodness for Wikipedia.

I scratch my stubble and flick back to random profiles, then I place my hand inside my track bottoms. 'Let's have some you and me time.' Wait, I have to finish my profile. I hit the smiley icon that tells this woman that I'm interested. I click on a couple of other profiles and hit more smileys. Might as well cast the net widely amongst the women who fitted my criteria.

Tonight I'm going to do me a bit of following, get out there and do my research. So many options and so little time. My fingers itch for a real, breathing version of you.

I glance back at the woman's profile and frown. This site doesn't promote love, it promotes lust. Not what I want, but, hey, it's a start. I'll quite happily arrange to meet this one for a hook-up.

I just need to get her here with me. Once she's here, she'll never want to leave.

'Why are you looking at her?' You stand above me, a tear running down your face, haunting me.

'You know why.'

You shake your head slowly in a disapproving way before fading into the darkness of the hallway.

'I'm doing this for us,' I shout as I hit the wooden arm of the chair, bruising my knuckles.

'You're doing this for you,' you whisper.

I want to storm out of the room and pin you against the wall but I know I can't, it's impossible. Then my phone pings, grabbing my attention. A smiley lights up in front of a photo. Women love a muscly man. It pings again and again.

'Don't do this.' Your shaky cries fill the room.

I head over to the record player to drown you out as I always do. Cranking up the volume, I let the music take me away to another place. A place where the memories are still raw. A place you and I go to together.

It's two in the afternoon. I know where a certain girl will be right now and I need to be close to her. Close but so far away. The smell of her perfume will tantalise my nostrils and I may even feel warmth emanating from her skin. That would be perfect. I grab my coat, leaving the record running.

'I'm coming with you.' You wipe your eyes as you step out of the darkness.

'No you're not.' I hate that you want to follow me everywhere. You never leave me alone.

You barge past me and you're already out the door. The record still plays as the back gate slams.

'Am.' You stick your tongue out and laugh, having the last word. A raindrop hits your cheek and resembles a tear. *'You don't need to do this.'*

Shaking my head, I move *you* aside. I do need to do this and I will do this because I don't have you in my life any more. I pull my phone out of my pocket and press the app one more time. The smileys keep on coming.

'I'm here. I'm always with you. Stay, please.' You hold out your arms trying to lure me back home but I'm not going. I'm on a mission now.

'Shut up and go home.'

'Or you'll…?'

I point to my lips and then to you. 'You know.' I will shut you up and you know it. You sit cross-legged on the wet path that leads to our home as I walk away. For once, I've had the last word. Changes are happening around here, in fact, they've happened.

I'm in control now.

CHAPTER NINE

'Okay. Guv said we're heading back to the station after speaking with the bus company and she said can you find out who teaches Amber Slater's course and get back to us?' Wyre paused. 'Yes, we're here now, just pulling up outside the bus garage. Speak later.'

Gina parked alongside the chemist opposite the large open garage. Several buses were lined up and one stood over a large hole in the ground as a mechanic worked underneath it. The smell of diesel caught her nostrils as she stepped out of the car reminding her of Terry's oily clothes when he used to come home after working as a tyre fitter – one of his many jobs. The memory of him almost turned her stomach. 'I think I got the gist of that phone conversation. The appeal for witnesses is about to go out on radio and will be on the local news, and our victim's father has been informed by uniform.'

'Yes, Mr Slater is driving down from Tamworth in Staffordshire now. He's desperate to be here. Jacob and O'Connor are heading to the morgue where they will meet him.'

Gina didn't envy DS Jacob Driscoll and DC Harry O'Connor. Witnessing the heartbreak on a parent's face when they saw their dead child always haunted her for a long time afterwards. As a mother and a grandmother, she couldn't imagine how that must hurt. They stepped over a couple of oily patches and headed across the vast space full of echoing voices and people in blue overalls covered in grease.

Wyre checked her notepad. 'Can we speak with a Mr Sale? He's expecting us.'

The man raised one eyebrow as he wiped a dark streak from his cheek. 'And who are you?'

'DI Harte.'

'DS Wyre.'

They held up their identification.

'Okay. Follow me.' He ruffled a few flecks of dirt from his hair with his grimy hands and pulled a rag out of his pocket to wipe them on. 'Just through there.' He pointed a dirty fingernail to a Perspex box of an office.

'Thank you.'

The man behind the glass looked to be in his sixties and stared at a screen with a pencil in his mouth. His jumper didn't quite reach over the bottom of his belly, exposing a thick line of hairy skin. Gina knocked.

The man's seat creaked as he stood and walked over to the door. 'Ah, are you from the police?'

Gina nodded as she held her identification up. 'Yes. Mr Sale, we spoke to you earlier about the CCTV from the bus.'

'Call me Ted. No one calls me Mr Sale.' His bulbous nose shone red in the strip light. A faint smell of smoke wafted from his clothing as he moved back to his chair, which creaked again as he sat. 'Take a seat.'

'Thank you.' Gina pulled out her notes. 'We need footage of all routes running past Bulmore Drive from seven on Friday evening to the last bus. The same for the stop outside the Fish and Anchor.' Although Amber was meant to be on the seven-twenty bus, there was a chance that she changed her mind, got sidetracked; even got on a bus going the opposite way. No one saw her arrive at the Fish and Anchor but that doesn't mean she didn't get off the bus on the road outside and go missing from there. All angles had to be covered. She made a mental note to task someone with looking into other methods of transport. Maybe Amber decided to get a taxi. It was cold that night.

'Several routes pass that road. We had the bus that leads from Bulmore Drive to the Fish and Anchor at seven twenty. From our footage, I can see that was on time. The bus was quite busy. Then there was the bus to Stratford and another smaller bus that goes through the estates. They pull up at that stop too. It goes without saying the buses on the opposite side of the road were also running. They go to Cleevesford Town Centre, Redditch, and through the industrial estates. All the footage is on here and all routes finish up at the main bus station at the far end of Cleevesford on the Headley Road.' He passed a portable hard drive across the table. 'It hasn't been chopped down. So for route 227, the cameras run all evening but are switched off when the bus is parked up. That particular bus was stationery for forty minutes for driver changeovers but was running from seven until eleven that night. It's the same for all routes.'

She placed the hard drive in her bag. 'Thank you. You've been really helpful.'

The man cleared his throat and scrunched his eyes as he read something on his computer screen. 'Is this something to do with the woman who was found at the park this morning?'

'We can't say at the moment as the investigation is ongoing.'

'Poor girl. I just heard the news on the radio before you came. I have a granddaughter just a bit younger. It's a horrid world out there. I hope you catch whoever did this.' Mr Sale pulled his jumper down.

Gina's phone beeped. Both she and Wyre looked at the message from Jacob as Gina opened it.

Mr Collins, the accountancy lecturer, has information about the case. He's with students until about three thirty but can see you after that. O'Connor and I are heading to the morgue. He said he really needs to speak to someone about a confidential talk between him and Amber Slater.

'Thank you for everything... Ted. We're really grateful for the footage.' Gina headed towards the door as Wyre packed her pad into her bag and followed.

'You're more than welcome. If there's anything else you need, you know where I am.'

Gina smiled and Wyre re-tucked her white shirt into her trousers where it had ridden out.

As they headed out into the misty day, a few snowflakes began to fall. Just a light flurry as the weather forecast had predicted. If it was accurate, it was set to freeze again overnight.

'I wonder what he has to say.' Wyre's boots clicked on the road until they reached the car.

'And me. I was hoping to call a briefing before we carried on but this is good, the leads are coming to us. Let's get over there now. You never know, this may be a first. We could have this case solved by teatime.'

Back in the car Wyre pulled a salad pot from her bag and began scooping tuna up with a plastic fork. 'Want some?' She held a forkful up. 'Sorry, I only have one pot and I'm famished. You're welcome to half.'

Gina shook her head. 'No, you enjoy your tuna. I'll save myself for later. I have a date with a packet of dried noodles.' That was a far cry from the fish and chips that Briggs had brought over for her the evening before so they could just chat, as friends.

As they pulled off, thicker snowflakes hit the screen. Gina was eager to hear what Mr Collins had to say.

CHAPTER TEN

The car park at The Hive in Worcester was as busy as the one at the university campus just down the road. Its golden honeycomb exterior was a landmark that everyone around these parts knew. A central hub, the library, a place for people to meet and where students worked. 'We've come at a busy time. Everyone isn't quite leaving for the day.' Gina drove around, tailing another car, competing for the first space that becomes vacant.

'What do you think so far, guv? The killer didn't try to hide the body.'

Gina stared out of the window through the few snowflakes that began to settle. The wipers automatically activated, swiping them away. 'No, she was easy to find. Face down on the bank of the lake, her face immersed in water. Looking at the stab wound, I don't think she was drowned but I'm waiting for that to be confirmed. No time has been confirmed for the post-mortem yet; we'll hear about that later. I think it will be tomorrow.' She paused as the car in front nabbed the first space. A woman was packing her shopping bags in the boot as she took them from underneath a pram. 'We're having that space. Why don't you use the app to pay for parking?'

Wyre smiled. 'Will do.'

While Wyre tapped away on her phone, Gina's thoughts went back to the lake. She shivered as she imagined their victim, Amber, trying to speak through torn lips and a pond weed-filled mouth.

'Her body wasn't placed with much thought. Whoever put Amber there wanted her to be found, or should I rephrase that, they didn't care if she was found. There was no attempt to disguise her body, no trying to immerse her in deeper waters, no attempt to weigh her body down. The killer didn't try to cover her up using branches or twigs. She wasn't wearing the same clothing as when she left her apartment on Friday evening. Lauren said she'd left in a pink jumpsuit and heels but when we found Amber, it looked more like she was wearing a nightshirt. I wonder if she took a change of clothing with her, knowing she was going to be out all night or if this is the outfit the killer had chosen for her. So many ifs.'

'Let's hope some of those ifs are narrowed down by the post-mortem.'

'Let's hope so.'

'What stands out the most is Amber Slater's lips. Bernard seemed to think they might have been glued. It's like she was being silenced. Quiet, unable to speak – that's how the killer wanted her.' A horn made Gina jump. The space had become free. 'Whoops.' She held her hand up so that the person behind could see and drove into the space. 'Let's see what our Mr Collins has to say. He's her lecturer, isn't he?'

'One of them. He specialises in management accounting.'

'Sounds riveting.'

CHAPTER ELEVEN

Darkness was beginning to fall. Gina clenched her hands to ease the cold numbness of her fingertips.

A couple of couches filled the university reception and led to a stairwell and a small café. The smell of coffee made Gina's mouth water. It had been a while since she'd had a drink and her throat was drying quickly. A few minutes after checking in, a man appeared through a door and smiled. 'Are you from the police?'

Gina walked over to him. 'Yes, and you're Mr Collins?'

The man nodded.

'DI Harte and DC Wyre.'

'Follow me. Oh, I forgot my manners, it's been a long day. Can I get you both a drink?'

Gina checked her watch. After speaking to so many people, time was racing away and they really needed to get back to the station for a briefing and to tie up with O'Connor and Jacob. 'We might have to pass on that one.' That statement was a painful one. She'd just turned down a coffee.

They followed him up the stairs until they reached a small room with a couple of tables in it. 'We can talk here. Come through, take a seat.' He grabbed a couple of crisp wrappers and an open can of pop and threw them into the bin.

'Thank you for seeing us at such short notice.' Wyre opened her notebook as they sat.

'When your officer called me and said what had happened… well, it floored me. Amber was so well liked. She was popular, funny and really clever. Such a waste. I can't begin to understand how her family must be feeling.'

Gina glanced at the email containing some of Amber's information that O'Connor had sent to her. 'So, she was a year two student and you lecture in management accounting. How often did you see her every week?'

'About three times.'

Gina listened as she took in his features. His dark hair was glossy but messy and his pinstripe shirt tucked into black jeans, topped with a smart jacket, made him look the part of a lecturer. He pushed his round glasses further up his nose. Jaw: chiselled and slightly stubbly. He was handsome in a slight, 'I'm not trying' kind of way. Gina guessed he was around thirty-five years old. 'Would you have a list of people she socialised with during lectures and breaks? We really need to speak to her friends.'

'I knew you'd want to know that. I've printed off some of their details. These were her close group of friends from the course. I don't know who she would hang around with outside the course though.' He placed the printouts on the table in front of Gina.

A list of four names, complete with addresses filled the page. Gina glanced at the names, none of which she recognised. 'Thank you.' She passed it to Wyre. 'You mentioned to my colleague that you and Amber had spoken in a confidential setting. Can you tell me what this was about?'

He swallowed. 'She came across as confident most of the time but I saw another side to her. A few weeks ago, I don't remember exactly when. It was before Christmas and I was just leaving for the night. She was standing outside, back against the wall by my car. It had been raining and she was soaking wet. She looked shaken. I asked her what was wrong and wondered if she needed any help.' He paused and stared out of the window at the falling snow.

'And…'

'She was freezing. I took her to the café that you saw on the way up. No one was there. I bought her a machine coffee and sat her at the table. After a couple of minutes she'd warmed up a little. She told me that when she'd reached her car, someone had been hiding around the side of the building, looking at her and taking photos on his phone. In her words, she said they freaked her out. She said she'd been alone and it was dark except for the flash from the phone. She told me that she called out to them, asking who they were and what they wanted, but there was no answer so she ran. I checked with security for CCTV but our cameras on the car park were out of action so there was nothing we could do. Anyway, I walked her to her car and she left the campus safely. After that, she reported no more incidents so I assumed everything was okay.'

Gina leaned back in the plastic chair. 'Did no one report this?'

'I did ask Amber if I could call the police but she seemed to want to get home after she'd calmed down and she said it was nothing and that she wanted to leave it. I reassured her that I was always here to talk if she needed someone.' He scratched his stubble and placed his elbows on the table.

'Is this something you do with all your students? Offer to talk, I mean.' Gina knew she sounded abrupt in her questioning but it was too late to take it back.

The muscles on his face tightened. 'Of course. If they have problems, their study suffers. I can point them in the right direction if they need counselling or help. Do you have a problem with me caring for my students?'

Gina looked down at the table. 'It's just routine, Mr Collins.' She cleared her dry throat. 'How did she seem after that night?'

The little twitch on his temples subsided. He was no longer grinding his teeth. 'Pretty much back to normal. She thanked me for helping her that night after a lecture. She said that maybe she'd exaggerated what she saw and not to worry about her. She seemed happy and was with her friends so I didn't worry about it, not until I found out what had happened. Is it definitely her?'

Gina thought back to the body they found in the lake and the photo that Lauren Sandiford had sent to her, it was without a doubt, Amber Slater, although formal identification hadn't taken place. Unless Amber had a twin, it was Amber. 'It's looking like it is Miss Slater although we haven't had definite confirmation of that.'

The man's eyes reddened after he rubbed them. 'She will be sadly missed. Is there anything else I can help you with?'

'Have you ever had any kind of relationship with Amber Slater that goes beyond professional?'

Mr Collins stood and pushed his chair under the table. 'No, and I don't like where this is going. Now if there's nothing else, I have to go. My wife is waiting at home for me and we're meant to be going out for dinner. Is that it?'

For now, it was. Gina nodded. As he left for the door Wyre's gaze locked on Gina's as if to ask why. Gina broke their eye contact and headed after him.

'You know the way out, Inspector, it's the way you came.' Within seconds he was gone, not even his footsteps echoing in the stairwell.

As they left Wyre reached out for Gina's arm, stopping her just outside the entrance. 'What was that about, guv?'

'Did you see the way he tensed up when I asked about his and Amber's relationship?'

Wyre shook her head.

'Well he did. I don't know what he's holding back but there's something there. And he should have reported that someone was taking photos of Amber in the car park, regardless. Would it not be the responsible thing to do?'

'I suppose he should have.'

'Maybe he didn't want anyone to delve further into these things for his own reasons. Maybe it suited him that Amber didn't want to report it or maybe the conversation didn't go exactly as he said and he convinced her not to say anything.' Gina paused and smiled at Wyre. 'Come on. Let's get back to the station before I die of thirst. We can pick up this conversation in a bit.'

'Fancy not saying yes to a coffee, guv. Unbelievable. I am now parched.' Wyre jokingly shook her head.

As they headed to the car park, Gina nudged Wyre and pointed towards Mr Collins as he got into his car. 'He just kicked his car door in a temper. That's what I mean about suspicious. Without a doubt, there is more to his story and we're going to get to the bottom of it.'

CHAPTER TWELVE

'I'll see you in the morning, Nanna.' Madison grabbed her coat and blew a kiss to her great-grandmother as she left. She'd be okay until the following evening, though. Madison was confident that she could get around with her walking frame and there were plenty of sandwiches made up in the fridge, ready for her to eat.

'Maddie, come here.' Nanna's crackly voice filled the hallway.

'I have to get back, Nanna. I'd love to stay all night, you know I would, but I have an assignment to finish and I don't want to be getting into trouble, do I?' Madison gave her nan the fake stern look she always gave but then her smile formed. The cream carpet underneath her nan's feet was stained from all the spillages over the past few weeks but it was clean; Madison had made sure she'd scrubbed it well to banish the germs.

Nanna laughed and pulled her purse from the side of her large recliner chair. 'Here, my love, take this and buy yourself a drink.' The elderly lady pulled out a fiver and pressed it into Madison's hand. She did this occasionally and Madison would always try to hand it back. Nanna would always look insulted and insist that she took it.

'Nanna, you shouldn't be doing this. You don't have much and I want to make sure you have enough money to look after yourself, don't I? We can't have you sitting here starving with the heating turned off all winter.'

'Don't be daft, you silly mare. I have a bit tucked away for a rainy day. You're my great-granddaughter, the only one who bothers with me and you don't know how much I appreciate you helping me like this. You're just a girl. You should be out having fun with all your friends, not here helping me in and out of the bath.' The lines around the old woman's eyes were more pronounced as she thrust the five-pound note into Madison's coat pocket. 'Don't forget to live a little. Go out, have fun, make friends, meet handsome men for wild nights. You're only young once.'

Madison's face reddened. Her nanna had talked so much more over recent weeks about her life, her youth, and all the things she'd got up to. Maybe Nanna was right but Madison wasn't about to discuss any of her romantic encounters with her nan. 'Thank you, Nanna. I love you too. As it happens, I'm heading home to study then I'm meeting friends at the pub so I best get going. When the carer comes in the morning, tell them that I'll be back tomorrow night to help you with your evening meal, but it won't be until after six.' She bent over and hugged the old lady, careful with her frail, hunched-over body. The last thing they both needed was for Nanna to break another bone when the last one hadn't even healed, but her nanna was a trooper. She'd fight for her strength and hopefully be independent again, especially as she had Madison's care.

Nanna pinched Madison's cheek and brushed both hands down the sides of her long black hair. 'Go on. You don't want to be late. Just remember that I love you. Put the key in the key safe when you've locked me in. I'm all fine and I promise I'll eat my sandwich in a bit. One last thing.' Madison smiled. 'I'm so proud of you. Little Maddie is going to be a nurse one day. Who'd have thought?'

A slight tear formed at the corner of Madison's eye. After caring for her mother to the end, she knew this was what she was meant to do. That had been her calling. 'Love you, Nanna. See you tomorrow.' As she went to leave the room, she glanced back.

Her nanna was already engrossed in the start of some repeated old quiz show on an obscure Sky channel. She smiled as she left, placing the key in the key safe as instructed.

Trudging through the slush underfoot, she felt a cold wetness seeping through her cheap boots. The orange street lamp reflected in a puddle ahead, lighting up the way between the trees and the side of Nanna's bungalow. The lane that ran parallel to the path seemed quiet. She glanced up through a cut in the trees, one where the old chopped down oak tree had left a gap that Madison used to play in as a child. She and a few of the local kids used to build dens there with old sheets and long sticks. They'd got into such trouble when they tried to light a small fire so that they could cook a piece of toast, setting the sheet alight. She let out a small laugh as the path met the lane.

Nanna's was only a five-minute walk from her flat on Bulmore Drive. She picked up the pace a little – maybe she should have driven, especially as they'd found the body of a woman in the lake that morning. She'd heard the news. Everyone on campus had been talking about it.

She hadn't known Amber Slater that well but they'd hung out as a part of a larger group, attended the same parties and she only lived a short walk away from Amber's block. She remembered the time outside the Angel Arms when Tyrone had been passing a spliff around. Amber was working behind the bar and had told them to go for a walk up the lane so she wouldn't get into trouble. Way to live… She smiled. It was all part of the student experience.

She thought of Nanna and all her stories. The handsome young men she spoke of. How she experienced the sexual revolution of the sixties, much to her parents' disapproval. Nanna had upped and left home, travelled half the world and had a love child by the time she was twenty-two. She smiled as she thought of all the fun she was going to have. Maybe she should let her hair down a bit more, meet some handsome young men just like Nanna had. She wasn't going to have a love child though. A slight titter escaped her lips.

She stopped, noticing that the bulbs had gone in the street lamps above her. The darkness was suffocating. She stared ahead at the next glowing light. It wasn't too far away. Her heart began to flutter. Take a deep breath. Everything is the same at night as it is during the day, it's just darker. Nothing to be anxious about.

A sound came from behind, from the small path that fed onto the lane. She turned to see a long shadow under the last working street lamp. There was someone standing just out of sight and not moving. She placed the long straps of her satchel over her head and across her chest in readiness to run if she had to. The shadow moved and she heard heavy footsteps sloshing on the pavement. A silhouetted figure stepped into sight and remained still, facing her. The person didn't move. She also remained still, both of them facing each other.

Fear ripped through her chest, causing her heart to miss a beat. As she gasped, she felt a light-headedness wash through her. She had to run. She turned and scarpered uphill, not stopping until she reached the next light, the sound of his heavy footsteps slapping on the puddles. He was coming for her.

On reaching the main road, she glanced back as she puffed and panted to get her breath back. The figure was gone. She looked to the right, then the left, ahead and back. He was nowhere to be seen. Had he been chasing her or had she imagined it? Maybe the sound of feet hitting puddles had been her own. She wiggled her soggy toes as she tried to calm her breathing down. She was safe. She was back on a busy road. No one was going to hurt her.

Her phone beeped. Her friends were at the pub. She needed a drink. She reached into her pocket and gripped the five-pound note that Nanna had given her. Her studies could wait until she got home. It wouldn't be the last time she was ploughing through her assignments at three in the morning after a couple of drinks. Glancing back into the darkness of the lane, she spotted a shadow.

Maybe it was a tree, maybe it was him. She shook her head. Was she being silly? Maybe it was nothing at all and the person standing on the lane had a good reason. Or, maybe it was some sicko that got off on scaring women who were walking alone in the dark. She thought back to the news, to Amber, and wondered if she had been stalked by her killer. No specific information surrounding the murder had been released. The only thing the media had concentrated on was a call for witnesses to get in touch.

Amber could have been killed by someone she knew, a boyfriend or a relative. One murder didn't mean there was a stalking killer prowling the streets. She was letting her imagination run away with her and it had to stop otherwise she'd send herself into a panic. She shivered and carried on towards the pub, searching for any sign of life or safe looking human activity.

Time to let her hair down and live a little, maybe even take some risks. Like Nanna said, you're not young forever and she was only going to be twenty for another month.

CHAPTER THIRTEEN

Gina smiled as she grabbed the steaming hot mug of coffee that DCI Chris Briggs had left for her in the kitchen. He'd started doing that a bit more often. He'd make her a drink when he made himself one and send her a message to say it was in the kitchen. She hurried to the incident room and watched Briggs quietly from the entrance.

He faced the board that had been covered with writing and photos of their victim, Amber Slater. Her long dark hair splayed out, bobbing on the water. A slimy film covering the sides of her face and her shoulders, which jutted out of the shallow lake water. His broad figure covered the rest up. If they weren't at the station, she would have loved to give his arm a reassuring squeeze. He reached across with his bulky hand and pinned another photo to the board. 'Gina.'

How did he know she was there?

'I could smell your body spray.' It was as if he'd sensed what she was thinking. Like they were in tune. The thought of him recognising her smell made her heart jump slightly. She'd used the same perfumed deodorant for years. 'It smells good.'

'I'm surprised I don't smell like a cesspit after the day I've had. It's been a here, there and everywhere day, sir.'

'You always smell lovely.' She glanced back, checking that they were alone. He continued. 'Your first thoughts?'

She hated it when he asked this question. It was early in the investigation and she always had so many threads running through her mind at this stage. She swallowed and paused for a moment as she got her thoughts in order. 'Amber Slater was placed in that spot to be found. Her body was almost on the bank where the lake water meets the earth. Looking at where our killer could have parked, it would have taken a lot of effort to get her there but there was no further effort to weigh the body down in the water. We don't know how she got there yet but I'm hoping the crime scene crew have found some drag marks or footprints. The weather hasn't helped though. We've had frost, ice and a thaw. It's been wet, windy and the lake was still busy with joggers and dog walkers regardless of this.'

'You've spoken to a lot of people so far. What are your initial thoughts on them?' He slid a chair out at the head of the table and sat. His lilac tie was loosened at his neck.

'Okay, the first person Wyre and I interviewed was Otis Norton. He called in after discovering the body. He said he was out walking, but he seemed to be dressed in his best clothes while taking a break from looking after his ill wife. It seems odd for him to be there, dressed like that for no reason. I mean, maybe I'm wrong and that's just what he does but it didn't feel right. Something was off and at the moment I can't think what.'

Briggs smiled. 'Suspect everyone until we've eliminated them, that's what we do.' He leaned back and began to play with a Biro, twiddling it between his chunky index finger and thumb. 'Who else?' As he leaned forward a little, the light from above the table caught the grey flecks in his dark hair.

'The chef at the Fish and Anchor, a Jake Goodman. He's a young man, not much older looking than Amber. When I showed him the photo of Amber, I knew he recognised her but he said he didn't. We need to check him out further.' She could feel the warmth coming from his body and she wanted more. It had been so cold in the station but Briggs was rarely cold. She moved to sit at the opposite end of the large table and the strip light flickered. The fan heater clicked off and the room was plunged into silence.

'Anyone else?'

Gina pressed her lips together as she thought back to the university visit. 'Mr Collins, the management accountancy lecturer. He took some of Amber's classes and he told us that Amber had become scared after she thought someone was taking photos of her in the student car park, but he failed to report it. He seemed to get the hump when I probed about how well they knew each other. Again, we need to keep him on our radar for now.' Gina glanced up at the photos again. 'Bernard said that it looked like the killer had glued her lips together.'

'An attempt to silence her?'

Gina nodded. 'Looks that way. About what? That is the question. Did he think she knew something or was she simply making too much noise?'

Briggs paused. 'I miss you when you're not around. I miss your company. It's not just the—'

'I know.' She stopped him mid-sentence as voices echoed through the corridor. DC O'Connor and DS Jacob Driscoll were approaching. Gina checked her watch. Wyre should be back with the sandwiches at any moment. Her stomach rumbled. She gripped her mug and took a long drink of the almost cold coffee as the heater whirred back into action.

Briggs stood and massaged his chin. 'Right, you're going to be the Senior Investigating Officer on this one, Harte. Report straight to me on everything you find. Any problems, call. I'll leave you to the briefing while I deal with the press updates. Obviously, I sent out a holding statement earlier, including an appeal for witnesses, so that we had a chance to speak to Mr Slater, Amber's father. The victim wasn't named but, as per usual, local social media are on our tail. It looks like her friend Lauren has already posted that it must be Amber on the *What's Up Cleevesford* Facebook page. Amber's father will be at her apartment in the morning and will be coming in to the station again. After the viewing with Jacob and O'Connor, he was so distraught they thought he might need an ambulance for shock but he came round a little and said he needed to be alone for now. He's given full permission as her next of kin to enter her property and search everything. It's good that we have his complete cooperation. He wants her killer found.' And there he was, straight back into his DCI role.

The human element of all the cases she'd ever worked on was the worst. She thought of Amber's father and the pain he must be going through. 'I'll obviously be available in the morning to speak to him. I'll try to arrange to meet him at her apartment.'

'Great, I'll leave you to the briefing. Get everyone up to date and work out a plan.' Briggs hesitated for a moment longer than needed before leaving. A prickle ran up her neck. He still hadn't fully forgiven her for her distinct lack of trust in him during the last case. She still had some work to do if their friendship was to survive.

Jacob burst through the door, deep in conversation about an episode of *Queen of the South* that he and O'Connor were watching on Netflix.

'No spoilers, I said. Damn you!' O'Connor gave Jacob a friendly shove as they entered. His usually bald head had a layer of prickly fair hair growing from his scalp. His cheeks were rosy from coming out of the cold and into a room where the heater had been chugging out warmth for hours.

Gina glanced at the condensation on the windows and listened to the pattering of rain that scattered over the panes, rattling the frames occasionally. She twisted her damp hair at the nape of her neck and tucked it up in a bun. Wyre entered with the sandwiches and placed them in the middle of the table. It was going to be a long evening. She glanced back at the photos that Bernard had sent. Ligature marks on Amber Slater's wrists, ankles, neck and waist. Her sore-looking lips made Gina shudder. She licked her own cracked lips and flinched at the thought. She hated the feeling even when she had a slight crack in them.

Grabbing a cheese and pickle sandwich from the pile, she opened the plastic wrapper and pulled the wholemeal triangle out, careful not to scatter grated cheese all over the floor as she took a bite.

Her phone beeped and an email from Bernard flashed up.

As she scanned down his preliminary findings, she felt nauseous at the last thing on the list. Stomach turning, she threw the sandwich on the table. Whoever could do that to a person had to be a complete sadist.

'Aren't you eating that, guv?' Wyre tucked her long fringe behind her ear.

'I've just lost my appetite. I think you will too when you read what Bernard's just sent.' Jacob and O'Connor glanced over as they took a seat.

Wyre flicked through her emails on her phone and winced. 'Oh hell. There's a definite confirmation as to why the skin on her lips was torn. I hoped it wouldn't be true.'

CHAPTER FOURTEEN

Two of Madison's friends had commandeered a booth by the window. She gave them a wave and a smile. The pub was dead. With the partygoers paying off their Christmas credit card bills and everyone deciding that their body was a temple, the party was well and truly over in the short term. That and with it being a Monday. The Angel Arms was the only place to be in Cleevesford, especially since the new licensee had taken over. As she hurried over, Madison glanced at the bar – the one which Amber had once worked behind. She began removing her coat and shuffled into the curved window booth that the other two were sitting in.

'I can't believe Amber, the girl they found dead this morning, used to work here part-time. I mean she lives in your apartment block, Ty,' Alice whispered across the table.

Tyrone gave her a nudge. 'You know when you whisper, everyone can hear?'

'And who exactly is everyone? There's no one in here or haven't you noticed the complete lack of atmosphere. Boring.' Alice yawned for effect. 'It's a good job Maddie turned up or it would have been shite sitting here with you all night getting slowly wasted.'

'Now, now, children.' Madison gave Tyrone a nudge and moved along a little more before she began ruffling through the receipts in her purse, searching for the emergency tenner that she tried to always replace. That and Nanna's fiver should make the night a good one. 'What can I get you?'

'Ooh, as you're buying make it a double vodka and Coke.' Alice burst into laughter. 'Half a lager.'

'Same.' Tyrone pulled his woollen hat from his head and popped it on the seat beside him. 'It's warmed up a bit in here.'

The fire crackled as a log began to burn in the fireplace. Flames danced and filled the lounge with an inviting warmth that told Madison that it was safe to relax and forget the feeling of being followed back in the lane. She headed to the bar, money gripped in her closed hand.

'What can I get you?' The landlady had the longest red nails she'd ever seen and wore her hair in a huge messy bun on the top of her head.

'Three halves of lager, please.' As the woman began pouring the drinks, Madison nervously leaned on the bar with one hand. 'I heard about what happened, on the news. I can't believe it and I'm sorry. I know she worked here.'

The woman frowned. 'We can't either. She was a lovely girl and the customers loved her too. Some bastard out there killed her.' She shook her head. 'We're having a collection for her family.' The woman tapped a tin on the bar with her nail. 'It's to help with funeral expenses and all that. I mean, no one expects to have to bury their child.'

Madison handed over her ten-pound note and received a little bit of change. 'It's so sad. I hope they find who did it.' She placed the coins in the box.

'And me. They should throw away the key. Anyone who can kill a young woman and leave her like that needs stringing up. Anything else?'

Madison shook her head and awkwardly carried the three drinks back to the table, only spilling a little bit of the frothy head down the sides of the glass. Tyrone and Alice were tittering over something on his phone.

'What are you both laughing at?' Madison shook the spilled drink from her hand and wiped the rest on her jeans.

Alice's face went red as she slammed Tyrone's phone on the sticky wooden table. 'I've just set Tyrone up with a profile on AppyDater. He's hoping to meet a tall dark handsome fit man anytime soon. I said he needs a better photo though.' Alice lifted the phone up and thrust it close to Madison's face.

'That couldn't be any less flattering. He has one eye shut and his nostrils are flaring. Check you out! Oh my, you've got your first smiley.' Madison bit her bottom lip.

Tyrone leaned over the table. 'Give it here.'

Madison moved back a little as she checked out the hottie who had sent the smiley. 'He is one handsome beast. You, my friend, are lucky. Get a better photo and quick.' She slid the phone across the table and Tyrone snatched it up.

'It's only been live for a minute. What the hell. I've died and gone to heaven. He's sending me a message.' He paused, his eyes fixed on the screen. 'Now he's stopped. Damn.' He slammed it on the table and picked his drink up, sipping at the head before taking a huge gulp of the amber fluid and letting out a belch.

'It's a good job the hottie isn't here now.' Alice pulled out her own phone. 'I haven't had a single smiley yet. What the hell am I doing wrong?' She passed the phone to Madison. 'It took me an hour to get my make-up right for that photo.'

Madison pressed on the photo so that it filled the screen. Alice's strawberry-blonde hair fell just over her shoulders. Her necklace glinted and her striking make-up made her green eyes look huge. She scanned her profile. Loves cat cafés and reading. 'Maybe you need to work on your interests more. It's definitely not your pic.'

'What's wrong with cat cafés?'

Madison scrunched her nose. 'I don't know. Maybe it's just a bit crazy cat lady sounding. You need to cast that net out wide and you might just catch a prize fish.'

Tyrone snorted lager from his nose. 'I agree. The cat café thing, it's a bit dull.'

'Well I don't think so.' Her serious expression quietened them both, then she grinned. 'If a boy doesn't like cats then I can't date him – seriously.' After a moment of silence, Alice piped up again. 'Maddie.'

'Mm.'

'You haven't got a profile, not in your own name anyway. Do you have a secret one?' Alice tapped her fingernails on the table as she tilted her head and stared into Madison's eyes. She reached over, grabbing Madison's phone.

'Give that back!'

Alice bolted from her seat and hurried past the bar out towards the toilets.

'Give that back.'

The woman behind the bar stood back and smiled at their antics, possibly pleased that something was taking her mind off Amber Slater's murder. Madison ran, hot on Alice's tail, running through the pub and out to the corridor that led to the beer garden. She glanced out to the empty garden, then she burst through the two doors to the toilet to be faced by three cubicles. 'Alice. Give me my phone, now. This isn't funny.'

The cubicle at the end was shut. Madison stomped over and slammed her fists on the door. 'Open up.'

'It's hilarious. Which photo do you want? The one of you standing outside a bratwurst stall at the Birmingham Christmas market or the one of you in your bikini around the pool in Tenerife?'

'Neither. Damn you, no bikini shots. Give me my phone back, you cow. I don't want to be on another dating app.' She kneeled on the floor, insistent on trying to get a look at Alice under the gap at the bottom of the door. 'Alice?' All Madison could see was Alice's boots tapping on the lino flooring.

As Madison laid her head on the floor, the whiff of disinfectant turned her stomach a little. 'Alice, this floor is gross. Just unlock the door.'

'I've nearly finished. Pressing the go button now. Madison, you are now on AppyDater.'

Exhaling, Madison shuffled away from the door and stood. 'Okay, you can come out now and then I can delete it. All that effort, wasted.'

Alice's laugh echoed through the room.

'What?'

Silence.

'Alice, what's going on?'

'You have two smileys. That's what's going on.'

In defeat, Madison headed to the mirror and wiped a bit of smudged make-up from the corner of her eye.

The cubicle door bounced off the wall as Alice flung it open. 'I can't believe it. I've been on it a week – nothing. Tyrone – on it a minute, gets a smiley. You – I've barely pushed the button and two of them are lining up and they look the biz.'

Madison snatched her phone back. 'You used the Christmas market photo. I don't believe you. I'm about to eat a bratwurst. How could you? Since when did I do burlesque dancing.'

'Shut up! Have you seen the two that are interested? You can thank me now. I think I'll swap cat café to pole dancing or something. What do you think? It must be the cat café thing that's putting my potential dates off.'

Madison clicked the first profile that sent her a smiley. He was just a little older than her, chiselled features and looking for a good time. Local too. Enjoys competitive swimming and running. The next one lived in a town close by and was equally handsome but with more of a sparkle. His smooth dark hair and the slight look up at the camera made it feel as if he was trying to seduce her. Loves squash. 'Wow! I mean okay… I forgive you. Thank you.' Remember what Nanna had said. *Live a little.* She bit her bottom lip and smiled. 'Would it be wrong to accept a date with both of them?'

'Absolutely not! You go for it. That's what AppyDater is. No one on there is looking for marriage. It's about dating as many people as you can. The fun is always in the date.'

Madison stared at her friend's reflection in the mirror. 'I'm sorry no one has dropped you a smiley.'

'Rub it in why don't you!' Alice nudged Madison, fluffed her hair up and headed to the door. 'You coming?'

'I'll be there in a minute.' Madison made a rubbing motion along her teeth with the side of her finger. 'Lipstick... teeth.' As her friend smiled then left, she locked herself in the end cubicle and pulled down her pants before sitting carefully on the unstable loo seat. The main door opened. 'What now?' she called out. She was met with silence. 'Alice.' Footsteps led the way to her cubicle. She tugged at the last three sheets of loo roll and wiped herself, quickly dressing then flushing the chain. As she went to unlock the door, she stopped. 'Alice. Is that you?' She bent over and saw the tip of a flat boot underneath. Those weren't the boots that Alice was wearing, they were more like the type a man would wear. The flushing of the toilet quietened to a trickle. 'Please get away from the door.' Whoever was there, remained in place. She edged back and slid the lock. The lights went off, followed by the loud crash of the inner, then outer door.

Bursting out into darkness with only the sound of a dripping tap in which to gain her bearings, she stepped forwards, hands outstretched in front of her. The windowless room gave her no clues as to how far away from the door she was. She gasped as she bumped into something hard and let out a scream as the hand dryer burst into action. Reaching to the right, she grappled for the door handle and darted out into the corridor. Whoever was just lurking outside the toilet had done it to scare her, or maybe it was some sort of joke. She wasn't laughing. With trembling fingers, she took a deep breath and gazed out into the dark beer garden. Beyond the festoon lights, she couldn't see a thing. A shaking tree at the bottom left caught her attention. She ran through the door and tried to focus but whatever might have been there was gone.

Shivering, she hugged herself as a biting breeze swished past. She was getting nowhere standing in the cold. She hurried back and stared at Tyrone. 'Where were you a minute ago?'

He shrugged his shoulders. 'Here. I did go for a slash just before, didn't I?'

Alice nodded. 'You sure did.' She finished her drink. 'Anyone for another?'

Madison ignored the question. 'Did you come into the ladies, while I was in there?'

He pulled a face like he was sucking on a lemon. 'And why would I do that?'

'Because sometimes you can be a dick with your silly pranks.' She remembered the time he'd put a very real-looking plastic spider on her pillow while she was checking her post box – done to scare in the guise of a prank. He thought things like that were funny whereas Madison didn't. After that incident she'd checked her bed every night for spiders. Then there was the time he refilled her shampoo bottle with chocolate sauce. It had taken her a week to forgive him. He didn't even live in her block, he merely visited her and Alice.

'Well, I wasn't tonight's dick.' He glanced at his phone. 'Ooh, I'm onto something here. I've gone and got me a date. See you both later.' He grabbed his puffy coat and pulled it over his long-sleeved T-shirt, finishing off with his black and orange stripy scarf. The firelight caught his deep, chocolate-coloured eyes, making the pupils look like they had little fires burning within them. She glanced down at his boots: black. Were they the same boots she saw under the toilet door? Maybe, maybe not. 'Madison, you need to chill a bit.' With the last word said, he was out the door quicker than she could reply.

Alice tilted her head and played with her hair. 'He's a dick.'

Finishing her drink, Madison stood. 'I think I'm going to head off now, I have a stack of work to do and my assignment is due in tomorrow.' That was a lie but she needed to get home and she was going to get a taxi with Nanna's fiver. She'd been scared too many times already that evening, there was no way she was going to risk another. 'I'm getting a taxi, do you want to come with me?'

Alice flicked through her messages on her phone. 'Nah, I'm heading to Rachel's in a minute. It's still early. Don't forget to look at your messages, Miss Popular. Your phone hasn't stopped lighting up.'

Doing her coat up, Madison headed for the door and stepped out into the car park. She exhaled and a plume of white mist coiled in the air. It had to be Tyrone in the toilets, trying to scare her.

Her thoughts flitted back to the figure on the dark lane. Was someone following her? Had someone been following Amber? She took a deep breath and forced that thought out of her mind as she lifted her phone to check AppyDater as she walked to the taxi rank.

CHAPTER FIFTEEN

Tuesday, 26 January

'Residue of superglue found on her lips? That's just revolting.'
DS Jacob Driscoll finished the rest of his chocolate bar and put
the wrapper in his pocket.

Gina stared up at the old converted house on Bulmore Drive,
the place where Amber Slater's father had agreed to meet them.
It must have been a grand family home many years ago. 'Was
that your breakfast?'

He nodded. 'Jennifer has obviously been working through all
the forensics stuff most of the night. We normally have something
together but she was showered, up and out before I was properly
awake.'

'That's dedication for you. I like Jennifer.' The chunky heel
on Gina's boot cracked through an icy puddle, sending a wave
of cold water over her toes. She wrapped her scarf around her
neck as they crossed the car park, weaving in and out of several
badly parked old cars.

'I do too.' His hair had grown a little longer on top but the
sides were still short and defined neatly against his face. He was
definitely more Clark Kent than Action Man now. He shivered
a little and zipped his coat up further.

'You two make such a sweet couple.'

He shook his head and carried on walking. 'Give over. Sweet.
What kind of word is that?' Pressing one of the bells, then another,

he soon realised none of them worked. He finally knocked, hoping that one of the residents would hear and answer the door.

The main door opened and a grungy looking lad stood there. His checked shirt opened onto a black T-shirt. Black skinny jeans reached his ankles. 'Yeah.'

Gina inhaled and the smell of stale sweat hit her, turning her stomach a little. She wished she'd had a little bite to eat before coming out as tummy rumbling nausea was plaguing her now. 'DI Harte and DS Driscoll. We're here to meet Mr Slater but we will need to speak to all who live here in turn, including yourself.'

His shoulders dropped. 'Sorry, I thought you might be a reporter. Someone knocked earlier, trying to get a story. A guy from the *Warwickshire Herald*. I told the man to sling his hook.'

'Thank you for that.' The last thing she wanted was for the press to start coming up with a million and one theories of their own and they could not get wind of the superglue. That information was just for her department and the killer.

He pulled a hairband from his pocket and scraped his greasy curly mane into a bun on the back of his head. 'Mr Slater is in Amber's apartment, waiting. He had a spare key.' He paused. 'We can't believe what happened to Amber. It's a shock, you know? Losing a friend.' A faint smell of weed wafted from the man's clothing.

Gina nodded as he pulled the door open. 'We're sorry for your loss. What's your name?'

'Curtis.'

Jacob pulled out his notebook and passed it open on a page to Gina. It contained five names. Amber, Corrine, Tyrone, Curtis and Lauren. 'Which flat is Amber's?'

'Up the stairs and left.'

'Thank you,' Gina replied. The entrance hall was quite roomy for the size of the building, with a staircase ahead. Her back brushed against the post boxes as she passed, all of which were overspilling with takeaway flyers and unopened letters. Jacob led the way up to the first floor and another thinner set of stairs led up to another level. As they reached the flat, Gina knocked. A shuffling noise came from behind the door. 'It's cold out here.'

Jacob moved from foot to foot, trying to keep warm.

She heard the catch click.

'Come in.' Mr Slater didn't ask for their names or any identification. He opened the door, moving aside to let them in.

'Thank you.' Gina stepped into the dark hallway. 'We're so sorry for your loss, Mr Slater. I'm DI Harte, you met DS Driscoll yesterday.'

'Come in. I was just...' He gasped for breath and led the way to his daughter's bed where he sat on her strewn clothes that covered it.

'It's okay, just take a moment.'

He rubbed his eyes and clasped his hands as he hunched forward, revealing a tiny balding patch in the middle of his dark hair. 'I can't believe she's gone. Just like that.' He clicked his fingers, his stare meeting Gina's. Jacob shuffled into the small room and stood beside Gina. She nodded to him. That was his cue to take a discreet look around.

As Jacob left again, Gina caught sight of the man in the full-length mirror. His brow was scrunched as he toiled over what had happened to his daughter. Gina wondered how she'd react in similar circumstances and she couldn't envisage it. She and her daughter Hannah weren't close but she couldn't imagine being where Mr Slater was now. She needed to approach things gently, sure the man would crack if she didn't and that was the last thing she wanted. 'Mr Slater, can you tell me a little about Amber?'

He grabbed a purple jumper from the bed and held it close to his chest, then he inhaled it and hugged it. 'She was my everything. It has just been her and me for the past ten years since her mother left us for some man she met when we holidayed in

Spain. That's where she lives now. I called her and told her. She's not even coming back, can you believe it? Her only child has been murdered and the woman isn't even going to help with the funeral.'

Swallowing, Gina hoped he'd go on without further prompting but he went silent instead and that silence continued. 'So, it's been you and your daughter for the past ten years. Did Amber call you regularly?'

He nodded. 'I live in Tamworth, Staffordshire. She popped in whenever she wanted but her visits had lessened. I popped over to help her with DIY running up to Christmas. Her landlord is useless.' He paused. 'I was lucky to get a visit from her once a month but I did make the effort to call her weekly. I understand what it's like, living away for the first time in your life, having a good time, establishing independence. I get why she didn't call me every five minutes and I didn't want to be that parent who smothered their grown-up child. The parent she dreaded the call from every five minutes, so I backed off.' He paused and let out a tiny laugh. 'I was trying to find myself too. Make sure I had things in my life to do and to enjoy now that Amber had left home, now that just feels selfish. I should have been around much more than I was.'

'When did you last hear from her?'

He placed the jumper over his knee and stroked it like it was a cat. 'About a fortnight ago. The last time I saw her was Boxing Day. She spent Christmas with me and her nan, and she stayed overnight, then left the next day to come back here. She said she was preparing to hit the sales with her friend Lauren. She loved clothes shopping. Everything was as normal as it could be. I drove over to visit a few times but she was never in. I thought she was having too much of a good time to see her old man.'

'Go back to that phone call a couple of weeks ago. How did she seem?'

'Full of life. Excited about her course and her future. She said she really wanted to be a management accountant and was looking into the CIMA qualification. That's chartered management accountancy. Apparently her tutor had said she had a natural flair for it and should really think about doing it, when the time was right. I was so happy for her. I don't know where she gets her brains from – got, where she *got* her brains from – but it's not me or her mother. I can't get used to saying that, referring to her in the past tense. I mean, I can still smell her in this room. There is a dent on her pillow from when she last lay on her bed. The milk in her fridge isn't even sour.' His hair looked like it was once a short back and sides but some bits had grown longer than others at a different rate, making him look a little scruffy. He clenched his jaw and straightened his back. 'Someone took her from me. If I find out who, I'm going to kill them! I'm going to torture the bastard and shove him face down in a freezing cold lake to drown, then I'll stamp on his head, crack it like a watermelon. I mean it…' His hands began to tremble. 'How could anyone have hurt Amber like that? I should have been there more.'

Gina could see his clenched knuckles shaking. 'Mr Slater—'

'Theo. Mr Slater is getting annoying. I never get called that. Sorry.' He took a breath and composed himself. 'I shouldn't have shouted.'

Jacob stood in the doorway as she continued. 'I have to ask you this. Do you know anyone who might want to hurt Amber? Anyone she'd had a disagreement with, fallen out with, anyone she was seeing?'

'She never mentioned anything when we spoke and I think I'd have known if she had a boyfriend. I don't know how anyone could not like her. She was kind, loved her friends and family.'

Gina knew that it wasn't likely that Amber would have spoken to her father if she'd fallen out with someone or met someone.

She'd more than likely speak to her friends, the people she was around day in, day out.

'I told you all everything I knew yesterday, at the station. And, what I do know is nothing. Not a thing. If I knew something, I'd tell you. I want her killer found.' He seethed at the end of his sentence, slightly spitting on the back of his hand.

Gina bit the dry skin on the edge of her lip and flinched at the thought of tearing lips trying to free themselves after being glued together. A metallic taste swirled on her tongue; they had cracked again. 'We will need to take Amber's laptop and any other devices that might help with the investigation. I would also like to take a look around her apartment if that's okay.'

'She'd hate anyone snooping around her stuff.' He stood and walked over to the window still holding the jumper. 'I understand though.' He placed a key on the windowsill. 'The rent is paid in advance until the end of February. I know because I pay it. Please be gentle with her things. They're all I have left of her. I wished now that I'd moved closer so she could have stayed with me at home. I could have protected her.' He walked back to the bed and placed the jumper back on it. 'I have to get out of here for a bit, clear my head with some fresh air.'

'Of course – and thank you. I'll make sure everything is put back in its place.'

Gina glanced around the room. It was a stereotypical student pad. A bit shabby and scratched, old-looking mismatched furniture and a scraggy rug. Mess filled every corner. Textbooks mixed with clothes. Make-up dust covered every surface.

'You have my number,' he said and left the room. The door slammed a moment later.

Jacob walked over to the window and stared out. 'Poor man.'

'Did you find anything?'

'Laptop on the worktop in the kitchen-cum-living room. And there's something else. Come take a look.'

Gina hastily followed Jacob through the hall, past the bathroom and into the kitchen area. With a gloved hand, he slid the top drawer open and pulled an old phone out, one that was only capable of sending messages or making phone calls on.

'It was already turned on. You should read these messages, guv.'

She glanced through them, hoping that the last bar of charge wouldn't turn it off mid read. 'Book this in now, along with her laptop. We have full permission from Theo Slater to be here so I want PC Smith to hurry over and organise a small team to search for anything that might be relevant. I don't see any evidence that her murder was committed here but we need to stay focused. We need her phone records too. I can't believe for one minute that this old phone is her main one.' She glanced at another message and shivered.

CHAPTER SIXTEEN

Theo hurried back towards the car and drove as fast as he could, away from the police and his daughter's digs. He drove into Cleevesford and along the high street until he found the pub, the one Amber worked in.

He charged through the heavy door and made his way to the bar. Maybe he should have come earlier, checked out where his daughter was working but she'd told him to stay away and he'd respected that. He glanced at the collection box and swallowed. They must have thought a lot of Amber, too.

'What can I get you?' The woman with bright red lips that matched her nails leaned on the bar, waiting for an answer. Her leopard print top flapped open as a button slipped from the hole. His instinct was to tell her to do it up, just like the many times he'd told Amber to change before she went out with friends. That had caused a lot of arguments between them. In any other circumstances, he might have tried to chat this woman up but right now, all he needed was a drink.

'A pint of Wonky Elm, please?'

'Good choice.' As she turned to pour it, her heels clipped on the tiled floor behind the bar. Too spiky and too showy, she wasn't his type at all. He stopped himself from thinking about when he confiscated half of Amber's clothes and shoes for this very reason. And now, he'd finally taken a look in her wardrobe, never daring to do so before in case the clothes she was wearing were despicable. The short skirts, the tight dresses, the high-heeled thigh-length boots – and she had a vibrator in her bedroom drawer. He shook his head trying to cast all these images out of his head. His Amber. His little girl.

'One Wonky Elm. Can I get you anything else? We have a brunch menu.'

He shook his head. 'I'm good thanks. Thank you for what you are doing.' He pointed to the collection tin. 'I'm Amber's father.'

'I'm so sorry. We all loved her here. She was such a lovely—'

He held up his hand to end the conversation. He couldn't talk about it, not yet. Taking the pint, he found a quiet corner in the pub and stared into the fireplace, watching as the flames licked the edges. A breeze blew through the chimney. Little flecks of black swished along the hearth until one piece hit the carpet.

Pulling the phone from his pocket, he clicked on the app one more time and stared at his daughter's face. His beautiful girl had been 'looking for a good time'. Holding his finger on the app, he dragged it away, deleting it forever. He no longer had to watch over her. Swigging the ale, he felt his emotions beginning to spill. He swallowed them down, closed his eyes and slowed his heart rate down with a few controlled breaths. The app was deleted and no one would know he'd ever used it.

He should never have gone there, to that place within himself that he tried so hard to bury. It was unforgivable. Some things can't stay in a box. They escape, consuming you until you let them out and now he could never forgive himself.

CHAPTER SEVENTEEN

Gina read through the messages again, sent from multiple people. This time she read all the replies to the original messages.

> *BigBoz*
> *Amber, I really lurved last night. You do something 2 me that I can't explain. Fancy a repeat performance? Just tex if u do.*

No reply and no further messages to BigBoz.

> *NoName*
> *I need to speak to you. Please, Amber.*

> *Amber*
> *What we did wasn't right and you lied to me. Don't message me again.*

> *NoName*
> *Don't do this to me. Answer your phone. I need to talk to you.*
> *NoName*
> *Why aren't you answering?*
> *NoName*
> *There's someone else, isn't there?*

Amber
You're stressing me.

NoName
Me stressing you.

Amber
I can't stand this any more. I'm turning the phone off.

NoName
Don't do that. You can't ignore me.

NoName
Why won't you pick up?

NoName
Just answer your phone.
NoName
Stuck-up bitch. There are plenty of others who'd like to have what you have.
NoName
Amber, I'm sorry about the last message. I didn't mean it.

That was the end of the message chain for NoName.

AdamzFun
You didn't turn up.

Amber
I turned up you shit. That wasn't your photo. Go do one.

AdamzFun hadn't replied again.

BearBoy
I can see U puttin it about. You don't have to do it! You're
a nice girl.

Amber
I tell you what, you and the morality police can FO!

The phone let out a beep and turned itself off. Gina bagged it
and placed it in her pocket. 'Bloody hell, some people just don't
take no for an answer. I'm talking about NoName. So, she had
been active on the dating circuit and all these messages were sent
over the course of three weeks. Why would she use this phone?
I'm sure this isn't her main phone, she would have taken that with
her when she left to meet her date. Will you check the number?'

Jacob leaned against the wall in the hall and flicked through
his notes. 'Her main number is different. Her father gave it to us.'

'It's possible that this is the number she gives to her dates
so she doesn't have to change her main number if any of them
become a nuisance.'

'Sounds reasonable.'

Gina took a slow walk around the apartment. The fraying
leather sofa was half covered in snuggle blankets and several
used glasses and cups were dotted around the room. The tiny
kitchen at the other end looked to be barely used, except for
the toaster, which had a pile of crumbs underneath. A box of
opened peppermint teabags and a jar of value hot chocolate sat
next to the kettle.

She left the room, nudging past Jacob as he checked his emails.
The tiny bathroom was more like the size of what a person would
expect in a caravan. The tiniest wet room ever with no window
and black mould seeping through the corners. She opened the
mirrored cabinet. A half-used packet of antibiotics and a variety

of moisturisers and hair serums and filled it. She closed it and glanced around. Nothing seemed out of place.

Gina's phone beeped in her pocket. She pulled it out and spotted Wyre's name at the top.

Hi guv, we can confirm from all the CCTV that Amber Slater never arrived at the Fish and Anchor for her date. Also, there is no footage of her getting on any buses. We've been watching them all morning and there's not one sign of her. The post-mortem is going ahead earlier than anticipated so I'll head over now and I'll keep you posted if that's okay. O'Connor and PC Smith are on their way over to help with interviewing the neighbours.

Earlier was better than later. Gina had hoped she could be there. She glanced at the time. She could still make it for the second half if she got a move on.

'Jacob. Amber never got on the bus. What happened to her between leaving here and getting to the bus stop?' She hurried along the hallway and stared out of the window.

He joined her, holding the curtain back. 'The person who sent those messages, NoName... they sound angry, and they're not taking no for an answer.'

Gina pictured someone hanging around, watching the young woman and waiting for her to come out. So consumed with jealousy and rage, they had to know what she was doing all the time. She'd left her apartment all dressed up. Had they seen red and done something reckless or had it been more premeditated than that? With any hope the car park and the path to the bus stop may hold the clues that they were looking for. A snapped fingernail, a clump of hair, a torn bit of her clothing, a shoe, anything.

The front door led to a large car park. Beyond that car park was an underpass and the road that eventually led to Cleevesford High Street. Through the trees, she could just about make out the post with the red sign that was the bus stop. 'I need a team searching the car park. Can you get down now and start cordoning it off. Monitor who comes and goes while I speak to Curtis downstairs. Someone must have seen something or heard something.'

'On it, guv.' Jacob moved his hand from the curtain and it flopped across the window as he moved. He nodded and left the apartment. Moments later, she watched him surveying the car park.

She pulled a pair of latex gloves from her bag and, kneeling on the floor, gently began pushing through the mountain of mess in the corner. The textbook had a refill pad sticking out of it and what looked like equations covered the page. She flicked through a few more but there was nothing of interest to note. She lifted a few more items of clothing, dirty mixed with clean, all creased, the heel of a shoe getting tangled in a bra strap. Shifting closer to the bed, she lifted the valance and peered under. Boxes of under-bed storage filled the space. Gina gasped and hit her head on the bedframe as a disturbed spider shot out from the darkness.

She took a deep breath and laughed to herself before getting back to looking under the bed. A tiny ornate box had been pushed against the wall. One that looked hand-decorated in an amateur manner with little jewels stuck onto the wood, some fallen off.

Stretching her arm out, she grabbed the lid of the box and slid it across the carpet until it had cleared the bed and she opened it. A little plastic package containing five sugar almond-coloured tablets that Gina was sure would turn out to be MDMA, more commonly known as Ecstasy.

Jacob called and she answered immediately. 'Guv, O'Connor is here and he's handling the cordon with Smith. You have to see this. We think we've found the spot where she was taken. I say taken because the street lamps have been purposely knocked out in one end of the car park, exactly where Amber Slater would have passed to get onto the path for the bus stop. There's also something else you need to see.'

Adrenaline coursed through her veins. A clue to how Amber might have been taken could lead to a clue as to who killed her. The thought of the poor girl's lips being glued together almost made her feel like gagging. Whoever did that to her had to be pure evil and she was going to stop them doing it to anyone else.

CHAPTER EIGHTEEN

Hurrying across the car park, Gina met with O'Connor and Jacob. O'Connor bumbled around, looking for anything he could see in the verges that led to the underpass. PC Smith was starting to drag the cordon around the various posts and street lamps to keep any potential pedestrians away from what could be a crime scene. 'Show me.' She bent over to see what Jacob was looking at.

A shred of muddied pink material was encased in a chunk of ice between the two street lamps, each of which had smashed glass from their light bulbs scattered underneath.

'She was wearing a pink jumpsuit when she left to meet her date last Friday, that's what her friend Lauren told us. Get forensics here straight away and let's all step away for now to preserve the scene. Who knows what else we might find.' Gina backed off, away from the shattered glass and the others followed suit. She pulled out her phone and pressed Bernard's number. 'I know you're up to your ears in it with yesterday's scene but we need a team to hurry to Bulmore Drive, the car park that is outside numbers seventeen to twenty-two.' She could imagine Bernard stroking his beard with a ruffled brow while he considered what she was saying. She could picture all the evidence bags that had been tagged and brought in overnight in boxes, ready to be processed and examined.

'I'll send Keith and Jennifer over now while I carry on with all the evidence that's piling up over here.'

'Thank you. Will you be joining us at the briefing later today?' Gina flinched as a cool splat of hail came from nowhere, stinging her face.

'I'm hoping to. You just can't imagine how much stuff we pulled from the lake scene. We have the contents of most of the bins, and everything picked up from the car park. We had a team out dredging the lake too after you'd left. So much stuff and any little item could be the thing that solves the case. We are literally drowning in objects to analyse.' He paused and made a smacking sound with his lips. 'I'll be there.'

'Thanks, Bernard. I'll make sure there are snacks. Look, I know you must be shattered like the rest of us so it's all much appreciated. Speak later.' She ended the call and Jacob nodded across to PC Smith who was filling out a log sheet, ready for the influx of officers and crime scene attendants to turn up. The young man with dark greasy hair stood outside the apartment block smoking what looked to be a roll-up. 'I think we should speak to Curtis Gallagher, see what he might know.'

Jacob wiped the wet trail from his face. 'Anything to get out of standing in this.' They hurried back.

Curtis's gaze met hers as he exhaled a plume of smoke. Someone who was always outside smoking may just have seen something that might propel the case forward. Maybe Curtis had seen Amber on the evening she went missing.

CHAPTER NINETEEN

'Curtis, may we speak with you now?' Gina spoke as Jacob waited beside her.

The young man took one last suck on his roll-up, stubbed it out between his thumb and index finger, and then placed the rest in his pocket. 'I can't go wasting 'em, being a student and all. Come through.'

They followed Curtis along his hallway and into his lounge and kitchen studio area, which looked to be a mirrored layout of Amber's apartment. The sparse room had a two-seater sofa in it and an oil radiator. A large television sat on a scratched wooden unit and a games console was strewn across a mustard-coloured rug. A desk piled with folders stood flush against the wall.

'Sit.' He gestured at the sofa.

As they sat, Gina felt herself being wedged in by Jacob. The sofa was far too small for two average-sized adults. Glancing around, she spotted an ornamental-looking bong and a pair of underpants in front of the washing machine. A jewelled black skull had been placed in the middle of a coffee-ringed table and looked to be peering in Gina's direction. 'We'd like to speak to you about Amber. We'll be speaking to everyone in the block so this is routine. Going back to last Friday evening between seven and half past seven, did you hear or see Amber Slater?'

He began to pick a dried-up spot on his chin. 'Not really, the only thing I heard was her coming down the stairs. I can't remember what time exactly but it was about then. These apartments aren't really soundproof and she stomps loudly on her heels as she's coming down the stairs. We can all hear each other coming and going. I heard her and Lauren talking on the landing, it sounded like Lauren was pleading with her to stay home. I don't know what it is with that pair. One minute they're the best of friends, the next minute they seem to ignore each other for days.'

'Can you expand on that a little?' Maybe there was more to Amber and Lauren's friendship.

'We all hang out together now and again, have a few beers in one of our apartments. It's cheaper than going out. Look, you'd have to be from another planet to not see that Lauren has a crush on Amber, the way she looks at her. Amber is a serial dater, loves meeting new people. Lauren is the opposite. She sits on her own at home with only Amber as a friend. I can't really tell you any more than that as I don't really have too much to do with either of them.'

Gina thought back to the little box under Amber's bed. 'Does Amber use drugs?' If nothing else, she needed to add 'drug purchase that may have gone wrong' to the killer's list of motives. Sometimes the simplest of reasons can be behind a murder and drugs and the money associated with them were powerful in the motive department.

He awkwardly shifted his weight to his other leg before grabbing the torn office chair in front of his makeshift desk made from a piece of old worktop. He slid the folders out of the way and placed his elbow on the wood. 'No.'

Gina cleared her throat as she and Jacob stared at the man.

'Okay. She may have dabbled on nights out. I know she had an occasional smoke or a tablet when she went clubbing, but that was it. Was she a druggie? No way. It was a special occasion thing. It's nothing unusual. Everyone does it. Not me, of course.'

Jacob relaxed his stare and caught up with his notes.

'What was Amber like?' He was opening up. Gina was sure that if she could get him to talk, he wouldn't stop.

He pulled the hairband from his hair and ruffled it, freeing it before bending over to flick the heater on. 'It's getting cold in here.' He grabbed a thick, mangy-looking cardigan from the back of the chair and put it on. 'Amber… she always seemed happy. She was popular. She had endless amounts of energy for going out, experiencing new things and life in general. She was so glad to get away from her strict home, it was like she'd won the lottery or something when she moved out from her dad's house. She told us that at home she had to be in by ten and even then Daddy would constantly call. He moaned about her clothes and her friends. He turned up here a few times even when she wasn't in. It was like he was trying to catch her out with a man.' He grinned. 'Anyway, living here, she was free and she was making the most of her freedom by dating, going out. I even recall her saying that she did a parachute jump last year. She didn't tell Daddy that either. The man would have freaked at his cotton wool-wrapped daughter jumping out of a big bad aeroplane.'

'Were you and Amber close?' Gina wanted to get down to the crux of any relationship they may have had although looking at him, she couldn't see that he'd be Amber's type, but then again, she always told herself, determining who a person would chose to be with was impossible. Maybe she liked his laid-back demeanour. She inhaled the combination of week old sweat and burger grease that came from his cardigan as he shuffled.

'No closer than anyone else in the building. We just hung out and drank together on rare occasions and as a part of a group. That was it. The things I mentioned are just what came up in mostly group conversation.' The spot on his chin had begun to seep a little. He swiped his finger across it. 'I should eat better really.'

'Who lives in the bungalow at the back of this building? The one with the private road that passes alongside this block.'

Curtis started biting the inside of his mouth. 'The biggest party pooper around. If we even fart too loudly, he's over, telling us to keep it down or our tenancies will be terminated. That will be the landlord. His father owns this block and he makes sure we know it. Toilet is leaking? Three weeks to fix. I cough? He turns up telling me to shut up. That's a bit of an exaggeration but you get my meaning. When we do drinks in the block, we have to keep all the windows shut and try not to be too obvious.'

Gina nodded. 'What's his name?'

'Vincent something or other. Don't know his second name. It's probably Arsehole, Vincent Arsehole. He's not even that old for a landlord, probably mid-thirties, maybe forty if he had a hard life. I don't know what his problem is.' Curtis laughed.

'Are you a student too?'

He nodded. 'I'm a mature student, I mean twenty-six is old, definitely mature. I attend college though, not university like Amber and Lauren. I'm doing a two-year mechanics course at the college in Bromsgrove. Hoping to have my own garage one day. I always loved tinkering with cars so after a few years of working in pubs and cafés, I thought it was time to sort my life out and follow my dream.'

'Just to clarify, where were you between six and ten on the evening of Friday the twenty-second of January?'

Curtis's brow furrowed.

'That's last Friday?'

He pulled the half roll-up from his pocket and placed it behind his ear. 'Now I need a puff. I was here all night gaming and like I said, I was here and I heard Amber coming down the stairs. My curtains were shut and I didn't see or hear anything else. I don't go out that much. I'm always pretty broke so I stay in and game until late.'

Gina listened to Jacob's pen hastily scribbling away. When he stopped, she continued.

'Did you go out for a smoke at all?'

He shook his head. 'I don't go out at night, it's too cold. I'd get into trouble if Vincent Arsehole found out but I smoke in the bathroom and blow my smoke out of the window. The fire alarm doesn't pick it up.'

Gina's shoulder dropped slightly. She was hoping that he would have been in and out on that evening, and that he'd have noticed something, however small. 'One last question, have you seen anyone suspicious hanging around the car park or outside the apartments?'

'Now that you mention it, yes, a figure in the bushes.' He got up from his chair and beckoned Gina over. She hurried to the window where he pulled back the yellowing voile and pointed. 'Right there, just to the side of the underpass. I've noticed this weirdo around since the New Year, only now and again, and it looks like he stands and stares at the flat. He wears a hat, like something Frank Sinatra would wear, but even under the street lamps all I saw was a shadow but no features. Was he stalking Amber? Is that what you think?'

Gina moved away from the window and headed back to the sofa, not sitting this time to Jacob's relief. 'At the moment we're investigating and this is something we will look into. Can you describe this person?'

'Yeah, a shadowy figure that looks male. Broad shouldered and average to tall. That's all I know. I really didn't worry about who it might be as I only saw him through the window now and again, never when I went out.'

'Can you remember when or how often you saw this person?'

He scrunched his nose and paused. 'About two, three times per week. I joked in my head that it was probably killjoy Vincent trying to gather evidence of our bad behaviour to catalogue, just in case he wants to chuck any of us out.'

'Did you ever think to report this person?'

'Nah. I just closed my curtains and got on with life. In hindsight, I wished I had now. Sorry.'

Gina checked her watch, she was missing Amber's post-mortem and it was looking highly unlikely that she'd make the meeting with the pathologist after. She made a mental note to message Wyre and ask her to cover everything that was needed in readiness for the briefing. Curtis began to chew his thumbnail, his teeth making a clipping noise as he gnawed away.

'Thank you for your time. If you remember anything else, can you call me straight away?' She passed him her card.

'Of course.' He read it. 'DI Harte.'

'Can you confirm your surname?'

'Gallagher.'

As they stepped into the hallway and out of the main door, Gina watched as the teams gathered to begin the search of the area for evidence. She watched from afar as O'Connor spoke and everyone listened. Her phone went and Briggs's name lit up.

'Sir.' She waited for him to break the silence.

'There's been a lot of digging going on at this end into all the people you said to investigate further and Wyre gave me her notes when she left for the post-mortem. There's one thing you will want to see in all this and we can't leave it too long. Get back as soon as you can.'

She glanced back at the road that led alongside the apartment block and she could just about see the bungalow amongst the naked tree branches. Vincent the landlord would have to wait.

CHAPTER TWENTY

Madison closed her textbook and glanced across the desk at the rest of the library. Other students worked away in silence and a couple of girls about her age were whispering as they picked up a few books and carried on past her, down the stairs towards the ground floor. The bright and airy space was one of the reasons she loved studying at The Hive, the striking new library in the centre of Worcester City.

The window beyond framed a misty sky, one that made everything outside appear milky white. A fog was descending which would blanket the whole of the charming city. She loved gazing at the river when she went for a walk and she knew it would look just as stunning on a day like this. Time to wrap up warm, stretch her legs and get some lunch.

As she packed her books away, she spotted a pair of heavy black boots under one of the bookshelves. Had it not been for the shelf, the person behind it would be staring right at her. She swallowed and zipped up her bag, throwing it over her shoulder as she stood. Her twitchy hands were telling her to run, to get away but something deep inside was saying, *you need to know who's there.*

She took a few steps closer and flinched as she kicked the bin. A student who looked to be studying microbiology glanced up.

'Sorry,' she mouthed.

He smiled and carried on with his studies. The boots, they were gone. She hurried around the shelf to see that the whole row was devoid of people. He had to be somewhere. She ran between the other rows, glancing back and forth, checking out everybody's footwear but he was nowhere to be seen. As she reached the last row of books, she took a deep breath, her hand gripping her bag so tight it felt like her skin had melded to the plastic strap. Her heart began to thud as she turned the corner. No one. She was alone, at the back of the library. As she turned to head back, she gasped as she crashed straight into a man's chest.

'Tyrone, what the hell are you doing, creeping up on me like that?'

'Firstly, I am not creeping up on you. I was looking for a peaceful place to study and this is my favourite place to sit and secondly, why the hell are you shaking so badly? You look like you've just seen the dead rise in the aisles of the library.'

Madison's gaze stopped on the single desk and chair under the window. 'I just… last night at the pub… just tell me the truth, did you come into the ladies toilets to play a prank on me? Just answer honestly as I'm freaking out here.'

He brushed a couple of his errant dark hairs away that had shed onto his coat. 'I swear it wasn't me. Is something going on?'

'I don't know. Someone is following me. When I left Nanna's last night I was sure someone was keeping back on the lane. The lights were out and I got scared. Then, in the pub, while I was in a toilet cubicle someone was standing outside the door…' She glanced down. 'They were wearing boots like yours which is why…'

'You thought it was me.'

She nodded. 'Yes. The same person…' She gulped and tried to hide her trembling hands but Tyrone had already seen them.

'Here, sit down.' He pulled the chair out from under the desk.

'After they stood there for what seemed like ages, they then turned off the lights and left. That's when I ran out. I heard rustling at the back of the beer garden but it didn't look like there was anything or anyone there from what I could see. That's when I brushed it off as a joke. We're always pranking each other and I just thought it was that. But when I saw your boots under the bookshelf, I thought it was him.'

He sat on the edge of the desk dropping his heavy bag down. 'Maddie, I swear on my life, it wasn't me.'

She bit her lip and looked down. 'Well someone's trying to scare me then.'

'You should go to the police.'

'And say what?'

'Someone's following you.'

'Right, I can see how that would go. *Hi, police, last night I think someone else was walking on the lane in the dark and they stopped and stood still for a few seconds. Then they were in the pub toilets and they turned the light off on me while I was trying to pee...* It sounds stupid now and I don't think they'll do anything. Besides, I haven't seen this person. I have no evidence that the person on the lane was following me. They could have been innocently waiting for a dog to do its business.' She slumped in the chair.

'Or they could be dangerous. You hear about these things happening all the time. Look at what happened to Amber. You just watch yourself, mate, okay?' He looked down at her, his warm eyes making her feel safe and he opened his strong arms and gave her a huge Tyrone bear hug.

'Anything else happens, I'll report it.'

He released her from his embrace. 'Okay. Tyrone will be angry with you if you don't.'

His phone beeped and he smiled. 'Get in there.'

'Another smiley?'

He nodded. 'I love this app. This is going to be the best year of my life, I can feel it.'

'Can I see?'

He held his phone down to reveal a broad man with the shiniest dark skin she'd ever seen. 'Whoa. You lucky man.'

He grinned. 'Yes, last night's was good too. Woohoo.'

'I best get going if I'm to grab lunch before my next lecture. Is it cold out?'

'Fecking freezing. Wrap up warm.'

She did up the buttons on her coat and flung her bag over her shoulder. 'I'll catch you later.'

'And you.' His attention was immediately diverted to his phone as she left him and headed towards the stairs. Just as she'd passed the café on the ground floor, her phone began to vibrate. She glanced at the man who'd sent her a smiley last night. A message had appeared in her inbox.

Hey, how about we meet up later or sometime soon? We could catch a film or grab a bite to eat. I'm a nice guy – promise.

She smiled and began to type back. Her dark-haired Adonis was waiting for a reply. Should she do it now and look keen, or wait and not look too keen? AppyDater wasn't about waiting for the right one, it was about trying many and seeing what happens. It was about fun and she tried to remember that. She quickly replied:

I'd love to do something. Surprise me. I love a surprise.

She shuddered at the thought, then wondered if she'd done the right thing. After the incident last night, she wasn't sure she liked surprises any more.

Leave it with me.

Nice reply. It didn't sound weird, just friendly. He looked to be not much older and was fairly local. If nothing else, they'd have a good night out and if they didn't gel, they could both move on to the next date.

Her phone rang, a number that wasn't stored in her phone. 'Hello.'

There was no reply.

She held the phone to her ear trying to listen for clues but then the sound of people walking along echoing corridors filled her ear. 'Hello.'

'Sorry, hello. Is this Madison Randle.'

'Yes. Is everything alright?' There was something in the woman's tone that worried her. Her brow furrowed as she left the library and walked out into the freezing fog, taking the steps down towards the river.

'I'm Angie, an A&E nurse at Cleevesford General Hospital. Your great-grandmother, Betty Falconer, has been admitted. I'm sorry to tell you she's had another fall but don't panic, there are no broken bones and she's sitting up in bed having a cup of tea. We know she was recently admitted with a broken leg following a previous fall and it looks to be taking longer than expected to heal, so Occupational Health will also assess her while she's here, see if we can offer her more assistance at home.'

'I'll be right there.'

A man bumped into Madison as she stopped in the middle of the path. 'Sorry.' She held her hand up and smiled as he passed. 'Thank you. When you see her, will you tell her I'll be with her soon?'

'Of course I will.'

The call ended and Madison arrived at the river. The whooshing of water was running violently under the bridge, dragging whole branches with it. She glanced across, unable to see Worcester Cathedral in the distance today. There was no time for lunch now. She hurried back to the university car park for her car and checked her watch. It would take her a good forty minutes to get back to Cleevesford so best not to delay. As she half ran and walked, she called one of her classmates to excuse her from the next lecture. She'd have to catch up on her missed lecture notes over the course of the week. As she reached her car, her phone beeped again.

I've booked something exciting for tomorrow night. Please say you're free. ☺

She dropped the phone in her pocket. He could wait. Without knowing how things were going to be with Nanna, there was no way she'd be able to answer that question. She only hoped that he hadn't gone to much expense. As she turned her engine on, she spotted someone standing alone in the mist, nothing more than an outline. She revved the car up and pulled away, leaving whoever it was behind without looking back.

CHAPTER TWENTY-ONE

'Well, how about that? Mr Collins, the lecturer, has an allegation on file against him for inappropriate behaviour.' Gina threw her coat over a chair in the incident room as Jacob shivered a little on entering. The heater cut out, leaving the room silent until Briggs coughed and sat at the head of the main table. When she'd seen Mr Collins, she knew something was off but she couldn't pinpoint what it was. Now she knew. All she needed was the finer details.

Gina and Jacob sat at each side of him.

Jacob pulled out a bag of crisps and Gina opened a cereal bar, both of them eager to eat something while they worked.

'Where are Mrs O's cakes when you need them?' Gina knew that O'Connor's wife would be treating them to something lovely soon as she'd been working on her brioche, but it wasn't today and today she craved something more than a cereal bar. It had already been full-on and it wasn't about to stop. Her mind flashed back to the sight of Amber's body lying in the shallow water and then forward a little to Amber's father, Theo Slater. She had to work this out and quick. He deserved to know who killed his daughter.

'What have we got then?' Jacob crunched on a crisp and leaned back in his chair.

Briggs ran a hand through his hair, his eyes looking a little shadowy around the edge. He gave her a glance and she smiled. 'We have Mr Collins in interview room one. I want it recorded even though he's come in voluntarily.'

Gina crunched on the chewy nut bar. 'What do we know so far?' A spec of nut hit her arm as she spoke.

Briggs flicked over a few sheets of paper in a refill pad. 'He's thirty-seven years old, married with twin daughters, aged four. This report goes back twelve years, when he was twenty-five. He started out by teaching various elements of management accountancy through home courses but this involved monthly meetups for the students. One of the meetups took place in a room that was rented at the back of a café in Birmingham. After the tutorials were over, one of the students stayed behind to ask a few questions and this led to them having drinks in a bar together. She claims that he met up with her at other times under the guise of helping her through a tricky module, but on the fourth occasion she said he'd tried to kiss her, then groped her. She claims she pushed him off and left but then the messages started. In them he'd claimed she'd been leading him on all this time. He kept sending the messages and she was sure he'd been following her too. She thought she'd seen him outside where she lived and on the street when she'd left work. The only other thing outside her statements is a neighbour's. A woman next door to Miss Gregory saw and described Collins watching Miss Gregory from the street. She reported it to the police but there wasn't enough evidence.'

Gina's mind flashed back to when she worked part-time in a shop while at college. At seventeen, she couldn't forget the manager, his breath stale with coffee, who happened to accidentally touch her bottom every time he brushed past her. If only she knew back then what she knew now. At the time she'd been too scared to say anything, not wanting to be dismissed from her job. Her mouth suddenly felt dry as a memory of Terry pinning her to the bed flashed through her mind. Sexual assault was more common than people thought. She swallowed and cleared her throat, trying to ignore the prickling sensation that was creeping up her neck.

'How about the messages? Didn't they offer enough as evidence?' Gina wondered what enough evidence meant in this case.

Briggs cleared his throat. 'Looking at the case, it seems that it was dropped by the victim. The messages alone weren't strong enough to take the case to court anyway and there was never any direct evidence of him following her. There were talks of a restraining order but in her words, the harassment stopped and she just wanted to forget him.'

'So he gets away with it.' She shook her head. It was a story that was all too familiar. Small-time harassment, stalking, domestic abuse, it often went without punishment or the case was dropped. Evidence was hard to find in a lot of cases. She only hoped that Mr Collins hadn't been harassing Amber in the same way, leaving her worried for the future of her course if she spoke up. Again, she thought back to her first job and she knew that her slimeball boss had done this on many occasions to the many girls that worked there. The other staff even joked about him making the whole thing seem less serious, making Gina believe that he was untouchable.

Jacob screwed up his crisp packet and threw it in the mesh bin. 'What was the victim's full name?'

Briggs flicked to another page. 'Scarlett Gregory, age nineteen at the time. She was working for a company in Birmingham called Revelation Logistics as a trainee accountant. She lived with her parents in Hall Green back then.'

'I suppose we best see what he has to say for himself?' Gina stood and pushed her chair under the table. 'Any news on the contents of Amber Slater's laptop?'

Briggs scrolled through the emails on his tablet. 'I'm expecting an update soon. I'll keep you posted. Hopefully we'll have something back before the briefing.' He gave her a small smile before grabbing his pile of work from the table and leaving.

'I suppose we best see what our Mr Collins has to say. Given what has happened to Amber, his past behaviour is nothing short of creepy.'

CHAPTER TWENTY-TWO

Gina placed her fresh mug of coffee on the desk in the interview room.

Jacob pressed the record button and the machine began rolling.

Mr Collins looked up and smiled. The muscles around his mouth were betraying him and his eyes were telling a different story. The faint odour of sweat that filled the room on such a cold day told her that their suspect was nervous. 'Mr Collins. I know you've already been told, but you are here voluntarily, you can leave at any time but we'd like to talk to you about Amber Slater. For the tape, DI Harte…'

'And DS Driscoll are conducting the interview.' Jacob kept a neutral expression as he spoke.

Mr Collins shuffled in his seat, keeping his hands on his lap, under the desk.

'Of course. I just want to help.' He pulled his blue tie loose and unbuttoned the rest of his grey overcoat. The top of his black hair almost looked white with shine as the light from above caught it. Gina was sure there was more warmth coming from that than the whirring heater.

'Can you confirm you full name and age?' Gina crossed her legs under the desk and leaned in to meet the gaze of Mr Collins.

'Clayton Collins. I'm thirty-seven.' His dark eyes felt like they were drawing her in. Despite how unkempt he looked, Gina could see that he'd perfected his demeanour to be almost flirtatious. The slight smile when he said his name, the intense look but not quite a stare, only held to the point of possible uncomfortableness but not a moment longer.

'Thank you for confirming that. We have your address and lecture timetable on file.'

She glanced at Jacob and he nodded. 'Yes, I can confirm that we do.'

'We spoke about how well you knew Amber Slater yesterday and you mentioned that you'd tried to help her when she thought someone had been watching her in the university car park before Christmas.'

'I've told you all I know.' He brought his hands up from below the table, linked them and leaned back. He was beginning to relax.

Now Gina was going in with the thing that was going to raise his hackles. 'Tell me about Scarlett Gregory.'

'What?' His jaw clenched. 'No way. What the hell does that have to do with Amber Slater?' He pinched the top of his nose and scrunched his brow as if he was trying to relieve a headache.

'We know there was an allegation of inappropriate behaviour. She was your student and she was asking for your help.'

'That was all dropped. It was a lie. I don't need this. I have a family now, children and a wife.' He grabbed his glasses and dropped them on the table as he began to massage his temples.

Gina didn't say a word, sometimes she knew it was best to remain silent and the interviewee would talk without further question.

A moment passed and he sighed. 'It didn't happen in the way she said it did. She kissed me after a drink and then told everyone that it was me that kissed her. She then got so full of herself.' He shook his head. 'She seemed to think I was following her. I mean, she got me suspended all over nothing. I just want to forget it now. I didn't do it. Charges were dropped.'

There was a knock at the door. She spotted Briggs through the small window and stood.

Jacob spoke for the tape. 'DI Harte is leaving the room.'

'Keep the tape running.'

Mr Collins remained in silence looking away from Jacob as she left. Once the door had firmly closed, Gina walked a few paces down the corridor. 'You've got something, haven't you? What is it?'

'Three emails dated early January between Clayton Collins and Amber Slater. We found them on her laptop.'

As Briggs handed her a printout, he touched her arm with his finger sending a little electrical wave of pleasure through her. She scanned them quickly. 'This puts a whole new light on the case. Anything else?'

He paused and moved his hand away. 'Yes, an email confirming that she subscribed to a dating site about a month ago.'

'Thank you. I'll catch up with you in a bit.'

As she entered, Jacob announced her return.

'Mr Collins, we've found something interesting, emails between you and Amber. You can stop lying to us about your relationship with her.'

His Adam's apple bobbed as he swallowed. He grabbed his glasses from the table and pushed them up his nose. His frown now hidden by the round lenses.

'Tell us about this one.' Gina began to read the email aloud. 'Amber, last night was special to me. I hope it was as special to you. I'm desperate to see you again. Clay.'

He shrugged his shoulders. 'I suppose you've already made up your minds. What the hell is the point?'

'I'd rather hear it in your words. We have her replies too, and further emails that were sent between you both.'

The heater whirred into action, fanning the room with a fresh burst of most welcome warm air. 'After the incident before Christmas, I began walking her to her car after lectures to make sure she was safe. She was nervous, I could tell. I just wanted to help her but we got chatting. She liked talking about anything she was watching on TV and I enjoyed listening to her. One night, early January, she kissed me. It came from nowhere. I tried to ignore her attention but then she'd send me little notes saying what she'd like to do with me and I suppose I was flattered. I mean, she was so young, confident and fun to be around and I'm thirty-seven and bogged down with life. She was showering me with attention. I suppose I got carried away, swept up in it all, but I didn't hurt her. It all lasted about three weeks then it was over as quickly as it started.'

'Were you and Amber Slater in a sexual relationship?'

He scrunched his brow. 'What do you think?'

'Please answer the question, Mr Collins.'

He began to grind his teeth. 'I don't see why I should have to answer that. It's private. It was all a mistake and I love my wife. I was stupid and I messed up.'

'Mr Collins, was your relationship with Amber Slater sexual?'

'Yes, for God's sake. We had sex, of course we did.'

'When and where did this take place?'

He shrugged. 'Really?' After a silent void, he continued. 'I booked a room at a hotel twice in the first two weeks of January and we did it once in my car. Believe it or not, she wanted to do it in the car. Then before I knew it, it was over. By the end of January we weren't in contact any more.'

'How did that affect your relationship as lecturer and student?'

'We were fine. We were both adult about it, agreed it was fun and moved on.'

Gina glanced at her notes about Scarlett Gregory. 'When Scarlett Gregory told you to leave her alone, she claimed that you followed her and watched her flat.'

'As I said, the charges were dropped and that was a lie. I didn't follow her. I didn't stalk her and I just got on with life. That girl really thought she was special, she was nothing but a trouble-maker. She asked me for drinks and kissed me, then accused me of assaulting and harassing her. She had a screw loose. I mean, Amber didn't come to you saying I was harassing her, did she?'

Gina had no evidence to say that Clayton Collins was following or harassing Amber. The mere mention of the term 'screw loose' gave Gina a slight headache. 'Mr Collins, can you account for your whereabouts from Friday the twenty-second of January at eighteen hundred hours until Monday the twenty-fifth of January at nine in the morning?'

'I was at home with my family. You can't tell my wife about me and Amber. It will destroy us. Things haven't been all that good at home and after Amber, I realised how much I wanted to make my marriage work. I love my wife and I love my children.'

'We will need an alibi.'

'Am I a suspect?'

The chair creaked as Gina shuffled it slightly. 'Due to your relationship with Amber Slater, you are a person of interest. The best thing we can do is eliminate you and the only way to do that would be to check your alibi.'

He placed both hands on his cheeks and exhaled. 'What am I going to tell my wife? I have twin girls. They're only four. They need me. This is going to ruin everything I've worked for.'

Gina wished she could feel sorry for him but at the moment she only felt sorry for Mrs Collins. 'We won't be divulging any details of the case, we just need to confirm that what you say is true. It's routine, that's all.'

'But my wife will ask questions, she'll want to know why you questioned her.'

Gina couldn't help him. She wouldn't help him. 'Mr Collins, a young woman has been brutally murdered and you had been in a recent relationship with her. We will do everything in our power to bring this killer to justice. Is there anything else you can tell us?'

'Will I be called again once my alibi is confirmed?'

There he went again, only concerned for himself and not the dead woman who was currently lying on a slab. 'I can't say for sure.' In Gina's mind, that would depend on how that went and if his wife could confirm his whereabouts.

'Can I go now? I want to go.'

'As I said, you are here voluntarily to help us with our enquiries. You are free to go. We have your address and phone number and we'll be in touch if we need to speak to you again.'

The man stood, stared at both Gina and Jacob one last time before leaving. When they left the interview room, the door at the end of the corridor was already swinging shut.

'We need to call his wife, now. Can you follow that up?' Gina left Jacob standing and hurried to the incident room. She checked her watch. It would soon be time for the briefing. She sat in front of one of the computers and logged on, doing a search for the dating site. Within moments the site came up. Frivolous first date fun – that's what it touted itself as. A site where dates with many people were encouraged. Several faces flashed up, those of men and women, all seeking dates. She tried to click on one but without a profile, couldn't access the file fully.

Wyre burst through the door and dropped her bag on the table. 'You looking for a date, guv?'

'No, it's just Amber was registered on this site and I wanted to take a look.'

'Everyone's on it. I found George on it too but that's another story. I wonder if the killer met Amber Slater through it.'

Jacob entered with two hot drinks. 'Paula, I didn't know you were back. I'd have made you one.'

'It's okay, I'll grab one now before the briefing.' Wyre smiled as she left.

'Seeking a date, guv?' Jacob winked.

'You're the second person to ask me that. Do you think if I was looking for a date I'd be doing it at work, in the incident room, in front of you lot?' She laughed. 'When Briggs called me out of the room, he said there was an email on Amber's laptop confirming her registration to AppyDater. I was just taking a look.' She reduced the icon to the corner of the screen. She'd take a look later, when she was on her own.

'I knew that really.'

'Yeah, right. What did you make of Mr Collins?'

Jacob paused. 'I'm trying to see the other side but then again two relationships with students, that screams inappropriate. He's not worried about pushing boundaries. Could there be more than two?'

'Did you try calling his wife?'

He nodded. 'There was no answer and the call didn't even connect. It could be that she has her phone turned off. I found the number for her workplace, she's a teacher by the way. The school receptionist confirmed that there's a staff meeting this evening and she will be in it for another half hour.'

Gina glanced out of the window, through the dripping condensation. Darkness had fallen and she could feel the chill in the air. 'That's great news. Is the school local?'

'Cleevesford High.'

'Bingo, we'll head over there before the briefing. Drink up.' Gina stared into her cup.

'What are you thinking?'

'I don't trust Clayton Collins. With Scarlett Gregory's allegations of stalking everything was dropped because it was short-lived and there was no real evidence. She went to the effort of trying to get a restraining order against him and then she withdrew because the stalking and harassment stopped. We really need firm evidence.'

'It does appear that Mr Collins likes to be a bit of a knight in shining armour. He said that he walked Amber to her car after his lectures to make her feel safe.' Jacob scrunched his brow.

'Am I the only one thinking that he could have engineered that fear in her? Turning himself into her protector.' Gina glanced at the emails. 'It was Amber who ended what they had after only a couple of weeks. He takes it well when you read the emails but then she received a lot of texts from a person she has called 'NoName' who came across as a bit of a stalker, calling her a stuck-up bitch after Amber ignored whoever it was. I checked his phone number against any that Amber had in her burner phone and it wasn't a match… but if he was having an affair it stands to reason that he may have another phone too, one which his wife didn't know about. Was it really over for him or was Amber's rejection just the start? Or, was Amber going to say something to his wife and did he need to shut her up? Maybe he took her somewhere to talk and it all got out of hand. Would he have gone as far as to glue her lips together in a temper and then stab her to death as she struggled?'

CHAPTER TWENTY-THREE

I pace back and forth, hidden by the darkness of nightfall. With each step, I crunch through the thin layer of ice that has settled on wet pavements. Rewrapping my scarf around my neck, I gaze up. She got home later than I expected and that worried look on her face tells me something has happened. My beautiful Maddie. Seeing her appear as a local on AppyDater made my day because I've been watching her. It has to be fate.

She crosses her living room, walking right past the front window with her phone to her ear. I'm excited. I can't wait to have her and I think the time is right.

Madison captivates me. My pretty student nurse at the University of Worcester. I imagine her tending to people with love and care, then I realise my teeth are clenched. She loves the old woman she visits. I wonder if she's a relative.

I shake my head as an image of Amber creeps in. All I wanted to do was love and care for her but she couldn't shut up and talking leads to bad things. People get to know your business and they ruin your life. Amber should have just kept her mouth shut. I urge the tension to go away, to leave me alone. I need to play my part if I'm to achieve my objective and I can't think about Amber while I do that. This is all about Madison now. As long as she accepts her fate and shuts the hell up, all will be fine. I shake my body and tilt my head from side to side until I loosen up – that's my warm-up complete. Transformation wasn't complete with Amber but now I get another chance to get my perfect life back.

I stare at the window again. Madison's long black hair is now tucked up into a cute beanie hat. The redness of her lips can be seen all the way from the back of the car park which is only minutes away from Amber's apartment.

Another resident peers from the top window so I duck behind my car, not taking any risks that she might see me. It's Miss Cat Café. Her stupid-looking friend.

The orangey glow from a street lamp to the left of the dilapidated old house shows up the pile of dumped rubbish at the bin store. A mattress leans up against the side of the building. My heart rate picks up as I hear a rustling noise. I peer over the bonnet of my car and wait for whatever lurks amongst the litter to show itself. A fox maybe, a hungry crow or maybe it's a cat. No, none of the aforementioned. It's a filthy rat. I watch as it scurries from behind the mattress and heads for one of the industrial-sized bins.

The curtains close on Madison's room and I can no longer see into her world, but that's okay. She's all dressed to go out and I'm waiting.

I glance at the time. Why is it going so slowly? It must be because I'm freezing to death out here. Miss Cat Café has now closed her scraggy curtains. Standing, I begin to pace once again to keep warm. Come on, Madison, come to me.

More minutes pass. Hurry up. Hurry up. Those words keep repeating themselves in my mind. My plans keep churning away. I think back to my mother. She always said that a person had to go out there and take what they wanted. Nothing is handed to a person on a platter. I think she meant through ambition and hard work. Back then, she had something about her but that fizzled out when my father left. It was soon replaced by venom and nastiness. I wonder if she got everything she wanted.

Come on, Maddie. Show me your face.

I step onto the pavement, never allowing my gaze to leave the building in front of me, then I tread on broken glass. All my fault for smashing the street lamps. I can't have her seeing me. It only took me four attempts with the rock in my pocket and now I have my cloak of darkness, my corner of the car park where no one will see what I'm up to.

Brr. I shiver and flex my fingers. That's good, I can still feel each and every digit. My toes are thickly quilted in the walking socks from when I did the Three Peaks, and the walking boots are the best. Not a spec of water has seeped through them. Both the socks and the boots are keeping my feet warm. A few flakes of fresh snow begin to fall and a perfectly formed flake settles on my nose. Hopefully it will be a fleeting flurry. I almost go cross-eyed trying to get a closer look but it's too dark to see properly. Hurry up, Madison.

Apartment block is too kind a description for what I see before me. It's a typical house of multiple occupancy with some shared bathrooms. Each floor has a kitchenette. I know this – I've been in. I've looked at living here myself once I knew that Amber lived nearby, thinking I could spend time getting close to her but something better came up. I wished I'd taken it now. But still, I like watching them from afar. Half of the fun came from orchestrating ways to bump into Amber. I was charming, kind, and complimentary but doing everything right doesn't always pay off. They don't see you until you make them. My fists are balled. Why do I allow myself to get worked up?

I flinch as the main entrance door clicks and she steps out. 'I'll call you from the hospital,' she shouts back to her cat café friend.

Now, I have to act. I kneel down on the floor and begin making cutesy noises at the nothing that is under my car. What will it be? A hedgehog maybe, or a cat. She's always going on about how much she loves hedgehogs if her Instagram is anything to go by.

'Come on little hedgehog.' I'm good, so good even though the voice I'm using sounds pathetic. I'm wasted in life. Maybe I should have taken up acting. As she clanks past me in her awkward heels, I turn to catch her eye but she can barely see me. My hood half covers my eyes and I put on my telephone voice. 'There's a little hedgehog sitting under this car and it looks hurt. I think it might be a baby. It's probably lost its mother.' I can see her trying to focus in the dark but she can't see me properly under the overhanging trees.

She stands for a second and glances over, trying to focus on me in the dark. 'Poor thing.' She pops her phone in her pocket and gets down on the ground. 'Let me help. If we can get hold of it, I can drop it at a rescue centre. Should it be hibernating?'

'Yes, definitely. Can't have it dying out here in the cold. I'd never forgive myself.'

She ignores me as she shines her phone torch under the car before cooing and calling.

Freezing wetness creeps through the knees of my jeans. The light from her phone almost catches me under the car. I jerk up, just in time to miss it.

I can smell her perfume as it's carried with the breeze. It's rosy, flowery, but not strong. It might even be the scent from her shampoo. I stand near the boot, just behind her as she continues. 'Hedgehogs don't have young at this time of the year. They normally have their babies about July.'

She's only just clicked. That was slack of me trying to lure her here to save a baby hedgehog. I grip the rock in my pocket. Now – I have to do it now, before she tries to get up to run. Smash it against her head and bundle her in my boot, that's what I have to do. I take a step back into the darkness as the main door of the block clicks open. 'Erm… maybe I got it wrong.' I loosen my grip slightly as the person calls.

Cat café woman is heading towards her car. I slip away, hurrying through the cut in the bushes as Madison turns to speak to her and I watch from behind a tree. She's shouting about going to the pub later and meeting Maddie after she's been to the hospital. At least I know where she's heading. I will have her tonight, that's for sure.

Miss Cat Café continues. 'At least she's only at Cleevesford. Oh, send your nanna my love. I hope they let her out soon.'

'Will do. Thanks, Alice. That man, the one who was looking for the hedgehog…' I know without looking that Madison is wondering where I've gone. 'Did you see him?'

I press my back against the tree and try not to move a muscle. 'No.'

'I think I'm cracking up. I'm talking to an invisible man and searching for a hedgehog that doesn't exist. No seriously, there was someone here. We were looking for a hedgehog… Never mind. I'll give the pub a miss.'

I'm not going to tail her to the hospital. It will be too obvious now. I wonder if she recognised me. Had it been lighter, she might have.

I've shown my interest on AppyDater but she's gone off radar. It's humiliating. I pull the rock from my pocket and feel my stare harden. My mother always said I looked like I was about to kill someone when I stared like this. Maybe she knew me better than I ever thought. I mean, hitting her with a rock. There was always a chance that I would kill her in the process. Thinking of Amber, I know I'm capable.

Glancing around, I realise that Madison has pulled away in her car and Alice has gone back in. I'm now alone except for the rat, which is on its hind legs, licking its paws after its bin feast.

Once I'm in my car, I check AppyDater again. Madison still hasn't got back to me, which is why I can't wait any longer. There is a void in my life and I need to fill it before I implode.

My thoughts fall on earlier. I need something, someone. I need you but all I can do is find second-rate replacements like Amber and Madison and hope that I can mould them into what I need them to be. Madison has to work out. But first, I need to break her. Break, then rebuild, or in Amber's case, break and fail.

My phone beeps. I reach down. For the first time on this app, I have a smiley. Oh, hello. The dark-haired woman looks down in a demure way. I can't quite see her whole face. She's older than what I need but hey, maybe I've had it all wrong so far. I scan her information and I'm sure that she's the woman from the lake. No mention of her being in the police and she's left her hobbies blank, maybe she thinks working for the police will put people off. I click on the photo I took on my phone from afar and compare the head shape and features, nose contours. It's definitely her, without a doubt, trying so hard to conceal her full identity. I call it being discreet. Clever woman. How can I bump into her? I ponder that thought. She was already on my radar so seeing her here is like Christmas has come early.

There's an earnestness in her look, a bit like you used to have. It's like you're back. I can't lose you again.

I look again at her photo. She's kind of special. More special than Madison? The likeness is closer. I flick back to Madison. I'm not sure what to do any more. 'Give me a sign. Eenie meenie…' I can't decide but having backup options is always a good thing. I know where she works and, if all fails, I can follow her home.

Right now, I'm not sure who will be the main feature and who will be the backup. A member of the police force will be more of a challenge but maybe the results will be better. I can't afford to fail. I messed up with Amber and that can't happen again. I'm craving closeness, company and warmth and I'm not prepared to exist without it. I deserve it.

I flick through the phone again.

It's always good to have options. My heart flutters with excitement as the car begins to warm up.

Decisions, decisions.

CHAPTER TWENTY-FOUR

Disinfectant and gravy, a nauseating smell that took Gina right back to school. It wasn't the dinners being unpalatable that she remembers, in fact she enjoyed them, it was the disinfectant that was turning her stomach – that and the hunger that had taken a hold. Jacob was ahead of her, tailing the kind teacher that was taking them to the waiting area outside the staff room where Mrs Collins was still in her meeting – running late, apparently.

She lifted a hand up and saw that she had the jitters. Maybe having that last cup of coffee was a bad idea. She shook her head, trying to clear the slight lightheaded feeling that was taking over. Before heading back to the briefing after speaking to Mrs Collins, she had to get some food.

'If you take a seat there, she should be out very soon. She knows you want to speak to her. I'll head back to reception. If you need anything in the meantime, just ask. Can I get either of you a coffee or a tea?' A few strands of the young woman's ginger bun were starting to escape.

Gina glanced at Jacob. He shook his head and she could do without another caffeinated drink. 'We're fine, thank you.'

'In that case, I'll leave you to it.' She smiled before turning and clip clopping on her heels back through the dining hall door.

'That smell is making me hungry,' Jacob said as his stomach rumbled.

'I'm the opposite. That smell makes me feel like throwing up. But I am famished.' Gina glanced through the glass pane on the staffroom door. A woman who looked to be in her mid-thirties, with a black shiny plait dangling down her back, glanced over as she flicked over a page on the huge pad and began writing on the blank sheet. She flashed her watch to Gina and then five fingers. Gina nodded back.

'I have some lovely memories of the school dinner hall. I was quite disruptive back then, not quite the model citizen I am today.'

Gina stared at Jacob and laughed.

He continued. 'I always ended up standing facing a wall and counting to one hundred for starting the food fight. Forever in detention, I was. It just goes to show that the worst behaved kids can grow up to be okay.'

'Oh, you rebel.' Gina sniggered.

'I bet you were a right swat.' Jacob turned a little, waiting for her to answer.

He was right, the one detention she had during senior school for accidentally leaving her homework in her bedroom had been an upsetting ordeal. Her mother and father knew when she took the letter home and they had shown their disappointment by grounding her for a week. It had been an accident. 'I did my best.' She remembered the other kids teasing her because she had frizzy hair and a brace on her top set of teeth. A loner, she struggled to fit in and that lack of solidarity with any of her classmates had left her craving attention, even the wrong kind. These days, the last thing she wanted was attention but she craved some close human contact, which is why she'd been seeing Briggs again. It had started with a takeaway, then wine, then laughs and warmth. One thing had led to another and now she couldn't get him out of her head but this wasn't the time. She thought of their victim, Amber, then about dating and the dangers. She could see the excitement too as she'd researched the site. It promised fun and frivolity. Jacob was still waiting for her to answer and did a mock yawn. 'Okay, I was a model pupil at school,' she conceded.

'Knew it.'

She glanced at Jacob as he watched Mrs Collins. He'd have been the popular kid, the cheeky chappie who threw a few chips across a table with his cute laugh. The joker of the pack, maybe? She'd never know.

The squeaky door burst open and several weary-looking teachers filled the corridor and brushed past them. Only one woman stayed behind. She popped her pen in the little cradle on a table and beckoned them in. Her plait swung as she headed over. Her long, checked skirt reached her black boots and she pulled a cardigan over her shoulders. 'I'm Mrs Collins, you wanted to speak to me. Please come in and take a seat.'

A cluster of dirty coffee cups were gathered on a tray on the table. Gina pulled the chair away so she didn't have to smell them. Fresh coffee was a wondrous smell but stale coffee, not a good thing – ever. Mrs Collins picked up her lipstick-stained cup and drank the rest of hers. For some reason, Gina expected Mrs Collins to look a bit like Amber. Except for their hair colour, there was no likeness at all. Mrs Collins looked homely and voluptuous. Her neatly trimmed nails tapped on the cup before she placed it down.

'How can I help you?' Mrs Collins picked up her beeping phone. 'Dammit, I have several missed calls. Can I just have a moment?'

Gina knew they would be from Mr Collins, trying to pre-warn his wife that they would be seeking to clarify his whereabouts. 'Actually, Mrs Collins, could you please wait a moment? We need to speak to you first.'

The woman looked at her phone one more time and placed it in her pocket. 'What's going on?'

'We need to ask you something. Do you want to take a seat?'

She took the pad from the flipchart and placed it next to them on the table. 'I'm fine standing. Look, I have twin girls waiting for me to pick them up from the childminder's so I really need to get going and all those phone calls might be to do with my children. My husband is trying to get hold of me. What's happened?'

'Sorry, we won't keep you long.' Jacob took out his pad and flicked to a clean page.

Gina cleared her throat and kept her trembling fingers in her lap as she spoke. 'We need to confirm your husband's whereabouts between six on the evening of Friday the twenty-second of January and six in the morning of Monday the twenty-fifth. Can you please take a moment to think and tell me what you can remember of your weekend?'

'Are we in some sort of trouble?' Three lines appeared across the woman's forehead as she sat.

'We're just making routine enquiries at the moment. As you may know from the news, a body was found at the lake in Cleevesford. Mr Collins was the young woman's lecturer.'

'Are you saying that my husband could have done that to a girl? No way!'

Gina leaned back on the creaky plastic chair. 'We're not saying that at all. Your husband knew her. We have spoken to him and he said he was with you all weekend. We just need to check that information.'

She began to twiddle the end of her plait. 'He was with me all weekend, at our home. We value our weekends as you can appreciate, even though we spend a lot of that time working. We had a takeaway together at about four on Friday, then the girls were picked up by my mother who had them for the weekend. I had a lot of work to catch up on, marking and lesson planning so she offered to help me out. Clayton… Clay had lots of work to do too. He was in with me all weekend, even when we went to Tesco together on Saturday morning. That was about ten in the morning – the Tesco just outside Cleevesford, off the bypass.'

'He didn't pop out on his own for anything?'

Mrs Collins scrunched her brow and stared at the space between her nose and the cups on the table. 'No, as I say, we had a lot of work to do and after a long week, we were both tired so we went to bed quite early. He never left the house without me, not once. I can wholeheartedly confirm that.' She paused and her gaze met Gina's. 'Is there something you're not telling me? What's going on?'

'At the moment, we can't reveal all the details of the case as we're investigating. Thank you for your time. One last thing, do you know if Mr Collins knew Amber Slater well?'

Mrs Collins swallowed and shook her head. 'I believe he knew her as well as a lecturer would know his students. He always took the time to help them all. Teaching is more than just a job to him, he wanted them all to get the best results and always gave everyone the time they needed to get there. I often hear him talking over an accountancy problem on the phone with his students, patiently explaining things. He's a good man.'

Gina didn't doubt he was good at his job but she did doubt his intentions and she wondered right there and then if Mrs Collins knew of Mr Collins's past. 'Have you ever heard the name Scarlett Gregory?'

Mrs Collins went to open her mouth then paused. 'No, I don't recognise that name.' She pulled her phone from her pocket. 'Look, I really have to go. My childminder will be charging me extra if I don't and she hates me being late and I'm already working over tonight.'

Gina stood and scraped the chair under the table. 'Thank you for your time and thank you for clearing that up.' She passed her card to the woman. 'If you or your husband think of anything else, please call me.'

Refusing to take the card, Mrs Collins placed her hands in her pockets. 'I've told you all I know, so now if you'll excuse me, I need to lock this room. You know the way out, don't you?'

Regretfully, Gina did and it was through the smelly hall. Within minutes they were getting back into the car. Gina pulled her seat belt on. 'She knows about Scarlett Gregory, of that I'm sure. How do you feel that went?'

Jacob pulled a mint from his pocket and popped it into his mouth. 'She looked worried, really worried. Especially when you asked for Mr Collins's whereabouts at the weekend. I don't think we can exclude him from our list of suspects.'

'I know it's a feeble start but maybe the least we can do is confirm that they were at Tesco's on Saturday morning, just to establish whether that part was true. They were both lying, I'm sure of that, but being sure isn't enough. We can't arrest anyone because we think they are lying.' She stared onto the dark playing field with only a glint of street lamp hitting the edge of a goalpost at the back. 'But we do need to know what they're lying about.'

CHAPTER TWENTY-FIVE

Madison stood outside the hospital, taking in the freshness of the crisp winter air. It had been stuffy in the medical assessment ward her nanna was in but, thankfully, the damage wasn't too bad. Just a minor cut and a couple of small bruises. She swallowed as she thought of the poor old woman lying in the corner of the kitchen after she'd slipped on some spilt milk. A whole hour had gone by before the carer visiting had called the ambulance her nanna didn't really need. *Best to be safe than sorry and get her checked out,* the carer had said.

She tried Alice's number again and this time she answered. 'Alice. Glad I caught you. I don't think I'll be back tonight. Can you keep an eye on my apartment and feed my fish?'

'Of course, mate. I still have your spare key from when you went on holiday.'

Madison smiled. 'Thanks.'

'Is everything okay with your nan? I tried to call you earlier but I couldn't get through.'

As Madison spoke a plume of white mist coiled in the air. She shivered as she walked away from the main entrance of the hospital and stood beside a stationary ambulance. Cold, she continued to walk. She passed the smoking hut and headed towards the car park. 'She had a fall, that's all. Not a serious one but they just needed to check her out as she's still healing from the last fall. I'm going to stay with her tonight, if they let her out. I need to be there to settle her in. She's a bit shaken and needs to get her confidence back with the Zimmer frame.'

'I'm really sorry to hear that. Tell her to get well soon from me. Are you okay? Is there anything else I can do? Do you need an overnight bag making up?'

Pausing, Madison stared into the darkness, just about able to make out the large expanse of land ahead with the helipad in the middle and a thick row of trees beyond the car park. She shivered and not because of the cold this time. It felt as though the darkness was about to swallow her up. As she turned back to the hospital entrance she almost crashed into a man in a wheelchair. 'Sorry,' she called.

'Madison? Are you okay?' Alice's voice came through the phone.

'Yes, I nearly crashed into someone. I best go and thanks for the offer but I'm okay. I have a spare of everything at Nanna's. Are you alright?'

'Don't worry about me. Even Tyrone has brushed me off tonight. I bet he's got another date with that man he liked. Anyway, I've decided I've been a wimp. I'm about to land a few smileys on a whole load of profiles so who knows where that will take me. I might be out on a hot date this weekend or even sooner. I think I'm going to head to the pub for a couple, see who's there.'

Madison let out a chuckle. 'Well, have a good one and have a drink for me, even if you are going to be a Billy no-mates. Speak soon.' The signal dropped as it had done a few times while she'd been at the hospital and Alice was gone. She walked around, holding her phone in the air until she reached the smoking hut.

A young man wearing a dressing gown and trailing a drip held a cigarette to his lips. 'Want one?' He held the packet in her direction.

'No, thank you.' She smiled then walked past and stood on the grass. She had one bar left on her phone, then it would die on her. A notification flashed in the corner of the screen. That orange AD logo with a smiley face in the D told her that she had more interest on her AppyDater profile. Now wasn't a good time. She clicked on the app, headed to profile and deactivated her profile before deleting the app. She looked ridiculous with that mustard-filled hotdog sticking out of her mouth. The notification was now gone, along with the app. Maybe it was what her friends were doing and she wished them all the best, but she preferred the more conventional ways of meeting dates; at uni, at the pub or on holiday – any way but the AppyDater way.

Her mind flitted back to the pub toilets and the person who tried to scare her; then there was the dark lane. The shadows and rustling of trees – she shivered. She'd bumped into a couple of men. Had they moved into her path on purpose? *Stop it*, she told herself. Her paranoia was getting out of hand.

'See you.' The young man left the smoking shelter and shuffled back towards the hospital, leaving her alone next to a tree. For a moment, she tried to weigh up how much effort it would take to fake a drip and stand in a smoking hut. She wanted to slap herself. No one knew she was coming here. She didn't even know she'd be at the hospital today. Even her practical course components didn't take place at Cleevesford General; she was often based in Worcester. She glanced at her watch. Nanna's discharge papers should be ready. As she took a step, she glanced around one last time and in the darkness she saw a still figure, just a silhouette against the moonlight on the path alongside the fenced-off helipad field. She stared at it and was sure he was staring back. He was whistling something, a melody that sounded like a lullaby she vaguely recognised. The whistling broke up and he stopped. She took two steps closer but the figure turned and walked away into the misty night.

She ran back to the entrance, knowing she had to get Nanna and hurry to Nanna's house, where she felt safe.

CHAPTER TWENTY-SIX

Gina took the last bite of the large cheese sub. She wiped her lips with the napkin and sat back as the team started to join her at the table in the incident room. She'd bought plenty of snacks for everyone. As she swigged her water, she headed to the front of the room where she scanned the boards to recap on all the information that they'd garnered so far.

Bernard accidentally kicked the doorframe as he rushed into the room. 'Bloody hell!'

Gina had heard the crack so she knew it must have hurt. His ashen face told her that he'd been working nonstop. He slammed a takeaway coffee and a folder on the table before slipping his coat off and grabbing a roll. Jacob and O'Connor entered with hot drinks and proceeded to take a seat. PCs Smith and Kapoor placed down some extra seats and shuffled in. Kapoor pulled a stray black hair from her uniform and dropped it on the floor. All of them grabbed some food.

Wyre hurried in, her face buried in her phone as she bit into an apple. She pressed one last button and placed it in her pocket and smiled across at Gina.

'Right, thank you. Let's get started.' Gina placed her water bottle down on the damp window ledge and flicked the switch on another heater. 'I know it's cold but hopefully the heating will be sorted tomorrow.'

'Thank God for that,' O'Connor said as he put his scarf on.

Briggs sidled in from the back and walked over to Gina. As the chatter in the room got louder he came a little closer, almost touching her. He gave her that smile, the one only she saw.

'How's it going with the press, sir?' she asked.

'All the information we want out there is out. As discussed we have left out the bit about the superglue. I just hope someone comes forward with something. I got an update from Annie just before heading here. Corporate Communications can confirm that a few calls have come in and they're being looked into. If anything comes of those calls, uniform will report straight to us and we can get onto it.' He paused. 'I haven't stopped thinking about the other night. Maybe we could do something together soon.'

She placed her finger to her lips. 'Thank you.' She smiled as she spoke over him. There was a look on his face, like he was faraway.

'No one can hear,' he whispered as he pointed at the board.

The chatter turned to a quiet hum, then silence.

'Right, gather round.' Gina leaned over the desk and smiled at Bernard. 'I know you need to get off as soon as you can and I appreciate you coming given your workload is so huge. Can you please go first?'

Bernard nodded and opened the brown paper file that lay flat on the desk in front of him. 'As you know, the post-mortem happened earlier today. DC Wyre was present throughout and we spoke after. I'll start with the stab wound to the chest. Her heart was pierced and the wound is six inches deep. The blade used was not serrated and the thickness of the knife was four millimetres. That would mean we'd expect a lot of blood at the scene where she was killed. From the nail samples, we found some skin cells and there were enough to obtain DNA. It didn't belong to the victim so I'm surmising that she fought with her attacker at one point.'

Wyre nodded, confirming that fact. 'No matches have been found to those we have on the database.'

Gina picked her dry lip. 'So we are looking for someone without a record.'

Bernard continued. 'The cause of death was the stab wound to her heart. She did not drown. There was no presence of diatoms from the lake in her body and the state of her lungs wasn't consistent with drowning.' He flicked to another page and held up a line drawing of a body sitting with elevated feet in a chair with shading of the buttocks, thighs and calves. 'I mentioned this when I saw the body at the lake. Lividity – this shows the position she would have been in at the time of death. It looks like she was sitting in a chair with her feet elevated.' He grabbed a pen and drew black lines across the neck, wrists and ankles on the picture. 'Ligature wounds show that she was restrained in these places. Then there were the marks on the sides of her mouth. She'd been gagged too at some point.'

'And talk us through the superglue residue on her lips.' Gina turned to look at the boards.

'Our tests are conclusive. The superglue residue that was left is layered on top of the wounds on her mouth suggesting that she was first gagged, then the gag was removed and then her lips were superglued together. There's something else.'

The room went silent.

'A minute strand of green fibre found in her nose, just the tiniest strand.'

Jacob dropped his pen on the table. 'Any sign of sexual assault?'

'There was no evidence of sexual assault or rape.' He checked his watch. 'I'll move on to the scene at the lake. After going over it again, we found what looks like a drag mark on the verge at the back of the car park and traces of blood, but the drag mark completely vanishes, suggesting that the perpetrator lifted the body up. We have loads of footprints and partial footprints, all over-trodden by others including dogs and birds. With the thaw, we couldn't take a clear mould of any. Same with tyre tracks leading in and out. So many people had been there and parked after, the evidence has literally been trampled on but we will keep going through it. No weapon was found at the scene after an extensive search by us in the immediate surroundings and uniform over the wider area.' He paused again as he tried to read his messy writing. 'I estimate that the body had been in the water from the time of midnight to three in the morning of Monday the twenty-fifth of January but this is just an estimate based on water temperature during the early hours.' He checked his watch.

Gina knew time was clocking on and she wanted Bernard back on the case without delay. 'Can you tell us what forensics found at Amber Slater's flat on Bulmore Drive and the car park?'

He stroked his neat beard and clenched his teeth momentarily. 'The pills that you bagged were definitely MDMA. There were also a lot of prints to work through but nothing that matched to the database. No sign of blood. She wasn't killed there. As for the flat itself, it was secure. The windows were locked and the door lock hadn't been tampered with and that goes for the main door to the block too. Due to staff shortages, we're going to have to go back to do a deeper search so I'll keep you updated. The victim's father is happy for us to go back. It definitely wasn't the scene of the crime. As for the car park, apart from the bit of pink material that was found out there we didn't find anything else that was directly linked to Amber Slater. There's evidence bags full of litter and cigarette butts, which we're still working through. It's going to be a mammoth task. All bins in the vicinity were checked for the murder weapon but again, no knives or blades were found. I will have to keep you updated on that. There are eighteen bags of rubbish to sift through. In fact, I'm heading back in a minute to help Keith, Jennifer and the team. It's going to be a long night. I can't yet confirm how the covers for the two street lamps were smashed but it could have been a rock or a brick, something had been thrown at them until they shattered. They are the old-fashioned type with the large bulbs which are in keeping with the older part of Cleevesford.'

Gina took a step back and glanced at Amber's photo on the board, the one of her alive and looking well. Then she glanced at her waxy body on the shore of the lake and shivered. 'Thanks, Bernard. Anything else that will help us right now?'

He shook his head. 'Not that I can think of but I will email you my full report when I've finished it. Obviously what I've just said is only a brief summary. We're not finished processing everything from the known scenes but as I find out anything, I will let you know in real time and then after, you'll have my detailed report.' The man rubbed his eyes and yawned.

'Thank you. I won't keep you any longer.'

He smiled and packed his notes back into the file and stood. 'Back to work it is and thanks for the food.' He gave a little wave as he left with a tuna sub under his arm.

Gina underlined the word CCTV on the board. 'Have we found anything useful on the CCTV we've obtained or from the door-to-doors?'

Wyre rubbed her hands together to warm them. 'I've been collating all that information, guv. We already know that Amber didn't make it to the Fish and Anchor and she didn't get on the bus. Uniform conducted the door-to-doors in the area and it appears that no one saw anything or anyone who was out of place. She lives in a large converted house that is set back behind trees, which would have worked to the killer's advantage. We have managed to gather a bit of private CCTV from some of the houses on the main road but the images are poor. We're working on it at the moment. I'll keep you updated.'

'Good work. If we can get any registration numbers – any one of those cars could have had Amber in them.'

'I have seen a bit, guv. That might be wishful thinking.'

Gina ticked CCTV off her list. 'Persons of interest.' She turned to the board and pointed to the list of names. 'Top of the list, we have the Collinses, that's Clayton Collins and Mrs Collins. Jacob, will you please follow up on her statement and head over to Tesco for the CCTV footage. It's only a small thing but I want to confirm how true her statement is. She claims to have been at the main Cleevesford Tesco at ten in the morning on Saturday and that she and her husband were together all weekend. I want to know if she was there and if he was with her. Get the car park footage too. Whoever did this to Amber would have needed a lot of time over the weekend. They took her on Friday, she turned up dead on the Monday morning. What did they do with her all weekend? We know she was restrained and held against her will.'

Jacob leaned back. 'I'll do that before heading home.'

Gina glanced up at the list again. 'Other people I want you to keep in your minds at the moment – Otis Norton, the man who found the body. Again, what was he doing at the lake? He also claimed to have seen someone suspicious hanging around. Any follow ups on that?'

O'Connor lifted his head up, his round chin red at the bottom like he'd shaved too closely that morning. 'I looked into Mr Norton. No record at all. I can confirm that he does have a sick wife at home who he cares for.'

'Great work. I still don't feel he was giving us the full story. He wasn't dressed for a walk. He was up to something. Maybe we need to follow up on that. Next… Jake Goodman, the chef at the Fish and Anchor. When I showed him the photo of Amber Slater, I'm sure he recognised her.'

PC Smith interjected. 'That name does come up on our records. He got into trouble as a teenager for basically stealing women's clothes off washing lines, including underwear.'

'That's a worry. I'll head back over to the Fish and Anchor at opening tomorrow. What about Amber Slater's neighbours and the landlord, Vincent? Do we have a surname for him?'

Wyre nodded. 'It's Vincent Jordan. He lives in a bungalow at the back of the apartment block that he manages. He's in his late thirties and lives alone. I know uniform have taken a brief statement. He said he didn't really know any of the tenants and only saw them when something needed fixing or when he cleaned the communal areas. In his words, he had nothing more to do with any of them as long as they paid their rent and kept the noise down.'

'Any CCTV on his property that may just have covered the back of the apartment block?'

Shaking her head, Wyre continued. 'No, he said he's never had any CCTV. He said he lives close by so is able to keep an eye on the property himself.'

Gina pointed to the board. 'Moving on to the other tenants. I spoke to Curtis Gallagher. Lauren Sandiford came in to report Amber missing. Who else lives there?'

O'Connor tapped his fingernails on the table. 'Uniform managed to speak to Corrine Blake and Tyrone Heard, both students too. Corrine and Tyrone claimed that they barely knew Amber and only spoke to everyone else when they got together for a drink in the block. Both of them also said that they were at home between seven and seven thirty on Friday night. Corrine showed uniform the log of a call she was on with her mother and Tyrone was Facebook messaging another man during that time.'

'Facebook messaging. I suppose he could have done that on the move.' Gina glanced across at the other details on the board. 'The superglue. Why do it?'

Wyre scrunched her brow. 'It's like whoever did that wanted to permanently seal her lips.'

'Budgets don't allow us the luxury of a profiler so we have to bear that in mind all the time. Okay, let's bat a few theories around.

Why? Maybe our killer would do anything to keep something a secret. Did Amber know what that secret was? Maybe she was going to say something, which is why her lips were glued. We need to allow ourselves to think like this person, imagine why they'd do this. What is it they don't want anyone to know? Look as deeply as possible into everyone who flags up. It's about the detail, something small from their past.' She stared at the board wondering what the killer didn't want Amber to say. Clayton Collins? Did he do something to Amber that he couldn't bear the world to hear about? Mrs Collins? Gina was seeing her as a pawn in his game, nothing but an alibi. Her mind mulled over Amber's injuries and an image of blood, lots of blood flashed through her mind. Poor woman, murdered before being dumped in a lake, early on a cold January morning. Her date… 'Anyone here have experience with AppyDater? I'm sure I've heard a few of you mention it.'

Kapoor put her hand up and started speaking too quickly. Gina could barely process her words. 'Say that all again but slower.'

'It's an app that really is for dating. It encourages lots of dates, as many as possible. It's not about finding the one, it's about finding fun company but it's not as crude as a hook-up.'

'Okay, slow down a bit more while I catch up.' Gina began writing a few bullet points on the board.

'Sorry, guv. Talking fast in Brummie is my speciality. I forget that a lot of people struggle to catch every word. It's about the going out and the socialising and more, if you want it. I joined about a year ago and have had a couple of dates. It's fun and easy. If you like someone, you just click on the smiley and that alerts the other person that you want to go on a date. After that, you can private message. You arrange a date and the guidelines recommend that this is always in a public place. A restaurant, a busy park, something like that.'

The young police officer waited for further questions and smiled, glad to be able to have an input.

'Anyone else on AppyDater? I'm not prying but we will be looking deeply into it so best say now. I joined earlier today for research purposes. No one is making a judgement here, I just want to understand the app better and the way it works and I'm likely to come across your profiles. We know Amber was on it as she had an account set up.'

Briggs looked away. 'I am.'

Gina's stomach sank and her legs came over with that jellied feeling. She glanced at Briggs but he wouldn't look her way. The other night... it was obviously nothing to him. Again, she had been the one taking all the risks. If their relationship, fling or whatever it was, had come out, she would have been sent to work somewhere else, not Briggs. He was her senior. She glanced at the table leg and wanted to kick it. She'd been stupid, so stupid. Maybe AppyDater was her own pathetic future. If it was good enough for Briggs and he was moving on, maybe she could. Maybe anyone would do and maybe there would be sex after. She kept her eyes on him but he wouldn't look her way.

Clearing her throat, she continued. 'Okay, I'm not suggesting our killer operated through this app. Amber was meant to meet her date at the Fish and Anchor but she never arrived. The booking was a no-show but her date would have known what time she'd have had to have left to arrive on time. This seemed well planned. Smashed street lights, being there at the right time to snatch her.' Gina paused. 'We don't have Amber's main phone but we have applied for the records. What we do have is another phone that Amber used. We need to find out who AdamzFun, BearBoy, NoName and BigBoz are. NoName stands out. I want to know who this is. I'll be checking out AppyDater later to see if I can find any links. Are we all clear on what we're doing next? Wyre, first thing tomorrow before the Fish and Anchor opens, we're going to see Vincent Jordan. Okay?'

Everyone nodded and began to disperse, including Briggs who was the first to leave the room. Wyre held back. 'I'm on AppyDater, guv. I didn't want to say anything in front of everyone because they don't know what happened between me and George and part of me feels stupid as it's so soon. I was curious.'

'Thanks for telling me. Like I said, you won't get any judgement here. I'm glad you're putting yourself first.'

'When those smiley's hit, it's a boost, do you know what I mean? I want to meet new people.'

Gina smiled. 'Of course. You have to think of you and if it's making you happy, right now, then that's good. Just be careful.'

'Careful is my middle name.'

Kapoor ran back in, grabbing the notebook that she'd left on the table. She stopped and smiled as she checked out the beep on her phone. 'I got me a date.'

'Stay safe,' Gina called as the woman left as quick as she entered.

Wyre let out a titter. 'It surprised me that Briggs was on it. I mean he virtually comes across as celibate. I only remember him dating Annie for a short while and that was it. Hey, you really get to know everyone when you ask a question like "Who's on AppyDater?" Fess up.' She laughed.

'And now it looks like we're all on it.' Gina checked her phone and noticed she had a smiley on her fake profile. 'Looks like I've pulled. I only joined for research purposes.'

'Yeah right, guv. No one will judge you either. You do know that, don't you? I'll see you in the morning. There's a ready meal for one calling me home.'

'Catch you tomorrow. I'll message you the times in a bit.' Gina glanced at the smiley. If it was good enough for Briggs, it was good enough for her. She headed towards his office and saw him standing in the corridor staring at his phone.

'Gina.' He started walking towards her.

'I don't want to talk about it.' She swallowed as she headed back and turned the fan heater off.

'Can I see you tonight? I need to explain. Nothing is going on, I promise.'

Feeling his breath on her forehead, it would be so easy to believe him right now and say yes to seeing him. He'd been in her bed, telling her how much he thought of her, making her feel like she was worth something and now, she didn't know what to believe and felt the fool in all this. 'You lied to me.'

'I haven't lied.'

'Come on, all those things you said at my house. It's easy when you're about to get laid.'

'Gina, you're being unreasonable. This app, I haven't done anything with it.'

'Nothing?' She stared at him and he looked away. 'Right, another lie. I'm too old for this. I should know better.' She pushed past him and hurried out of the room, leaving him standing there. Flicking through the app one more time, she wondered if she should… if she could. What the hell. She deserved to have a bit of fun. Everyone else was doing just that.

CHAPTER TWENTY-SEVEN

Madison pulled the awkward, bulky wheelchair to the entrance of the hospital, leaving her nanna next to a seating area in the foyer. She flicked on the brakes with her foot.

'I'm sorry to be a burden, Maddie, love.' A tear formed at the corner of her nanna's crinkly eyes. It had been a long day for the old woman.

She bent over and hugged her. 'Never say that, Nanna. You are not a burden. We are going to get you home, get you washed and in your nightie and I'm going to make you some dinner, then we'll watch TV together. I'm staying the night so we can spend some girly time together. I saw a huge box of chocolates in your cupboard and there are some reruns of *Morse* on later. We like Inspector Morse, don't we?'

Her nanna wiped her eyes as Madison stepped back. 'Thank you. I don't know what I'd do without you.' The woman grabbed Madison's hand with her shaky fingers and rubbed it with her thumb before letting go. 'Now go and get that car so we can bust out of this joint.' The twinkle in Nanna's eyes had returned.

Madison winked with her mouth open, making Nanna laugh again. 'I've parked in the overflow car park at the back so it's quite a walk. You just hang out here and I'll hurry back with our getaway car.'

Madison stepped back out into the crisp night as she walked into the cloud of white mist that was her breath. She shivered and zipped her coat up to her neck, eager to get a move on. The cold was biting, her fingers already numbing and a twinkle of frost covered the main car park. It reminded her of Christmas. It never snowed but it was often frosty or rainy. The twinkles changed colour as she stepped under each street lamp, then they ran out and the only twinkling came from the moon's light and even that kept hiding behind passing clouds. Taking a shortcut, she climbed in her low-heeled boots up the mound of grass that led to the overflow car park until her feet hit the rugged tarmac.

She glanced around and felt a few twitches in her body. It was as if they were telling her to go back, to get out of the solitary darkness and run back into the light. Only four other cars were parked up at the back. During the day it had been full, in fact she had to drive around the whole car park three times for a space. Now, she could've had her pick of spaces closer to the hospital.

For such a busy establishment, the atmosphere was eerie. A light breeze blew an empty carrier bag across the car park. She grabbed her keys from her bag as she glanced back. No one had been following her. The trees beyond the last row of spaces, just behind her car, rustled in the biting breeze. She imagined the person who had lurked in the pub toilets now hiding and watching. Shaking her head, she picked up her pace. This wasn't the time to scare herself. She was near her car. She had her keys ready and her nanna was waiting for her.

As she stepped between her car and the next, the other car door opened on her, preventing her from stepping any further forward. She shuffled back, heart booming away. 'Sorry, you go first.'

'Thank you,' came the muffled reply. Whoever was emerging had a walking stick and wore a scarf across their mouth. Their hat and the darkness ahead made it hard for her eyes to focus. All she could make out was an outline of a bulky frame in a long overcoat.

He closed the door and shuffled on the uneven car park between his car and hers. She stood back, giving him some space. His stick skewered as it hit a pothole and the man began to tumble. Madison instinctively reached down to block his fall.

'Thanks, Maddie.' He snatched her keys from her hand.

How did he know her name? Her gaze darted in all directions. It was the man who was pretending to look for a hedgehog, the one who'd vanished into the night. *Run.* She had to head back to the hospital. She stepped forward but he already had her around the waist. Tumbling to the ground, she reached ahead, trying to drag herself away from his grip, scratching his wrist and reaching for his face under his dark hood. She felt a nail on the other hand bend back and snap as she dug it into the road.

'Get off me! Help!'

There was no one around to hear her screams. She tried to turn, to see his face but his bent arm was pressing against her jugular, almost throttling her. With one swift movement, she gasped for air and brought her elbow back catching his ribs. 'Get off me.'

He wheezed as she rolled him off her and stumbled to a stand. Within seconds, he was up too swearing and circling her. She had to head the other way or he'd tackle her to the ground again. Heading straight into the dense foliage, she would hide until he gave up. Hopping over the uneven grass, she darted through the spiny brambles, their branches slapping her face and arms, thorns pushing into her as they scratched and tore at her skin through her clothing. She felt the wind of his chase behind her.

Darting to the left, she stepped into what was probably a dip.

He stopped. 'Nowhere to run, nowhere to hide.' He spoke in a whisper. A speckle of light through the trees caught her attention as the breeze ruffled the trees. So close to the main road but so far away. She wiggled her foot out of the dip and took a step back.

Then white pain hit her head. He'd struck her with something, a stone or a piece of rock. Dots prickled her vision and she slightly wobbled. She couldn't give up. He grabbed her collar and proceeded to drag her back towards the car park. She wasn't going. She couldn't. Fight – that's what she had to do. As he turned her way to get a better grip, all she could see was the scarf and a dark outline.

Without warning, she brought her knee up to his groin with all the strength she had. She pulled him close and hooked the back of her arm around his neck and brought him to the ground. That basic self-defence class she'd taken not so long back was paying for itself now. As he groaned in agony, she stepped back from his loosened grip and wandered further into the thicket, lowering her stance as she tried to blend into the trees.

'You bitch,' she heard him mumble. Then the branches below cracked beneath his weight. She held her breath, hoping that he wouldn't come any closer. A hazy feeling came across her and the world seemed to tilt. She was dizzy, maybe concussed. Blood dripped down her head. She felt the wetness and she was sinking into unconsciousness.

Sirens blared out from the road as an ambulance hurried to accident and emergency. No one would hear her if she did scream, not over that shrill sound. She tried to open her mouth but nothing came out. She thought of her nanna waiting in the hospital for her to come back with the car. How long would she wait for her to get back? Nanna didn't like making a fuss. Maybe she would think that Madison had stopped to make some phone calls first, or maybe she thought Madison had popped to the shop. Nanna would wait patiently, leaving Madison stuck.

Bringing her hand to the top of her head, she felt the blood matting her hair and as she touched her wound, the sting brought tears to her eyes. The wooziness was getting worse and her pulsating heartbeat was all she could hear. No longer could she track his movements. The whooshing in her ears got louder and the world began to tilt and spin. She closed her eyes and everything went blank. That was it. Game over. He was coming.

CHAPTER TWENTY-EIGHT

Lying in bed at seven in the evening eating a garage sandwich, laptop whirring, electric blanket on, Gina couldn't get warm. There was something missing in her life or someone. She loved Briggs. She couldn't say those words to him but she did and he'd lied to her. They'd had a heart-to-heart while lying in bed a few nights ago. She'd confessed to sleeping with someone she'd met in a pub when they'd been moving on from each other and the disappointment had been pasted across his face. Not something she was proud of but she was a woman with needs. After her outburst during the last case, when she'd blamed him for trying to expose her past, their friendship had suffered and they'd distanced from each other. Only over the past few weeks had they been getting closer again, their friendship restored and the old chemistry creeping back in. He should have told her that he'd been dating, instead he'd made her feel guilty for what she'd done. Her cat, Ebony, was curled up by her ankle, purring. She missed the warmth of another human being. A message pinged through on her phone.

I'm sorry. Please can I come over? I miss you. B.

She opened up AppyDater on her laptop and logged into the profile she'd set up for research purposes. She typed in his first name, then searched through the million and one Chris's that were registered on AppyDater. She narrowed it down to Warwickshire.

Again, nothing. She sighed. He was hardly going to register using his own name. She did the same with Wyre and Kapoor. Again, nothing came up. The more she looked at it, the more she saw that a lot of people made up names. She typed in AdamzFun, BearBoy, NoName and BigBoz – again nothing. Maybe those were names that Amber gave to these people to put them in her phone. She glared at her own fake profile. Jill the florist with a photo of herself about five years ago wearing a hat covering most of her head as she looked down. No one would know it was her.

She had several smileys already. Jill's half-concealed face was obviously desirable. She clicked on the succession of men and gave them a tentative glance before throwing the phone on her bed, disappointed that she was nowhere nearer to finding out who Amber was meeting for a date. She searched for Amber's profile again and nothing came up. What name had Amber been using? She wondered if anyone on this whole system was real. Gina glanced at Briggs's message again and replied.

I'm glad you're getting out there. No need to say sorry. It seems everyone's on it. You're not alone anyway. I'm just checking it out now! Might get me a date or two, or three! Go me.

She added a laughing emoji, a bit like the smiley on the app. She waited for a reply but it didn't come. She bit into her sandwich and opened the files on her laptop as the cheese and bread mulched in her mouth. All CCTV had now been uploaded, all records were up to date and on the system and Bernard had sent his report through. She opened the bar CCTV from the Fish and Anchor and watched as Lennie Dack greeted a succession of couples on the night in question. He showed people to their tables and came back, waiting for the next customers to arrive. All she could see were happy faces of people looking forward to a special night out. One table remained empty, a no-show on Amber's booking. She had been the one to book the table in her name. Maybe she'd messaged whoever she was meeting to say she wasn't coming. Maybe Amber was lying to her neighbour and friend, Lauren. But the booking had been made and she hadn't cancelled. She'd fully intended to go out for dinner that night.

Gina watched as the couple nearest to the door smiled and looked into each other's eyes, leaning over at one point for a kiss. So intimate and the whole process familiar like they'd been together years. He placed his hand over hers. She bit her bottom lip and smiled at him. This scene was teasing her, showing her something wonderful that she'd never have. Terry had robbed her of intimacy, he'd robbed her of love. It was because of him she knew she could never trust anyone else with her heart. She glanced back and the couple were now eating bread. A glimmer of movement caught her eye in a wall mirror next to the couple. The chef, Jake Goodman, stood in front of the door, his stare on that couple reflected in the mirror. It was if he was watching the woman as she removed her delicate scarf.

A second later, he glanced at the empty table and around at the others before heading back into the kitchen. She noted a question on her pad. Was he looking for Amber?

She slammed her laptop closed. A break was in order. She grabbed the second triangle sandwich and shoved the corner into her mouth. It was unappealing, exactly as she felt right now as she lay in bed at such an early hour, eating food. As she tried to swallow the bread in her mouth, it almost lodged as she felt herself begin to choke up with tears. Why had she been unfortunate enough to meet Terry? She could have met someone like Briggs right from the start and had a whole different life.

She glanced to the side and threw what was left of the sandwich on her bedside table. Self-pity was making her ugly and she didn't want that.

Her phone beeped again. It was an AD notification. She clicked onto it and glanced at the man's photo, the man who was interested in Jill the florist. He was about her age, claimed to be a plumber and had a nice smile.

AppyDater was research, that was all. She wasn't meant to use it. But everyone else was using it and it was becoming ever more tempting. What harm could it do? Her finger hovered over the message button then her phone rang. She held it to her ear. 'Sir.' Her tone was formal.

Briggs paused before speaking. Was he going to talk to her like he used to, at least in a friendly way. Was it the message she sent?

'We need to talk at some point and I'm sorry okay but I'm not calling about us so thank you for answering. We have another potential missing woman. Young, long dark hair, been missing over an hour. That normally wouldn't be a worry but it's the circumstances. Her great-grandmother, Betty Falconer, was waiting for her to get her car at Cleevesford Hospital and she never came back with the car. Her name is Madison Randle and she's a twenty-year-old-student at Worcester. The great-grandmother is still at the hospital in reception.'

It was time to put her emotions aside and get on with her job. 'I'm on my way.'

CHAPTER TWENTY-NINE

As Gina walked across the car park, she spotted Jacob standing outside the hospital, shivering against a brick pillar. He waved when he spotted her. From afar, he had a classic timeless look: long overcoat, perfect facial profile, light glinting off his jaw and nose.

'Alright, guv?' He placed a stick of gum in his mouth. 'Can't believe it, I was just about to get in the bath and then I got the call. Jennifer is now soaking in my bath drinking the bottle of wine we were going to share.'

A splash of rain hit the side of Gina's face. She hurried under the entrance canopy where the smell of smoke hit her. The no smoking signs were obviously being ignored. 'Maybe you can pick up where you left off later.' She smiled.

He nodded as they entered the hospital, not having to go far to spot the lonesome, frail old lady sitting in a wheelchair. She was nursing a plastic cup that looked like it had been empty for ages, drip marks where she'd been sipping dried down the sides. Someone placed a few coins in the slot of a coffee machine and the machine gargled and spluttered to life, the only sound breaking up the evening silence.

'Ms Falconer?' Gina headed towards the woman.

The woman nodded and replied in a whispery voice, 'Yes.'

'I'm DI Harte, this is DS Driscoll. You called about your great-granddaughter.'

A few strands of Betty Falconer's white wispy hair had stuck to the shoulders of her navy blue cardigan. 'She was meant to get the car and take me home but she hasn't returned. I'm worried about her. I told one of the nurses and they kept saying to wait a bit but then an hour passed and I knew something was wrong. I got the nurse to call you.'

Gina glanced up the corridor. The café had closed for the evening and the newspaper stand was deserted. She sat on the chair next to Betty's wheelchair.

'Ms Falconer, what time did you last see your great-grand-daughter?'

'What? I can't hear very well. Can you speak up?' The woman tapped at her ear and Gina noticed the skin-coloured hearing aid as the woman moved her white curls back.

'Sorry, Ms Falconer.'

'And it's Betty.'

Gina took a deep breath and checked her notes. 'Betty, what time did you last see your great-granddaughter, Madison Randle?'

'I'm not one hundred per cent sure but it was about six this evening. The doctor had just given me my discharge papers and Madison parked me here to go and get the car. I've been here since. At first, I thought she was catching up with her phone calls in the car or maybe she'd just popped to the garage for some petrol. She knew I was safe and warm here. I was certain that something was wrong after a while. I tried to call her but her phone kept going to voicemail. She wouldn't just leave me here. Madison is a caring girl. She's training to be a nurse. We were going to go back to mine and watch *Inspector Morse* together.' The woman stared at the unmanned reception desk.

'Do you know where Madison had parked her car and what type of car she drove? We can check the car park for her car?'

The woman's brow furrowed and she looked a little vacant. A clopping noise distracted her. A nurse stopped in front of them. 'Are you okay, Betty? Can I get you another drink?'

Betty Falconer shook her head. 'If I have another, I'll need to pee again. I just want Madison found. I'm worried.' Betty swallowed.

Gina walked to the side, leaving Jacob while he took the description of Madison's car. 'Any thoughts on what might be going on here?'

The young woman shook her head. 'No. I was here when her great-granddaughter came to take her home. I wasn't alerted to the fact that Ms Falconer was still here until she asked one of the staff to call the police. I just thought I'd come back to check on her. I'd half expected her to be gone and for all this to be a misunderstanding.' The nurse paused.

'Can you please sit with Betty while my colleague and I check out the car park? We can see if the great-granddaughter's car is still there. Betty is clearly worried and upset and I don't want her left alone.'

The nurse checked her little clock. 'Of course. I'm actually on a break. I have half an hour but we're really short-staffed. I need to get back to MAU after that, sorry.'

'Just a quick question, sorry to keep you. How did Madison Randle seem when she collected Ms Falconer?'

The nurse shrugged and paused. 'Upbeat that there were no major problems resulting from Ms Falconer's fall and keen to get her home. She mentioned that she was training to be a nurse and seemed to enjoy talking to the staff about her course. Ms Falconer is very proud of her. There was nothing to suggest she was worried. She did seem distracted by her phone earlier on and grimaced a few times but that's nothing unusual with people in general. They always seem to be buried in their phones.'

'Thank you.' Gina turned to Jacob and Betty. 'Betty, this lovely nurse,' Gina read her name tag, 'sorry, Nurse Becky, will sit with you while we see if we can find Madison's car.'

'You will come back, won't you?'

'Of course we will.'

The old lady smiled and began chatting to Nurse Becky.

As they exited through the sliding doors, a cold wall hit them. Gina hugged herself as she followed Jacob. 'Where did you say her car was?'

'Apparently, there's an overflow car park right at the back. It's a blue Corsa and the only other thing Ms Falconer can remember is Madison has an ice-cream air freshener dangling from the rear-view mirror.'

As they climbed up the mound of earth that separated the main car park from the overflow, Gina instantly felt the difference. There was no street lighting and the back was lined with dense trees and shrubs that blurred into blackness at the back. She squinted to get a better view.

Jacob pulled out a pocket torch from his pocket. 'This should help.' The beam reflected off a windscreen at the back, the only car on that part of the car park.

'Her car is still here.' Gina stepped into a pothole and let out a little shriek as she regained her balance. It had been filled with slushy water. She felt her boots beginning to soak through. That would deaden her toes within minutes.

As they got closer, Jacob shone his torch through the window of the dark-coloured car. The air freshener dangled in the window.

Gina peered through the window and pulled out a pair of latex gloves from her pocket before trying the door. 'It's locked but I suppose that was to be expected.' She glanced up and she couldn't see any CCTV. 'We need a team here, ASAP. She could be anywhere by now. Get uniform to check her address. I'm sure we have it on file from the original call.'

Jacob stepped to one side and made the call.

'Madison,' Gina called as she held up her phone to get some light on the area. It was a long shot but worth a try. She crept onto the earthy back that led to the shrubs and noticed footprints that looked to have been sliding through the mud. Careful to not follow the same path, she continued forward, pushing through the brambles. In her mind, she could see a struggle. Maybe Madison tried to run. A snapped branch on a tree hung down, just holding on by a thread. 'Madison.'

No answer.

'They're on their way, guv. Guv?'

'Over here. There's some footsteps and the opening there.' She pointed. 'It looks like the earth has been recently disturbed.'

'Should we leave it until the others get here? We might destroy evidence if she's been taken.'

'I'll take a different route. Stay there, there's no need for both of us to look but I have to make sure she's not here.' She yelped as her ankle caught the spine of a bramble.

'Be careful, guv.'

She took a few more steps forward, flashing her phone in front of her. Inhaling almost hurt as it was so cold and the hum of traffic was making it difficult to hear. A twig cracked. Glancing across she saw a fox turning to run away. With her pulse running through her head, she took a few more steps forward. It was hopeless. He'd chased her and caught her and now she was gone, just like Amber. Sighing, she glanced around one more time. Left, right, even above, then ahead. A glint of something sparkled back.

Taking a step closer, Gina could see a finger with a ring on it. Running over, Gina kneeled over and peered behind the tree. That's when she spotted the unconscious girl. Blood ran down her face, meandering over her cheeks and settling into the groove of her neck. Gina felt for a pulse. 'Madison... Madison. Wake up.' There was no response. The pulse was faint. 'Jacob, get a medic here now. I've found her but she's unconscious.'

'On it, guv.' In the distance, she heard the gravel under his feet shifting as he headed back to the hospital.

Gina placed the back of her hand on the girl's arm and it made her shiver. It was like one of the bodies they keep refrigerated. A small flurry of rain began to fall.

Gina removed her coat. As her teeth chattered, she placed it over Madison and began talking to her gently. 'Madison, you're safe now. Help is on its way.' She shone her phone over the girl's face. She shuddered as she saw how much she looked like Amber – and she shuddered even more when she saw the raging, bloody wound on her head.

A rustling could be heard and the girl made an incoherent sound.

'Madison.'

It was no good, however hard Gina listened, Madison wasn't making any sense.

A man in a blue tunic pushed forward, followed by another. 'We really need you to get back so that we can treat her.' She stepped out of the way, stomach churning as she saw how bad the head wound was. Rushing out, she met Jacob back on tarmac. 'I don't know if she's going to make it. She's covered in blood and her breathing is shallow.'

CHAPTER THIRTY

That bitch got me good and proper. Damn! The kitchen door shudders as I slam my fist into it. Reaching down, I stroke my tender crotch and wince. The mission had to be aborted. It forced the wind out of my sails and now I'm here, pants around my ankles, trying to sooth my pain away.

'I told you not to go, not to leave me.' You stand there, a smug look spread across your face. You're relishing the fact that I got hurt.

'Just piss off, will you?'

You shake your head, knowing that you have no intention of ever leaving me but when I finally find your replacement, you'll have to go.

I hobble to the record player and set the needle on the soothing record that neither of us will talk over. A tear slips down your cheek, that smug smile now gone. I know you don't want me to do the things I do but I miss us and I need to recapture that feeling. The moment I saw Amber, I thought she would be the perfect replacement and that ignited something in me. Even the way she placed her hair behind her ears was identical to how you do it.

'You enjoyed what you did to Amber, didn't you? You're sick.'

'Shut up!' I pull my black boot from my foot, struggling as it's such a tight fit. In a fit of fluster, I fling it at you but all it does is create another dent in the door. I rock back and forth taking in the song and then it ends. It's finished and the bungalow is silent. The chair is empty and I am alone. I am hollow and I don't deserve to be hollow.

I grab my phone and glance at the app again. I need to fill my life with purpose. Amber didn't work out; Madison turned out to be a disappointment and she paid for that.

'I promised I would find another you to make my life complete and this time, I'm sure I've found her.' I gaze at the profile. Police or not. She's the one.

I send a message, not wasting any time. The whole night doesn't have to be a write-off yet. I followed her home earlier while Madison was in the hospital so all I have to do is be patient. When I came back and Madison's car was still there, my night was made. I have been a busy boy but that's far better than sitting idle, as my mother would say. At the back of my mind, I knew I had to have a backup plan. The pain in my crotch is starting to ease so I stand and walk around a little.

I learned one lesson tonight. They fight back, which means from now on I take no chances. Strike quickly. I grab my coat and head to the door.

You walk into view from the darkness at the end of the hall and you begin to sing our song as you cry. Tears spill from your eyes and you can't get beyond the first line. As your voice cracks, you step back, falling back into the darkness. I can't see you now but you're always there. You never leave me.

My phone beeps. It's a message and she's interested but I don't think I can wait until her proposed date night, a week from now. I know she's a busy woman but that's too long. I need her now. Maybe this is fate playing out. Madison was never meant to be but this one who works for the police, she's the closest match so far. Our eyes met. That had to be a sign. The more I think of her, the more I can't get her out of my head. There's a void in my life. Since Amber, there is no going back in my quest to find the right one and when she is presented to you on a platter, you know it's time to act.

I punch the wall and my fingers crack. That's how hard it has to be when I strike them dumb. No walking stick or sick hedgehogs.

Such a scenario won't work on this woman and I want her. No, it's more than that, I need her and I will have her.

One last message, play it cool.

I'd love to meet up! Wow, we have so much in common. :)

We don't but we soon will. I will help you to emerge out of the chrysalis and become the butterfly that I need you to be. We'll have each other. I glance back at the chair, the one with all the binds and plastic covering, ready to receive another woman for conversion. Maybe I should call myself Dr Frankenstein. I'm no scientist but I will work on my creation until it's perfect and if that means breaking her down totally so that I can rebuild her, then so be it.

'Please don't do this.'

I can't see you but you're everywhere, haunting me. Are you cowering in that dark corner of my mind? I slam the front door, leaving you behind.

I know you're not real but I like that I imagine your voice so vividly, even though in my mind you now hate me. When the right person replaces you, she and you will meld into one and I will have you back.

We will be happy and we can live again.

I glance at the woman's photo and smile. The more I think about it, she's perfect. Dark hair and a look that tells me she can become what I want her to become. The slight distance in her gaze makes me want her more.

It's going to be a long night but I'm not coming home empty-handed. That is not an option and that woman is mine.

CHAPTER THIRTY-ONE

'Doctor Nowak, can you spare me a moment?' Gina recognised him from previous encounters at the hospital.

He hurried along the corridor and put his round glasses on. 'You want an update on Madison Randle?'

'Yes, please.'

Jacob came and stood next to Gina, clutching two cardboard cups of coffee. He handed her one.

The doctor opened his file. 'It's a really cold night. She has the onset of hypothermia. She's also not making much sense at the moment but I think that's due to concussion and shock. I'm organising scans. We want to take a closer look at her injuries. I know you want to go in there and ask questions but she's really not in a fit state. She's not even getting her full name right at the moment.'

'Thank you for the update. Do you know how long it will be?'

'How big is the universe? As soon as she can talk to you, I will call you. I do know how important it is that you speak to her. An assault was committed on hospital grounds. We want this cleared up as much as you do. For now, I suggest you get some rest or go and get some food. I'll call you when I have some news. She's also in a lot of pain with the head injury, we may end up sedating her a little as she's so agitated and confused.'

Gina's shoulders slumped. It was no good trying any harder. If the doctor said she wasn't up to talking, she believed that Madison really wasn't up to talking. 'We will need her clothes as they may contain vital evidence of her attack. Also, I'll get someone from uniform stationed here. We will need fingernail clippings and some swabs. This could help us catch her attacker. Would that be okay to arrange those?'

'Of course. As soon as we've stabilised her, we can do that for you. For now, the patient comes first.'

'Thank you so much, Doctor Nowak.'

The doctor smiled and left her standing by the nurses' station. Phones rang, monitors beeped and staff walked back and forth with samples and equipment. Everywhere she and Jacob stood, they ended up moving and apologising. She left accident and emergency and stood outside to make a call. PC Smith answered. 'It's me, Harte. Could you or a colleague please come over here and keep guard in A&E? We need to get samples from Madison Randle and I need someone to be here to supervise, bag and tag.'

'I'm on my way.' Within minutes she spotted PC Smith walking across the car park from the scene that he and his officers had cordoned off while they searched for evidence.

Jacob finished his coffee and dropped his cup into the bin. 'I'll head back over there for now. See you in five.'

She smiled and sipped her coffee, waiting for PC Smith to amble over. The fluorescent strips on his jacket shone as they caught the signage lights, passing the smoking shelter.

Nurse Becky pushed Betty Falconer through a door just inside the entrance to A&E. The old woman's frown told Gina all she needed to know. 'Push me to her, Nurse, please. I need to be with my Maddie.' It was going to be a long night for Betty Falconer too.

Gina stepped back inside. 'I'm so sorry, Betty, but it's such a good job you got someone to call us. We found her and she's being treated. Will you be okay?'

'I need to be with her. She's always there for me, now, I'm going to be there for her.' Gina didn't doubt that for one moment. 'Just catch whoever did this to her.'

The nurse continued to push Betty onto the A&E ward. Gina moved away as an ambulance pulled up and its doors burst open.

Smith met her under the A&E sign. 'I can take over here, guv. Everyone's suited up and the search has begun.'

As she walked across the near empty car park, she checked her phone. Another message from AppyDater. She ignored it. Maybe she could look at it later. She glanced at the diary app on her phone. Tomorrow she was meeting Wyre at Amber's apartment block before they went on to the Fish and Anchor to speak to the chef, Jake Goodman, to discuss his previous for stealing women's underwear from washing lines. It sounded as cliché as it came but she knew this to be worrying early behaviour that could lead to something more serious.

For now, she was going to treat this attack on Madison Randle as being possibly linked to the Amber Slater murder. Both students at the same university. Both of the same age, similar build, similar in looks. There were too many similarities for it to be a coincidence. She dabbed her dry lips with a bit of lip balm, the slight slit in the middle stinging like mad. She thought of Amber's torn lips. *Why, why, why did he want to shut you up?* Answering that question was the key to solving the case.

Damn it! She wanted to kick something. If only she could have spoken to Madison. She might have been able to give them a description or something further to work on.

Her phone beeped again. That app was going to go as soon as she finished with the case. She glanced down. It was the same man again. He certainly did have appeal. She bit her lip as she thought of Briggs and the fact that he'd let her down. Stuff it. She typed out a reply.

CHAPTER THIRTY-TWO

Wednesday, 27 January

I wait and my patience is paying off. After falling asleep for a couple of hours I feel a bit more refreshed although sleeping in a car isn't easy. I see her through the bedroom window. She's dressed in her white shirt and dark suit jacket. Her hair falls over her shoulders and she checks in the mirror one more time before heading to wherever for another day of crime fighting.

Little does she know that today, she gets to be star of the show. At this time in the morning it's still pitch-black. She must be dedicated, being up this early. I think back to the lake on the morning she was there, one of the first on the scene, looking down at Amber. Was she searching for me when she glanced back and forth? Had she looked harder, she would have probably found me but no one walks along the old overgrown bridle path, definitely not at this time of the year. Not even a dog walker came by. I was neatly tucked away behind the trees, watching and waiting to see how it all panned out. I know our eyes didn't really meet but in my mind I like to think they did, because all I see is her begging me to come for her.

For a while, I even stood, blending in amongst the crowd in my winter wear, but then they started taking names and details. I managed to slink away again. I'm good at that, at being the unmemorable person that I am.

The light to her bedroom goes off and every room is now in darkness. Her car is the silver saloon. I know that because I saw her come out of the station yesterday and I followed her home. I mean my attention had been on Madison but my time is my own. I don't have a boss to answer to or a workplace to be at. I have commitments but they are on my terms. Finding an excuse to not be where I should is easy and nothing unusual.

I don't need much to exist and I have a bit of a steady income although it's a paltry one. I live my life freely without the burden of employment. No one tells me where to be or what to do which is why I'm here. The main front door will open at any minute. No pussyfooting around with this one.

Grabbing the pepper spray and the rock, I gently close my door and slink behind the car, then I scuttle along to the next one and I'm right where I want to be, behind hers. I'm ready and it's dark – perfect.

I hear her boots clipping on the ground, getting louder as she gets closer. Two words to myself, *Don't hesitate.*

As her lights flash and the car beeps, she goes to open her car door and I stand and bring the rock down hard, straight onto her head as hard as I can. Then comes the pepper spray, just a touch. She's going to scream. 'Don't you dare scream or I will kill you – just don't.' Her gaze is confused and wavering, like she's losing her focus. I bring the rock down one more time and all her muscles go at once. She slumps between her car and the next, perfectly hidden from anyone who might pass by.

I did it. She's mine. Come on police person, detective or whoever you are. Who cares? Let's go home.

I will break you and remake you. That's a promise.

I cannot fail again. I refuse to fail again.

CHAPTER THIRTY-THREE

Gina paced in the car park outside Amber Slater's apartment. Every car that passed had her attention. It wasn't like Wyre to be late, ever. She could barely feel her phone as her fingers were so numb from the morning frost but she managed to call the station to see if Wyre had got their meeting time mixed up.

O'Connor picked up. 'Alright, guv?'

'Yes, I'm at Bulmore Drive waiting for Wyre and she's not picking up. Have you seen her?'

'No but I think we have a staff problem today. A couple have called in sick. 'Tis the season for the flu.' He sang the last line.

'Must be something in the air. So, you haven't seen or heard from Wyre at all today?'

'Sorry, guv. On a good note, I'm going through all the CCTV cameras from the Tesco Superstore, looking for Mr and Mrs Collins. I'll hopefully have something to report soon.'

'Don't let me keep you. Is Jacob there?'

A scuffling sound came through the phone, sounding like O'Connor was holding it against his body or covering the receiver and Gina caught O'Connor's muffled words as he asked around. 'He is, guv.'

'Would you ask him to meet me at Amber's landlord's, Vincent Jordan's, bungalow as soon as? I want someone else with me when I speak to him and let me know if you hear from Wyre.' Gina listened as O'Connor relayed her request.

'He said he's on his way. Be ten minutes. On a good note, Mrs O has made some pecan and maple twists, I'll keep one aside for you.'

'Mrs O is too kind. Tell her "thank you" from me.'

'Certainly will.' O'Connor ended the call and Gina stared at her phone. She'd tried Wyre three times and no answer. She did a half-hearted jog on the spot to warm up a little but it wasn't working. Her fingers may as well have been three times as chunky as she missed the redial button and cursed her failed attempt under her breath. Her phone lit up. It was a message from Wyre.

I'm not too good. Sorry. Paula Wyre.

Gina's brow furrowed. This wasn't protocol. Each and every one of them had been sick at some point. The first thing they were required to do was actually call in. She exhaled a white mist and wondered if her break up with George had been affecting her colleague more than she was making out. The usually pristine Paula Wyre had seemed a little dishevelled but she'd also been eager to work so that her mind was off her problems.

Gina stared at the message. Had her response been a little cold? It wasn't as if their messages or emails had ever ended with kisses but there was something off. She scrolled back to Wyre's message. Since when had she ever been that brief? Wyre trusted her enough to say what was wrong and why would she end with her full name? Paula Wyre. Paula or Wyre would have been sufficient or even nothing. Gina knew her number.

She tried to call Wyre again and the call was cut off. She tried again but her phone went straight to voicemail. An uneasy feeling began to swell in the pit of Gina's stomach. In her mind she pictured Wyre still in bed, depressed and unwashed, not wanting to get up and face the world. As a colleague, it was Gina's duty to leave her be; as a friend, there was no way she could sit back and see Wyre head into some dark descent. After her visit to the Fish and Anchor, she was going to head to Wyre's apartment to see if there was anything she could do to help.

Jacob pulled around into the car park and drove straight into a space. The booming of his music could be heard from outside. He turned the Kings of Leon off and stepped out of his car. 'Anything from Wyre, yet?'

She nodded. 'She sent me a text saying she wasn't good, whatever that means.'

'A text?'

'I know. Something's not right.'

Jacob pulled his gloves on and did a comical shiver. 'I know Smith's team is a couple of PCs down too.' He pulled his hat further over his ears. 'It's like the arctic out here.'

Gina rubbed her hands together. 'I suppose we best get on with it then.' They walked down the winding lane together at the back of the apartment block. It was sectioned off by a row of lopped off conifers that seemed to reach the height of the block. A ray of winter sun reached through the gaps in the foliage, glistening off the ice-tipped branches and fallen needles.

A rugged road led them to a bungalow that looked condemned. The aerial seemed to be attached with old rope to some plastic piping that was swaying on the side of the building. A collection of old used tyres were piled up beside the front door and a shopping trolley sat in the middle of the mud garden as if it were a feature.

Jacob glanced up and down. 'This place looks condemned.'

Gina almost slid on the icy uneven slabs as she put her hands out and regained her balance using the front door. 'You're not wrong.' She knocked as hard as she could with her balled up hand. There was no knocker and no bell, only a little exterior post box attached to the right side of the door. Several flyers were leaking out, threatening to escape. She knocked again and placed her ear against the door. 'I can't hear anything.'

'Wait.' Jacob stepped to the side. 'I just saw a curtain twitch down the far end.'

The front of the bungalow had four large windows and the curtains were drawn across all of them. She knocked again and then an interior door slammed. Moments later, after listening to about three locks being slid across followed by the turn of a key, the door creaked open.

'What? Don't you know what time it is? I don't want to buy anything. I don't do charity or religion.'

'It's eight thirty in the morning. I'm DI Harte and this is DS Driscoll. We'd like to have a few words with you. May we come in?'

He scrunched his face up making it look like his mahogany brown eyebrows were meeting in the middle. His thick lips smacked. 'No.'

'It would be easier if we could talk inside.' Gina was hoping to take a look at how he lived and his body language was not sitting well with her – plus, it was cold. From what she knew, Vincent Jordan claimed to be in on the night of Amber Slater's abduction and now, for some reason, he wasn't going to let them in. He didn't have to let them in but he was looking more suspicious by the second. He didn't respond in anyway. If anything, he pressed the door closer to his body, leaving no room through the gap for Gina to see in. 'We need to talk to you about Amber Slater's abduction and murder. She was your tenant and neighbour. Either you invite us in or we book an appointment for you to come and speak to us down the station, this morning.' That was enough to make him open up.

He rattled the flimsy door open and folded his arms as they stepped inside the dark, flowery-wallpapered hallway. A scurrying sound came from above. He pointed upwards. 'Rats in the loft.'

Gina shivered. The one wall was filled with pictures, a ramshackle mixture of old photos of places and prints of famous paintings. She glanced up at the loft as a rat ran above her. The dirty pink runner led to a kitchen that looked like it had been fitted in the sixties. Tidy but scuffed doors were hanging off cupboards by their hinges and the old freestanding cooker stood against the wall, grease melded onto every part of it. She glanced out of the window, which revealed a huge garden with several large sheds at the bottom. The smell of grilled cheese hung in the air, then she spotted the pizza box leaning against the bin.

'I'd offer you a drink but I don't want you to stay. I don't do visitors so just say what you have to say so we can all get on with our day. I have to clean the communal areas today and sweep up leaves.' He pulled his vest down further over his maroon bed shorts. His feet padded along the dirty lino flooring before he stopped and leaned against the worktop.

'Amber Slater was last seen on Friday night. Evidence is pointing to the fact that she was taken from the car park in front of the apartment block you manage. She was later found dead at Cleevesford Park. We need to ask you a few questions. Did you see or hear anything from the apartment block on Friday evening after six?'

He let out a snigger. 'I don't see or hear anything. Have you seen how far back I am? The conifers also provide a screen. I don't have anything to say because I don't know anything.'

'That's not what the tenants say. They say that you've gone over to the block a few times when they have music on and asked them to turn it down. So you can hear from your bungalow.'

'Yeah, when it's turned up so loud it sounds like they're having a rave. I bet they didn't tell you they played it that loud.'

Jacob leaned against the fridge. 'Where were you between six and nine last Friday evening?'

The man's gaze flashed to Jacob where he stared at him. 'I was here. I'm always here. Always around, always on call, that's me.'

'Mr Jordan.' Gina stared at him and paused, wanting to unnerve him a little. He fitted their bill. He seemed to be a loner, he was cagey. He was everything they could be looking for, on paper. 'Tell me a bit about yourself.'

He opened his mouth, then closed it, not expecting her to say that. 'There's not much to tell. I live here. It's my job to maintain and manage the apartment block and I do the general maintenance for a few others. My parents own a few properties and they leave this one with me to look after. It comes with the bungalow so that I'm always around should anyone need me. This is my main and only job. I'm forty-five. Anything else?'

'Do you have an alibi for Friday evening?'

'No and I don't like where this is going.'

'May we take a look around?'

'No. Please leave. Unless you have anything to charge me with or any evidence that I have done anything wrong, I'm not saying another word without a solicitor.' He stepped forward, ushering them out of the kitchen and back into the hallway. As they passed a slightly open door, he slammed it closed. Gina tried to glance through the next door but he did the same again, ending her view abruptly. He literally nudged them out the door and back into the cold. 'At about seven thirty on Friday evening I was on a phone call to my electrician, Eamon. One of the lights in the block is out and he normally comes to replace the bulbs. I don't do electrics. He is listed under EL Electrical Contractors and I called him from my home phone. I'm sure you're both skilled enough in detective work to verify that, look him up, and ask.' He smiled as he rubbed his stubble and slammed the door.

'We meet them all in our job.' Gina said to Jacob. As she led the way along the slippery path back to the road, she stared through the trees at the apartments. 'What did you make of him?'

'Shifty.'

'We definitely need to check his alibi out and I'd like to see if the electrician's phone call log shows that Vincent Jordan called from his landline on Friday evening about seven thirty.'

'I wonder what he was hiding behind all those doors.'

'He wasn't about to let us look. We'll see if his alibi checks out and take it from there.'

Jacob stopped at the end of the road and looked up at the apartments. 'The other day, you were going to tell me something but then you forgot and I forgot to ask. What was it?'

'Oh yes, it was about Wyre, but you can't repeat it. It's not common knowledge yet.'

'Okay.'

'Wyre's engagement is off. I thought she was handling it okay but today, I don't know. She hasn't called or come into work. All I have is a text from her.'

'I thought they were solid.'

'And me.'

'Have you tried calling her again?'

Gina nodded. 'I'll try now. Her phone went to answerphone last time.' She pulled her phone from her pocket and pressed Wyre's number. 'Answerphone again. I'm going to pop by hers when we've finished at the Fish and Anchor. There's just time to catch up back at the station before heading over there while they prep for lunch service. I called ahead and Lennie Dack the landlord said we could come after ten thirty.'

Gina's phone rang in her hand. 'O'Connor.'

'Guv. I've been through the footage showing the times that Mrs Collins claimed she and her husband were at Tesco and she was lying. We only have her walking around the shop. Her car is clearly visible on the cameras, coming and going – she was alone.' Gina felt her head begin to hurt. The Collinses had lied and she wanted to know why.

'Another thing, guv. Doctor Nowak called and said Madison Randle is well enough to speak now.'

'Will you message me the ward details? And double, triple check that footage at the supermarket. We can't get this wrong.' She turned to Jacob. 'Skip the last plan. We're heading straight to Cleevesford Hospital. A good description or a positive ID of Madison's attacker could fix everything at the moment. Let's go.'

CHAPTER THIRTY-FOUR

I saw the fear in her eyes as I brought the rock down on the side of her head. All done efficiently and no one saw, that's the good thing. The trail of blood down the side of her face has dried up and she stirs. Opening her red pepper-sprayed eyes, I register her confusion. She looks momentarily blank.

She makes some half-hearted whimper. I don't have long before she'll try to escape or summon up the strength to fight back again so I tighten her binds. She cries a little. She may feel all-powerful in her policing role, fighting crime and making the streets safer but here and now, she is brought down a peg.

'It's okay. Don't be scared. You're safe here with me.' My mother was wrong about that look in my eye. That wasn't the look that said I was about to kill. I'm saving that one for later and only if I need it. If she turns out to be like Amber, it will be all her fault. She will have brought it on herself.

CHAPTER THIRTY-FIVE

Gina checked her phone as she and Jacob hurried onto the ward, swiftly being buzzed in by a nurse who caught sight of them from behind a counter. Still nothing from Wyre. As she approached the desk, she held her identification up. 'DI Harte and DS Driscoll. Doctor Nowak left me a message telling us we can now speak to Madison Randle.'

'Ah, go through those double doors, carry on down the corridor and it's the first room to your left. There was a PC there but he left for a comfort break.'

'Thank you.' As they reached the room, Gina spotted the young woman lying there with a white sheet covering her body. Another girl appeared from the corner of the room holding a pair of tracksuit bottoms and a jumper. Gina knocked.

Madison beckoned her in with a shaky hand. The dressing on her head covered up the sticky bloody wound that Gina had seen the night before. A piece of surgical tape dangled from her dark hair. 'Hello. Are you from the police?' She slurred a little as she spoke and her eyes opened wide. She shook her head. 'I'm so not with it yet. I asked for something to help me sleep last night and I feel zonked too.'

'DI Harte and DS Driscoll. We'd like to ask you a few questions. You probably won't remember but I found you last night, in the bushes at the back of the car park.'

Staring blankly, Madison shook her head. 'I'm sorry.'

The other girl stood awkwardly by the door. 'Shall I come back in a bit?'

Gina turned. 'Would you mind?'

'Course not. Shall I get you some chocolate, Maddie?'

Madison nodded. 'Thanks, Alice. I'd love some. I think I deserve it. Won't be counting calories while I'm stuck in here feeling sorry for myself.'

'Back in five.' Alice left the room and the door softly closed behind her.

Madison pushed the overhead television away from her body. 'Have you found him?' She winced as she sat up a little.

Shaking her head, Gina sat and Jacob pulled his notebook from his pocket. 'Sorry, not yet, but we need to ask you some questions. I can see you're in a lot of pain so I'll try not to keep you long.'

'Don't worry about that. I just want him caught.'

'Please tell us what you know from the beginning. Include everything, however small.' Gina gave Madison a warm smile to put her at ease.

Rubbing her head, Madison stared at the sink on the opposite wall as she thought back. 'Nanna was taken into hospital yesterday. She had a fall but she's okay. I stayed with her while we were waiting for her to be discharged.' She paused and swallowed. 'I left Nanna in the foyer to get the car. I usually park outside the entrance as she's not very mobile. When I'd arrived earlier the car park was full, but there's a patch of rough tarmac at the back that is used as an overspill car park. When I went back to get the car it was dark.'

A tear trickled down her cheek.

'I know this is hard but you're doing really well. You've been through a lot so just take your time.' Gina placed one hand over the other and leaned back to put Madison at ease and not rush her.

'That's when I saw him, well his outline. It was dark. He had a walking stick and looked a bit wobbly. I think I offered to help him or if I didn't, I intended to. It's a bit of a blur. I remember being scared and I remember fighting him off me. I can't remember how I came to be doing that, it happened so fast. I kneed him in the groin at one point and he yelped but that didn't put him down. He was still coming for me and I ran towards the bushes. I thought, if I can just hide, he'll give up and go. He hit me with something hard but I can't remember when. If it was before I kneed him, or after…'

'You're doing great.'

'I remember my heart pounding. I thought I was going to die. I kept thinking about the other student, Amber, and I didn't want to end up in a lake, dead. I tried to be quiet but my head… it was spinning and next thing, I was out of it. I don't remember being brought into the hospital and I don't remember last night. I had weird dreams and woke up this morning wondering where I was and then I called Alice – she's one of my best friends. Apparently the staff persuaded Nanna to get a taxi home in the night.'

Gina tilted her head. 'Can you tell us what your attacker looked like?'

Madison pulled her sheet up a bit further, almost up to her neck. Gina could see the trembling of her hands under the sheet. 'It was pitch-black. There are no lights up there. I remember him being bulky; either he was wearing layers or larger built. It felt like layers when he grabbed me, not muscle if you know what I mean. A scarf covered the bottom of his face and he wore a hat, just a woolly hat or hood but I couldn't make out any features. I'd just walked straight up from the lit area into darkness. My eyes hadn't properly adjusted to the change in light then it all happened so quickly, I panicked. I fought like mad and I think I hurt him but I wasn't going to make it easy for him to take me. I read that most attackers don't think that people will fight back, that we freeze. I fought knowing that my life probably depended on it and I hid. I didn't want to die.' A few tears became a sob.

'Did he speak to you?'

She nodded. 'It was more of a murmur or a whisper. I didn't recognise his voice but then again, I wouldn't if he was speaking like that.'

'Is there anyone I can call to be with you?'

'No, I have Alice here and my friend Tyrone will be around when they let me go later. I just want to feel better so that I can leave.' Madison nervously scratched her arm. 'I live close to where Amber lived. Is there someone stalking our area? We both go to the same uni.'

Gina flicked back a couple of pages in her notes and glanced at Jacob. She knew they were both thinking the same thing. 'You mentioned someone called Tyrone?'

'Yes. Tyrone Heard. He lives in the same block that Amber lived in but he was waiting for someone to move out of ours so that he could be with us. We've been close friends over the past year, Tyrone, Alice and I.' She paused. 'It wasn't Ty before you ask. He's the gentlest guy anyone could meet.'

Gina begged to differ. How people often presented themselves to the world didn't always tie up with the real them behind closed doors. She only had to think of her ex-husband Terry. No one would have believed he could have raped and beaten her for years. She held back on questioning Madison any further on Tyrone but made a note to look further into his whereabouts on both occasions. 'Is there anything else you can think of that might help us to find your attacker?'

There was a knock at the door. Alice held up a takeaway cup and a chocolate bar. Madison put her hand up and nodded. Alice disappeared from the window. 'On Monday this week, I thought someone might be following me but they probably weren't. I think my imagination just got the best of me.' She wiped her eyes.

'Tell me anyway.' Gina felt the life coming back into her feet from being in the cold too long. She undid a couple of coat buttons as she waited for Madison to start – the hospital was stuffy. Jacob leaned against the back wall, standing with his notepad cupped in one hand and his pen in the other.

'When I left Nanna's I saw someone on the lane, the one that leads to the side of the Angel Arms, well just a little back from the pub. That person was loitering by the trees but they might have been waiting for a dog. There's something else... When I got to the pub, I went to the loo. I was in a cubicle and someone came in and stood outside the door. They were wearing black boots. I know that because I crouched down and looked underneath. A moment later, whoever it was turned the lights off and left. I ran out of there as quick as I could but I couldn't see anyone around. I heard rustling out the back of the pub, by the bushes. Thinking about it, I do know if you carry on through them they lead back to the lane. Do you think he could have been stalking me? I thought it was Tyrone and Alice playing a joke but they swear they weren't.'

Jacob noted down what she was saying.

'We'll secure the CCTV from the pub, see if we can see anyone loitering around on that night.' Gina loosened her shirt. 'Can you tell us what time this was?'

'About eightish, I think. And there was something else.'

'What was that?'

'When I left to go to the hospital to see Nanna, there was a man looking for a hedgehog under a car. He said it was a baby but I know that it couldn't have been. It's not the right time of the year. Again it was dark and I barely got a glimpse of him but I think it was same man. Alice came out to speak to me. When I turned around, he'd gone and she didn't see him. That was weird. My head's hurting. I think my painkillers are wearing off.'

'Is there anything more you can remember about that moment? His height, features, anything?'

'No. I didn't look at what he was wearing. I was looking under the car for the hedgehog most of the time.'

'We'll get that area checked out too. Thank you for all your help. We have your address. Can I take your number? When you get home, can you call the station? Given what's happened, we'll also send someone over to make sure your apartment is secure.'

Madison grabbed the pen that sat next to the hospital menu. 'I'm going to stay with Alice for a few days now that I know Nanna has been settled in back home. I know Alice is only next door but I don't want to be alone and I'm not in a fit state to care for Nanna at the moment either so I'll have to call her carers. Alice lives at number one, I'm number two.'

Gina nodded. 'That's good. We'll do the check anyway ready for when you do go back to your apartment. One last thing, are you familiar with a site called AppyDater?'

'Yes, everyone has it. I didn't until Monday night but I ditched it last night, just before my attack.'

'I know this is personal but can I please have your login so that we can see who messaged you?'

'Do you think my attacker used the app?'

'We're investigating various lines of enquiry at the moment.'

Grabbing the pen again, Madison wrote down her login and password for the app and passed it to Gina. 'I didn't meet anyone or send any messages. Alice set it up for a laugh and I didn't want it so I deleted it. I only deleted the app though. I didn't delete my account. That's something I was going to do later, so you should still be able to log in.'

'Thank you. If we have any developments I'll let you know, otherwise someone will be in touch soon. Here's my card. If you remember anything else, please call me straight away, anytime.'

Jacob opened the door and Alice peered in. 'Am I okay to come in now?'

Madison nodded. 'Just in time, I need to get dressed and I think I need a hand.' Madison seemed unsteady as she threw her legs over the side of the bed and stood. 'I feel like I have the hangover from hell. I just need to get out of here.'

Gina smiled and left them both to it. As they reached the exit and hit the wall of cold air, Gina couldn't wait to check her phone again. She had a message from Wyre.

I'm feeling a lot better now, guv. I'm heading to the station. Sorry I was a bit vague, I slipped in the shower and was trying to get the feeling back in my leg when I texted. I'm okay now, be there in half an hour.

Gina smiled. 'Wyre's okay. Looks like she fell over in the shower but she's okay now.'

Jacob pressed the central locking on his car and got in. 'Poor, Wyre. She's going to be sore for a while.'

'In more ways than one. Will you call the Angel Arms and get hold of the footage for Monday night? That'll be more to add to O'Connor's pile. I'll meet you back at the station for a quick break, then we'll head over to the Fish and Anchor. See what our underwear thief has to say.'

As she headed to her car she glanced ahead at the overflow car park and saw that the area was still cordoned off. PC Smith was talking with another PC. She jogged up the mound. 'Have forensics finished with this scene?'

'For now.' PC Smith began chewing on a bacon bap that the other PC handed to him.

'Are you here for the day?'

'I wasn't meant to be. Kapoor should have been here but she didn't come in for her shift? So here I am and it's bloody well cold.' He bit into his sandwich again. 'It's okay though. Got my trusty thermals on.'

'I've never known Kapoor to take a sick day. Must be bad.'

PC Smith shrugged. 'I just hope it's not contagious. I don't fancy the flu or norovirus. January's gloomy enough.'

'I'll leave you to it then.' She waved as she carried on back down the mound, waving at Jacob as he pulled out of the car park.

Her phone went. 'O'Connor? What you got?'

'Kapoor's mother has just called. She says she's been to see her consultant about her test results and she was meant to call Kapoor as soon as she received them. She said her daughter hasn't answered and she's worried, which is why she called us to see if she was okay as Mrs Kapoor knew her daughter was working today. She said they're a close family and her daughter wouldn't ignore her, let alone when it came to something so important.'

'I didn't realise Kapoor had that on her mind.'

'Me neither. Kapoor's father also has a spare key and is on his way over to Kapoor's apartment.'

'Keep me posted.' Gina glanced back at Smith who rolled his tissue up into a ball and popped it into his pocket. Kapoor never had a day off sick. Her stomach began to churn just a little. No, Kapoor wasn't a student… but she is on AppyDater… and she did look a little like Madison. A sick feeling passed through Gina's body. What if Kapoor was the next victim?

CHAPTER THIRTY-SIX

Jhanvi Kapoor's eyes begin to flicker as she tries to prise them open. The crackling melody surrounds her in the darkness. A calming voice sings about a beautiful dreamer while she drifts in and out of consciousness. In her half-dreamy state, she pictures herself lying on an old-fashioned four-poster bed, surrounded by drapes. As she tries to sit up and reach beyond the netting, the drapery swirls around her wrists and pulls her back.

'Don't fight me.' He turns her phone off, removes the SIM and places the phone on the floor.

That voice. It's real, not the sounds of a dream. A buzzing sound comes from below as her legs elevate, then the record skips a beat before continuing. She tries to open her eyes again and this time she succeeds, but they need a moment to adjust to the candlelight. It's him, the man who attacked her in the car park outside her apartment and she sees his whole face – every mark, every line.

Her breaths quicken and she feels her heart hammering until her sight prickles. Hyperventilation, her training told her as much. She needs to calm down. Breathe in, hold that breath, and breathe out, but the gag is making that difficult – like breathing through a blocked straw. She knows she is staring at him with a stark expression. She can feel the tension in the muscles around her weepy eyes.

'I'm going to reach over and remove the scarf from around your mouth. If you scream, I am going to knock you out again. Are we clear?'

She's not in a position to do anything else but nod in agreement. A tear drizzles down her cheek.

He holds up a bottle of water and a small blister pack of tablets. She squints but can't quite focus well enough to read what it says on the packet that sits in his lap.

He places them down and leans forward. The smell of something oily and savoury lingers on his clothes and in the air. She sniffs a couple of times and now she knows that smell is grilled cheese. The place smells like a pizza takeaway.

'I made your favourite. Cheese on toast. That's what you normally ask for.'

I've never asked you for anything. Jhanvi thinks it but doesn't speak. She leans back a little, wondering if she should say something or if that will anger him. Whichever drug he has beside him, she doesn't want any more of it in her body. Things are fuzzy, it's hard to remember. She doesn't want to be forced into a sleep and to have to wake up again still not knowing where she is or why she's here. A flashback to another moment enters her mind. She's woken up in this chair before, maybe more than once. The buzzing noise comes from the leg-stand. It rises as the back reclines so that she can lie down in the mechanical chair. It's built for comfort and is similar to the one her dad uses since his bad back worsened.

'Right, you keep comfortable and I'll be back in a second.'

He leaves through the wooden door and a light flashes on in the hallway. She tries to struggle but the rough binds hold her in place and she can feel them gnawing away at the top layer of her skin with every movement. He's drilled holes through the chair to thread the ropes through that bind her wrists; it's the same around her waist and feet and, worst of all, there is a thinner rope tightened around her neck so she can't sit up. Her hair has been plaited and each plait falls over an arm.

The candle flickers as a slight breeze wafts through the room. There's a draft coming from somewhere. Maybe he has opened a window to get rid of the smell.

There has to be a way out.

An old-fashioned portable television with a deep back sits in the corner on a tiny stand. The windows are boarded up with planks of wood and there is another smell; it's musty, like the place has never been cleaned. An old looking hi-fi system in a dark wood cabinet sits next to the television.

He barges through the door and starts that song playing once again as he forces a corner of toast into her mouth. 'Eat.'

Saliva fills her mouth. Everything is surreal but for some reason, she's hungry. It's as if she's been starved for hours. She nibbles on the toast as he waits patiently for her to finish the first quarter. Questions run through her mind. Does he ever go out? Why her? She glances at him again as she chews. She definitely recognises him. She's seen his photo in the case files but she can't match a name to the face. Remembering might be the key to getting out of this situation intact.

A surge of panic travels from her stomach to her fingers. She can't eat any more. If she does, she knows she'll be sick. Hunger and nausea – the feelings are similar. 'I've… I've had enough. I can't… manage any more.'

The plate bounces on the wooden floor and he looks disappointed.

'Please untie me. People will miss me. I'm a police officer and they'll wonder where I am.'

He smirks. 'Oh, Hailey, you haven't even made the news yet. No one is missing you.'

Her body is stiff and there's a sore forming at the base of her spine. He must be mistaken about her identity but she tries to hold back from saying anything until she can process the situation. She looks down. She's not wearing her black trousers and her duffle coat, she's wearing a Minnie Mouse nightshirt and a pair of bed socks and as she shifts, she hears the rustling of plastic beneath her and a tear rolls down her cheeks. Has he cleaned her up and changed her while she was asleep?

She goes to yell but he clamps a hand across her mouth. 'What did I say? If you make a noise you will be punished.'

She whimpers as she remembers the case they were investigating. Amber Slater's lips had been glued together. Tears slide down her face as she thinks of her lovely mother and father and her two brothers. They will be looking for her. The police will be looking for her.

'I want to go home, please untie me. My parents will be worried and my mum is sick. She needs me.' She speaks in an almost whisper. Her poor mother might be thinking that she doesn't care and that is the hardest thing to bear.

'I've already told you, time and again. You are home. Your home is here, with me.' He strokes her head.

She wriggles in her chair, trying to get a feel for any pain or any sign of being hurt but there isn't anything apart from her throbbing head. A thought flashes across her mind. An AppyDater message she was about to delete. She didn't want to date him and he'd sent her one word back: *slag*.

'Are you going to kill me?' Her face flushes, she can feel the heat creeping up her neck.

He pauses and shakes his head. 'Do I look like I'm killing you?' His grip on her thin arm burns. He pinches her tighter causing her eyes to water.

She knows she might be punished but the urge is too great. She screams at the top of her voice. 'Help!' If there is an open window someone will hear. They have to. A fleck of his saliva hits her arm as he seethes, then he releases his pinch on her arm and gags her again.

He grins as he turns the music up and begins to sway in the middle of the room making some odd contemporary dance moves as Roy Orbison's voice fills her head with more of 'Beautiful Dreamer'. Everything is surreal. She clenches her eyes shut and reopens them – he's still there, being weird. When it finishes, he plays it again, and again, reaching out like he can feel the musical notes in the air. He leaves the room and it still plays until she can't bear to hear it any longer but it keeps on coming, then he turns out the lights, leaving her gagged with that same record playing on repeat. She doesn't know if it's night or day, not with the way the windows have been covered in some sort of blackout material.

There has to be neighbours. Someone must be able to hear the music even if they missed her scream. She wriggles again but the ropes are beginning to burn through her tender skin.

Someone will come. They have to or he'll either kill her or this song will drive her insane. Did he just come back in? A shuffling sound from the other end of the room gets her attention. The hairs on the back of her neck prickle. Then the music stops and a shiver runs down her spine. She's not alone in the room, she can feel hot breath on her neck and she can't stop trembling.

CHAPTER THIRTY-SEVEN

Gina could see Jacob pulling up his car behind her at the Fish and Anchor. Mist hovered above the rolling fields beyond and the wind chill was far from pleasant. The fine rain turned into small snowflakes. So far, the snow hadn't settled too badly but extreme weather was something she didn't want them to have to add to their list of battles.

Jacob grabbed his satchel from the back seat, taking out a pack of cup a soups, which he threw on the back seat, replacing them with his notepad. 'I delivered the CCTV from the Angel Arms back to the station. Brr, it's cold... The new licensee seems nice, very helpful, not like the last one.' He shivered.

'Any news from Kapoor's father? I know he was going to check to see if she was okay in her flat.'

'Nothing as yet. No one said anything. Are you worried about her?'

A melting snowflake dangled from a stray wisp of hair that kept blowing around her face. 'It's just this AppyDater thing. I'm finding it unsettling since this case came along.'

Jacob rubbed his hands together, not enjoying getting wet. At least his hair wasn't getting frizzy, not like hers. 'She texted in. I don't think we need to worry about anything. I'm sure she'll be fine.'

'Heck, you're probably right but...' Gina wouldn't settle until she'd heard from Mr Kapoor that their colleague was okay.

'But what?'

'It's out of character. I'm worried about her with all that's going on. You've got to admit, she looks a bit like Madison and she's on AppyDater.'

'You think…' Jacob's brows furrowed.

Gina shrugged. 'I don't know. Give the station a quick call, tell them to keep trying her phone, email and everything. Even Facebook and WhatsApp.'

Jacob nodded and stood on the pavement as he made the call.

In the restaurant, Lennie Dack was there to greet them.

'DI Harte, we have people booked in for midday and I really need Jake Goodman working his socks off by then. I thought you'd be here a little earlier.' The man smiled and accompanied her to the bar. 'I'll just get Jake so that you can speak to him but I don't think he knows anything. He doesn't have any contact with the diners at all. He's always in the kitchen and from our CCTV you can see that the woman you were asking about didn't even come in last Friday.'

Gina leaned on the shiny bar. 'It's just routine and we'll try not to disrupt your service. Is there anywhere private we can take Mr Goodman to talk?'

'You can use my private living quarters but, please, I really need him to be in the kitchen as soon as possible.'

It was their fault. She'd added in a visit to the hospital and other things had come up that needed addressing. She was later than she told Lennie Dack she would be. 'We hopefully shouldn't be long.' She smiled warmly, hopefully putting the man at ease.

'Thank you.' Lennie headed through the flapping kitchen door and Jake came out a moment later. He rubbed some dark red sauce from his hands onto his white apron. Lennie led the way through the door marked 'Private' into a cosy living room. 'I'll leave you to it. If you need me, I'll be by the bar.' He left them alone.

Gina sat on the leather couch and motioned at the chair for Jake to sit. The sofa dipped as Jacob sat beside Gina.

'Hopefully we won't keep you too long but something has come to light that we need to speak to you about.'

'I don't know anything. I don't even know the girl you were asking about.'

Gina took a photo of Amber from her bag and placed it on the coffee table and Jake looked away. 'When I showed you her photo the other day, it looked like you recognised her.'

'Well I don't.' His spiky brown hair shone in the light and he began to pick a spot in the crease of his nose.

'Are you sure. Take another look at the photo.'

His stare met hers.

'Go on.' She pushed it further across the table.

He glanced down and rubbed his now sore nose as he began shaking his head. 'I don't know her but I did recognise her when she came in the last time, maybe before Christmas. She flagged up as being a local on AppyDater and I saw her profile. I even left her a smiley but she never responded. When I caught sight of her, I made sure I never came out of the kitchen because… I suppose I was embarrassed.' His Adam's apple bobbed as he swallowed. 'I mean look at me and look at her. I thought I might be in with a chance but, no, she didn't want to date me. That's the only reason I recognised her. I'm not some oddball that likes hurting people.'

Gina knew she had to bring up his previous conviction. 'Mr Goodman, we know you have previous.'

'Frigging hell! That was years ago and it was stupid. I was a stupid kid. It was just a few items of clothing and I was deeply sorry and… I didn't do anything. Do you know, the kids at school found out and picked on me for the rest of senior school? I don't want this to all come out again. I came here for a fresh start and I didn't hurt Amber Slater.' The young man hunched over and began hugging his knees. 'Please don't tell Lennie. If anyone here knew about my stupid past, they'd think I was a freak.'

'Where were you on Friday the twenty-second of January between six and eight in the evening?'

'I didn't do anything?'

'Please, Mr Goodman. If you just tell us where you were, we can clear this up. Mr Dack sent us the schedules through and it showed that you started work at eight as you had an appointment. What appointment did you have?'

He shook his head and wailed. 'I didn't have an appointment. I was depressed and I couldn't get my ass out of bed and showered. I lied. I was at home and my brother kept calling me. I did answer his call. It was the anniversary of our mum's death. It's only been a year and I loved my mum. She was the only person who knew me properly and she had to die. We only have our dad left and he's a right bastard. You can check with my brother… please don't tell Lennie. I can't afford to lose this job and he's been really good to me.'

'Where were you yesterday evening?'

He shrugged. 'Getting rat-arsed at home. I worked the day shift and was off last night.'

'Were you alone?'

He wiped his nose with his arm. 'Of course I was alone.'

Gina glanced at Jacob who was scrunching his brow. Jake Goodman may have had opportunity, however brief, for Amber's abduction but Gina wasn't sure. She could tell by Jacob's expression that he felt the same and they would definitely be checking his call times with his brother. Jake's past crime was definitely a red flag. 'We will need you to come to the station to make a voluntary statement. We will also need your brother's details and to see your call log to verify your movements on Friday night.'

'My past isn't what you think. I wasn't obsessed with the women. Neither was I gawping at them through their windows or stalking them. You've got me wrong, so wrong.' His face looked paler than before, making his newly picked spot stand out.

'How have we got it wrong, Jake?' Gina leaned forward and tilted her head. Whatever he was holding back, she needed to know.

'I'm not a perv and I'm not some dangerous saddo who got off on stealing underwear for sexual kicks.'

'It's okay, Jake. Just tell me what you need to tell me.'

The door flung open and Lennie pointed to his watch.

Jake sat rigid to attention.

'We're going to need a few more minutes.'

Lennie stood with his mouth open. 'Oh hell. I suppose I'd better don an apron.' He shrugged and left.

Jake hurried to the door and checked to see if Lennie had gone before sitting back down. 'I don't know how to…'

Gina wondered if she should say something. The torn look on Jake's face told her it was best to stay silent. Jacob remained looking down at his pad, not focusing on Jake.

'I took the clothes for myself… to wear… and I've never told anyone that except my mum and she understood and helped me through my emotions and feelings. I was a teen and I couldn't go into a shop to buy any, I just couldn't, but I wanted them so badly. I don't expect you to understand.'

'Thank you for being honest with us, Jake. We're not here to judge you in any way.'

A tear streamed down his face. 'I didn't know who I was or how I felt. I still don't. It's confusing… I…'

He took in a huge breath and sobbed.

'I couldn't bear to tell my father or my brother but my mother was the best and she stood by me. The only person in the world I trusted with my secret and she died.'

Jake wasn't their killer. The best actor on earth couldn't fake the emotions she saw before her. 'I'm so sorry about your mother, Jake, and thank you again for sharing the truth with us.'

He shrugged. 'It's all going to come out now, isn't it?'

'We won't be telling anyone, Jake. We will still need to check your calls with your brother, but that's all. If you come to the station after work, we can go through that with you.'

'You might wonder why I liked Amber enough to leave her a smiley.'

Gina leaned back. Amber was pretty and sounded outgoing, she had no problem understanding how she attracted people.

Jake stood and looked out of the window. 'I thought she'd accept me. In her profile she said she didn't mind who she dated, men or women, that she sees people as people because she liked them. I thought she'd be accepting of me. That's how I choose the people I leave smileys for. I look for people who can love a person for who they are. I can't and don't want to change who I am. I want someone to like me for me. Can you understand that?'

Gina nodded. At the end of the day, all everyone in life wanted was to be loved and accepted and everyone has a past. Everyone has done things and we think we know the reasons why but sometimes those reasons are the complete opposite. 'I can understand that, Jake.'

He wiped his face with the sleeve of his arm. 'I finish the lunch shift at four thirty after clean up. Can I head over to the station as soon as I finish?'

'Of course. If we can just take your brother's details in the meantime, that would be helpful. It won't be too painful, I promise.'

Jake pulled out his phone and handed it to Gina on the call log page. 'That's the call I made to my brother. As you can see, I was on the phone for nearly forty-five minutes while we were talking about Mum. He misses her too.'

Gina glanced at the time on the call log and held the phone up for Jacob to see. He was talking from six fifteen to nearly seven on the Friday evening. Jacob noted the number and name down. 'May I see your AppyDater profile?'

'Why not? You know everything else about me.'

She clicked on the AD icon and went straight into Jake's account and his records. At no time had he used any of the names in Amber Slater's phone. He had only messaged two other people, both men, and none of his messages or smileys were met with any interest. The photo was clearly of him. 'Thank you for your cooperation.'

'Didn't have a choice really. I can't have anyone thinking I'm a murderer but you know something, I still feel like I'm bad somehow. I think I need to spend some time finding myself properly.'

Gina felt herself getting slightly choked by the young man in front of her, and didn't quite know what to say. 'You've really helped us and we thank you.' She smiled. 'I don't want to keep you any longer or Mr Dack won't be too happy.'

The man took a deep breath and fanned the wetness around his eyes. 'Lots to do.' He opened the door and led the way out.

'I need four duck and three pigeon, now,' Lennie shouted as he threw his apron at Jake. 'Sorry both. Duty calls and some of these lovely people are on a lunch break.'

'Apologies for the disruption and thank you.' Lennie ignored Jacob and began showing another group of people to their seats.

As they headed outside, Gina walked into the flurry of chunky snowflakes and noticed that they'd settled on their windscreens. 'Well, that didn't go as planned. If you can check out his alibi, I'd be grateful.'

'I'll meet you back at the station.' Jacob ran across the car park and hurried into his car.

Gina watched as he reversed out leaving a trail in the thin layer of snow. Her phone rang.

'Wyre, good to have you back.'

'It was touch and go, guv. I ache like mad. O'Connor asked me to call as he's now looking at the footage from the Angel

Arms. He said he's watched all the Tesco footage several times. Mr Collins definitely wasn't with his wife at Tesco.'

'Any news on Kapoor?'

'It's not good, guv. Her father just called. She's not in her apartment. He said he's really worried. He's tried calling her many times and it's off. Something's wrong.'

'I want Collins and his wife brought in. She lied to us and I want to know why. I'm heading back now. In the meantime, keep trying to contact Kapoor. She is our priority right now.' She felt her fingers trembling and it wasn't from the cold.

CHAPTER THIRTY-EIGHT

Theo had called all the relatives to break the news of his daughter, Amber's, murder. Before long, the phone calls had got to be too much. He unplugged the home phone from the wall and turned off his mobile. He'd already called the police about the release of Amber's body and they weren't releasing it for the foreseeable. He couldn't even organise the funeral properly. All these people sending cards and condolences were filling his head and he needed to shut them all out. The noise was too much.

He cranked the music up, wanting all his thoughts to disperse. He allowed himself to be carried away with the melody but thoughts of Amber crept back in. He'd betrayed her in every way possible and no one could ever know.

He ran to the garage, gathering up his secrets. The snow was falling faster now and landing like a pure white blanket, just waiting to be spoiled. Leaving a trail of footprints, he grabbed the old rusty shovel and grimaced as he tried to dig out a patch of earth. It was no good. The ground was too hard. He threw everything into the metal bin and ran back to the garage, grabbing the lighter fuel and a box of matches.

The stench of fuel rose. He stepped back and stared at the contents of the bin. Wondering if he was doing the right thing, he lit the match regardless and placed the lid on the bin. Smoke bellowed out of the hole in the top. Lifting it slightly, he could see everything shrivelling away as the flames licked the contents of the bin. The metal wouldn't burn, he knew that. He'd try to dig what was left into the earth after. Maybe the ground would soften overnight. For now, he would leave it burning away.

He rubbed his chin and shivered as the snow landed on his long-sleeved jumper and began to seep through as it melted against his warmer body. There was still something else he needed to erase but it was all he had.

Slamming the kitchen door, he flicked the kettle switch. He grabbed his laptop from the chair and turned it on. It was time to bury the last of the secrets.

The music came to an end and silence filled his house. Always silent. The house that rarely saw any visitors was seriously lacking life. The only people that had frequented his home were two women found on AppyDater but all that had now gone. No one could know he had the app.

He almost stumbled as he went up the stairs and lay on his bed. The pillow still smelled of the last woman's perfume. The video footage ran through his mind as he closed his eyes. He opened up his burner phone and deleted everything relating to BearBoy. Amber telling him where to go had been the last straw. He only wanted to make sure she was making good decisions and keeping safe. His aim as a father was to protect her but he'd failed in every way possible.

Standing, he walked to the mirror. He hadn't shaved for a couple of days, hadn't slept and felt sick every time he thought about food. He needed to escape his own head. He pressed play on a video on his phone, one showing the bedroom he was standing in. AppyDater date number one lay on his bed, half-drunk as she peeled her clothes off and beckoned him over. He watched it again and again but his body wasn't responding. He had no feelings at all. They were now tainted. He hadn't meant to start dating but while using the app to keep an eye on Amber, he'd met people and had got carried away. Now, all he could think of was Amber, his only child. He should have kept his focus and not got sidetracked. He missed the little girl who used to love colouring and singing along to Disney films as a child while dressed as a princess. He'd lost her and all he wanted was to keep her safely here with him, forever.

Falling to the floor, his grief and guilt poured out. He had to go where no father should go. It was the only way. Nausea began to rise in his throat as he faced the thought of what came next.

CHAPTER THIRTY-NINE

Keeping her coat on, Gina burst through the incident room door. She could see that O'Connor was still examining CCTV footage. 'Anything else?'

He shook his head. 'Heard nothing from Kapoor.'

'Damn.' She glanced at her watch. 'It's hard not to jump to conclusions but we need to keep trying to contact her.'

O'Connor swallowed and nodded. 'We will.'

'Right, what have we got?'

He paused and glanced back at the CCTV. 'There's nothing from the Angel Arms. They have no CCTV on the beer garden, which is where Madison Randle said she thought she heard someone. But look at this, guv.'

She bent over to get a better look, moving slightly to avoid the reflecting strip light. 'I recognise him.'

'This is a couple of hours before Madison arrived at the pub and an hour before her friends Tyrone and Alice arrive. This man arrives but we don't see him leave. I called the pub and the new landlady said that sometimes people leave out the back but it is rare. Looking at all the statements, it was pretty much common knowledge that Madison used this pub all the time and we know Amber worked there. I know this doesn't really tell us much but it is odd given what happened there a couple of hours later.'

'Vincent Jordan. He manages the block of flats that Amber lives in. He lives at the back. We went to see him this morning and, believe me, he's an odd character. He couldn't get us out of his bungalow quick enough… If he left around the back and cut through the bushes, he'd be on the lane. And Madison thought someone was following her when she'd left her great-grandmother's place.' Gina paused. 'I feel like we're getting everywhere and nowhere with this case.'

'I wish the footage showed us more but that's it I'm afraid.'

'You've done a good job going through all this. It must have been long and tedious.'

O'Connor nodded and smiled. 'I've had enough of screens for a bit so if it's okay, I'm going to help locate Kapoor next.'

'Please do. I just need to know she's safe then we can relax.'

Jacob entered with a steaming cup and blew on it. The smell of tomato filled the room as he stirred the soup. 'I've just called Jake Goodman's brother and he verified that Jake was in a bit of a state on Friday night. He confirmed that it was the first anniversary of their mother's death and he spent forty-five minutes talking him around so that he'd go to work.'

'That backs up his phone records?'

'I know what you're thinking, guv. We need to confirm that both of them aren't in this together.' Jacob took a sip of his soup.

'I don't believe he did it but we have to make sure we follow up properly.'

'Jake Goodman's brother said the neighbour knocked while they were on the phone with a parcel for Jake. It had been delivered earlier in the day when he was out. I asked uniform to check this out and they found the neighbour who has confirmed that Jake was in at the time Amber was taken. Given when he arrived at work, he could not have been involved.'

'Great work in eliminating him. Any news on Mr or Mrs Collins?'

Jacob shook his head. 'Both of them are apparently off work today, unauthorised absences, and neither are at home, which is odd.'

'Try to track them down. She's a teacher and he's a lecturer and it's a school day. That's not sitting well with me and neither are their lies. Keep digging and put out an ANPR on their vehicles. I want them brought in.'

He sat at the main table and made a note. 'I'll get straight on to it.'

Wyre entered with Briggs, mid-conversation about the press release. She reached up and rubbed the large bruise on her head.

'Sorry about this morning, guv.' Wyre sat at the table and Briggs headed to the board where he glanced back and forth at the updates.

'That's okay. You got me worried and that text didn't seem like one you'd send.'

'I think I knocked myself a bit sick. One minute I was about to step out of the shower, the next I'd hit my head on the toilet bowl and I knew I was going to be late.' The red lump on the top of Wyre's head was evident.

'Have you been checked out?'

'I was going to but after half an hour and a cup of tea I felt okay so I thought I'd see how things go. I'm just a bit sore, that's all.'

Gina raised her brows.

'Okay, if I feel anything that I shouldn't, I'll go straight to the hospital.' Wyre shivered and did her jacket up. 'I can't believe the heating's still out. These fan heaters are rubbish. I thought it was getting fixed today.'

'No, the company have cancelled because of the weather. I'm seriously worried about Kapoor.' Gina glanced around the room. 'She wouldn't just go off radar like this. Does anyone know her outside work, maybe a little more on a personal level?'

Everyone shook their head.

Briggs turned. 'All I know is that she's never had a sick day.'

'I'm calling it now. Kapoor not being at her home or contactable is a worry. Her father called again to say none of the family have heard from her.'

Briggs pointed at the board. 'Look.'

'I know. Amber Slater, Madison Randle and Jhanvi Kapoor – similar in features, same build. Amber and Madison are both twenty, Kapoor is in her mid-twenties. All three were on Appy-Dater and live locally. We've been grasping at the student link.' Gina felt the weight of what they were seeing bearing down on her chest. She gasped a little before staring at the board. 'This can't be happening. Maybe she's just…'

The room was silent.

'No.' Gina stood and paced, accidentally kicking the waste-paper bin over. 'We need to put out a press release. Get her face out there for everyone to see. We need to see her flat, now. Where's her car?'

'Her father said it's still in her parking space, behind her apartment block. Just before coming here, I asked uniform if they'd head over and cordon it off. I haven't had any word back yet.' Briggs sat down.

Gina glanced at the board. Their persons of interest list was still high. The Collinses, Vincent Jordan and there was another. 'Otis Norton, the witness at the park. He'd have seen Kapoor there on the day we found Amber Slater's body. While we're in process with everyone else, I want him brought in. Can you do that, Jacob?'

He nodded.

'O'Connor, Jacob, I have the login for Madison Randle's AppyDater account. She's given us permission to take a look at it. I'll leave that with you both. It may throw up some leads. Cross-check any names with Amber Slater's burner phone contacts, see if there are any patterns in the way the messages are worded – anything!'

'Yes, guv.'

'Wyre, are you up to heading over to Kapoor's apartment with me?'

'Definitely, guv.' She rubbed her head.

'Right, don't let me stop any of you.' As everyone prepared for their next tasks, Gina headed over to Briggs. She pulled her gloves from her bag. 'Are you going to prepare the press statement? Do you need me to do anything?'

He rubbed the back of his neck. 'I've got it in hand. I'll get on to that right now. I can't believe this might be happening to one of our own. We have to find her.' His stare met hers.

'I know we do. I'll keep you posted.' She hurried out, knowing that time was of the essence. Amber Slater's timeline was all she had to go on. Amber went missing around six thirty on the Friday night and was found dead on the Monday morning. Several hours had already passed. The clock was ticking.

The incident room phone rang and O'Connor grabbed the receiver. 'Keith. What have you got for us?' O'Connor stopped biting the end of his pen and gazed at everyone in the room as he listened to Keith in forensics. 'It's Amber Slater's apartment. With her father's permission the team went back and did a more thorough search. They found some very discreet wiring running from a dummy burglar sensor in Amber's hallway that is next to the airing cupboard. Whatever was in the sensor has been snipped out with a pair of scissors. Following that lead, it led to a false cupboard that originally looked like the back of the wall and inside that was nothing but a lead and a plughole. If the dust is anything to go by, it looks like someone has recently removed some equipment from the base of this hidden cupboard. There were also several old unused sensors and all were untampered with except one.'

'Are you saying that she could have been under surveillance and whatever was there has been removed recently? Maybe it was run through the Wi-Fi, enabling whoever was watching her to see her every move.'

'Yes.'

Gina felt her face flushing and her heart rate pounding. 'Someone had been watching Amber and it looks like they had easy access to her apartment as this equipment has now been removed.' Her mind flitted between the landlord or maybe one of her neighbours. 'We need to find out who had a key to her apartment? Vincent Jordan isn't sitting well with me. He'd definitely have a spare key being her landlord. His father owns the block. He manages the block and he maintains it. Contact all her neighbours and her father too. I know he has a key and maybe her friend Lauren Sandiford did too. O'Connor, Jacob, contact Madison. We need to check to see if she was under any kind of surveillance.' She checked her watch. 'Right, I have to get to Kapoor's apartment.' She swallowed and took a deep breath.

CHAPTER FORTY

Gina hurried up the stairs to the third floor of Kapoor's apartment block with Wyre hot on her tail. Only one of them was breathing heavily as they reached the top. 'I'm getting so unfit,' Gina panted. Knocking on Kapoor's door, they waited a few seconds and Mr Kapoor opened up.

'Thank you for getting here so quickly. We are so worried about our daughter.' His creased polo shirt hung over his large belly. He rubbed his eyes, leaving one of his brows sticking out a little.

'We're so sorry and we'll do everything we can to find her.'

'She's my only daughter, the baby of the family… we're beside ourselves. Her brothers are out looking and my wife is having a nervous breakdown. If anything happens to her, I don't know what we'll do.' He gasped and walked through to the kitchen, then stood at the worktop staring out at the car park.

Gina and Wyre followed. 'I know this is going to be hard but I need to ask you a few questions. We have everyone at the station on alert and looking for her. Are you okay to talk?'

He went to speak and placed his shaking hand on the worktop. 'Yes. I just want her to come home.'

'Can you tell me when you last had any form of contact with Jhanvi?'

'My wife was on the phone to her last night. She's a wonderful girl, always calls us. We always say that we are blessed to have her. Jhanvi knew my wife was getting her results this morning and she was desperate to know the outcome. She wouldn't not call, you know. Something's happened to her, I know it has. This is so out of character. Look.' He pointed out of the window where the uniformed officers had set up a cordon. 'Her car is still there. She didn't even go to work.'

Gina led the trembling man over to the tiny kitchen table against the wall and he sat. 'Can you tell me what Jhanvi and your wife spoke about?'

'I heard them chatting about her brothers and her niece who's just started nursery. They spoke about my wife's cancer and how nervous she was of getting the results. And they always ended the conversation with the words "love you."' He placed his head in his hands and slumped over the table.

Shivering, Gina sat opposite him. The heating must have gone off when Kapoor left. From looking at the rotas Gina knew she had been due in at six thirty that morning. 'We know PC Kapoor as a lovely person and a brilliant police officer but we don't know much about her personal life. Can you tell me a bit about her? Was she seeing anyone?'

His face scrunched a little as he thought. 'She didn't have a boyfriend. She was seeing someone three years ago called Ben, but I think she slowly became married to her job so that didn't last long. She never mentioned anyone else to us. She spent most of her free time with her older brother and niece. She loved little Alisha and often took her out to give her parents a break.' He began to bite his thumbnail.

'Is there anywhere you think she could be or might go?' Gina had to ask the question. Deep down, she hoped that Kapoor could just be working through something no one knew about but the sick feeling in her stomach told her that was wishful thinking.

He shook his head. 'No. She was always at home, shopping or hanging out at one of our houses when she wasn't working. If she did go anywhere else, she never told us.'

'May we take a look around her apartment?'

'Of course. I'll just go outside to give my wife a call. She's beside herself and she keeps messaging me.' Standing, he walked to the door. 'I'll be back in a minute.' The front door slammed closed.

Gina made a quick call to PC Smith. 'How are the door-to-doors going? Has anyone seen PC Kapoor this morning?'

'No luck, guv. Not one person saw her. The resident underneath her heard her door bang around six in the morning but that's it. Not many people are at home but we've left cards and we'll knock again at the end of the working day.'

After ending the call, she placed her phone in her pocket and followed Wyre through to the other rooms. She checked the corners, not noticing any alarm sensors. Glancing up, she saw a smoke alarm and stared at it, wondering if a hidden camera could be inside the device. There was a knock at the door and Keith entered. 'Good to see you. Could you carefully check the fire alarms or anything else that could hold a small surveillance device? We need to know if PC Kapoor was being watched and I want that checked before Mr Kapoor comes back up. The last thing I want to do is worry the man even more that he already is.'

Keith walked lopsided, the weight of his toolbox causing him to lean. 'Yes, I'll get started.' He pulled a forensics suit over his shirt and trousers and popped some latex gloves on.

Gina and Wyre gloved up too as they entered the bedroom. The smell of washing powder lingered in the air. Kapoor's quilt lay in a crumpled heap on one side of the double bed and a pile of books sat on the floor, empty crisp packets being used as bookmarks.

'I had no idea she was living like this, guv. It looks like she eats crisps in bed and there's empty pop bottles lined up against the wall and her clothes are just piled up on a chair. Her curtains don't quite cover her window and her carpet is coming up round the edges of the room. This flat is cold and it's not one bit homely.' Wyre walked over to the window and looked out to the large wall of the block of flats opposite.

Gina didn't want to say that she often had empty sandwich wrappers on her bedroom floor and she lived in chaos too. She imagined Wyre to be pristine at home, just like she normally was in appearance. 'She has a busy life.'

'Don't we all but this room still makes me sad.' Wyre glanced around. 'Anything seeming out of place?'

Gina shook her head. 'I'm going to head to the bathroom.' She left Wyre in the hallway and took a turn into the small wet room. She placed the back of her hand on the hanging towel. It was damp. She pictured Kapoor getting up early, taking a shower. In her mind, someone was watching through her bedroom window, catching small glimpses of her getting ready through the gaps in the curtains. How long had they waited for her? Maybe they waited in the knowledge that today might not be the day they take Kapoor but the opportunity arose and they took it. Maybe they had studied her routine and knew her shift pattern well enough to be sure that she would be coming out of her apartment at a specific time in the morning.

They had no idea who they were dealing with. An image of Vincent Jordan virtually throwing them out of his bungalow filled her mind.

What did they have? Kapoor was missing and not answering her phone. Kapoor's car was still in her allocated parking space. Kapoor had got up for work, took a shower and left around six to start her shift at the station, but she never arrived.

Keith made her jump as he poked his head around the door. 'There's no sign of any surveillance wiring or equipment in the fire alarms or any of the cupboards. I'm going to take a more thorough look around so it might be best if you head out soon so that I can work my way through the apartment. Mr Kapoor has given me the go-ahead to check whatever I need to. Oh, I didn't tell you what I did find after I called you earlier. This, you're going to like.' He flinched and held his back as he straightened up.

'What?' Gina felt more awake in that moment than she had all morning.

'We found a nice full fingerprint on one of the pipes in Amber's airing cupboard behind the hidden cupboard where we think some of the surveillance equipment might have been set up. The same print also appeared on the sensor in the hallway where we found remnants of a surveillance device. The print is being run through the system as we speak. There were a few partials too, all fresh and not Amber's.'

A smile formed across her face. 'There has to be a match. We could have a name soon and, in turn, a lead on Kapoor.' A lump in her throat formed.

'I like Kapoor. She's a good constable.'

The skin around Keith's eyes crinkled. She'd never heard him pass a comment on anyone. 'She is, and we're going to find her. Now get me a match on that print. Call me as soon as you know anything.'

'Will do.' He turned away and headed to the kitchen.

Gina met Wyre by the door. 'Anything of interest?'

'I found a pad in her kitchen drawer and she's written something on it. I'm not sure if it's anything to do with the case but she's written down a time and date, three a.m. this morning, and then there's the briefest of descriptions. Tall, male, too dark to see. Then she drew a line through it. I wonder if she saw something in the night and, being a police officer, instinctively noted it down. On the other pages she has random notes and dates but nothing for the past three weeks.'

'What type of notes?'

'Things like youths hanging around by bin cupboard. Drunken woman falling asleep in communal area. Graffiti appearing on the fence at the back. Kids having a fight but no one hurt. The smell of weed. It's like her own personal little log.'

Gina headed through to the kitchen to see for herself. 'Let's bag it up.'

Wyre took an evidence bag from her pocket and sealed the notebook in it.

'She saw something in the night and then thought nothing more of it. If only she'd called it in for us to investigate.' Gina placed her hand over her mouth and grimaced.

Wyre didn't reply. They both knew that if their killer had Kapoor, there was a chance they'd never see her again.

Gina's phone rang. 'Jacob,' she answered. 'Right. We're on our way back now.' She ended the call and headed to the door. 'We've had a breakthrough.'

CHAPTER FORTY-ONE

The record comes to an end and Jhanvi hopes it's the last time she has to hear it. She sees the flashing lights again. *Keep your calm – he's trying to confuse you.* He hadn't left earlier. She'd felt his breath on her neck as she remained in pitch-black darkness. It was like being with a ghost. Maybe he'd gone for a while, maybe not, but he was definitely back now.

She then hears him breathing from all parts of the room and pictures him watching through some night vision goggles.

Trying to loosen the binds around her wrists, she knows there is no point. The sores are just getting deeper and deeper and she's not getting any closer to escaping.

He wants something but what is it? Think like a police officer not a captive. Better still, think like him. What does he want? The constant music is messing with her senses. He's trying to break her, but why? What happens if it doesn't or if she tries to yell and escape? She shivers as she thinks of Amber and what the post-mortem report had said. Amber's lips had been superglued.

Panic builds up and the urge to throw all her strength into trying to break free overwhelms her. Her whole body aches for the chance. She wants a free hand so that she could punch him in the throat if he comes close enough. She might be small and slight but people underestimate her strength.

'I'm not the enemy, you know.' His voice is gentle.

Her chest feels as though her heart might explode from it at any moment. Her eyes searched for any glint of light in the darkness but there was none. Not a spec. She didn't try to answer, leaving him to do the talking. Everything she could think of saying might antagonise him. He'd expect the following: *Please let me go. Why me? My family will miss me. Someone will know I'm missing. They're on to you. Please don't hurt me.* Amber Slater must have said all those things but he didn't let her go. He stabbed her through the heart and dumped her body in the lake.

His hand brushes the back of her neck as he loosens the thin piece of material tied to the side of her mouth.

'Who are you?'

'PC Jhanvi Kapoor.'

'You are not Jhanvi. She is dead. Do you hear me?' A fleck of his spit hits her cheek.

A burst of perfume comes from nowhere, one that smelled of lilies.

She has an inkling of what he desires and she would give it to him. The superglue. Amber. The stab to the heart. She swallows, knowing that if her idea doesn't work out, she'd be his next murder victim.

'I won't leave you and I'll be quiet,' she says.

She wonders who he thinks she is, if not Jhanvi Kapoor. Maybe him calling her Hailey earlier wasn't a slip of the tongue.

'Just go away, will you,' he spontaneously shouts, then pauses.

Who is he speaking to? There is no one else in the room and his voice travels away from her. Maybe her only way out of this is to become Hailey.

CHAPTER FORTY-TWO

Jacob held a piece of paper in the air and flicked it. 'We have a match on the fingerprint.'

Gina almost fell into a chair at the incident room main table, her mouth dry with anticipation.

'Who?'

'Theo Slater.'

'Her father?'

Jacob flicked the printout in his hand and dropped it on the table. 'Yes. He's on our system. Drink driving conviction three years ago.'

'I want him in, now, and I want a search warrant for his house on the basis that we've found his prints on surveillance equipment in the home of our murder victim. Wyre, can you get onto that?'

Wyre nodded and headed off to one of the computers. 'Why would he put surveillance in his own daughter's hallway? What the hell is going on?'

Gina only wished she knew the answer to that question as she paced past the board. 'Whatever we do, we mustn't drop the balls that we're juggling. I still want anything we can find on Vincent Jordan and I still want Mr and Mrs Collins. Any news on them?'

Jacob flicked through a couple of screens. 'Nothing yet. It's like they've vanished.'

'Do we have an address for their parents? We need to look further. Their car hasn't been flagged by an ANPR. Are there any connections between any of these people? We can connect Tyrone

Heard to Amber and Madison. He lived in Amber's block and wanted to move into Madison's. I'm all over the place with this investigation. I also want Tyrone here, today, but first we need Theo Slater. We need to press him hard on this issue. Not only did he let himself into Amber's apartment before we got there, it seems he may have removed evidence. He's in big trouble and it's enough to search his home and bring him in. Go gently to start. Anything he can give us voluntarily will be easier than him going "no comment" non-stop once a solicitor gets involved. I want any phones, computers, digital storage devices looked at as a matter of urgency. Any resistance, we're going to have to arrest him on suspicion so that we can investigate him further.'

CHAPTER FORTY-THREE

Wyre stood next to Gina with the search warrant in her hand and a team of officers ready to go in. A police officer's life was at stake and if Theo Slater had anything to do with all this, he was going to tell before the day was out.

Gina rapped her knuckles on the door as hard as she could. The snow beneath her feet was now about an inch thick. She shook her boots as she heard Theo unlocking the door from the other side. As he opened up, a stark look spread across his face and he stared. 'Theo Slater, we've met before. I'm DI Harte, this is DC Wyre, we have a warrant to search your premises.' She took the piece of paper from Wyre and passed it to Theo. As he read through it, his shoulders slumped. 'We've found your fingerprints on what looks to be surveillance equipment in your daughter, Amber Slater's, apartment.'

He stepped back opening his mouth but no words coming out. 'Phone.'

He pulled his phone from his pocket with shaky hands and handed it over. The wind blew and a flurry of snowflakes followed them in. Gina bagged his phone and passed it to the officer behind her. 'We need you down the station. You have a lot of explaining to do.'

'I was just doing some jobs at her apartment. You know, decorating, DIY. Of course my prints were there.'

'Your prints were found behind a false cupboard made to look like a wall.'

His face reddened and Gina swore she could see him shaking. 'This is ridiculous. I've just lost my daughter.'

Several officers continued forward, heading into each room to conduct the search methodically.

'We also found remnants of a surveillance device inside an old alarm sensor and your prints were on that too. You'll have plenty of time to explain yourself when we get to the station.'

PC Smith entered.

Gina caught his attention. 'Can you stay with Mr Slater while I assist with the search? And please explain to him what will happen when we get to the station.'

'Of course, guv.' PC Smith took Theo to one side.

Tension was plastered all over Theo's face, from his twitching face muscles to his clenched jaw. His beady eyes were flitting from side to side, trying to take in everyone's movements and failing spectacularly.

Leaving Mr Slater behind, she glanced through the living room door and pulled a pair of latex gloves over her hands. Two officers were already making headway. Another came in from the garden. 'The metal burning bin is still warm.'

Constant rustling and the sound of opening drawers came from above, then an electric screwdriver began to whirr. 'Guv, come here – quick.' Wyre's voice boomed down from the landing.

Running up the creaky stairs, Gina could feel the weight of Theo's stare on her back. 'What is it?'

'They've just found a surveillance device in the fire alarm in Mr Slater's bedroom and we've found the same sort of wiring that was in Amber's cupboard. And look,' Wyre pointed along the ceiling, 'the tiny wire had been painted to blend in and it leads to the back of the fitted wardrobe. There's surveillance equipment inside.'

'Bag it all up. I want to know exactly what he's been recording.' She shook her head as she thought of his daughter. Amber had not known her father was watching her comings and goings. She clenched her hands. They had to find the recordings and her big hope was that they'd be on his laptop or a hard drive of some description. She ran from room to room. 'Mark any recording equipment as a priority.' Running down the stairs, she noticed that Mr Slater was now staring at the door. He turned away slightly so that she couldn't see his face and she wondered what expression he was trying to hide.

All the kitchen drawers were open and two officers were reaching into cupboards. Gina looked down and saw a scrape mark on the lino flooring. Bending down, she began to press it and pull the kickboard, trying to work out how to loosen it. She knocked the one end and the other side flew forward. 'Can I borrow your torch?' The officer passed it to her and she shone it under the cupboard and spotted a rectangular chunk of metal. Reaching through the grime and cobwebs, she grabbed it and slid it out, bagging it immediately.

Kapoor's image kept running through her mind. What if her colleague was on this hard drive? She swallowed and bit her bottom lip, knowing she had to see exactly what Mr Slater had been up to. She hurried along the hallway, almost tripping over the runner. 'What have you done with her?'

Theo Slater slowly turned, shrugged his shoulders and made a zipping motion with his fingers across his lips.

CHAPTER FORTY-FOUR

The tape had been rolling for several minutes and Gina knew that Briggs was watching from behind the interview room screen. Jacob slid the file to her. With PC Kapoor missing, they were all on the case and would stay fully on it until she was found. As Theo Slater tried to pull another one of his eyebrow hairs out, Gina took a photo from the file. The dark-suited male solicitor whispered in Theo Slater's ear. 'This is a photo of the hard drive found under the kickboard of your kitchen.' She placed another photo next to it. 'This is the recording device found in your bedroom.' She slid two more photos across the table. 'The device in which it records to and finally the bits of equipment and lead we found in your daughter's apartment. I've seen the footage.'

'I didn't hurt my daughter.'

'You think recording her in her own home, without her knowing, wasn't hurting her?'

'I wanted to protect and look out for her, that's all. She'd never lived alone before. I mean the camera was in the hallway where people come and go.'

Gina pulled out another photo. One of a woman lying next to Mr Slater in bed. 'Did you want to protect and look out for this woman? Who is she?'

He shrugged his shoulders and sighed. 'I don't know.'

'You don't know. Your computer tells us that you uploaded a clip of you and this woman having sex to an online porn site.

Did you have her permission? Did she even know you were recording her?'

'No comment.'

Gina leaned back, the creaking plastic chair filling the pause. The heater clicked on and began to whirr.

Theo brushed a few specs of dandruff from around his ear and leaned forward.

Glancing back at her notes, Gina knew exactly what he had been doing. All the sound from their encounter had been recorded. The AppyDater app that he'd deleted was easily restorable and that woman was one of his hook-ups. 'You met her on AppyDater. I've seen the messages…'

A bead of sweat formed at his hairline even though it was bitter cold.

'The day after, you talk in your message about having a lovely date and how you came back to yours for sex; consensual sex by the sounds of it. After watching the recording in full, I see you, glancing up at the camera grinning, but she doesn't do that once. She is totally unaware that she is being filmed. Then, the evidence on your laptop shows that you've edited the footage to blur out your own face and uploaded it to The Horn House, an online user community porn site that anyone can upload to. There is something else that bothers me…'

The man began to waft his jumper. The heat that his own nervous body created was getting to him.

'The name BearBoy.'

'I'm not saying anything. I want to leave. Can I leave?' His glare met that of his solicitor. The man whispered to his client once again. Theo sighed and leaned back.

'This is serious, Mr Slater. Take this as a warning. If you do this again, this as evidence will be used as a course of conduct. Going back to BearBoy. We found a phone at your daughter's house, one that she used to message her dates and there was an interesting message from BearBoy. For the tape, I'm reading the message from the file. "I can see U puttin it about. You don't have to do it! You're a nice girl." Can you explain why you sent that message to your own daughter?'

He stood, knocking his chair against the back wall.

'Sit down, Mr Slater.'

The man glanced at his solicitor.

Jacob leaned forward and smiled warmly in Theo Slater's direction. 'We've seen the recordings on the hard drive that were taken from your daughter's apartment. We just want to know why you sent her that message.'

Theo seemed to be less antagonised by Jacob and he sat. 'My solicitor has prepared a statement.'

Gina slouched back. Great, not what she wanted. Just as she thought he might open up. She glanced at her watch. The clock was ticking and the thought of Kapoor being kept hostage and taunted with death was getting to be too much. The sickly feeling in her stomach was being further exasperated by the heat blasting on her feet and the coldness above that was making her nose feel like it had frozen solid. They were getting nowhere fast.

The man pulled out a piece of paper. 'My client wishes to express that he didn't place the surveillance equipment in his daughter's apartment for any reason but to ensure her safety. It was her first stint of living alone and, as her parent, he was worried. He knows he went about things wrongly and for that he's deeply apologetic, but it was all done with the most sincere of intentions. He hoped by connecting with her on AppyDater that he would make her see that she didn't need to be on there. He admits that he was being overprotective and by being like that, he overstepped the mark but he had no intention of hurting her.'

Gina felt her hackles rising. 'If your daughter was here now, how would she feel knowing her own father was spying on her? You can see right through to her lounge from the hall.'

'I'm sorry. I just needed to know she was safe and that none of the people visiting were weirdos. That's all,' he yelled.

'You betrayed her trust. Did you go one step further and begin to stalk her because you couldn't bear her starting a life without you? Maybe she didn't call you often enough and you couldn't bear not to know what she was up to at all times.'

'No.'

'Did you watch her every move, angry that she was enjoying her life without you, going out and having fun after being under the same roof as a father that stifles her?'

'No.'

'Mr Slater. Did you kill your daughter, Amber Slater?'

'No! I would never hurt her. I was stupid. I watched her because I couldn't bear to let her go. I love her and she was all that I had and I feel like there's a big gaping hole in my life. I just wanted to protect her and keep an eye on her. I was stupid, so stupid but my intentions were good.'

'And how about the woman in your bedroom video?'

He shook his head and gasped. 'I recorded a woman while I had sex with her. Why? Because I'm an idiot. I sussed out the surveillance equipment and I don't know, I got carried away. I admit it. I was wrong. I was stupid and you know something, I'll never forgive myself for not keeping a closer eye on Amber. I wish I had stalked her now. I sent those stupid messages as BearBoy because I wanted her to be put off that stupid app and look where it got me. I tried to explain that she was too nice to be on it.'

'You used spyware on Amber's computer too. We found it.' Jacob dropped another photo on the pile so that Theo Slater could see it. 'We found it linked to your computer. You knew everything your daughter was up to. She had no privacy at all except for the burner phone we found in her apartment. Did you get angry when she gave her number to BearBoy? Upset that you couldn't see what she was up to?'

Gina remained still even though she needed to shiver. 'And that must have driven you crazy knowing that she'd broken away from your constant spying on her. Is that why you killed her?'

'I didn't.'

'Where did you take her?'

He stood again and threw the chair at the door. 'I. Did. Not. Kill. My. Daughter.'

It was no good. Gina had to push him harder. Kapoor's life was at stake. 'Where were you on Tuesday evening? Were you anywhere near Cleevesford Hospital?'

'I was at home.' He began to pace and seethe. 'Get me out of here.'

'Can anyone confirm that?'

He slammed his palms on the door. 'Get me out. Now.' His booming voice filled the room. 'Bastards! You're trying to fix me up. I want to leave. I need to get out.'

'Where is Jhanvi Kapoor?'

'What?' He kicked the door over and over again.

'My client has had enough for now. I'd advise him not to say another word and he is clearly distressed.'

Gina scooped up the photos from the table and stared at the solicitor. 'My colleague is missing and believed to have been taken by the same person who took Amber Slater. A young woman has been killed. Another young woman was attacked on Tuesday evening and is in hospital.'

'And my client needs a break or I report you for misconduct. That's enough for now.' The solicitor placed his Montblanc pen in his top pocket and went over to Theo Slater. 'We can talk about this in a bit okay? You need to have a drink, something to eat and a break.' As they left, Mr Slater's yelling and swearing filled the corridor.

'Interview suspended at sixteen fifteen on Wednesday the twenty-seventh of January.' Jacob stopped the recording.

Briggs hurried through. 'Damn it! You went in too quickly. Even with his solicitor's statement, he was talking. We could have got more out of him.'

Gina's brows furrowed. 'He knew exactly what he was going to confess to and what he was going to hold back on. He couldn't dispute the chain of evidence that we had but we don't have any evidence linking him to the murder of his daughter. We don't have any evidence linking him to Madison Randle's attack and we have no evidence that he's ever come into contact with PC Kapoor. We went in with nothing apart from a man who was guilty of a shameful act and we hoped that it was him and that he'd crack. It's not him. He doesn't have Kapoor.'

'I'm sorry. We're all on edge. I shouldn't have gone off like that.' Briggs lowered his head and shook it. She glanced up at him, feeling the tension between them. This wasn't about the interview, it was about him being on AppyDater and her finding out.

Jacob leaned on the back wall as he gathered up the file.

Backing down, she swallowed. Now wasn't the time. 'I know I could have played it better. We're desperate. Every time I think, Kapoor is in my mind. I picture her bound to a chair waiting for a painful death. I see the knife wound through Amber's heart, driving through Kapoor's and I—' She slammed her fist on the table, making the recorder jump. 'We have to find her and it's desperate. Time is running out and we're no further to the truth. In Mr Slater we have a despicable person who has committed a despicable crime, but murder? We are no further forward. That's the frustrating thing.' She knew that to Kapoor every minute would seem like forever and the not knowing what would happen, or anticipating the worst, would take its toll. 'Right, I think we need to call a briefing, find out where we are with everything. Back to the bloody drawing board.'

Jacob led the way out and Briggs placed his large warm hand on her shoulder. She shrugged it off.

O'Connor stomped down the corridor and held a hand up at Gina. 'We've found Mr Collins's car.'

Gina followed O'Connor to the incident room. 'Just the break we needed. Tell me everything you know.'

CHAPTER FORTY-FIVE

I pick up the kitchen knife, then the loaf of bread and I cut a couple of slices. My hands feel jittery. I grab the cheese from the fridge and pop the bread under the grill, then turn it and put the cheese on it. Cheese on toast was always her favourite so this is what I'm making.

I stare at the corner, that same corner that her memory often haunts me from. Things are different now I have someone else.

I have a living, breathing version of you in my living room, a good copy. I am going to turn her into you. I feed her the food you liked, play her the music you enjoyed and dress her in your clothes. She will become you.

The smoke alarm starts to sound. I grab the burnt toast from the grill and begin wafting the tea towel in the air and for a second I'm stunned. I'm back there on that day all those years ago, the smell of grilled cheese in the air. I'd burnt my food on that day, the day my life was ruined. I clench my fists. In the past I've been sad when allowing myself the luxury of thinking about that day but now, I'm livid. You are making me do this, you!

Closing my eyes, I imagine I'm underwater, the same image that plagues me often and I see you attached to me by a rope but you're drifting. I pull and pull, trying to haul you closer but the rope is more like stretchy elastic and you get further away. I try to swim but the water is weird. Still clear but it's thick, like honey and I can't swim, I can't float. I'm drowning, you're drowning. My lungs are choked and I feel the panic. The last thing I see is your vacant stare as the cord snaps and you drift into the darkness.

Jolting back to reality I grab the knife and stab it so far into the chopping board it slices through and pierces the worktop. I snatch the charred grill pan and unlock the back door, walking through the wall of snowflakes along the patio to the bin, that's when I give the shed a little glance. If my little police officer doesn't work out, that's where she'll end up. No more lakes; I can't have her found. Not this time.

I look at my watch and the music comes on automatically as per my programming and all I imagine is my beautiful dreamer and I hate myself for getting angry just then as I thought about her. It's complicated.

The snow blankets the landscape. The houses beyond are capped in pure white and the sky almost matches that colour so I can barely see where horizon meets it. Shivering in my T-shirt, I hurry back into the kitchen and enjoy the melody as I decide that a cheese sandwich might be the best course of action given my failure in toasting the last one.

As soon as I've made it, I hurry into the lounge and a shaft of light from the hallway catches the one side of her face, lighting her profile up beautifully. There's something poetic about it all. The policewoman is Hailey. She looks like her. She acts like her and she will be her. I just need to teach her how.

'The darkness won't last forever, Hailey. I promise. When you're better, we'll have the loveliest life. I promise.'

Her glare searches for the light behind me, scoping out the bungalow. The home she never knew. Soon, it will be hers as well as mine.

'Are you hungry?'

She nods so I remove the gag that I had to put back on her. I hate doing this but it's the only way. I want this one to work.

Her searching lips clasp around the bread as I hold it to her mouth, her dark eyes bore into me as she chews. I close my eyes for a second and I'm back in the water pulling the cord and she's coming back to me. Her dark hair splayed out framing her gentle features, making her look like a willowy angel. My Hailey is coming back.

As she takes another bite, I smile. She needs to build her strength up. 'My Hailey.'

CHAPTER FORTY-SIX

As Gina bit into the chocolate muffin that O'Connor had left on the table she continued to listen. Maybe some of her anxiety could be alleviated with a bit of food. It had been a long time since she'd last eaten. The rest of the team gathered around.

O'Connor pulled a hat over his bald head and shivered. 'The Collinses car is parked up at his parents' house. They've only gone for a break in their caravan.'

'In this weather?' Gina said.

'I know.' O'Connor shrugged. 'That's what Mr Collins's mother said. They also borrowed his parents' Land Rover Discovery, claiming it made towing easier. At least we know which car we're looking for now.'

'Do we know where they've gone?' Gina licked a crumb from her lips.

'They didn't say. They tended to go everywhere in their caravan but quite often went on local breaks for short periods, preferring Warwickshire or Worcestershire. His mother mentioned that they liked a particular site in Evesham. I contacted that site but it was closed for the season.'

Briggs cleared his throat and sat at the table. 'I think we need to put out a press release and I need to make a statement. We need the Collinses out there, state that we are looking for witnesses, not suspects. We need them to stop running.'

'We can't send Kapoor's photo out there, not yet. Whoever is holding her can't be alarmed. They've already killed once and they might kill her if they feel we're closing in,' Gina replied as she finished the muffin and stared at the board. The doughy texture began to clog in her throat. She took a swig of her drink.

'Yes, agreed. We definitely won't mention Kapoor yet but we need to work harder, longer and I'm afraid this is going to mean cancelling all personal plans for now. I know this is hard but we owe it to Jhanvi Kapoor to do everything we can.' Briggs's eyes creased at the corner.

Gina stared at the photo of Amber's body by the lakeside.

'I miss her accent ringing through the station.' PC Smith stood and left the room. They'd worked closely together for years and Gina could see the veil of worry that was smothering him.

'Can one of you see if he's alright?' Gina felt a knot in her throat as she tried to swallow. Their colleague had been missing all day. Mr Kapoor had called several times, almost in tears, and everyone in the room had been stunned into silence.

Wyre nodded and headed out after PC Smith.

Gina turned to address the room. 'Let's work with what we can. Otis Norton, our witness at the lake. He's due in, isn't he?'

O'Connor nodded. 'In about half an hour. He said his wife had a medical appointment and he'd come as soon as it was over.'

An appointment. To satisfy Gina, Otis Norton would have to back that up with some evidence. 'Have we confirmed that?'

'Yes. Mrs Norton was due to see her doctor at five this evening so I suppose he could be here anytime now.'

Briggs's phone rang and he headed to the corner of the room to take the call.

'Vincent Jordan, Amber's landlord. Where are we with him?'

Jacob checked through a batch of notes. 'No prior.'

'But there's something off about him. I don't trust him.'

O'Connor piped up. 'With good reason, guv.'

'What do you have?'

'Just before the briefing, I finally got hold of EL Electrical. Mr Lehman recalled seeing a missed call from Vincent Jordan but is adamant that they haven't actually spoken since the first week in January. There was a message on his phone asking him to pop by and change some bulbs in the apartment block and that it wasn't urgent.'

'That's a far cry from the conversation he said he had. How about the timing?'

'Mr Lehman claims it was at six twenty-five on the evening as stated on his message.'

'A half-truth. Sounds suspicious to me and he couldn't get us out of his bungalow quick enough. Actually, later this evening, I want to head back to Amber's block. I can't get over the fact that Mr Slater had a camera in his daughter's hallway. Maybe one of the men or women who came back to Amber's is the person who killed her. Can we identify anyone in those videos? I know they're grainy but it's worth a shot. I recognised the girl in one. Lauren Sandiford. When we spoke to Lauren, she didn't say anything about being in any type of relationship with Amber but the video tells us otherwise. They were kissing in the hallway.' Gina looked down. 'I hate this, it feels like we're violating Amber using the videos in this way. What happened between her and Lauren should have been private.' The thick snow falling outside caught her attention as it settled on the ledge.

'But looking might lead us to her killer.' Jacob grabbed a muffin. Wyre re-entered and leaned against the door frame.

'It seems that everyone had been in Amber's apartment, sometimes just to hang out and eat food. We saw clips of Curtis Gallagher with her eating a takeaway. Corrine Blake and Amber had been trying on clothes together at one point in the lounge. We don't see Tyrone Heard at all but from what I've heard he doesn't hang around with them much. So, tonight, we'll head back to Amber's block and talk to everyone again. The weather is diabolical so I'm hoping that they'll all be in. After that, I'm going to perch up outside Vincent Jordan's bungalow. We can't take any risks of him being dangerous if he's cornered or of us being wrong, which is why I want to observe him for a short while. Any sign of Kapoor or anything even remotely odd, I'll be calling it in so be on standby. Anyone care to join me?'

Wyre put her hand up. 'I'll sit it out with you, guv. I don't have much to go home for and I'd rather be doing something practical tonight. I want to help find Kapoor.'

'Great. We have a plan then. Wyre and I are on surveillance and interviews. O'Connor could you keep ringing around various campsites looking for the Collinses and let me know if the ANPR flags up the Discovery? The press release will also be going out soon so we're expecting to be busy back here. I need everything followed up thoroughly. Kapoor is out there somewhere. She may be tied up. She may be cold and hungry or hurt. She is our absolute priority. Every crumb of information matters.'

'I'm on it, guv.'

'Jacob, could you liaise with forensics, find out if there are any updates and go through all the interviews and the case so far? Maybe we've missed something. Look at everything again. Photos, timelines, the lot. Right, what are we waiting for?'

PC Smith headed in through the door, his face ashen and arms folded. 'Otis Norton has arrived. I've put him in the last interview room.'

Everyone began to work on their tasks and the hum of the room got louder.

'I can't express how scared I am that something bad has happened to Jhanvi. She wouldn't hurt anyone.' PC Smith took a deep breath. 'Count me in for an all-nighter. I'm not leaving until she's been found safe.' His throat bobbed as he swallowed. 'We have to find her.'

CHAPTER FORTY-SEVEN

'Otis Norton, as we've already explained, the tape is rolling and this interview is being recorded.' Gina waited for the man to acknowledge that statement. Jacob sat up straight in the chair next to her.

'I'm not in any trouble, am I?' His sovereign ring flashed light across the side of the plain wall as he fidgeted to get comfortable.

Gina made a mental note that he was dressed far more casually than the day she spoke to him at the lake. Jeans, a worn-looking jumper and a navy blue puffy winter coat. 'This is a voluntary interview. We just need to speak to you again about your discovery of Amber Slater's body on the morning of Monday the twenty-fifth of January. Hopefully, we won't have to keep you too long.'

He exhaled and a slight smile spread across his face. 'Of course. I absolutely understand.'

Did he? Gina couldn't help noticing how undisturbed he looked after finding her body. He seemed relaxed and as far away from upset as a person could look. 'There's something I need to speak further about. You told me you were walking but you looked dressed up, like you were going somewhere rather than the walk around the lake you say you were doing. You also drove for about fifteen minutes to get there. Why were you really there?'

His smile cracked. 'I told you.'

'Yes, you were taking a walk. The problem is, it seems odd. Do you see where I'm coming from?' There was no time to waste and drawing the interview out was wasting precious time when PC Kapoor was missing.

The man began to bite the inside of his cheek. 'Look, I found her. I had nothing to do with what happened to her and I called you. I should have just left her and got on with my day. If I'd known it would cause this much hassle, I would have.'

'Hassle? A woman has been murdered. The least she deserves is that we investigate thoroughly. Can your wife confirm you were with her before you left for your walk and the evening before?'

He shook his head. 'My wife? Are you serious? She barely knows what day it is. Late stage Parkinson's disease, that's what she has, and the dementia is worsening. Besides, she was still in bed and we've had separate rooms since her illness took over completely. She has to use a hospital bed and I didn't want to wake her. A carer normally comes in to do that as I can't cope.'

Gina remained silent for a few seconds, trying to read his body language but he wasn't giving anything away. 'See it from my point of view. No one can vouch for where you were from Sunday evening and you are clearly lying to us about where you were going? You need to be honest with us.' She threw her pen to the table and leaned back in her chair.

Jacob cleared his throat. 'Mr Norton. It would be better for us all if you just told us the truth.'

He shook his head and stared into space. 'You're trying to pin this on me.'

Gina felt the urge to grab her pen and snap it. 'Why were you at Cleevesford Park on Monday morning?'

He started twisting his ring round and round and all Gina could think about was how Terry had scared her on so many occasions with his. She fought the urge to flinch as she replayed the punch to her chest. She focused back on Mr Norton, noticing that he wasn't wearing a wedding ring. 'I was meant to be meeting someone but that never happened because I called you.'

'Okay, now we're getting somewhere. Who were you meant to meet?'

'HappyGoLucky1207. We messaged on a dating app.' He pulled his phone out of his pocket and selected the app. 'Happy now?'

Gina picked up his phone and clicked on the message centre. Message after message filled his box. Some explicit, others arranging dates. There was even one from the evening before.

'Go ahead and judge all you like but I get lonely and sometimes I meet people just to talk, sometimes we screw and sometimes we grab a drink. Do you know what it's like seeing someone you love deteriorate? She is barely present any more and her weeks are numbered. I'm scared of the silence in our home and I have to get out or I'll go insane. The nursing staff come several times a day, which gives me some sort of life. I don't want to be alone when she's gone. I can't be alone, which is why I meet people. I don't lie to these women about my situation. They get the whole truth, each and every one of them, and I won't apologise for what I do. It's me who is soon going to be left in this shitty world alone.' He placed his head in his hands and leaned over the table. 'HappyGoLucky gave me her phone number. Call her. Her real name is Ellen and she lives in Worcester. She's also married to a man who forever sleeps around on her, which is why she probably agrees to meet people like me. What's good for the goose, and all that. Nothing changes the fact that we're both married so we decided to meet at the lake, out of the way from anyone we might know. A snatched hour, that's all we had and now she's not picking up her phone if I call. Maybe if you get through to her, you can tell her I'm sorry for standing her up on Monday.'

Scanning down the whole message chain, Gina knew he was telling the truth. 'I'll be back in a moment. May I take your phone for a minute?'

He shrugged then nodded.

So Otis Norton had been cheating on his sick wife. That's all they had on him and that wasn't against the law. She walked up to O'Connor and popped the phone down. 'I'm just going to grab a glass of water. Can you call this number for me and ask the woman, Ellen, if she was set to meet someone called Otis Norton on Monday morning at Cleevesford Park?'

'Yes, no worries.' He took the phone from her.

She continued to the kitchen and ran the tap. The lights were giving her a thick head. The cold was making her bones ache and a night of watching Vincent Jordan's bungalow sounded like a recipe for cramp. She filled her glass and headed back out. 'Did you get through?'

O'Connor read the notes he'd just taken. 'She said she was meant to meet someone she knows as FunnyLoverMan who was in his fifties and from what she said he matches Otis's description. She said that he's tried calling her a few times but she decided that she wanted to work on her marriage so she ignored him. She asked that we don't contact her husband as she's ashamed.'

'So he is telling the truth. That's the end of that chain of investigation. I'd look into it further but I've seen the messages, they go back to last week and their little date was arranged before Amber was even taken. You can cross Otis Norton off the list.' She held her hands in the air. 'Kapoor is out there and going through something that none of us can comprehend and we're getting nowhere. I'm going to spend the evening going over old ground with the other tenants and spending the night in a car hoping that Vincent Jordan is the killer and that he slips up somewhere so that we have an inroad. We have so little to go on. When you can, please make sure the system is fully updated with the other tenants' details and interviews and those of Vincent Jordan. It'll give me something to plough through over the course of the evening.'

'We'll find her, guv.'

All hope was slowly diminishing. If they didn't find her alive within the next day, Gina wondered if they would ever see their chirpy, much loved colleague ever again. 'If the person who killed Amber has escalated, they might kill Kapoor earlier to get the same high. She might not be given two whole days. What if the killer's frustrations at not managing to kidnap Madison drives this too?' She checked her watch and carried her water to the door. 'I best get this phone back to Mr Norton and let him go. Any further on tracking down where the Collinses might be?'

'I've eliminated another four campsites.'

'Keep up the good work.'

Water sloshed over the sides of the glass as she entered the interview room. Jacob began introductions again as he rolled the tape. 'Here you go, Mr Norton.' She put his phone on the table. 'You're free to go.'

'Is that it?'

She shook the water off her hand onto the floor. 'That's it. Your alibi has come through. We thank you for your cooperation and I'm really sorry to hear of your wife's illness. Interview suspended at nineteen-twenty hours on Wednesday the twenty-seventh of January.'

Mr Norton scooped his phone up. Jacob stood and led him out.

Gina stared at the magnolia walls with all their scuff marks and tea splats. O'Connor knocked and entered. 'Sunny Side Caravan and Camping Park in Evesham confirmed that the Collinses checked in earlier today but then left after they'd paid. We don't know where they are now.'

'Can you head over there and speak to them? Get any CCTV footage and keep me posted. They're looking more suspicious by the second. Firstly, why would you go off camping when you both have busy jobs teaching and your children should be at school? Why would they turn up at a site then pay and leave? They're on the run.'

O'Connor folded his arms and shivered. 'I'll see if Jacob wants to come with me. Wyre's going with you, isn't she?'

'Yes and nice work. Keep me posted.'

'Will do. The car park has been gritted by the way. Should make driving out easier, I don't know about the roads though, the snow is coming down thicker now. Mrs O loves it but me, I hate the stuff. Roll on summer.' He paused. 'Drive safely, guv.'

'You too, especially down those winding roads. They're less likely to have been gritted. Wait, it's odd that the caravan site is open now, don't you think? Who goes caravanning in the snow?'

'Mrs O and I used to go caravanning all year round early on in our marriage. It's true that a lot close and some of the ones that we've called have been shut for the winter but a few are still open. People don't always stay in their caravan for a holiday, it's cheap accommodation when visiting relatives in different areas and the new ones are so cosy, they're like home from home.'

'Thanks for the insight into the world of the caravanner.' She glanced out of the tiny slit window high up in the wall and shivered as she watched the snow fall. 'We don't know where Kapoor is being kept. She could be being transported from place to place in a caravan. That's a possibility but they have children.' She tried to picture the Collins family and Kapoor tied up at the back of the caravan and it wasn't sitting right as a theory.

'The children are with the grandparents. It's just Mr and Mrs Collins that have left.'

'Why didn't I know this?'

'It's in the file.'

'Dammit!' She'd missed this vital piece of information and she could've kicked herself. 'I bet they left the caravan site, knowing they'd left a record of their whereabouts. We need to get uniform driving around woodland areas and tiny country lanes in the area. Something tells me that they might not even be at a formal site. They've probably parked up down some tight road, gone off grid.' Her heart began to pound as she thought of them taking Kapoor, here there and everywhere. For what reason? They didn't even have a motive as far as she could see but their behaviour was increasingly becoming more suspicious.

O'Connor frowned. 'I'll get Smith onto the case, then I'll head straight to the caravan park, see if the person who booked them in can help in any way.'

After he'd left, her mind toiled over everything and led her into a jumbled mess. She stood and hurried out trying to force away an image of Kapoor tied to a chair in a condensation-filled caravan that was parked up on a verge with the Collinses torturing her. Gina took a sip of her water to alleviate her dry mouth as she imagined the terror in Kapoor's eyes as her lips were being superglued.

CHAPTER FORTY-EIGHT

As I drift in and out of this strange dream world, I try to fight my way to consciousness. He must have put something in the sandwich that made me sleep. *I'm not Jhanvi Kapoor, he called me Hailey. I am Hailey and I mustn't forget. Who are you? Hailey. You want to live, don't you? Yes I do. So, who are you? I am Hailey.*

Something smells fresh. I think it's my hair. Shaking my head as far as the binds will let me, I feel the two braids hit my cheeks and I shiver. I can't cry. It won't help. My skin feels soft and the grime of the food I'd dropped in the crease of my chin has gone. He's bathed me or given me a wash. The thought of his hands touching my skin makes me cringe. I prise an eye open but the room is as dark as when my eyes are closed.

There's a coolness around my legs. My legs are bare, that's why they're colder than the rest of me. When I last saw daylight it was either frosty, slushy or snowing. Where are my trousers? Then, I remember the nightdress. He'd already changed me into it earlier. My heart begins to race and my mouth is dryer than ever. I don't know if he's touched me or not. I can't feel anything I shouldn't feel but would I know? I feel panic rising and in my mind I'm bursting from the binds. Every twitch in my body is vying for me to attempt to break free but I know I can't. Did Amber try to break free and scream and shout? Is that why she died?

I take a deep breath through the cloth in my mouth. It's suffocating me. I can't breathe. I bite down and my gums itch as they clench the cold damp material that tastes weirdly of toothpaste.

'You're not suffocating. Just calm down, Hailey.' Again, he is there in the darkness. He can see me but I can't see him. That dreaded tune plays again. It's driving me crazy but he tells me that I love it. I have to embrace it, allow it to possess me so that I can be what he wants me to be. It's either that or die.

I'm trying to be brave. I'm a police officer, a pillar of the community, a much-loved daughter and sister, a respected colleague. I miss my family and my heart aches for my mother. I wonder if her news was good or bad. Me not calling her to hear her results will be seen as a let-down. She'll think I'm putting my job first or that I've forgotten.

Deep in the pit of my stomach, I know I'm never going to see them again and I want to shriek like a wild animal and lie on the floor, grieving for everything I've lost, including myself. I just wished that I'd called my mother last night and told her how much I loved her.

'Hailey. I'm going to tell you a story. The story of you.' His hand slams onto the chair and my heartbeat skips a beat. 'I don't have long so don't you dare interrupt.' I hear a click as he swallows. 'There was once a boy and a girl…'

And so he continues for a couple of minutes, describing them and all the shocking details.

'That girl was you, Hailey. I'll carry on next time but for now, you are going to rest.'

I hold back a tear. I'm trying to remember everything he said but my head is fuzzy. I was half listening while trying to think of how I can get out of here. He removes the cloth from my mouth and places a bottle to my lips, then moments after gulping the liquid down, I begin to drift to the warped sounds of that record. That's when the nightmares start. I can't fight the drug. A tear spills out of the corner of my eye. What will he do to me while I'm not present? I can't think about it.

CHAPTER FORTY-NINE

I feel a spring in my step and a lightness in my heart. This time, I know she's the right one. She said she is Hailey and she hasn't attacked me with loads of questions. She's not fighting. She's not calling me names. That's how I know she's really my Hailey. I knew I'd found her and I was right.

I remove my boots and grab a beer. It's too early to celebrate but while I'm here on my own for the shortest of time, I am going to allow myself the luxury of feeling triumphant. Soon Hailey and I can leave and start afresh, away from our past. When she fell asleep, I watched her for a few moments and stroked her hair before leaving the bungalow for the evening. The heating is on so she'll stay warm and I know she won't wake for hours.

I glance out of the window. My car is already covered in snow and a shiver runs through me. What if I get snowed in here and I can't get back to her? Shaking that thought away, I know it wouldn't be for long. A human can survive for ages without food. She'd be okay without water for a couple of days and it's not like she can go anywhere. I'm not planning on leaving her there for that long.

'She's not me.' Hailey's voice rings through my mind.

I throw my beer bottle and it smashes against the table but your voice remains in my head. *'You should have let me go.'* My hands are shaking and my jaw is clasped so tightly I fear I may crack my teeth if I don't loosen up.

I slam the front door knowing I have a list of things to deal with this evening and I'm expected to be somewhere.

I will never let you go. Never!

CHAPTER FIFTY

Madison hobbled over to Alice's freshly changed bed. 'Thank you for putting me up.'

'Don't be daft, girl! You'd do the same for me. And your nanna looked okay so that's another thing to relax about. You're like a regular Florence Nightingale the way you look after her.' Alice grabbed some extra pillows from the wardrobe and passed Madison the remote control.

'Thanks for taking me to check on Nanna first, and for making her some food. I don't know what I'd do without you.' Madison paused and clutched the soft Bagpuss toy that always sat on Alice's bed, holding it close to her chest.

'Don't thank me. I'll get you back when I have an accident or a shitty hangover. For now, my bed is yours and you can stay as long as you like.' Alice lay on the bed next to Madison. 'I will warn you, people tell me that I snore.'

'Great!' Madison laughed but then the sobs came. 'Who did this? Who attacked me?'

'Come here.' Alice pulled Madison towards her chest and stroked her hair.

'He must've known I was at the hospital and the only way he could have known is by following me. Even I didn't know I'd be there that day.' Madison's tears began to dampen the shoulder of Alice's jumper. 'I bet he's out there now, watching and waiting for me to leave so that he can try again?'

'You don't know that. It might have been an opportunist. Wrong place, wrong time.'

Madison pulled away and shook her head. 'I could have gone with that theory had that weird incident in the toilets at the Angel not happened. Seriously, someone was in there and they were trying to intimidate me. Then there was hedgehog man. Too many weird things have been happening lately.' She gazed into the stuffed toy's eyes and stroked it like it was a real cat. 'Where's Ty?'

Alice shrugged. 'I called him earlier and he was totally shocked when I told him what happened. He said he'd pop by to see you in a bit but he had something really important to deal with and it couldn't wait.'

'When I was in the toilets, Ty left you to go to the loo as well?'

'It was only for a moment. You know how long guys take to pee and he probably didn't wash his hands. He'd give me that look he does if he heard me say that.' Alice pulled an open bag of Haribo from her bedside drawer and offered one to Madison.

Madison took a sweet and began to chew as she allowed her thoughts to settle. 'Where is he now? What could be that important? He was always here or hanging out with us in the run up to Christmas. Since New Year, we've barely seen him. What changed?'

Alice's brow furrowed. 'I hadn't really thought about that but now that you mention it… What's he doing with his time? He didn't mention that his studies were getting on top of him but he does keep asking me if anyone is moving out of our block. He still wants to live here. I heard that Ali was moving so I texted him earlier with our landlord's details. He answered swiftly saying he was on it so he is reading his messages straight away. I don't think there's anything in it. He's been doing a lot of dating lately. Maybe that's all it is.'

'Maybe.' Madison's head began to twinge. She grabbed her phone and checked Tyrone's Facebook. He hadn't posted anything for about a week. 'It's odd,' she showed Alice her phone. 'Ty's normally glued to Facebook and Instagram. He hasn't even sent any of his silly TikToks to our WhatsApp group. Something's up and we have to find out what that is.'

CHAPTER FIFTY-ONE

Gina parked the car around the back of the apartment block off Bulmore Drive. She watched as Vincent Jordan trudged through the snow leaving fresh boot marks across the grass. He appeared to be carrying a cardboard box containing a few tools. The orange glow coming from the street lamp shone through the trees, just catching the back of him as he cut through to get to his bungalow at the end of the path. 'We have a good vantage point here. He didn't even see us when he passed.'

'I wonder what he's been doing. Fixing something maybe. It's late.' Wyre stepped out of the car and grabbed her scarf. 'It's beautiful, isn't it?'

'The snow?' Gina pressed the central locking and did her buttons up, wishing that she'd worn a thicker coat. She had barely got warm that day.

'Yes, it just reminds me of what Christmas should look like but never does.'

'Christmas is so overrated. Not only do all the idiots come out with their fighting and drinking, filling up the station, it's an excuse to part with lots of money to buy junk that's slowly killing the environment.'

'I can't argue with that.' Large flakes landed in Wyre's black hair and on her shoulder.

'Let's hurry before we turn into snow people.'

Wyre and Gina ran to the front of the building and pressed the main bell. As she touched the door, it must have been on the latch as it opened a little. Heavy footsteps thudded down the central staircase and Lauren was standing there in a dog onesie.

'Come in. Damn, I wish people would stop leaving the door open.' She flicked the latch off and allowed the main door to close properly.

'Hello, Lauren, may we have a word with you? Sorry to intrude on such an awful night.'

The young woman smiled. 'Don't worry. It's probably the best night to come. I think we have a full house so anyone you need to speak to should be in.' Lauren waved at Corrine as she came out of her apartment with a bin bag. Corrine did her coat up over her pyjamas and pulled her hood over her head. Curtis came out with a roll-up between his lips and as he opened the front door, he clicked the latch on again.

Gina followed Lauren upstairs and into her apartment. It was a far cry from Amber's. Lauren had a place for everything and her bookshelves were perfectly stacked in colour order and baskets for her work stacked next to them. She had a little table and her laptop screen was filled by a photo of a dog with a huge nose. Textbooks were stacked up to the right with little bookmarks and Post-its marking out reference pages. 'It's lovely and cosy in here.'

'Can I get you a drink?'

Gina thought back to their travel mugs in the car. Time was running short and she wanted to get back as soon as possible to not miss anything. 'Thank you but time is against us tonight.'

'I think I told you all I know.'

'There's something we found in Amber's flat that I need to tell you about. Would you please take a seat?'

The woman's chirpy expression quickly changed and worry lines appeared across her forehead. 'Okay.'

'There's no easy way to tell you this but our investigations have led to the discovery of surveillance equipment in Amber's apartment, more specifically her hallway, and you and Amber are on it.' Gina took a seat at the table as Lauren sat. Wyre gave her a sympathetic look.

'No… no way.' She swallowed. 'Not when we…?'

Gina nodded. 'I'm sorry.'

'Did Amber do that to me? She was my friend.'

'It wasn't Amber.'

'Who was it? Was it that bastard landlord, Vincent? He's always around here looking creepy and messing about with things under the guise of maintenance.'

Gina shook her head. 'We have made an arrest but I can't share the details with you yet. It isn't your landlord. We'll need to speak to you further about this when you've got over the shock. Are you okay to come to the station at some point and we can tell you where we go from here?'

Lauren nodded and held the back of her hand to her red cheek. 'I'm all hot now. I can't believe someone did this to me and to Amber.'

'You didn't mention that you and Amber were in a relationship when we interviewed you.'

'That's because we weren't.' Lauren began playing with the zip on her onesie, pulling it up and down by a couple of inches. 'It was one drunken night, that's all. Amber had well moved on from that. I still liked her but I know she wasn't really into me. I'm sorry I didn't mention it.'

'We've since found that she kept another phone, an unregistered phone.' Gina nodded to Wyre who removed her notepad.

'Oh, the "date phone" she called it. She didn't give out her main number to people on AppyDater. If anyone gave her grief, she said she could just vanish online and bin the phone. She wanted to keep her contract mobile number separate. The last person she was meant to meet, she gave him her proper number though. She seemed to like him more.'

'Did she ever mention being in a relationship with anyone from her course?'

'Yes, but that was over weeks ago. She slept with her lecturer a handful of times and joked about it. She just wanted to know what it would be like but then things got awkward for her in lectures. I didn't approve, obviously, but it was him doing the cheating. Amber wasn't married. Amber said she wasn't his first fling, he apparently had one on the go with every year group. She wouldn't really say much more to me, especially after our night together.'

Lauren stared at the dog on her screen. 'Amber was just enjoying life. Her father would never let her out when she lived at home and I suppose she went a bit mad, partying and one-night stands. He was really strict with her. When she first moved in he was here all the time. She had a big row with him and told him he was stifling her.'

'Did she ever take drugs?'

Lauren bit her lips. 'I don't, ever, but I know Amber took the occasional tab and those weird canister thingies, but then so does everyone.'

The sound of Wyre's pen scraping on her pad came to a stop.

'What will happen to that video of me and Amber? I know we were only kissing in the hallway.'

'It's currently in police evidence. From what we have, I can see that it hasn't been uploaded to any public sites.'

'At least that's some good news, I don't think my mother could take the shock. I still can't get over the fact that some sicko was spying on us while we were… It doesn't bear thinking about.' Lauren exhaled and wafted her hand in front of her face. She too had suffered a violation in all this.

Gina had read the notes that were on file about Mr Slater's laptop. He'd shared the video of his own sexual encounter to a porn site but not the one of his daughter kissing Lauren. 'How close are you all, in this building?'

'We're quite tightknit, I think. We sometimes have weekend drinks, albeit not noisy ones. When we do, we open all our doors and wander around the building freely. It has a house share feel to it even though we all have our private quarters.'

'Tyrone Heard, does he mix much?'

'He's not here as often. His best friend is Madison who, well… you know, the girl who got attacked. He's made it clear he wants to move out of this block and he doesn't really gel with the rest of us.'

'Great, thank you for your time and I'm sorry that we came bearing the news we did. Someone will be in touch soon about the case.'

Lauren stood and awkwardly fidgeted on the spot. 'I saw Tyrone staring through Amber's door when it was open one day but I thought it couldn't be him. I know Tyrone is gay so he wouldn't be interested in Amber, not in that way. I just don't get him.'

Gina smiled. 'Thank you for being so helpful. We'll be in touch.'

As they left, it worried Gina that the housemates left their doors open quite often and that the front door may have been on the latch – anyone could easily access the building.

CHAPTER FIFTY-TWO

Gina heard voices coming from downstairs. They peered through the bannister and spotted Corrine and Curtis passing a roll-up between them. 'May we have a quick word?' Gina hurried down.

'No probs.' Curtis put the cigarette out between his fingers. 'Sorry about smoking. There's no alarm in the hall on this floor and it's cold. Won't happen again.'

Gina ignored it. The last thing on her mind was Curtis smoking in the communal area. 'We're just following up on all your details.'

'Okay.' Curtis's greasy face shone under the stark light.

Gina whipped out her own pad. 'I have it that you're studying motor mechanics at Bromsgrove and, Corrine, you're studying hairdressing at Redditch, is that correct?'

Both of them nodded.

'Do you know if Tyrone Heard is in?'

'That dick?' Curtis popped the unlit roll-up between his lips. 'What makes you say that?'

'I don't know. He just doesn't make an effort to get on with us. It's like he thinks he's above us.'

Corrine nudged him. 'Don't say that. You can be a prick sometimes, Curtis.' She brushed her long blonde fringe from her eyes.

'Well, it's true. He never wants to have a drink with us and you only have to see the way he looks down his nose because we're not at uni and he is.'

'He doesn't do that at all. I think the problem is you. You feel inadequate when you see Tyrone because he's a finer specimen of a man than you are.' Corrine nudged him in the ribs and laughed.

He giggled back. 'Whatever, but it's true, I'm telling you.'

Corrine pushed him again. 'Tyrone seems okay. When Amber was sick once, he popped his head around her door and asked if she was okay or needed anything from the shops, she told me. He did the same for me too when I had a hangover. Once, when Amber had come back from partying and left her door open, Tyrone made sure she had a blanket over her and a bowl on the floor before closing her door. I think that was last October. He's a good guy really, he just has his own friends and prefers to hang out with them. Curtis is just jealous that Tyrone is a nice guy.'

'Like hell.'

Gina wondered if they were both talking about the same Tyrone. Now was a good time to find out. 'Thank you. Sorry to have kept you.'

Gina hurried up the stairs with Wyre following until they reached the top of the building. She knocked and there was no answer. Placing her ear against the door, she listened but all she could hear was her own heart beating. 'Can you hear anything?'

Wyre placed her ear on the wood and shook her head. 'There's a rustling noise behind this door. It sounds like someone's in there.'

Knocking again, Gina called out. 'Tyrone, it's the police. Please open the door.'

No answer.

Gina bit her bottom lip. 'It could be Kapoor. Tyrone seems to be the outsider here. The kind of resident that people barely notice. The one who comes and goes quietly and he's also a link between the two victims, Amber and Madison.'

Wyre stood back. 'What do we do? Go in?'

'Make a call to the station.'

As Wyre pulled her phone out and waited for an answer Tyrone came into sight behind them on the stairs and he stared directly into Gina's eyes. She could see his panic and the tremor in his hands made his keys jangle. Whatever was behind his door, he didn't want anyone to see.

CHAPTER FIFTY-THREE

Tyrone Heard pushed past and stood outside his front door, holding his keys out. 'Can I help you?' The angry scratch mark on his chin looked to be seeping a little.

'I'm DI Harte and this is DC Wyre. We just want to speak to you about Amber Slater. May we come in?'

Without speaking, Tyrone stared between the two women – a wide-eyed stare that was filled with dread. 'Err, it's a bit of a mess. Can we talk here or maybe I can come to the station?'

Nothing sounded odder. It was rare that people volunteered to come down to the station. 'There's no need for that but we would like to come in.' The sound of pans clattering to the floor came from behind the door. 'Is there someone else living with you?'

'No.' Tyrone swallowed.

'Mr Heard. As you know, Amber Slater was murdered and another young woman, Madison Randle, was attacked last night and we know her to be one of your best friends. What you don't know is that another woman has since gone missing. We really need you to open the door.' Gina felt her hands trembling. Maybe they should have called for backup but she wasn't stopping to do that now, not when he was about to let them in. Someone was in his apartment and those pans clattering may have been a sign from PC Kapoor, hearing them talking outside the door and hoping to be rescued.

He placed the key in the lock and led the way into the dingy attic hallway. 'I'm in big trouble.'

Gina kept back a little, holding her arm out to keep Wyre behind her. Standing at the top of a staircase made her feel particularly vulnerable. If Tyrone wanted to make a run for it, all he had to do was push her hard and she'd tumble to the landing, taking Wyre with her. The sound of the thud that Terry made as he hit the bottom of their stairs all those years ago made her legs feel slightly jellified. 'Please step away from the door. Back a bit.'

The young man scratched the dark hair on his head and stepped backwards into the bathroom. A tapping noise came from the living room. Gina could see Tyrone Heard shaking under his black skinny jeans as she passed him and headed to the living room. Wyre remained in place at the front door, keeping an eye on Tyrone's movements.

Gina placed her shaky hand on the door handle and pressed down. As she entered, she heard a scurrying noise heading to the kitchen. All the curtains were shut and the room was in pitch darkness. A stale smell made her stomach churn, that of rotten meat. She felt acid beginning to burn her throat and her mouth began to water, not in a good way. The last thing she could think about was food. She reached for the light switch and the whole messy room was illuminated by a single bulb in the centre of the studio apartment. She glanced around but all she could see was clutter everywhere and a desk by the window with a pile of paper next to it. 'It's okay, Wyre, come through.'

'Please don't tell my landlord.'

A meow sound came from the worktop and next to the microwave sat a scrawny black kitten.

'Having a pet is a breach of my tenancy. I'm sorry I looked cagey. You won't tell him, will you? I won't be here long. Alice messaged me, someone is leaving her block and she said they're allowed pets. It'll only be for a few more weeks.' Tyrone stepped into his living space and grabbed a pile of clothing, throwing them on the single bed that had been pushed into a corner of the sloping attic space.

The cause of the smell was now apparent, cat food in a bowl on the floor. 'No, I won't say anything. Why didn't you just say that you had a cat when we were outside?' All that anxiety that Gina had just felt had been for nothing. She was slightly angry with Tyrone. The cat meowed again and her heart rate slowed down a little.

'Sorry. I guess I'm an idiot. With all that's going on and all. That's Clover. I found her in the bins outside on New Year's Eve. I know she still looks a little sad and sick but she's in much better shape than she was a couple of weeks ago. I have to keep popping out of lessons to see to her though. She's already clawed my bed base and all my furniture. Oh well, at least it belongs to me and not Vincent.' He paused. 'I couldn't leave her there, in the bin, and I didn't want to take her to a cats' home just in case no one wanted her. Do you want to sit?' He grabbed more clothes off his wooden chairs and threw them into the growing pile on the bed. 'I know I live in a mess and I know the place stinks…'

'That's okay.' Gina and Wyre sat and Tyrone wedged his bottom on the edge of the bed.

Wyre flipped out her pad and leaned it on the desk that looked like it doubled up as a dinner table given the dirty plate that had been left there to rot.

'I know you have already made an initial statement which I have read but I just want to follow up. How well did you know Amber Slater?'

He shook his head, the black fluff on his chin catching the light as he shifted to get comfortable. 'I don't know her that well. I've borrowed things off her but we all do that here. You know, bread and sometimes coffee, things like that?'

'So you've been in her apartment?'

'Yes, but ages ago. We've all been in each other's apartment.' His gaze shifted to the floor, then back up. 'We don't always lock our doors, it feels more like a house share here than apartment living. Some nights the others have a drink together, then everything is open.'

Gina paused for a moment, trying to listen for anything that suggested that he was nervous, a crackle in his voice, hesitancy in answering, any display of nerves, but she couldn't see anything that alarmed her. 'The others say that you aren't always a part of their social gatherings.'

He shrugged. 'I don't always want to sit around drinking. Besides, my best friends live in another block. I spend more time hanging out with them. Me and Madison are on the same nursing course so we hang out at uni too. Alice is studying social work. I don't have as much in common with the guys in this block.'

'Where were you on Tuesday evening?'

'I was with a guy I met on AppyDater, at his bedsit.'

'Can I take his name and address, please?'

'It's Sully. I don't know if that's his real or full name but that's the name he used on the app and that's the name I called him all night.' Tyrone began scrolling down his messages and Wyre was poised to take Sully's phone number and address.

After he'd finished, Gina stood and walked over to the kitten on the worktop and began stroking it under the chin. 'She's beautiful.'

The young man's frown turned into a slight smile. 'Which is why I've kept my mouth shut. I'm keeping her.'

'It was mentioned by one of the other tenant's in this block that the main door is often left on the catch. Have you noticed anything strange or anyone hanging around that shouldn't be?'

'Not that I can think of. Although, I came back late one night and saw Vincent gently tapping on Amber's door. I tried to listen to what was being said from the top of my stairs but they spoke in whispers and he went inside for a couple of minutes. I thought that was weird as it was too late to be fixing anything, but I haven't seen anything else. The main door bangs at any time, day or night and occasionally one of the others has fallen asleep drunk in the communal areas, but not Amber. I've never seen her like that.'

'Can you remember how long ago it was that you saw Vincent at Amber's door?'

He stood and grabbed his diary. 'I remember, I'd handed in an assignment that day, a big one.' He flicked a few pages and pointed. 'It was Friday the eighth of January and I think I'd not long come back from the Angel Arms, where I'd met Madison and Alice. I go there most Friday nights. Money's been a bit tight after the Christmas spend so I didn't stay out late. I was probably back about ten, latest. It must have been about that time or not long after.'

'You've been really helpful. Now, can you think back to the Angel Arms on Monday the twenty-fifth of January? Madison said she saw someone suspicious on the lane that runs alongside the back of the beer garden. A little later, she said someone stood outside the toilets while she was in a cubicle, then they turned the lights off. Did you see anything that night?'

He scrunched his nose and stared into space. 'I remember her saying something about the toilets. She thought I was messing around but it wasn't me. I did pop out to the loo while she was in there… wait… when I was in the men's, I used the urinal. The cubicle was locked. I was literally in there for half a minute and the cubicle was still locked. I didn't think about it before now but there hadn't been any other men in the pub. It was dead, so I don't know who was in that cubicle.' He began biting his nails. 'Poor Madison, I think I joked about what she'd said. Are you saying that whoever was there might have attacked her?'

'We're not saying anything at the moment. It's just a line of enquiry we're following. Do you recognise this woman?' Gina held up a photo of PC Kapoor.

'Yes, she's a police officer, isn't she?'

Gina nodded. 'You've met her before?'

'I saw her on the day Amber's body was discovered. She was with another officer, asking questions. I spoke to the policeman and I think I saw her heading towards Vincent's bungalow. Is she the woman who's missing?'

'I'm afraid so. If there's anything else you can tell us that might help, however small, it might mean everything.' The kitten began chewing on Gina's sleeve. Patiently, she teased the material from its mouth before patting its soft head.

'I wish I did know something. I really do.'

'Here's my card. If you can think of anything, if you see anything, remember anything, call me straight away.'

He walked over and took the card from her before picking the kitten up and stroking it as he held it to his chest. Its little paw worked its way out of Tyrone's hold and began to hit his chin. 'You little minx.' He kissed it on the head. Looking at Tyrone, she found it hard to imagine that he could be the murderer but until his alibi had been confirmed, he wouldn't be completely off the list.

'Thank you.' Wyre stood and walked over to the door, closely followed by Gina.

'Can you show yourselves out? I don't want her to escape. Not until I've moved, had her inoculated and microchipped.'

Gina nodded. 'Of course. You've got my number.'

As they left, her phone rang. 'Jacob, everything okay?'

'Yes. News on the Collinses. Their car has been flagged up by ANPR. We've tracked them to the Bridgnorth area but the trail has run cold. I'd say they've headed along the country roads. I'll keep you updated.'

'Can you pass me Sully's address?' She waited for Wyre to open her pad to the right page and then she read it to Jacob. 'I need to know if a man called Sully was with Tyrone Heard on

Tuesday evening. Let me know what he says.' She ended the call and they headed off to the back of the apartments ready for a night of watching Vincent Jordan's bungalow.

As they got into the car, through the trees and shrubs Gina could see his hall light come on and he stood on his doorstep. The spark of a lighter flashed and he puffed out a plume of smoke. 'Why would he be at Amber's apartment late at night on the eighth of January? What were they whispering about?'

Wyre shivered as a smattering of sleet hit the windscreen. The drive ahead was blanketed in snow and it was still coming down. 'We've got to get a look in his bungalow. Tonight has to yield something.'

Gina agreed. They just had to work out how that was going to happen but it had to happen soon. Kapoor was being held somewhere and Vincent's bungalow could easily be the place.

Vincent looked each way, checked his watch and dropped his cigarette to the ground before stamping on it.

'Who's he looking for?' She grabbed the binoculars from the back seat and stared through the trees at Vincent. He checked his watch again before slamming his door.

CHAPTER FIFTY-FOUR

Thursday, 28 January

Madison lay on the bed half listening to the television that had been left on in Alice's bedroom. She glanced at the digital alarm clock. It was way past one in the morning but she was sure she'd heard Alice talking on the phone.

Alice peered around the bedroom door. 'You've woken up?'

Madison rubbed her throbbing head as she propped herself up. All the painkillers she'd taken at the hospital had long worn off. 'Do you have any paracetamol? I know there's none in my apartment. Why didn't I think to get some from Nanna's place when we popped by? She's got boxes of them lurking around.'

'You've had a lot on your mind. Besides, I do have some painkillers but they're codeine based so they will make you sleepy.' Alice placed a hand on Madison's forehead and smiled.

Madison forced a mock laugh. 'Durr, have you seen the time. Sleepy – who cares?'

'I'll go and grab a couple.' A round of gunshot firing came from the television and several bodies blew up into the air on the black and white screen. 'What on earth are you watching?'

'I'm not.' Madison switched to love songs set on a radio channel. 'That's better.'

Alice left the room and Madison could just about hear her rifling through the kitchen cupboards before she came back in. 'Here, take these.'

She took the two white tablets from her friend and swallowed them down with a gulp of water. 'I had the weirdest dream.'

'I'm not at all surprised. When I came in you were twitching and muttering away.'

'I dreamed I was at uni, sitting at the back of the lecture theatre and there was a line of men with no faces sitting in the front row. They all turned around at the same time and their faces were flat – as in no features. I don't know who attacked me. I might never know, but he's out there and I think my dream meant he could be anyone.' She exhaled. 'But I feel I know him, or I've seen him around but I never got a look at his face. I wish I could say I'd looked into his eyes but it happened so quickly. I didn't see a thing.'

As Alice sat on the cheap mattress, Madison almost rolled into her and winced as she held her head. 'Sorry.'

Lifting a hand, Madison brushed away her apology. 'I did what I had to do. I ran and I'm still alive.'

'You know, I spoke to Tyrone earlier and he agrees that you and Amber could be connected. I suppose you have similar features, you go to the same uni. We've visited Tyrone together at his place so there's another match in the places that we've all been to. Ty said something that breaks the mould though and you're not going to believe this. I wanted to wake you, to tell you.'

Madison could feel her eyelids getting heavier as the codeine-based painkillers began to work their way into her system. 'What?'

'The police visited Ty a few hours ago to follow up on the statements of everyone living in his block and they said someone else was missing, another woman. He said she was a policewoman. She's the anomaly. I don't think it's uni or the block but… there's something that we're not figuring out, that's what Ty said.'

A snort came from Madison as she fought to stay awake. Her hand reached over to Alice's. 'Don't leave me alone. I'm so tired.' She yawned and closed her eyes.

In her half dreamy state, Madison heard Alice's phone buzz and she left the room.

'I can be over in a few minutes. I'll meet you there.'

'Alice, where are you going? Did you just give me painkillers? I can't...' Her speech was slurring and her thoughts jumbled. Her body felt as though it was gently sinking into the warm mattress. So inviting and unwilling to let her go. The exhaustion had caught up with her.

Seconds later, the front door closed and Alice hadn't responded. 'Alice, where...' Her friend had gone and she was drifting into a sleep that she couldn't fight any longer.

Back to that scary dream. Those blank faces in the front row of the lecture room appeared again. This time, she walked down the steps while the whole audience stared at her, then she turned from the stage area to get a better look. Each figure now had a walking stick and a sickly grin with sharp animalistic teeth. She wanted to wake up, run away but her feet were stuck to the ground and the crowd had disappeared. All the lights went out plunging the room into darkness, then they clicked back on.

Only one faceless figure remained, the only person in the auditorium. 'Madison, I'm back.'

CHAPTER FIFTY-FIVE

Gina had been shivering for a while now. The snow had thankfully stopped falling but more was predicted. They had been staring at Vincent Jordan's bungalow through that same crack in the trees for well over three hours now. Since earlier, when it looked like he was waiting for someone, not a thing had happened. His lights had all gone off about an hour ago.

'Nothing. Not a thing and it's bloody freezing.' Wyre wrapped her arms around herself after having a quick swig of water. 'I'd do almost anything for a hot chocolate.'

'Light on behind us.' As Gina turned, the car rocked. She could just about see through the icy back window. 'The attic room. That's Tyrone's apartment.'

'Are we watching him now?'

'We're watching everyone. I'm prepared to change strategies if anyone is deemed to be acting suspiciously.' Gina paused. 'Light's off again.'

'Let's hope he's gone back to bed.' Wyre began to sniff; her nose beginning to run. She grabbed a small pack of tissues from her pocket. 'I hope Kapoor isn't cold like this.'

Gina had been thinking that exact same thing all evening, along with all manner of other disturbing things. 'I can't stop thinking about her. I keep imagining her trapped and bound, just like Amber had been. It sickens me to think of her lips being glued and—' She paused, imagining a knife plunging into their colleague's heart. 'We have to do something. Vincent's in bed.

Let's head over and take a look. We might be able to see through a window or hear something.' A flash of light came from behind the bungalow. 'What was that?'

Wyre reached for her gloves. 'I'll grab the torch.'

Barely making a sound, both detectives crept out of the car and stealthily made their way through the trees, staying off the road that led to Vincent's bungalow.

'Ouch, rabbit hole ahead.' Wyre bent over to rub her ankle then continued. After leaving a footprint trail in the snow, Wyre stopped in Vincent's garden, remaining in the darkness of a tall conifer. The light behind the bungalow flicked off and all was silent.

Gina led the way around the edge of the garden. 'If he comes out, we just needed to follow up on our interview and I don't care that it's the middle of the night, okay?'

Wyre nodded and followed.

'I can hear muffled voices. Listen.' They both stopped.

Wyre scrunched her brow. 'Sounds like there's a few people. What the hell is going on? Should we call for backup?'

'Send a message to Jacob. Get someone down here just in case. It can't hurt.'

As Wyre tapped away, Gina walked up to the dark windows but could see nothing at all. Either the windows were blacked out or the curtains were closed. The light in the hall flicked on. 'Keep back.' It looked like Vincent was walking back and forth through his bungalow. They ducked under the window as more lights went on. The tiniest crack in the curtains became visible as the light flooded through. Vincent might see them if he came closer. Gina flinched as the window cracked open. A cigarette butt flew out and fizzled in the snow until it had been extinguished.

Somewhere in the house, Gina could hear a woman's voice, not clear enough to make out if it could be Kapoor or anyone else. Vincent cleared his throat and pulled the stiff window closed again and the light went back out.

'That was close.' Wyre pulled her phone back out of her pocket and hit send on the message that she'd typed out for backup.

'I heard a woman's voice. It might be Kapoor. We have to get around the back, see what's going on.' Gina pushed her way through the bushes, cracking and crunching as she moved slowly. 'They're going to hear us. Damn.' As she reached the end, she caught sight of two figures who began to scarper towards the back of the garden. Gina gave one last push through the bushes. 'Police, stop.' They continued to run. Vincent stood in his back doorway, illuminated by the security light as it flickered back on. She turned to Wyre. 'You go after them.'

'On it.' Wyre burst from behind her. Being fitter, Gina was sure that Wyre would catch up with whoever was out there.

'Vincent Jordan, what's going on here?'

The man scurried inside and locked his door.

'Open up. We have reason to believe that a police officer's life may be in danger which would give me reasonable grounds to enter.' She felt the slamming of her heart in her chest.

He glared through the window in the top of the back door. His wide eyes almost looking bloodshot in the corners. 'You haven't got a warrant.'

'I don't need one if a life might be at risk.'

He opened the door and took a couple of steps forward. 'You're not coming in. Get away from my door.'

'Stand back, Mr Jordan.'

He began to seethe and took another step forward. 'Just get the hell away from my house. I said you're not coming in.'

'Don't step any closer.'

He ignored her warning, lifted his hand and went to grab her. Just in time, she blocked his arm and twisted him around, before grabbing his other arm and cuffing him. 'Attempted assault on a police officer.'

Seconds later, she heard Wyre scrambling back through the bottom of the garden. 'What happened here, guv?'

'He stepped towards me in an aggressive manner, then went to grab me so I cuffed him.'

'I wasn't going to grab you.' The man kicked the wall a couple of times.

'There will be plenty of opportunity to tell your side of the story down at the station.' She turned to Wyre. 'I gather you lost them?'

'I hate to admit it, but, yes. I recognised one of them, it was Tyrone Heard. At least we can bring him in later.'

'I think I just heard a car pull up in the distance. It's probably uniform and DS Driscoll. I'm going in.' She swallowed as she stepped into the kitchen, the cheesy smell cloying in her throat and her heart pounding at the thought of what she might find. 'Jhanvi?' She took another step and listened for an answer.

CHAPTER FIFTY-SIX

As PC Smith caught up, Vincent Jordan was left in his capable hands. Gina stepped across the crumby kitchen that they'd only recently visited and it still smelled of cheese and beer and all manner of sickly greasy things that were now coating the insides of Gina's nostrils. She only hoped that the smell of death wouldn't be coming next but she'd heard a woman's voice. Her stomach dropped. It may have just been the voice of one of his visitors but she knew Vincent Jordan had something to hide. It's possible that the something he was hiding was PC Kapoor. She stepped into the dark hallway, snapped on a pair of gloves and turned on the lights. Glancing back, she nodded over her shoulder at Wyre to stay close. 'The room we saw him going into, it was this way.'

Gina took a right, past the front door and along another corridor that led to a room at the end of the bungalow. The same room that Vincent had flicked his cigarette out of the window.

'Jhanvi, it's Gina and Paula. Jhanvi?' Gina listened for any kind of response but none could be heard. A shuffling sound came from the room ahead. Taking another step, her foot crunched on something below, broken glass. She spotted what looked like an ornament that had been smashed. 'Jhanvi?'

'She has to be here.' Wyre swallowed.

Gina pushed open the door to the room and pressed the light switch as she hurried through. 'Police. DI Harte.' Her shoulders slumped as she stared at an old workbench covered in a mini plastic filing cabinet containing what looked like compartments for screws and DIY oddments.

Wyre took a step forward and placed a hand on one of the slide-out boxes. Gina nodded. 'Tablets. Lots of them. Looks like Ecstasy.'

'Where the hell is Kapoor? Check the rest of the building and get some officers in here. This all needs to be bagged up and Vincent Jordan needs to go down to the station right now. Jhanvi?' Gina left the room and burst into what looked like a cupboard – nothing but clutter, coats and a vacuum. The next room – a scattering of porn magazines next to a filthy mattress on the floor. She hurried back towards the front door and burst into the living room. Again, no Jhanvi. She ran out of the bungalow where Wyre was instructing uniform on what to do next. She jogged to the back of the garden and peered through the shed windows and then the old crumbling garage at the bottom of the garden – nothing.

A flurry of snow shook from the trees as the wind blustered away. They'd caught a drug dealer, nothing more. He had to know something. He had to have seen something or someone. She walked around the back of the garage and leaned against the wall, shivering with her eyes closed. The general noise of everything around her and her thoughts were overwhelming.

'Guv?'

She opened her eyes. 'She's not here, Jacob. Where is she? We're too late. I know we are. What the hell is happening to Jhanvi right now?' She clenched her fists and followed him back.

'Quick update. We've found the Collinses, guv. A witness was driving back from his girlfriend's place in Bridgnorth in Shropshire and he spotted a man pulling a woman from the country road into a caravan, which he thought was suspicious. Police over that way headed over and confirmed that the couple were a Mr and Mrs Collins.'

'Was Kapoor with them?'

He shook his head. A snowflake landed on his eyebrow. She could see the darkness under his eyes. They were all tired but the night's work had just begun. 'It will take a few hours to get them back to us as police there are processing them but they will be brought back to Cleevesford.'

Gina's phone rang. 'DI Harte,' she answered.

'This is PC Eagleton. We're at the scene of the Collinses' caravan. They have been taken to the station in response to the ANPR that was out for them. Your colleague suggested that we give you a call if there was anything else.'

'What is it?'

'We've found a phone on Mrs Collins with what looked like abusive messages on it.'

'What phone number have they been sent to?' Gina gazed at Jacob. 'Grab a pen.'

He did as asked and waited for her to read out the number. Jacob flicked through a few of his notes. 'That's the number, guv. We have found out who NoName is.'

'You say that phone was on Mrs Collins's person?'

PC Eagleton verified her statement. 'It was also a burner phone with only that number stored in it. No other numbers have been stored or called on this phone from what we can see, no incoming calls either.'

'Thank you.' As the call ended, the messages whirled through Gina's thoughts. 'Can you access the system on your phone and read the messages from NoName out?'

Jacob pulled his phone from his pocket and began to log in. He pressed a few buttons and scrolled before reading them out loud. '"NoName: I need to speak to you. Please, Amber. Amber: What we did wasn't right and you lied to me. Don't message me again. NoName: Don't do this to me. Answer your phone. I need to talk to you. NoName: Why aren't you answering? NoName:

There's someone else, isn't there? Amber: You're stressing me. NoName: Me stressing you. Amber: I can't stand this any more. I'm turning the phone off. NoName: Don't do that. You can't ignore me. NoName: Why won't you pick up? NoName: Just answer your phone. NoName: Stuck-up bitch. There are plenty of others who'd like to have what you have. NoName: Amber, I'm sorry about the last message. I didn't mean it." That's the lot, guv.'

'So they have a phone taken from Mrs Collins that shares the same messages as Amber's phone. Where are Madison's messages or even something that links to Kapoor? So far, I'm seeing an obsession with one person and why did Mrs Collins have this phone? Was she toying with Amber after finding out about her husband's affair? Maybe we're reading too much into this. Damn, we need to speak to them. Like always, people are as closed as clams, not caring whether they send us on a stupid little merry dance while our colleague could be being stabbed through the heart as we speak.'

As they reached the bungalow, PC Smith came out with several bags of tablets. The creases at his eyes told her his emotions were strained. His partner hadn't been found. All they'd found was drugs. During any ordinary raid, this would have been a great result but now, all everyone wanted was Kapoor to be found and that hadn't happened even though their two main suspects were now in custody.

She shook her head. 'What are we missing?' Jacob and PC Smith stood in silence, both of them looking as clueless as she felt. 'We have to go back to the start. Go back to basics. What holes in our investigation haven't we plugged? What questions have yet to be answered? Jacob, we'll head back to the station and deal with Vincent Jordan while we wait for the Collinses to arrive and Smith, we will find her.' She instantly regretted offering him that reassurance. No one could guarantee anything at this point.

Wyre ran towards them. 'Guv, Tyrone Heard is in a police car and they're taking him to the station now. He was found trying to sneak past the police back into his apartment.'

'First thing I want to know is why he was running away. I knew he was holding something back when we saw him earlier.'

Jacob took the tablets off Smith. 'I'll finish up here and meet you both at the station.'

'Right.' Gina took a breath, brushed the snow off her coat and followed Wyre back to the car. 'Tyrone Heard isn't going to know what hit him.'

CHAPTER FIFTY-SEVEN

I try to prise my eyes open but they're stuck. The wetness that seals them is itching but I can't get to it to relieve the irritation.

I gaze into the darkness and I can't tell if he's here. I wriggle and feel a dampness in my underwear. The smell tells me I've peed myself. I couldn't hold it any longer.

Tears spill from my eyes and my nose is stuffy. With the rag in my mouth and the gag tied around my head, I feel as though I will choke. I can't breathe. I need to get out. My heart feels as though it will burst from my chest. I struggle against the binds in this contraption of a chair and I make funny little noises through my nose and eventually manage to blow it clear.

I want to shout and scream, everything I know I shouldn't do but staying calm is hard.

There's a spark of recognition. I know who he is. I've seen him and I saw him looking at me just for a second when I was at the lake. It hadn't clicked at the briefing when I saw all the photos and names on the board. He is hiding right under their noses.

Flinching, I feel the cord cut into my arm, like it's sawing on bone and I sob. Helpless and trapped.

I am confused by the dark, by my throbbing head, by my damp clothing and my screaming hungry stomach and the nausea. I'm confused by the song that won't leave my thoughts. Since waking, I haven't heard the tune for real but it plagues me. I'm losing it. In my mind's eye, I can see my sanity hitching a ride on the tune as it whirls around the room, out of one ear then back in through the other, a constant carousel. Each word, each note, the melody. It's as ingrained in my brain as the alphabet song I learned in preschool. The only difference is, I don't think about the alphabet song all day and night.

If only I could shout to relieve my frustration, to hear the real sound of my own voice as I hear it. Others say I'm a shrill, squeaky Brummie, but when I hear me, I sound friendly, accentless and warm. We never perceive ourselves the way others perceive us. How does he perceive me? He sees Hailey or he wants me to be Hailey. Did Hailey speak like me? I need to speak to him. Not plead, not beg – try to be Hailey. How do I become someone else? Someone I don't know. I have to assume that I look like her or share her characteristics. If I say too much, he'll glue my lips, I know he will. Clenching my fists, I know I need to find that answer otherwise I'm dead. A bloody image of a knife plunging through my heaving chest, crimson liquid spurting then dripping as he pulls it out and finally, the sound of my last rasping breath.

Trying to spit the rags out of my mouth, just a little, is near impossible. They've shifted slightly but sometimes the shift isn't for the better. The cloth tickled the back of my throat almost making me gag, which is why I should quit doing that.

Wriggling once again, I try to fight the binds. The skin is torn on my wrist and the wound burns like nothing I've ever felt. In my mind's eye, I see my skin peeling back as my wrist chafes back and forth, binds sawing deeper into my flesh. My logical brain weighs up my options. Knife through heart or binds cutting me to the bone to enable my escape? Just a bit further. I've seen the film *Saw*, where the only way to escape boils down to the victim being able to slice through a piece of themselves. Can I do it?

Sweat falls down my face as I cringe at the thought. My head shouts yes. The pain cries no. I ask myself again. Lose the skin on my wrist or get stabbed through the heart and dumped in a lake.

Which is it? That is the only question I need to ask myself.

If they don't find me soon, he will kill me.

CHAPTER FIFTY-EIGHT

Gina tapped her fingers on the side of the desk that separated her and Wyre from Tyrone Heard. Shivering, she couldn't wait to get back into the incident room where over the course of the day it had warmed up a little. Tyrone didn't look affected by the cold in his black padded coat and his hoody that was zipped up underneath it. His chocolate-eyed stare hadn't moved from a dink in the wood. He'd answered the basics; name, address, date of birth.

'I will ask you again. What were you doing this evening at Vincent Jordan's bungalow?'

For the first time since they'd all entered the room, he looked up. 'I was trying to catch him out, talk to him about Amber but to do that I had to pretend I wanted some tabs.'

'What tabs are you referring to?'

'Ecstasy. I overheard some of the other students mention that they'd bought a few from him and I wondered if that's what Amber had been trying to do when he turned up at her apartment. After I told you what I saw, it had me thinking that maybe I could investigate a little, find something out that might help.'

'Mr Heard. What would really help is if you told us everything you know and didn't play amateur detective. You could put yourself and others in danger.'

His shoulders dropped and he sat back in the plastic chair, slumping so far back, it looked like he was lying down. 'I know and I'm sorry. I just wanted to help. I managed to get his number and rang him. I've never felt so scared. I said I needed some tabs for myself and a friend. He said to come over later, much later, when there was no one around and to come around the back. He seemed nervous but I guess that was because of all the police activity. I didn't want to buy the tabs, it was just to get in there and talk to him, to get a look at his bungalow. I mean you can check. I don't even have any money on me. I was going to look at them, pretend I knew what I was on about and change my mind. All we wanted to do was to suss him out and get justice for Madison.'

Gina took a deep breath and exhaled. The last thing she needed was the students interfering. 'It's time to tell me who the other person was.'

'She only came because I asked her to. I was scared to go alone and she wanted to get to the truth as much as I did. It's all my fault though. Neither of us wanted the drugs, you have to believe me.'

'Tyrone, a woman was murdered, one of your best friend's was attacked and one of our officers is missing. I shouldn't have to spell that out to you again. Tell me who you were with.'

He bit his lip. 'Alice. Madison's neighbour and my other best mate.'

'Thank you.' Gina remembered Alice from the hospital when she spoke to Madison. Thoughts of a Scooby Doo mystery ran through her head with those meddling kids. If only those pesky kids had come up with more, but what Gina did have was still pointing to nothing more than Vincent Jordan being a drug dealer. 'Is there anything else you're not telling me? Think about that question carefully before answering. I don't want to have to bring you in again for withholding information or wasting police time.'

He shook his head. 'If I hear anything or think anything else, I'll call you straight away. Immediately. I totally promise. I know I've been an idiot.' He began to pick at the cat scratch on his chin.

'Okay. An officer will come to take a full statement from you with regards to Vincent Jordan and the drug deal that nearly went ahead. Next time when the police are chasing you, stop. It'll be less trouble in the long run and we don't take too kindly to people leaving the scene of a crime.'

'I will, ma'am. I promise.'

She kept her gaze on his. The way he said ma'am made her feel like the oldest person in the world. Even though he was in his early twenties, he could have still been mistaken for a boy in his mid-teens. Gina grabbed her notes. She nodded to Wyre who began to speak to the tape. She hurried along the corridor towards the kitchen where O'Connor was pouring a cup of coffee. 'I love a boiled kettle.' She grabbed a cup.

He scratched some sleep from under his eyes. 'We've just finished up with the drug dealer, Vincent Jordan. He's been charged. I've been in touch with the officers at his bungalow.'

'And.' She put a spoon of coffee into a chipped mug and poured.

'There is no evidence of Kapoor ever being in his home and no evidence that Amber has ever been there either.'

'You were looking into his family, his background, the lot, just in case he could be holding her somewhere else. I know it's a long shot but what do we have?' Gina took a sip of the hot liquid and her face contorted briefly as she burned her lip.

'His father owns the property business. We spoke to him and he claims that his son is a lazy layabout and that he set him up with this job to inspire him to take over the business one day but he despairs at his son's lack of ambition. He wasn't surprised about the drugs. Vincent doesn't have access to any other properties as his father doesn't trust him with anything better – those were his words. He was meant to start small and prove himself with managing this block but his father said he's blown his last chance.'

'Do we know his father? Has he come up in the investigation?'

'No, not at all. On the better news front, the Collinses are on their way. I've just got the call from a PC Eagleton so you might want to get that coffee down you. There's some pasties in the incident room if you need to refuel.'

Gina blew on the coffee and tried again. This time her lips didn't feel as though they were being singed to her gums. 'Have you started looking for those holes yet?'

'I have and there are a couple. Corrine Blake gave us her registered address; that of her parents' house, but they no longer live there. It's a Birmingham address. I don't know why she'd lie. We obviously need to wait for office hours to resume to chase up the colleges and universities.'

'First thing in the morning, make sure you're on that phone.'

'Will do. Two of the lecturers I needed to speak to weren't available last time I called and one was off sick and the administrator in charge was a temp.' He paused and stared at the ceiling for a few seconds. 'Do you think she's alive?'

'She has to be.' He swallowed and looked away. She patted him on the shoulder.

He turned away and held his hand up as he left. 'Don't forget those pasties.' Her big-hearted colleague, the one who quite often with his teammate Mrs O made sure they always had food during a big case, was feeling the strain, just like all of them were.

CHAPTER FIFTY-NINE

Gina checked the time again and it would soon be morning. She'd not even managed to have a nap in her office and exhaustion was taking its toll. She yawned as she stared at Mrs Collins. She and Jacob remained seated while the woman sobbed into her hands as Jacob had introduced her for the tape. She wondered how Wyre and O'Connor were getting on in the room down the corridor with Mr Collins.

'Mrs Collins. An unregistered phone was taken from you by police in Shropshire, one that contained messages sent to Amber Slater and, I must say, they appeared to be harassing in nature. I'll read some of them to you.'

'Please don't. I can't hear them again.' The woman shook her head and wiped her nose and eyes with the back of her hand. Her crumpled coat clung to her frame and was almost bursting at the buttons around her bosoms. Her sunken eyes reminded Gina of her own. She guessed that Mrs Collins hadn't been getting any sleep either.

'So tell me why you sent these messages to Amber Slater?'

She shook her head and ran her fingers through her damp hair. A sweaty smell began to permeate through the room. Mrs Collins was feeling the pressure but her lack of talking was getting more frustrating by the second.

'"NoName: Don't do that. You can't ignore me. NoName: Why won't you pick up? NoName: Just answer your phone. NoName: Stuck-up bitch."' Gina said the words as loud as she could and as pronounced as she could make them. 'What did you want to speak to her about on the phone? Was there a rage building up inside you because you'd discovered that your husband was sleeping with this young woman? She wouldn't answer, would she? Did that make you angrier? Angry enough to—'

'Stop!' Mrs Collins broke down. 'It's not my phone.'

'Now we're getting to the truth.'

'My husband told me to crush up the SIM card and bury it while we were in Bridgnorth but I couldn't, not after I'd read the messages. I told him I'd done it but I couldn't let the phone go. He's an expert in changing a story over time and making out that I'm crazy or make something into more than it was – I suppose you could call what he does gaslighting.' She bit her bottom lip and blinked away a tear. 'This phone gave me the proof I needed to believe in myself when the time came. I kept reading those messages over and over again and it hit me. He'd been cheating on me and the girl was now dead and he'd dragged me out of my home to go on the run. I know about Scarlett too. I had it out with him but he kept saying that she was a mad woman. That she tried to lead him on then shopped him to the police because she was an attention seeker. He said that what happened with him and Amber was different – but then I found this phone, in his study. He'd hidden it behind a loose skirting board. When I confronted him, he went mad, said we had to get away, which is why we left. He said you'd read it all wrong, that it wasn't him that was the problem, it was her. I didn't want to go and the children… he upset them. They were crying.' She paused. 'I'd never seen him like that before. I thought it was best to get us away from the children so that we could sort things out, which is why I agreed to go with him. He was…' She stared into space.

'He was what?'

'Frenzied. His eyes were stark, his grip on me, forceful. The kids, he didn't seem to care that they were cowering in a corner as we argued. Then, we turn up at his parents' house begging them to have the kids and to use their car so that we can take the caravan away. They were as confused as the kids but they could see that something was stressing us so they agreed. Our car had been playing up and given the weather, they were okay with us borrowing theirs. We often did that anyway.'

Jacob scribbled a few notes and looked up.

'What happened after that?'

Mrs Collins glanced at Gina as she continued. 'We travelled to one of the sites we'd stayed at before, in fact it was the only one that I knew was open at this time of the year in Evesham. We have friends that live close to it and when we've visited in the past we've taken the caravan there as it's cheaper than a hotel and they live within walking distance. It always meant we could have a drink.' She sobbed and continued. 'We obviously didn't visit friends this time. We started to argue as soon as we got there. The man who runs the site had booked us in and he knew us by name. He could tell by my red eyes and my husband's clenched jaw that something was wrong. We didn't even unhook the caravan. We left and just drove, heading towards Shropshire. I don't know why. It was as good a place as any.'

'You know how it looks, running away like that?' Gina leaned in.

She nodded and half hiccupped as she calmed down a little. 'I told him that but when he's on one, it's either his way or no way. I was confused, spurned and even jealous of the girl he'd had a fling with. Part of me wanted to tell him where to go, take the kids and leave. Another part of me wondered how I'd be able to tell people and if it was my fault? Did I love him enough, give him enough attention? I mean look at me compared to her.' Mrs Collins's lips began to quiver as she held back a sob. 'Anyway, I couldn't process what was happening. I let him take the lead and with a foggy head, I followed.'

Gina rubbed her gritty eyes. 'Why did you provide a false alibi for him? You said you and Mr Collins were at Tesco, together.'

Glancing between the two detectives, Mrs Collins began to tremble. 'I didn't. He was with me.'

Gina pressed her lips together and shook her head. 'We've seen the CCTV from every angle.'

'He stayed in the car.'

'It's not helping your case when you continue to lie to us. Perverting the course of justice is a very serious offence, Mrs Collins.'

She snatched her shaking hands from the table and placed them out of view. 'I'm sorry.' She began to cry again.

Gina pushed the box of tissues across the table and the woman pulled a couple from the box and snivelled.

'He was at home on his own. No one can verify that, no one. He wasn't online. He wasn't talking on the phone. He said if I didn't say that he was with me, he'd have Amber's murder pinned on him and the real murderer would walk.'

'What about the rest of the weekend?'

She looked away.

'Mrs Collins. Were you with him all weekend? By that I mean did you see him all day and all night or were there times when he was out of view or may not have been in the house?' Gina felt her hair itching the back of her neck as she waited with anticipation.

'He was at home but we weren't together. He spent the weekend in his study. He has a daybed in there and we'd been arguing about all this. About the messages.'

'Could he have left without you knowing?'

She slowly nodded, her large eyed gaze meeting Gina's. 'I don't know, maybe. He didn't do it though. He's the father of my children. He can't be a murderer.'

'Do you recognise this woman?' Gina held the photo of Madison up to Mrs Collins. 'Or this one?' Then the photo of PC Kapoor.

'No. I've never seen either of them before.'

'Monday night. Where was he? Did you see him?'

'Yes. We both sat at the kitchen table drowning our sorrows and bickering. I did see him that night – all night. We've been together since we left in the caravan too.'

Things weren't fitting together. If Mr Collins had taken PC Kapoor, what had he done with her?

'He cheated on me. It's clear from the messages he's an arsehole but that's everything. I was foolish. He was too. We should have known how this could escalate by running away and not being straight with you.' The woman scraped the legs of the chair along the floor and clicked her fingers as if to retrieve a thought. She waved her arms and her eyes seemed to widen. 'That's it. I can prove he was in on Monday night. Our neighbour popped by to deliver some Avon that I ordered from her, and my husband answered. If you don't believe me, you can ask her. Her name's Elaine. It's the house next door to ours. On the right if you're looking towards us.'

They would definitely be checking out her claim. O'Connor knocked at the door, smiling. He had something. Gina nodded for Jacob to continue with the formalities as he announced her leaving the room for the tape.

'O'Connor. What have you got?'

'Mr Collins has made a confession.'

CHAPTER SIXTY

As I return to the place I call my real home, I hear nothing, not even a chirping early morning bird. It's been a little quiet around here since the blizzardy weather started. Every creature with any sense is holed up right now. The snow is coming thick and fast against my face, clouding my vision. I can hear something now. The tick, tick, tick of my hot car engine parked on the drive. I glance each way, no one sees me coming and going, there's too much distance between each property. My mother certainly likes to live in a secluded manner and never did get the trees and shrubs pruned back around the perimeter of the garden. It literally resembles a jungle now, albeit a naked branched jungle. Each one defined with a strip of snow balancing on the top just waiting to be toppled by something as delicate as a robin.

I hurry through the door. 'Hailey, I'm home.' I will call her Hailey from now on as she is now Hailey. As I go to unlock the room she sleeps in, a memory hits me.

She isn't me. She isn't me. She isn't me. That voice in my head again. I have turned her into you. I can't bear to listen any more and my head hurts.

I slam the door to the kitchen shaking the frame.

A rustling noise comes from the other room. Where was I? I need to tend to my new Hailey, the real in-the-flesh Hailey.

Heading back, I unlock Hailey's door and enter, my eyes trying to adjust to the darkness. I pop the music on again and our tune plays quietly in the background. It's working. It's turning her into Hailey. If she eats what Hailey used to eat, listens to what Hailey listened to and sits in the dark, just like Hailey always did when she needed to think, she will have to become Hailey and my past will be brought forward to my present where the two shall finally converge.

I glance at the woman in the chair but her eyes are screaming fear and there is so much blood around her arms. Removing the rag from her mouth, I kiss her forehead. 'What's happened?'

She looks confused and screams at the sight of me then she stops as if regretting her decision to scream. She takes a few sharp breaths. 'I'm Hailey. I like cheese on toast.' But she's shaking and sweating. Nothing feels right. The ghost of my past screams through my head. *She isn't me.* I want to hush it away but it won't go.

'Which Teddy does Hailey like the most?'

The woman in front of me doesn't answer.

'What is Hailey's favourite song?'

'"Beautiful Dreamer". I love that song and you keep playing it for me.' She pauses. 'I love you.'

My neck prickles. Hailey never once said that to me. 'Wrong answer!' I pace back and forth, knocking things over in the half-light. I could tear down the blackout material and the cardboard from the windows but I won't. Hailey liked darkness and she did until the end where it consumed her.

'Please untie me. I can learn to be better.'

But I know better. It hits me. She's just like Amber. This is where it goes downhill.

'Please,' she yells. Her crying and wailing hits me. I've been kidding myself. That voice. How could I ever have thought that it would become Hailey's soft voice? The shrillness of it is going through my head and I want it to stop. Shut her up, that's what I need to do and I know just how to do that. I run out to grab what I need from the kitchen.

I hurry back with a tube of glue and I yank the cap off it.

'No, please. I'm quiet. Look.' She shuts her mouth and she's right, she's quiet, but it's too late. I can't trust her now. I was kidding myself that I could see Hailey as all I now see is Jhanvi.

Pressing the button on the chair's control panel, it begins to slide back and the leg rest comes up further. She's trying to resist. I grab her plaits that I lovingly created and yank her neck back against the back of the chair. Its slight tilt is just right for what I'm about to do, like a dentist preparing to examine a patient. As she wriggles, I press the tube of glue. The fast-drying liquid lands on her cheeks, her chin and her chest, then what's left lands on her lips. 'Now you have no choice but to shut up.' Tears spill down her face. A part of me feels guilty as I catch Hailey again in her features but I shake my head. It didn't work. What I need to do is start again and do better.

I was never good enough. In my mind I see my mother telling me what a loser I am and my hands shake. Now that she can't engage in conversation with me, I speak and I can't shut up, babbling on about everything. Then I stop and I see the alarm in her eyes. There's no going back now. It's all out there. She knows my deepest darkest secrets and more than anything, they must be contained. I stomp out of the room to get what I need.

In my mind I see Hailey sobbing, saying I told you so. It's not just about Amber. It's not just about Madison. I stare at the shed through the window. For a moment, I hate myself more than ever. Grabbing a knife from the block, I know what I must do.

This has to end, once and for all. Her tears are falling but I can't let that cloud my ability to see this through.

'You're breaking my heart. Now, I'm going to break yours.'

CHAPTER SIXTY-ONE

Madison heard chattering coming from the kitchen, something about what Alice was doing with Tyrone last night and mentions of having to go to the police station to make a statement. The door slammed and Alice rushed in, bringing a waft of chilly air with her. 'What are you doing, Alice?' Madison saw her friend pulling a fresh pair of jeans on. 'Who was that and where did you go last night?'

'I met Tyrone.'

'You left me.'

'He was convinced that his landlord, Vincent, killed Amber and attacked you so we set up a meeting to buy drugs from him so we could suss him out.'

'You what?' Alice ignored her and continued dressing. Madison forced herself out of bed, holding her head for a few seconds until the wooziness passed. A little stretch told her that she needed to go easy on herself and not overdo it. 'Wherever you're going, I'm coming with you.'

'Get back into bed. You're not well enough.'

'No and I don't care.' Madison discarded her pyjama top and flinched as she pulled a jumper over her head. 'If it concerns me, I want to be a part of it.'

'You're one stubborn cow.'

Madison forced a smile. 'Whatever. Grab your coat, girl. Where are we going?'

'I'm not going to win this one, am I?'

'Nope.' Madison shook her head as she dragged her hair from the insides of her jumper. Alice was right with that question.

'We're heading to Tyrone's. He said he saw something last night and he wants to be sure about what he saw before he tells the police.' Alice paused. 'It could be dangerous.'

'I've already faced danger. Count me in.' Madison dragged her hair into a low messy bun and pulled one of Alice's woolly hats onto her head. As she lifted her arms up, she grimaced. 'Wow, I stink.'

'You should stay here and have a shower instead. We've got this.'

'No. You go, I go.' She paused as she shivered in the thick coat. 'Do you think we're close to finding out who attacked me?'

Alice grabbed her tiny rucksack, the one she used as a glorified handbag and she fed her one arm through it. 'I hope so.' Within moments they'd left, slamming the main door behind them.

For several minutes Alice had been turning her car key but the little old Fiesta wasn't having any of it. About a foot of snow had settled on the roof and bonnet.

'I suppose we should walk. I'll tell Tyrone we'll be ten minutes.' Madison pulled out her phone and removed her gloves to call Tyrone. The phone rang out and went to answerphone after several rings. 'He's not picking up.'

'Try again while I check Facebook.'

'Still no answer.' Madison ended the call and they began walking.

'He hasn't been on Facebook for three hours according to when he was last active. He knows I'm coming. He called me then to say we were meeting at eight in the morning, at his. He should be up and ready.'

'What exactly are you both planning?'

Alice stopped, almost slipping on a patch of trodden snow. 'He wouldn't say.'

Madison tried his number again. This time it went straight to answerphone.

'Hurry, we're already late.' Alice grabbed Madison's arm.

'What if something's happened to him?' Alice continued hurrying without answering Madison and she wondered if Alice knew more than she was letting on. For the first time that morning, Alice looked worried.

CHAPTER SIXTY-TWO

Gina shook her head. 'With Mr Collins's confession, all we can possibly have him for is harassing Amber, nothing more and no further evidence to prove otherwise.' All their theories were slipping away, being disproven at speed when they had no time left. The metaphorical egg timer was running out of sand.

'We've made two arrests this evening but neither has brought us closer to finding Kapoor.' Jacob sniffed and sat back.

Mr Collins was being charged and so was Vincent Jordan – harassment and drug dealing. On a normal day, those results would be celebrated but now the team seemed more deflated than ever. The stench of frustration and failure filled the room and Kapoor was still missing. Gina stood up straight, trying her hardest to fight her body's need to curl up into a ball and ruminate. There was no time for that. 'Jacob, just run through things for us. Let's start with Corrine Blake's story.' Snow blanketed the outer wall of the car park but the road itself had been gritted earlier that morning. Gina wiped the condensation from the incident room window to get a better look and in it she could make out Jacob's tired reflection.

'I checked with her again and she says it was a slip of the tongue. Her parents had lived at that address all her life, as had she before leaving for university. She claims she didn't knowingly give us her wrong registered address and said she kept meaning to change it to the flat on Bulmore Drive but hadn't got around to it. She seemed to be more worried about her passport and driving licence still being registered there.' She turned, taking in the length of Jacob's stubble.

'Have we checked the addresses, old and new?'

He nodded. 'Uniform have seen to that. Her parents live at the new address Corrine gave us and the old address has a new family living there. It seems that Corrine Blake is genuinely just a little forgetful.'

'I honestly don't know how some people function in life.' She glanced at the board and three faces stared back at her. Amber, Madison and PC Kapoor. The photo they'd used was a professional shot with a pale grey background that was taken at an awards function. Her face so youthful, smiling in her pristine uniform. The classic shot. The type that families proudly displayed on mantlepieces. Gina remembered her earlier days in uniform and she had a similar photo but it was somewhere in the loft, boxed away no doubt until the day she died, when maybe her daughter Hannah would unearth it. Her stomach fluttered. They were seriously running out of time. She glanced at the other photos, the ones of Amber's body at the scene and post-mortem. In her mind, she saw Kapoor's next to them. The spritely young officer, dead and bloated then a y-incision on her chest as she lay on a stainless steel slab as her body gave up its secrets.

'Guv.' Wyre entered with a tray of steaming hot coffees. 'I think we all need these.'

Gina continued to stare at the board. All hope slowly diminishing. She dragged her fingers through her hair, pulling a few strands out before grabbing a coffee. 'Thank you. We're not going to find her, are we?'

Each detective was a realist in their own right. If a family member was asking the same question, it would be met with, *we are doing all we can,* not a promise to find their loved ones safe and alive. No one knew. There were no answers to be had, only a deep sense of hope that a lead would come in fast.

Gina took a long swig of the coffee and hoped that the caffeine would begin to work as she was now struggling to function. 'The Collinses: nothing. Tyrone Heard: again, nothing. Vincent Jordan: nothing unless you count the drug charges. That won't save PC Kapoor. The link was looking promising with Madison and Amber – both students, living close to each other, same university. But Kapoor – apart from having a similar hair colour – where does she fit in? They all have their similarities but looking for someone who targets dark hair and not knowing why isn't really helping us.'

'There's definitely a resemblance.' Jacob took a coffee and thanked Wyre.

She nodded. 'He glues their lips and stabs them. He's trying to shut them up. Why them? It's not them, it's who he thinks they are, or who they represent. What happened to him?' No one answered. 'Time is running out. He is going to kill PC Kapoor, I know it. Why?' She slammed her other hand on the desk and stepped back to the board, leaving a ring of spilled coffee around her cup.

'We definitely need a break.' Wyre sat at the table, head in hands.

There was one person on the board and she walked up and stared at the photo. It was a long shot but they had to dig deeper. His name had come up, he'd seemed okay but had she trusted all that he'd said? She placed her index finger over her lips as she tried to think back to the times she'd spoken to him.

O'Connor barged in as Gina placed her finger on the name. 'You read my mind,' he said. 'I've just come off the phone to his course lecturer.'

The tremble in O'Connor's voice told her that he had something. 'Spill it out.'

'The lecturer doesn't know of that student's name and has never heard of him. I emailed his photo over and he said he'd definitely never seen him before. He then delved into the records for me.

This student,' O'Connor jabbed at the name on the board with his finger, 'studied this course six years ago and didn't finish it. His name was in the old college records, way before this lecturer started two years ago.'

Gina turned, drank her coffee in one go and enjoyed the feeling of adrenaline that coursed through her veins. 'What are we waiting for? Get everyone ready. Get one of the team to delve further. Find his past addresses. His parents – look them up. Everything. Now.'

The room began to hum with voices as they all jumped to action.

'Kapoor's survival depends on us getting this right.' Gina paced out of the room and stood against the hallway wall as she waited for the trembling in her fingers to pass. It was time to go.

Briggs approached. 'Are you okay?'

She shrugged and left him standing alone. She was not okay. They were not okay and their colleague might be dead. Nothing about today was okay.

CHAPTER SIXTY-THREE

'Go check out the side window.' Tyrone pointed in the direction.

Madison kicked snow as she walked through the bin store leaving Alice and Tyrone fiddling with the sash window. She could almost taste the revolting odour from the bins as she passed. These apartments were a filth tip, she could see why Tyrone wanted to leave – well that and the kitten he was hiding. As she kicked the snow, she pushed the bottom of the gate with her foot and it pinged open. The frosted window that led to his bathroom was open, just a little. A couple of nub ends were balanced on the ledge where Curtis had been smoking out of the window. 'Here.'

Within seconds, the other two arrived. Tyrone stared at it. 'I'm far too big to fit in there.'

'I'm far too curvy.' Alice stood back with a puzzled look on her face.

Madison shook her head and pointed to her wounds. A shiver ran through her body and it wasn't from the cold sting in the air. Her mind flashed back to the night in the toilets at the pub, then the dark lane. The build of the man following her was covered up by clothing but now it was all coming back. She gasped as she thought of the hospital car park. Through the clothing, the scarf and the walking stick, she could now see his eyes. Her dream of the faceless man in the front row of the university auditorium had now been filled and it was as clear as daylight.

'Do you want to know who attacked you?'

'Yes, but—' Something was forcing her back – fear, apprehension. She gasped and turned away. 'I can't do this.'

Tyrone chipped in. 'You can. You have to if you want to find out the truth. He's not in. I saw him leave and I know what I saw through the window. Like I said, we have to get in there, see if he's left it behind. That's the evidence and we can't let him get away with it. If we find what we're looking for, we can call the police. Maddie, if you take your coat off, you'll fit through. You can then go straight to the front door and let us in.' His dark eyes had a pleading look about them, like a puppy begging for a snack.

'Okay! I can't believe I just agreed to this.' And she couldn't. It wasn't either of them who had been attacked. They had no idea how her stomach churned and her vision swayed. All her body's responses were telling her to run away as far as possible but running doesn't uncover the truth.

Tyrone ran into the bin store and came back with an old bedside table. He brushed the snow from the top. 'Just step up onto this and pull yourself through. Simple.'

'For you, yeah.' She rubbed her head. It already pounded. Alice was right. She shouldn't have come. She should have stayed wrapped up in Alice's bed with the television on. Sleeping in ignorance as to what they were up to, but she'd insisted. 'What am I going to fall on? Do you know the layout behind this window?' She pressed her nose to the frosted glass and could make out blurred shapes.

He shrugged his shoulders as Alice helped her to step up. A fine flurry of snow blew into their faces. Madison picked at the window, getting her fingers under it and pulling until it was open. 'Great, it looks like I'm going to land in the bath.' She pulled off her coat and thrust it towards Alice's face before pushing herself through the tiny gap. Squirming with a few groans and moans, she eventually reached down and fell into the bath. 'Ouch.' The tap dripped cold water onto her hand.

'Are you hurt?' Alice sounded worried.

'Why are you both still there? I'm going to open the door now. Hurry.' As she listened to them scarpering off, she heaved herself out of the scummy bath and regained her balance. She pushed the creaky door to the hallway and glanced through the other open doors. The sight of an ornamental skull made her jump back, her heart beating like a jack hammer. 'Chill, chill. It won't hurt you.' She swallowed, wondering what it was that Tyrone had seen.

Alice tapped on the door. 'Let us in.' She paused and tapped again. 'Maddie? Are you okay?' They both began to bang away.

Madison ignored them and glanced across the lounge and kitchen. The clutter that adorned every surface and floor was a distraction but there was something that sent a chill through her body. The photo that Alice had used to set up her AppyDater profile, the one of her eating the hotdog at the German Christmas market in Birmingham had been torn into four pieces and left on his desk. There was an open notebook. She glanced down. It had times and dates of where she had been on the Monday she was attacked and there was so much more. He'd been the one following her. She stepped back and gasped, her heart banging and stomach gargling. She couldn't swallow and the banging in her head almost knocked her sick.

'Open the door!' Tyrone was banging away. 'What's going on? Say something.'

As tears spilled down her cheeks, she breathlessly stumbled back into the hallway, banging against the walls until she reached the door. As she opened it, she fell into Alice's arms gasping for breath and sobbing. 'He was going to kill me. You saw the photo of me, didn't you?'

Tyrone nodded. 'It's still there then?'

'And there's more. So much more.'

Tyrone ran into the apartment, hurrying through like a gust of wind before coming back. 'I knew it.' Grabbing his phone,

Tyrone pulled DI Harte's card out of the sleeve in his phone case and began to tap the number in. 'I'm going to call the police.'

A loud knock instantly shut them all up, then the police entered the unlocked communal door. Tyrone instantly put his hands up and Alice and Madison cowered. 'If I have to do time, will you look after Clover, Alice?'

Alice stared tight-lipped and nodded as DI Harte stood there, her temples twitching with anger as the other officers followed her in.

CHAPTER SIXTY-FOUR

My lips, I can't breathe. It happened so fast, the binding of skin to skin and I can't bear to pull them apart. Only a short while ago, I was mentally preparing myself to tear the skin from the bone in my wrist so that I could escape but look at me. I can't even prise my own lips apart. It's like the thought of a paper cut or a pinprick or nails down a blackboard. Sometimes it's the smaller things that we fear the most. I shouldn't have yelled.

As soon as I said I loved him, he flipped. It should have worked. He should be crying in a ball now, releasing me from the binds and trusting me. I've screwed up and now he's going to kill me.

My stomach keeps cramping from the nauseating hunger and I want to hold it or bend over but I can't.

'Damn it!' His shouting is booming through the walls. Lots of banging and swearing and he's talking to Hailey again, the person who doesn't exist. The music still plays and I can't hear my breaths. That's probably a good thing.

Lots of people say that being mindful is good. Concentrate on breathing and feeling. I don't buy into it. When I sit in silence, I hear things and I get hung up on them not sounding right. I hear and feel my heartbeat and I wonder if everything's as it should be. When I swallow, I catch the sound my throat makes at the back and I don't like it. I don't like any of it. I prefer the sound of traffic or children playing or the hum of the television in the background. But not this music. I want it all to go away. All I want to hear now is my mother's soothing voice again and my brothers taking the pee or my father trying to discuss what's on the news with me. I begin to rub away at my wrists.

I try to lift my neck a little to get a glimpse of what I'm doing. My eyes have adjusted to the dusky room. I can see that a tiny flap of the blackout material has lifted at the corner of the window.

Out of the corner of my eye, I catch light on metal as he storms past and deadlocks the front door. Then the track ends and silence. With my stuck lips, I swallow and it sounds wrong. My ears pop and it's like the volume just went up. Shuffling and muttering – the words I cannot decipher. Again, it's me and the sound of my breathing and swallowing.

Saw away at the skin on my wrist, that's what I should do. A tear slips down my face as my flesh slices even further. The raw burning sting is like nothing I've ever experienced and I stop. I can't do it. Maybe this is why people give up. Death preferable to the pain of existence.

A few more tears slide down my cheek. I want to go home. I want to see my family and I miss my work colleagues. I'd never admit it to PC Smith but he's one of my best friends and I miss him too. DC O'Connor always gives me time and cookies or whatever his wife has been baking. I always liked him a lot. My team are my friends and I want to see them again.

It is as if the air in the room has shifted. That's what I mean about mindfulness, this intricate focus on the smallest of things. I didn't hear him creep up the hallway but he's there. It's as if he's staring right through me. My heart wants to escape. I can feel it banging away and the flutter in my throat gives me a sense of being choked. Sweat forms at my brow yet I'm shivering as the temperature drops. It's cold, so icy cold that I can't quite feel my arms and legs as much as I could a few minutes ago.

Panicking and pulling, I keep my focus on him, then I glance at the knife. This is it. I scream in pain and all I see is blood.

CHAPTER SIXTY-FIVE

'What are you three doing here?' Gina glanced through the open apartment door then at the three students bundled together on and by the stairs. 'Madison, shall I call you an ambulance?'

The student sobbed as Alice held her tightly.

'Madison, are you okay?'

Tears drizzling down her face, Madison nodded. 'He was going to kill me.'

Alice held her closely and stroked her head. 'It's okay, Maddie. You're safe now.'

Corrine came out of her apartment and Lauren stood at the top of the stairs rubbing her sleepy eyes as she spoke. 'What's going on?'

'I'm sorry, really sorry.' Tyrone stood. 'It's all my fault. I told Alice and Maddie to help me. I thought I saw something and wanted to prove it. I was going to call, look.' He held his phone up with one hand and flashed Gina's card with the other. Her number was half keyed in. 'We just wanted to give you the proof.'

Jacob nudged his way in between PC Smith and another uniformed officer.

Gina sighed. 'Is this tenant in?'

Madison shook her head. 'Not unless he's hiding in a cupboard.'

Corrine butted in. 'Look. What the hell's happening here?'

Gina's shoulders slumped. 'Just go back into your apartment, please. Someone will speak to you in a short while.' Corrine let out a snorty huff and slammed her door. Gina nudged Curtis's door and it fully opened. 'Why is his door unlocked?'

Tyrone went to speak but Madison put her hand up. 'It was me. I got in through his bathroom window and opened the door.'

'You broke in?' Gina stepped into the hall of the apartment. 'Curtis Gallagher. It's the police.'

Tyrone smacked his lips as he started to speak. 'Like we said. There's no one there but you should see his desk. Madison said he has a notebook and a photo of her.'

'There's so much more.' Madison rubbed her tears away. 'There are others. Amber is in his book. He'd been keeping notes on us.' She hiccupped and took a deep breath.

Tyrone placed a hand on Madison's shoulder and turned to Gina. 'Don't blame them. It was my idea. I thought I saw your officer's picture through his window in the early hours but I couldn't be sure. He was sitting in his front room with the light on. It was when I came home from the police station. He had his coat on and I wondered what he was doing at that time so I stood back in the dark and watched him. I've been keeping an eye out for days and he's been acting strangely all week. I know I should have called you and I know I promised but I had to be sure of what I'd seen. I couldn't just call you because I thought he was weird.'

Gina shook her head. So far, they'd broken in and entered, they may have messed with potential evidence and they could have put themselves in danger had Curtis Gallagher been in. She nodded to a uniformed officer beside her. 'We'll talk to you later. Will you take all three of them up to Mr Heard's apartment?' She needed them out of her way.

Stepping through into Curtis's hall, her stomach began to churn. She crept through into the kitchen and lounge and peered up and down, her attention immediately brought to the desk area. Tyrone had been right. There in front of her was a photo of PC Kapoor, her AppyDater photo. The same with Madison and Amber. She popped a pair of latex gloves on and flicked through the exercise book, page after page. He'd been recording Amber's comings and goings for ages before he took her, noting down details of her relationship with Clayton Collins and her other dates.

Madison's page soon followed and it was short compared to Amber's. The information gathered by him was brief but to the point. He'd needed a replacement after killing Amber and had given very little time to stalking Madison. A lump formed in her throat as she read on as he then wrote about the policewoman at the lake who he'd followed home.

Jacob entered. 'Blimey.' He began reading over her shoulder.

'If he's not here, where is he?' She felt her fists tighten as she clenched them. She darted through every room, falsely hoping that he'd be hiding Kapoor in the wardrobe or somewhere obvious but no, it was never going to be that easy. She slammed the bedroom door and it bounced on its hinges. 'Where is she?' She held her head in her hands as she calmly headed back to Jacob.

'O'Connor is looking into every angle as we speak.'

'We're too late. He probably knows we're onto him. He's probably running desperate now.' Her mind whirled with everything they'd been through over the past few days. Information never came back as fast as they'd hoped. So many people had lied or interfered with the case throwing them off on tangents that took their investigation away from finding the murderer. Now they knew who he was, they just didn't know where. She stared at the skull ornament and she saw him. Curtis Gallagher with his eyes sunken into his bone. He was a true reflection of his surroundings but not one item screamed stalker murderer. Just like every murderer she'd come across. They all seem like normal, perfectly fine people until you know they're not.

Gina spotted an envelope in the waste bin. It looked official and had a government logo in one corner. She reached in and pulled it out. A Mrs Gallagher was having her benefits increased by one pound and forty pence per week.

Her phone rang and O'Connor's name lit up. 'Tell me you have something and get forensics to this address now. I'm getting the place cordoned off at any moment. We've found our murderer, I just hope there's not another body to add to his count.'

Jacob looked down.

Gina listened as O'Connor blurted everything out. 'We have to go.' She darted to the front door with the envelope in her hand, gave her instructions to uniform and ran as fast as she could to her car. There wasn't a minute to lose. Lost time loses lives in this game and that statement had been proven right on so many occasions. Jacob hurried to his car. Wyre jumped into the passenger seat and the car wheels spun in the snow a few times before gaining some traction on the concrete below.

CHAPTER SIXTY-SIX

Gina slammed on the brakes, skidding to a halt along Chamberlain Way, the address on the envelope, the address that O'Connor had confirmed was Curtis Gallagher's mother's home. The sixty-five-year-old woman apparently lived here alone. She pushed the car door open. 'Do you want the back or front?'

Wyre began fitting her stab vest over her suit jacket and shrugged. 'Back. We should wait for the others.'

Jacob's car pulled up behind Gina's and a couple of police cars followed. 'Right, let's go.'

Gina tightened her stab vest as she trudged down a couple of steps, almost buckling on a cracked slab. 'Be careful.' Music blared out. It was a slow melodic song, one Gina had heard many times. Her parents used to have a Roy Orbison record. It was 'Beautiful Dreamer'. Gina glanced at the windows but each pane was covered from the inside.

Wyre nodded and crept along the side of the building with two uniformed officers. PC Smith reached Gina's side and held the battering ram up in readiness. Preserving life was all that mattered and they had to get in there. She nodded at Jacob to follow Wyre. If Curtis Gallagher was to escape out the back, she needed her fittest officers ready to chase him. The track came to an end and started again. Something wasn't right, that she was sure of. Her mind flashed to an image of Amber, was she his beautiful dreamer?

Slamming her fists on the door, Gina called out. 'Open up, police.' She placed her ear against the door but nothing could be heard over the music. Then there was a piercing scream that made her heart jitter. The scream turned into a laugh, a sadistic tittering with a hint of fury, or was it elation? 'Open up!'

Wyre ran back to the front of the building. 'Guv, there's a body in the shed.'

Gina ran as fast as she could, keeping up with Wyre. Her colleague pointed through the smeary window. 'Blooming hell! Call it in.' She almost pressed her nose to the window to get a better look at the corpse that was strapped into a chair.

Wyre looked away. 'Is it Kapoor?'

Gina swallowed and took a closer look. 'I can't see.' She leaned back and rammed her shoulder into the flimsy door and it pinged open to reveal the body.

CHAPTER SIXTY-SEVEN

Gina breathed a sigh of relief. 'No, I'm guessing it's Gallagher's mother. We have to get in that house now. We'll need to confirm the identity later. The rats have eaten the flesh. It's just bone.'

Wyre looked but quickly turned away.

She stepped into the overgrown garden and shivered. 'Wyre, cover the back door, I'm heading to the front. Count to twenty and go in.' Running around she gave the nod. 'Go now.' PC Smith began slamming the old front door with the battering ram. The deadlocks fought back but after three goes, it caved in.

'Police.' She nodded to two officers to head along to the kitchen and she went to open the living room door but it was locked, from the inside. The back door must have been unlocked as she could hear Wyre and Jacob entering. 'Hello, police.' She banged on the door where the music was coming from and the laughter continued, followed by a thud. Gina flinched and stepped back. 'Stand away from the door, we're coming in.'

As PC Smith battered the flimsy door down, Gina's ears were filled with the sound of the music. She entered and almost stumbled back as a spray of blood came from the pulled out knife. There was blood everywhere. On the walls, the green carpet, the chair and the music, it kept playing.

Jhanvi Kapoor straddled a gurgling Curtis Gallagher, his eyes wide and his laughter loud as she held the knife to his neck. Her own blood mingling with that coming from his arm. The flesh lying loose under her wrists made Gina heave a little. Tears ran down Kapoor's face.

'Put the knife down, Jhanvi. You're safe now.' She shouted to be heard.

Kapoor held it to his throat, pressing the tip against his jugular.

As he spluttered, he spat a glob of blood down his cheek. Gina could see that he had a couple of missing teeth.

Kapoor glanced up at Gina then back at Curtis and with shaky hands she held the knife out to Gina, who grabbed it and handed it to the officer behind her and Smith. Smith ran straight over to his colleague and helped her up, leading her gently into the hallway. As the record music came to an end and clicked off, the sound of sirens filled the street and an ambulance pulled up right outside. The room seemed hauntingly silent.

'Curtis Gallagher, you are under arrest on suspicion of the murder of Amber Slater, the assault of Madison Randle and the kidnapping of Jhanvi Kapoor. You do not have to say anything, but it may harm your defence if you do not mention when questioned something which you later rely on in court. Anything you do say may be given in evidence. Do you understand?'

The weasel-featured man gasped until he regained his breath and nodded.

'Are you injured?' Not that Gina cared but it was her job and she wouldn't have poor care of the perpetrator hamper their case.

He shook his head and rubbed his neck. The scratch on his shoulder was superficial but would need treatment, maybe even a couple of stitches. Plus treatment for missing teeth. Kapoor pushed Smith away and ran back, aiming to kick Curtis in the side but Gina stood in her way. As her colleague broke down on her shoulder, Gina hugged her closely and led the young woman into the hallway as uniform finished up with Curtis Gallagher.

Kapoor pushed her away and for the first time since she'd entered, Gina properly looked at her young colleague. Tears slid down her cheeks, blood seeped down her arm and wrists.

'I need the paramedic in here, now. We're getting you to the hospital, Jhanvi. Do you hear me?'

Jhanvi didn't reply. She brought a trembling finger up and pointed to her lips, which were sealed together. Gina placed an arm around her and led her to a waiting paramedic. Jhanvi turned back and nodded to Gina as she was led out. There would be time to talk later.

Gina hurried back into the living room and stared at the hellish prison that Kapoor had been trapped inside. A photo of a dark-haired teenager sat on a shelf in the corner. The mechanical chair was in the lean-back position. That's the position Amber had died in. Binds were tied through the contraption and in Gina's mind she could see Kapoor peeling off her own skin to free herself. The woman was a fighter and that had most likely saved her from a knife to the heart.

This very moment was just the beginning of the end and she wouldn't rest until she had answers. She closed her eyes and all she could see was Kapoor covered in blood, the feral fear in her eyes that said so much even though she was rendered speechless. She wondered if her lovely colleague would ever be the same again.

CHAPTER SIXTY-EIGHT

Curtis Gallagher slumped over the table in the interview room, the duty solicitor by his side. The young woman whispered a few words into his ear as Gina loudly exhaled. They had been questioning him for half an hour and all he'd replied with was requests to use the toilet, for a drink, a smoke but not a word had come from his lips about the crimes he'd been arrested for. Wyre checked her watch.

Curtis began to roll his shoulder in its sling then he flinched. His wounds had been superficial and only a few stitches had been required. Most of the blood on his body had been PC Kapoor's.

Images of Amber Slater's body and the remains of Curtis's mother filled her mind. The young man in front of her had murdered two people. He'd attacked Madison Randle and what he'd done to Jhanvi Kapoor made Gina grimace. Curtis glanced at her. It was as if he could tell what she was thinking. The glint of light in his dark beady eyes that peered up through the gaps in his greasy fringe gave her the creeps. 'Let's try again. Let's talk about your mother.' He put his thumbnail to his mouth and began to bite. Gina wondered if Kapoor's blood was still under his dirty brown nails.

He snorted and a broad smile filled his face. 'Let's not.'

He may not have replied in the manner she'd hoped for but it was a start. They were getting somewhere.

'What happened?' The woman's remains were undergoing a post-mortem as they spoke. They didn't yet know the cause of

death, all they knew was that she'd been restrained in a chair in
the shed where she'd died.

'She got what she deserved.' His smug grin turned to a wide-
eyed glare.

'How?'

He burst into laughter. 'I can see what you're trying to do.
You think I killed her, don't you? I didn't kill her, I just left her
there and she died.'

That was the same thing. She imagined the woman being
locked in the cold shed, slowly dying of hypothermia or starva-
tion. 'You left her there to die, your own mother, restrained in a
shed?' Gina felt her body shiver for just a second as she thought
of the woman.

He shook his head. 'Like everyone else, she wouldn't shut up
so I shut her up, alright. I was trying to get her to see but she
wouldn't.'

'See what?'

He began shaking his head rapidly, bits of spittle landing on
the table. 'No.'

He was cracking. Gina clenched her hands under the table in
anticipation. 'No, what?'

'Can I have another drink?'

'What were you trying to get your mother to see?'

'I need a smoke.'

'What did you want her to see?'

He stared straight at Gina. 'That she was a murderer.' Curtis
stood and flipped the table over, knocking the recording equipment everywhere. It was as if the pain in his arm was gone and
had been replaced by a surge of adrenaline. 'She's a murderer.'
He slammed himself against the wall. Gina hit the alarm strip
on the wall and PC Smith and Jacob ran in and attempted to
restrain the man.

Curtis slammed his fist into Jacob's jaw then he ran into the corridor. PC Smith grabbed him from behind and brought him to the ground. Gina ushered the shaken solicitor out. The woman's low heels clattered down the corridor where she stayed watching at the end.

Curtis's roars filled every inch of the station as he swore and shouted. 'She's the murderer, not me. I did it for Hailey. Justice for Hailey.' He began to scream and kick as he was led towards the cells. The rest of his shouts were incoherent babble.

'Do we know anything about his deceased sister?'

Wyre shook her head. 'They were twins.'

'You're shaking.'

Wyre looked at her hands. 'So I am. I just wasn't expecting that.'

Gina felt her own body trembling a little. 'I won't ask if you're okay.'

Wyre smiled. 'Thanks, guv. Ditto. What's happening with Jhanvi?'

'She called and wants to see us. I was going to head over there when we'd interviewed Curtis Gallagher. You coming with me?' Gina glanced at her watch. It was almost nine in the evening. Late for a visit but they all needed to know what Jhanvi Kapoor had to say before they stated their case to the CPS and the medical team had stabilised her now.

'Too right.'

Gina smiled at Wyre. 'Let's do this.'

As they headed back towards the incident room, Gina glanced into the main reception where she saw that Madison, Tyrone and Alice were about to leave. She peered through the door. 'Have you all given statements?'

Tyrone nodded. 'Yeah, just finished. Sorry again. We didn't mean to mess things up.'

The dressing on Madison's head had begun to peel around the edges where she was picking at it. 'I can't believe it was him. All this time, he must have been watching Amber, then me. When I visited Ty, he was there, always lurking outside with a roll-up in his mouth, trying to make conversation.' She shivered. 'It makes me sick to think about it. Is the other woman okay? Your officer?'

Gina didn't want to discuss Kapoor with the meddling trio. 'We're going to visit her in a while.'

Madison forced a smile and Alice linked arms with her. 'Let's get you home.'

'Stay safe and I shouldn't need to tell you again. Any trouble in the future call the police straight away and let them handle it. Don't go putting yourselves in danger. Anything could have happened.' Gina smiled back at them. For all their faults they had been trying to help. She couldn't be angry at their interference any longer. To her they looked so young, so vulnerable and she now knew they were safe from Curtis Gallagher and Gina hoped that tonight, Madison would sleep well knowing that they'd made an arrest. They were only a little bit younger than her own daughter, Hannah, and she felt this sudden urge to protect them, mostly from themselves and their own stupid decisions.

Tyrone pulled her card out of his pocket. 'Thanks, DI Harte. If I suspect anyone else of being a murderer, I'll call you.'

His wide grin made her smile. 'Look after that kitten of yours.' She waved them off and turned back to the incident room, bumping straight into Briggs's broad chest. As always, heat radiated from him. 'That was moving, Harte. Are you okay? I heard about what happened in the interview so I thought I'd check.'

She glanced at him, properly this time. His frown caused his forehead to crease. She knew he wasn't just checking up on her. He wanted to know if they were okay. She mulled over that for a second and she couldn't answer that question. 'You know, Wyre and I have made a decision never to ask each other if we're okay ever again. I'm standing and I'm present and I'm not hurt. We've made an arrest. Things couldn't be better.' They could. Briggs being on AppyDater had really played on her mind. She swallowed and looked away.

'I'm sorry you found out about me being on AppyDater the way you did. I know I should have said something.'

'It's none of my business. We've established that. Now all this is over, I might even resurrect the account I opened the other day just so that I can have a snoop. Might find me a hook-up. A woman has needs.'

'You're going to find a hook-up?'

'Yep.' She looked away but felt the weight of his stare on her.

Gina glanced up and down to make sure they were alone and he followed her into a small waiting room off the corridor.

'I'm lonely, Gina. I joined before what happened between us last week and I almost forgot about it. Believe it or not, I get lonely and I crave company. I want your company but look at us.'

'And that's my fault?' She ground her teeth.

'I didn't say that. It's just complicated but I'm not going to be meeting anyone on AppyDater. I've deleted it.'

She stared at the floor.

'Please say something, Gina. You and I have a past. We know things about each other that no one else does. I just need you to be okay with me.'

'I've been unfair with you. I know I have but the truth is, I don't know where we're going to end up. You should be free to meet someone else.'

'I don't want anyone else.' He brushed his fingers across her cheek. 'By the way, you should get out more. This weekend, drinks for the whole team are on me. Say you'll join us.'

Wyre was calling Gina from the corridor.

'I best go.' It was time to call it a night at the station and head to the hospital. She hurried back to the incident room.

Wyre bit her bottom lip then turned to walk towards the door. 'Right, guv. To the hospital?'

Gina nodded.

O'Connor bit into a chocolate bar as he swivelled on his chair. 'Yes, Jhanvi just called again. She said to hurry. I asked if we could visit but she said her family were fussing like mad and she just wanted to get the statement out of the way. She said she needs to tell you about Hailey and that it's urgent.'

Gina grabbed her thick coat from the end of the table. 'Right, the night is still young.'

CHAPTER SIXTY-NINE

As Gina and Wyre trudged through the ward they left a trail of snow behind them. Slowly it would turn into puddles. Something that was once so beautiful would be nothing more than a dangerous smear on the floor.

'I think we've found Kapoor.' Gina pointed to the side room where Kapoor's family were spilling out.

A nurse thundered past. 'Excuse me. Visiting is over and only two at a time in future.' The cracked veins on her nose looked more accentuated as she kept her angry expression.

'Sorry and thank you for all that you're doing for my sister.' The tall young man left with the child in his arms and Jhanvi's parents.

'See you tomorrow, my love,' her mother called, blowing a kiss through the window as she left. 'I'll be back first thing in the morning with some supplies.' As Jhanvi's mother passed the room, the woman burst into tears and fell into the arms of her husband.

The younger man carrying the whining child passed Gina and Wyre. 'Dad, I'll meet you both outside. She's getting restless.'

'Mr and Mrs Kapoor, I'm DI Harte – Gina – one of Jhanvi's colleagues. How is she doing?'

Mrs Kapoor pulled away from her husband's chest. 'She looks so frail and all those tubes. I can't believe it. My poor baby. Someone did that to her.'

'I'm so sorry.' Gina could only imagine how she felt. If she was in Mr and Mrs Kapoor's position she didn't know how she'd feel. If it were Hannah that had been through something so traumatic, would she be here now, feeling helpless and crying? Probably, and they weren't even close. The Kapoor family were as close as they came.

'She wants to speak to you. She said you were coming which is why we were saying our goodbyes until tomorrow morning.' The woman pulled a crumpled tissue from her jeans pocket and wiped her tears away, snivelling a few times before finally stopping completely. 'We have to be strong, for her.' She paused. 'She was getting tired. I think they gave her a sedative so you might want to hurry.'

'Thank you.' Gina smiled sympathetically as the Kapoors continued down the corridor and out of the main door.

The nurse came out of Kapoor's room. 'Not more visitors. Don't you know what time it is? I have sick people trying to sleep on this ward.'

Wyre tilted her head a little. 'We're really sorry. PC Kapoor called us at the station and requested that we come to speak to her. We're her colleagues, DC Wyre and DI Harte.'

'Oh, I see. Make it snappy, she needs her rest.' A buzzer went and the nurse hurried past. 'Coming.'

Gina approached the door and peered through the side window. Kapoor's long black hair that was usually tied up in a low bun under her hat was splayed out all over the pillow and fell way past her chest. A white sheet had been pulled up to her bust and her arms lay on top of it, connected to the drip and bandaged up. The cabinet next to her bed was piled high with boxes of cakes and chocolates, bottles of pop and crisps that Kapoor's family had brought with them. Tubes led to a beeping machine above and Kapoor lay there with her eyes closed. 'I think she's asleep.'

'I'm not,' she murmured, wincing as she forced her body to sit up a little. She reached for a cup with a straw in it and sucked with closed eyes.

'It's me, Gina, and Paula's here too.' The room smelled of disinfectant. Gina pressed the lever on the sanitiser dispenser and rubbed it into her hands.

Kapoor opened her red-rimmed eyes and squinted as she tried to focus. 'I'm so glad you're here. I have a lot to tell you. Grab some chairs. Do you want some of this food?'

Gina shook her head. She brought the plastic chairs close to Kapoor's bedside then she and Wyre sat. Wyre pulled out her notepad.

'We've been so worried about you. Smith told me to say he can't wait to see you. Mrs O is making you some of your favourite Chelsea buns for tomorrow and we all miss you.' Gina tilted her head to the same angle that Kapoor's was tilted at and looked into her weary eyes. The last time she saw the young officer she'd been covered in blood and on top of Curtis Gallagher with a knife in her hands.

'I had him, just before you came.' Her torn cracked lips formed a smile then she flinched. 'You think this would hurt more.' She held up her bandaged wrists. 'My lips kill.' A tear slid down her cheek then she laughed. 'Never superglue your lips.'

'We got you some chocolate but it looks like you're well sorted for goodies.' Gina pulled out a large bar of milk chocolate from her bag and popped it on the food mountain.

'My family are a bunch of feeders, I swear.'

Gina paused. 'How did you end up on him when we got there?'

'For hours, I'd been pressing through my flesh with the binds on that horrible chair and the skin on my wrists was literally peeling away. In my mind, I thought I'd scored them to the bone but when they were stitching me up, they said I hadn't sawn away at them too deeply.' She scrunched her nose. 'Eventually, I managed to pull them free, then I was able to untie my legs, waist and neck. When he went for the knife, I knew I had to take the opportunity to fight for my survival. I did it and something came over me, the biggest surge of adrenaline ever. I thought of my mum and I knew I'd get one chance. I brought my fist quickly to his throat taking his breath away. He went to stab me and I managed to slide off the chair and he got the knife wedged in it. I reached up and grabbed him between the legs and twisted as hard as I could and he yelped like a baby and fell to the floor. We fought and scrambled for the knife. I pulled the knife out of the chair and he reached over and fought me for it, that's when the adrenaline wore off and the pain seemed to take over.' She shook her head. 'The keys to the door were in his back pocket and I couldn't get them from him so I hit him again, hard. He lolled on the floor.'

Gina placed her hand on Kapoor's arm. 'You were so brave. That fight you had in you saved your life.'

'He started to come around a bit after rolling on the floor and I was still wrestling to get the keys from his pocket. He grabbed my bleeding wrist and began pulling me to the ground. Just as I reached the floor, I gripped the knife and knew I had to use it to get away from him. My wrists were stinging like mad and blood was dripping everywhere. I was sure I'd bleed to death. I awkwardly pushed the knife into the only place I could seem to aim which was his shoulder. He was going to kill me. I had to get him off me. He was shocked when I stabbed him, and I kicked him again but he still fought back. After a struggle, I managed to pin him down, then you arrived. I wanted to gouge his eyes out and smash his nose in. I saw red and that's never happened to me before. I didn't know I had it in me to feel that primal.' She let out a sob.

'You did what you had to do to survive, Jhanvi. You fought and you lived.' Gina felt Kapoor's hand grab hers.

'Thanks, guv.' She took a moment to gain her composure. 'There's more. Before he came in with the knife, he let me into his thoughts. He said other things and you need to hear them.' Kapoor paused.

'Are you okay talking about this now?' Gina hoped she was but the nurse passed and peered through the window, giving her and Wyre a stern look.

'Yes. I want to talk. Can you crack open a can of Coke for me? My mouth is bone dry and I'm sick of water.'

Gina gently eased a can of Coke from the pile and opened it, passing it to Kapoor who took a swig as her hands trembled.

'The painkillers are good. I'm dreading when all the meds wear off. Anyway, while he kept me there, he kept referring to me as Hailey. He thought I was going to become Hailey and he would talk to himself as if he was in conversation with Hailey herself. I found out that she was his twin sister. He was weirdly trying to turn me into her in an effort to bring her back to life. There was something that he kept mumbling about at the end. His mother found out about Hailey being pregnant by some boy at school and she recently told Curtis that it was she who gave the tablets to Hailey. I think that was the trigger for all this. Their mother bullied Hailey into taking her life because of the shame she'd bring on the family. He kept saying how his mother beat them and was nasty all the time.' She paused. 'I don't know where his mother lives.'

'He killed his mother, Jhanvi. We found her body in the shed. He was keeping you at his mother's bungalow.'

Kapoor took a couple of deep breaths. 'It makes sense. He blamed her for Hailey's death. He killed his mother and I think it sent him on a path looking for a replacement for Hailey. He fed me Hailey's favourite food, spoke to me as if I was going to be possessed by her and become her. I think that's what he thought.' Her voice cracked and she took another sip of cola. 'He kept playing this song over and over again and it was sending me crazy. Even when it wasn't playing, I couldn't get it out of my head. I can't now. Every time there is a moment of quietness, it starts again and I hate it…' Tears spilled down her cheeks and she dropped the can of Coke on her bed sheet.

Gina quickly grabbed it and Wyre pulled a handful of tissues from the dispenser.

'I knew I had to become her to survive. I tried to play along, then I failed and it sent him crashing into reality. That was the start of the end, I know it was. He was going to kill me like he did Amber then he'd probably have dumped me in a lake too. All that time I imagined my family finding out what had happened to me. I thought I'd never find out if my mother got the all-clear or see my brothers again. I faced my end. I thought that was it, so to be here now, even in this state, I'm happy. I'm elated and I've never felt so alive in my whole life. I want things I've never wanted before and when I inhale, it's like I've never breathed before. Everything is so vivid. The taste of this Coke, it's like the best thing ever. Hailey wanted to die and I feel for her. I've been thinking about her. She must have been such a confused kid.'

Gina finished mopping up the cola and turned the sheet down so that the damp bit wasn't pressed against Kapoor.

'My mother got the all-clear by the way. She is finally cancer free. I just want to get better, get out of here and go home so that I can celebrate with her. I was thinking something else...' Kapoor flinched as she sat up a little more.

'What's that?' Gina helped to adjust her pillows and arrange the tubes that were coming from the cannula in her arm.

'I'm going to study to become a sergeant. I'm ready for anything now. I fought him. I survived and here I am, standing to tell the tale. I have more to give, so much more.' She paused and dabbed a little Vaseline onto her lips.

'You just concentrate on getting better. You're going to need all your strength.'

'I'll be out of here in a couple of days. A week of my mother fussing will force me back to my apartment and back to work. Scrap that, I can walk so I'm going home.'

Wyre finished making notes and closed her pad. 'Is there anything else you want to tell us?'

Kapoor shook her head. 'No, that's the lot. One day I will get that song out of my head, these wounds will heal and I'll be back as a fitter and stronger version of myself. It'll take more than what has happened to crack me.'

'You know, if you need to talk, we're all here.'

Kapoor placed her hand on Gina's again. 'I know. We're like family.'

'I'll check in on you tomorrow.'

The nurse tapped on the window and pointed at the clock on the wall. It was nearly midnight, way past any visiting hours.

'We're going.' Gina and Wyre stood. 'See you tomorrow.'

'See you then.' Kapoor lay her head back onto the pillow as they left.

'She looks so frail, but what a fighter.' Gina threw her bag over her shoulder.

Wyre popped her notebook in her pocket. 'I don't know how she did what she did? She's amazing.'

As they neared the entrance, Mrs Kapoor was on the phone filling in all her relatives with the news of how her daughter was doing and her father sat on a bench smoking a cigarette. The woman ended the call and ran over to Gina. 'Was she okay? I didn't want to leave her.'

'She's doing as well as can be expected and more. I bet you are all so proud of her.'

'We are and we're so grateful to have her back. I thought she was dead.' The woman waved her hand in front of her face to ward off her tears.

Gina and Wyre walked back to the car park with the Kapoors before saying one last goodnight.

As they got in their own cars, Gina waved goodbye to Wyre then sat in the car park alone for a while longer. She glanced up at the mound and remembered what had happened to Madison in this very car park. She gave one last thought to Amber, the girl who had washed up in the lake. It had been a long week and she was exhausted. Then she gave a final thought to the Gallaghers; a mother and her twin children. If Curtis was to be believed, his mother had confessed to leaving the tablets for Hailey to deal with their family shame by ending her young life and once the mother had confessed what she'd done to him, Curtis had exacted his revenge and sought to find Hailey once again by trying to turn these innocent young women into her. It didn't get more messed up. Her phone began to ring.

'O'Connor. You okay?'

'Yes, I've just been digging a bit deeper. Hailey, the sister of our perp. She killed herself at sixteen and it was in her notes that she was pregnant.'

'We've just found that out. I'll fill you in later.' When the call had ended, Gina rested her head back on the headrest and rubbed her temples, giving her last thoughts of the day to Hailey, the young girl whose life ended too soon. Her phone rang again.

'Sir?'

'Harte.' Briggs's usually stern voice was soft, as it always had been when they were alone. 'Just checking on things.'

She smiled. 'I'm okay. Thanks for checking.' It had been a long day and all she could think about was getting some food and having a long hot shower before crawling into bed. That was still a few hours away but that thought would keep her going.

EPILOGUE

A cold wind blew Gina's hair but it didn't matter. She'd neatly tied it back into a high ponytail with the bobble that Wyre had given her. Her make-up was well fixed and her best jeans fitted a treat. She'd even bought a new pair of heeled boots. 'Are you sure you want to be here. Everyone else is at the pub and they're all queuing up to buy you a drink, especially Briggs. He's buying too so you can go to town on that tab.'

Jhanvi Kapoor swallowed and stared at the bungalow covered in police tape. 'I needed to see it one last time but I could do with a gin and tonic too.' She shivered and rubbed her hands together. 'I came and I've faced it. I won't let what happened or that place,' she pointed at the front window, 'beat me.' She paused and licked her scabby lips. Her eyes watered up.

'You know, you don't have to be brave about this. It's okay to feel upset.'

Jhanvi shook her head letting her long glossy hair follow her movement. 'I'm not shedding a tear for myself or for what I went through. I feel so sad for Hailey. He badly wanted his sister back and he'd been prepared to kidnap and kill to find the right replacement. That poor girl killed herself. I just can't get over that. Such a waste of life.'

'I agree. She must have been in a bad place. I suppose knowing she was pregnant and then the reaction from her mother, it had left her feeling like she had no way out.' Gina felt herself getting a little choked as she imagined Mrs Gallagher leaving all those paracetamol tablets for Hailey to take, knowing how low her daughter felt – that's if it were even true. For some reason, she couldn't imagine Curtis Gallagher making that bit up. After he'd finally talked, he'd sobbed his eyes out as he told his story.

'There's always a way out. It's sad no one was there for her to help her see that.'

Gina nodded. 'It is.'

'When I was listening to that song, I hated it but now, in my mind, I see her in her last moments and I like to think of her. She was the beautiful dreamer except she was never going to wake up.'

'She was beautiful, and kind, and caring.' The man standing behind them stepped closer. He had to be in his early sixties with a greying moustache and heavy bags under his eyes. 'I'm sorry, Hailey Gallagher was my daughter and I've just heard what happened to my ex-wife and son. I can't believe he did what he did, but his mother, she had a nasty streak about her. We were already living apart but after Hailey killed herself I had to get away and Curtis didn't want to come with me. I really wanted him to but he was sixteen and I had to respect his decision.' The man shook his head and looked at his booted feet.

'You've been away for a long time, Mr Gallagher. I'm glad one of the team managed to contact you.' Gina remembered that the last address they'd had for him was an apartment in Amsterdam.

'I still live close by. The people living in my last apartment forwarded the message on that police were trying to contact me. Curtis had my last address but never called or came to see me. He never forgave me for moving away at such a bad time so I guessed after years of trying, I should finally stop upsetting myself. So I moved again and never told him.' He paused. 'I suppose my ex-wife died in this bungalow?'

Gina nodded. 'In the shed at the back. Sorry.'

'I'm not. She was a cold person. She pushed my Hailey into killing herself and I'm glad she's dead.' He paused again and rocked back a step. 'I'm sorry for what my son did to you.' His stare met Kapoor's.

She looked away. 'It's not your fault, Mr Gallagher.'

'It is. When his mother and I split up, I wasn't there for him. They were both just kids and Hailey could have done with our parental guidance not my ex-wife telling Hailey that her only way out was to kill herself.' His eyes glazed over and began to water slightly. He closed them and swallowed before opening them again. 'After Hailey's suicide, I couldn't bear to call Curtis. When I saw him, which wasn't often, all I saw was Hailey… they were twins.' He clenched his fists. 'I was angry, I was grieving and, yes, I was also mad that she'd got pregnant at such a young age. I did what I've been doing ever since, I ran away and buried my head in the sand.'

'It must have been a difficult thing to go through.' Gina furrowed her brow.

'I can't run away any more. I need to sort all this out.' He pointed to the bungalow. 'It's my responsibility. The home where my son killed a woman and he held you.' He nodded to Kapoor. 'The house where he flipped and eventually killed his mother when he heard what she did. Up until then, he'd only thought she'd worn Hailey down causing her suicide, he never knew she'd shoved the tablets under her nose and pushed her into it. It's all my burden to bear. You can leave it behind, sweep it under the carpet and pretend it didn't happen while you carry on living but eventually, it comes back for you. My past has come back for me tenfold.' He shook his head.

Rain began to fall. 'I'm getting cold.' Kapoor shivered.

'Anyway, I'm sorry. I'm truly, truly, sorry for what my son did to you. I know you say it's not my fault but there's so much more I could have done. I'm sticking around now and I'm going to be there for him despite what he's done. I'll visit him in prison or wherever he ends up. It's my burden as his father. I have to be there for my killer son. Saying it sounds weird but that's how it is. I best get used to it.'

Gina looked away.

'I suppose I best go as I'm getting soaked. You'll let me know when I can go into the house and sort everything out and when my ex-wife's body will be released? I'm going to have to sort out a funeral. Someone has to.'

'Of course we will, Mr Gallagher.' Gina could see the guilt etched on the man's face and she knew that guilt would gnaw away at him until his last day.

'Thank you, and bye.' He forced a smile and began walking away.

'Guv, I can't feel my fingers it's so cold. Can we go to the pub now?'

'We're not on duty, you can call me Gina, Jhanvi.'

'Gina, Jhanvi. That sounds comical. Okay, Gina. Let's go and get something strong down our necks especially as Briggs is paying.' Jhanvi Kapoor led the way to Gina's car and waited for her to unlock it. 'And thanks for being there this week. My family are great but it's hard to talk to them. They mean well but they're overpowering sometimes. I couldn't wait to get back in my flat.'

'You can talk to me anytime. My door is always open. Oh, and Jhanvi?'

'What?'

'Next time you see some man lurking in your car park in the middle of the night, call it in.'

'Okay. I didn't call because I live by a pub, there's always some drunk person or people loitering around in the middle of the night. I'd become the station's number one nuisance caller which is why I keep my notebook.'

'Just be vigilant. None of us mind attending a call out if some weirdo is hanging around, okay?'

'Yes, okay.'

Gina smiled at the young woman as they got in the car, ready for an evening with the team. Kapoor was making a brilliant recovery and they had all the evidence they needed to make a solid case. Gina only hoped that Jhanvi Kapoor wouldn't be haunted by her past trauma like Gina had been throughout most of her adult life. She hoped the young woman could go on to be a sergeant one day and she'd have a long and happy life.

'We're never going to get there if you don't turn the engine on, Gina.' Jhanvi's screechy Brummie accent was a delight to hear.

A LETTER FROM CARLA

Dear Reader,

I'd like to say a huge thank you to you for choosing *The Broken Ones*. There are so many books out there, I remain grateful that you're reading mine.

If you'd like to be kept up to date with my news and new releases, please sign up to the following link. Your email address will never be shared and you can unsubscribe at any time.

www.bookouture.com/carla-kovach

I'm often asked where I get my ideas from so I thought I'd share the origins of this particular story. It came from the spark of an idea when I was visiting my dad in hospital while he was still alive. I'd left The Heartlands Hospital in Birmingham and it was dark and chilly. I'd also parked right at the back of the car park and it felt like I was far away from everyone else, especially as I'd left late at night. I literally scared myself silly walking back to the car as elements of this storyline ran through my head.

Thankfully, I reached my car in one piece and drove home safely – phew – and then I got to invent the rest!

If you loved *The Broken Ones*, I'd be hugely grateful if you'd leave me a review on Amazon, Apple Books, Google or Kobo.

I'm also a huge social media user and I love chatting to readers, so pop by and say hi.

Massive thanks once again for reading *The Broken Ones*.

Carla

CarlaKovachAuthor

CKovachAuthor

carla_kovach

ACKNOWLEDGEMENTS

Behind every book there is a team of professionals that make it the success that it is. It begins as an idea, then it's a synopsis, then a draft. After that, it's polished and edited, and the cherry that is a book cover and description is added to the top. There's so much going on behind the scenes and everyone involved is amazing at what they do. I'm hugely grateful to write for Bookouture and appreciative of everything that the Bookouture team do.

My editor, Helen Jenner, is amazing! I always feel so lucky to be working with her and the edits that she gives me elevate my writing to its full potential. I really think she's superwoman as I don't know how she does all this so quickly and is so brilliant in what she says. Helen, hugest thank you for everything. I couldn't do it without you!

Kim Nash, Noelle Holten and Sarah Hardy – thank you! They are behind the brilliant Bookouture publicity team and they work tirelessly. I'm hugely grateful for everything they do and I don't know where they get the never-ending stream of energy from. They're always there to chat, they're there on publication day and always waving the flag for our books at all other times.

There is also something else that's really special about being a Bookouture author and it's the support we give each other. I love being a part of the Bookouture family. It's absolutely awesome. Thank you so much for everything. Thanking authors doesn't stop with the Bookouture family, though. I'm friends with so many and they're an amazing group of fabulous people. I'm really grateful to be a part of this hugely supportive author club and some days, I feel like it's a dream. Well, it's a dream come true.

Bloggers and reviewers are amazing. Huge thanks to everyone who takes the time to read my work and then review it. I'm touched that so many people give my work a mention, write blog posts about my books or share news of my book releases. All this takes time and I'm grateful that some of their precious time is given to me. I'd like to say a huge thanks to The Fiction Café Book Club (group) on Facebook. The amount of support they've given to me and other authors is heart-warming. They're a group that are in love with books, reading and book discussion. I feel at home when I'm chatting away with them both as an avid reader and an author.

I'm lucky to have DS Bruce Irving as a friend and I'd like to thank him for answering all my questions on policing matters. If you find any errors they are my own or down to artistic licence. Another professional I'm grateful to is my other good friend Samantha Warren who works with the New Road Parents Support Group, for her advice on one of my characters. Thank you massively to Bruce and Sam.

My beta readers, Vanessa Morgan, Brooke Venables, Derek Coleman, Su Biela and Anna Wallace are lovely people and most of them are writers too. I'm grateful to have you all in my support group. We've all been friends for a long time and to have that bond is special. Thank you.

Book covers are immensely important and I have Toby Clarke and Helen Jenner to thank for mine, from coming up with the concept to the final cover design. I love all my covers and feel they represent the content of my books in the best possible way. I'm bowled over by how striking they look and this one is no exception.

It's always lovely to be contacted by Peta Nightingale in contracts and rights, huge thank you for everything you do.

Lastly, thank you to my husband, Nigel. He sees me when I'm nervously working through edits, when I'm flapping over a storyline niggle, when I'm panicking that no one will like my latest book and he often supplies me with coffee when I'm racing for a deadline. I'm hugely grateful for all his support and patience.

All in all, I feel really lucky to have so many wonderful people in my life. Thank you!